Under Vixens Mere

Also by Kit Fielding

Under Vixens Mere

KIT FIELDING

inkspt
PUBLISHING

First published in 2025 by Inkspot Publishing.
www.inkspotpublishing.com

ISBN (Paperback): 978-1-916708-15-0
ISBN (eBook): 978-1-916708-14-3

Printed in the United Kingdom by
Hobbs the Printers Ltd, Totton, Hampshire.

Cover design: Mark Ecob
Map of Vixens Mere: Taryn de Meillon

Typeset using Atomik ePublisher from Easypress Technologies.

MIX
Paper | Supporting
responsible forestry
FSC
www.fsc.org
FSC® C020438

To Mum: *Just One More Bend.*

Hunters Woods

Tow Path

Jetty

Farm Track

Canal

Vixens
Mere
Marina

Saddleback

Home Sweet Home

Bombardier

Morning Star

Summer Walker

Crystal Lady

Track

Toilet &
Showers

The
Shed

To Broome

Elson
Point

MORPHIC RESONANCE

by Stanley Drake

If you cut me in Bristol I will bleed in Birmingham, my veins will open in Cardiff, my blood will leach into the Mersey.

If you cut me in Bristol there'll be a shiver in the water and eels will pause in slither, silver dace will freeze in dance, and pike will pause in the hunt. A silent heron will cock his head to listen to the draining of water.

If you cut me in Bristol my arteries will open in the Grand Ship Canal. The barges will slow on the Avon and Kennet and all the brightly painted narrowboats will incline a bow.

If you cut me in Bristol there will be a flooding of field and ditch, the locks will stand dry and the canal will become a channel for gasping boats.

If you cut me in Bristol I will lose the centuries past, hewn stone tunnels, the ghost of pick and shovel and fireside tents. And accidental drownings. And deliberate submersions.

If you cut me in Bristol I will bleed my life away.

The verse is taken from his collection of poems Waterways *published in 1928. The inspiration came from the many hours he would sit by Vixens Mere and imagine the interconnectivity of water; gutter to ditch to stream to canal and river, ocean, pond and mere.*

PROLOGUE

Vixens Mere Marina.
Bombardier.
Sunday. One o'clock in the morning.
Moored barges. Tree-shrouded waters dark and deep and
silent. Glow of a cigarette from the deck of The Bombardier.
It's quiet and still, bitterly cold, and Harry Jones has belted
his bulky greatcoat, his army remnant, tightly around himself.
When he's smoked his last cigarette, he flicks the butt over-
board. He doesn't see the glowing arc clearly but he hears the
hiss as it hits the water. 'One sense making up for another.'
It must be true because, since his eyesight's worsened, he's
aware that his hearing has become so much more sensitive.

'You know, I think I can actually hear a pin drop,' he'd
told Karen and she'd laughed. But it's not only his hearing.
He feels the slight tremor of their boat as Karen turns in her
bed. He can read the mildest of vibrations; a quiver of movement, a foot on the gangplank, a visit to the bathroom, a pot
set onto the cooker. He imagines the sleepy warmth of her,
remembers how they'd wake in the mornings with not a fag
paper between them. But that was in the early days. When he
was a proper man. He's gone from Proper man to Useless man,
and she'd stuck with him through the transition and beyond.
And now? What fucking use am I, Karen? What fucking use
to anyone? She'd always calmed him when emotion and the
colossal injustice of it all combined in a bitter tirade or a black

1

outburst of temper. All of this is worming around in Harry's head, and now enough is enough. She's done her shift. *None of this is your fault, Karen. Please forgive me.* That's what he's written, slowly and laboriously; blurred letters formed into words on the note that's lying on his pillow. A note signed with love.

Harry stands up slowly, feels the weight of his loaded coat pockets, his trouser pockets, that are packed to overflowing with nuts and bolts and washers of iron. Harry slowly shuffles his way off-board the Bombardier, along the towpath, out onto the end of the jetty, and then painfully struggles to ease himself to sit and dangle his legs like he's a boy again; a blonde-haired child swishing the cool water against his bare legs on a hot summer's day. But this is a night twenty-five years later, the moon taking an occasional peep through ragged clouds. Its light falls onto this thin man in a baggy overcoat slowly lowering himself into the marina. Very slowly, so he makes no splash.

Harry knew it was going to be cold, knew that it would steal his breath, chill his body, and cause him to slow in his push towards the depths, until the water's at his chin, lapping at his mouth. Then he takes the deepest pull of air, a lung-stretch of filling that he's going to hold onto until he's under and it's impossible to turn back.

'Come on, Harry. One step at a time. Discipline. Discipline. No going back now.' The water's over his mouth, seeking into his nose, his ears, until all of his head is covered. Harry raises an arm, breaks the surface of the water in a last brief clutch at this world. Then he opens his eyes, peers into the liquid twilight where the fickle moon is showing a faint path through a thicket of floating weed. He breathes out, waits for the involuntary suck for air, waits for the choking. He's anchored by nuts and bolts and scraps of metal to the bottom of Vixens Mere expecting the end to start. But nothing is happening except ... *except for the muffled sound of voices, a break of laughter, the chatter of conversation.* Now the light around Harry has grown stronger, brighter, harsher, and the moon is the sun and the waterweed is prickled brush, and there's desert sand and pebbles under his boots. Through the brush there's a team of soldiers carelessly arranged around a billy-can brew up. And the wonder of it is that they're his team, his mates. His pack. There's Geordie, and Jason, Hoppy, and Tallyman, and Harry can feel their welcome wash over him. He's come home to his company. They're pleased to see him, these comrades in arms. Comrades who've been through a lot together. Stuck together. Always. Alongside the crew, waiting for their embarkment, the Saladin is in heavy tick-over.

Jason, dashing the dregs from his mug, says, 'Knew you'd make it back, Harry.' Hoppy says, 'Bet you've been having a rare old time without us to keep an eye on you, eh, Harry?'

Tallyman, stubbing out his cigarette, says, 'Enough prattle, let's get aboard. Get this show on the road.'

Geordie says, 'Couldn't have left without you, Harry. You know we never leave anyone behind.'

They climb into the Saladin and Harry, rifle resting on his forearm, takes his position against the door. They've been bumping along the rutted dusty tracks for an hour or so and it's broiling hot in the armoured vehicle. Oven hot. Geordie reckons that he'll soon be thoroughly roasted and ready to serve up with some apple sauce. Jason says that there's enough meat on Geordie to feed the entire division. Hoppy hopes he doesn't get the parson's nose and Tallyman says the last thing he'd want is Geordie's prick in his mouth. Harry's halfway through saying that he's thinking of becoming a veggie when *nothing happens. No explosion, no ear shattering eye-blinding blast, just a percussive rumble in the distance.*

Tallyman laughs without humour. 'Well. Glad we missed that one, boys.'

There's a collective nod of agreement and Geordie says, 'Be glad to get to base. Wash this fucking dust away.'

Jason reckons that he's counting the days until they're, 'back in dear old Blighty.'

Hoppy says to Harry, 'Bet you can't wait to get home to that cracker of a wife of yours?'

Harry says that Hoppy's right, he just can't wait.

He's lying on his back under eight feet of water. His bed is a soft mattress of fine mud, soft silt. His imprint, the shape of him, will remain for days after his removal. His eyes are wide open, like he's amazed to find himself in this place of murk and floating weed. But dead, cold, drowned flesh has no emotions, no feelings, and so there's no resistance to the nylon ropes as they are threaded around his body, tightened, knotted on his chest, for the dragging of him up to the light.

And that should be that for the Police Rescue team. All done. Mission completed. Body recovered. Morgue and post-mortem awaiting. All going well on this wet Sunday afternoon. Should be home in time for tea. That's the thought, except that the diver, treading water, facemask dropped under his mouth, is shaking his head and saying, 'I'm going in again. Need to check on something else.'

The something else has been down here a long time and the tarpaulin shroud wrapped around this body has rotted away in snapshots of exposure, frames of slime-greened bones, tatters of dress, a pale grinning skull, and a release of hair gently wavering in an eddy of current.

If these two drowned could speak and tell how they ended up in these freezing waters, he would gently say that he'd had enough of his painful existence, and that what he'd done was an act of sacrifice, of a selfless love to give a life to another. He had prepared himself to die. It was his duty.

That's what he'd say.

She would say that she could never have imagined laying lonely and cold and in this place for all of these years. She'd loved the warmth of the sun, mostly loved her life, and always loved her child in her own way. She'd tell that she hadn't been perfect but she was young and pretty and she wasn't ready to die.

That's what she'd say.

And if you could kneel beside her in the mud, in the black silt of these murky cold waters, and take her hand, draw close to her mouth, you might hear her softly, regretfully, whisper the whole of her story.

CHAPTER ONE

Vixens Mere.
8 am.
Lorrie Smith.
'To Let. Barge, The Morning Star. Excellent condition. Freshly
painted. Fully furnished on a permanent mooring. Landlords
are Mr Ethan James and his daughter, Dinah. Ethan, the
proprietor of Vixens Mere, also farms the surrounding acres
of countryside.'

That's the advert she'd seen. On this cold morning, ice spiking
the grass, and a half hour before her appointment with the
landlord of the Morning Star, Lorrie parks her car and walks
the towpath around Vixens Mere. She's a tall, slightly over-
weight, cropped-haired young woman, late twenties, in a
smart suit and she's looking out for a freshly painted boat.
Lorrie likes the serenity of this place at this time of day. God
knows she could do with some peace after what's gone on.
And there is a peace here that's not broken by a fisherman –
teenager by the look of him – as still as a heron, watching his
float and poised to strike.

'Well, Lorrie,' she says to herself, 'This looks a good place
to start again.'

Her thoughts of starting again are interrupted by the
romantic ringtone of her phone. Petra had chosen the melody.
When a *Secret Love* was no secret anymore. *'Our tune, Lorrie.*
So you know that it's me that's calling.'

Lorrie doesn't answer. She taps the off button. But she knows that tonight, on her own, she won't be able to resist listening to the message.

At first, a month ago when the messages are new, Petra is full of apology. Remorse tremors her voice.

'I can't say how sorry I am. It'll never happen again, I promise. Please come home.'

And Lorrie would visualise the woman behind the words, the pretty face, the tumbling of dark hair and even darker eyes. The softness of her body. But, like so much of Petra when she doesn't get her own way, her tone gradually hardens as she sends messages and texts. Voice and word. Again and Again.

'Look, I've said I made a mistake. Why can't you accept that?'

Then the appeal to jealousy. 'I'm going out tonight, Lorrie. Here's a selfie of me.' The picture is stunning. Petra has hitched her skirt up and unbuttoned her blouse. There's a lot on show and she's added to her text, 'I'm getting desperate, Lorrie.'

'Don't know what time I got home last night. Can't remember a thing after ten.'

'Bumped into Barbara yesterday. She asked after you. Told her you'd left me and arranged to have a drink with her.'

'Why don't you answer? We could at least talk about ... oh don't fucking bother.'

'If you don't come and pick up the rest of your things, I'm going to bin them.'

'Your things are at the tip!!!'

'Barbara's coming round for dinner.'

'I'm going to sell the house. You won't get a penny!'

The last text reads, 'What are you without me, Lorrie?'

Lorrie messages back, 'Happy,' although she's not, because there's so many nights when she's lain in her bed and dreamed that Petra was beside her. One morning she wakes to a disappointment so deep that, while the sleep is still in her eyes, she actually dials Petra's mobile. But she stops on the last digit because she must not do it, she cannot go back there. As Lorrie's mother always said, 'There's no point flogging a dead horse,' and Petra has to be the deadest of all equines.

So tonight Lorrie will listen to Petra's last – really last – message and then she'll delete her ex from her phone, block her on social media, cut the ties that bind. Completely. And then she'll have a bit of a cry, even though she's a big strong girl, wipe her eyes and begin this new life. She'll leave Desolation Row in the past where it has to belong.

By the time Lorrie's walked her meandering path her head is clearing and her appointment is standing by the pale-green Morning Star. There's two to greet her, a ruddy-faced man, dented hat on his head, a buttonless overcoat wisped with straw fitted to his large frame, a pair of caked wellies complete the picture; a young elfin-like woman beside him. She's the complete opposite; immaculately dressed, pristine Hunters on her feet. Perfectly made up. Lorrie can't help thinking Beauty and the Beast. Then she tuts at herself for applying this cliché as the Beast offers his rough farmer's hand to her, introduces himself in a gruff country accent.

'Ethan James.'

'Lorrie Smith.'

Then it's an introduction to Dinah, his daughter. A much softer handshake and a gentle, 'Hi, Lorrie,' and Ethan James adds, 'She'll show you round. Show you how everything works.' He laughs. 'She don't want me clambering about in there after she's done it spotless.' He points at the wellies. 'I've got to get back to work.'

He leaves them to it.

The showing around doesn't take long in this wide-beam boat.

Two bedrooms, shower and toilet, lounge, kitchen area. Dinah says that the electric's connected, water's on, gas bottles are full, boiler only needs to be fired up.

'And so there we are. What do you think?'

Another Lorrie, a long time ago Lorrie, might have said, *'What I think is that you're a very attractive girl, Dinah.'* Instead she says, 'I like it.'

'You'll let the agent know asap, Lorrie? There's quite a lot of interest.'

Before she leaves, Dinah says, 'If there are any problems, if you need to get in touch.' She draws a business card from her pocket. 'Here's my number.'

The card reads, *Dinah James. Hairdresser and Beautician. Looking to help you look your best.*

Lorrie, a little more of that long ago girl peeping through, says, 'Do you think I need smartening up then?'

Dinah's hand goes to her mouth, 'Sorry, I didn't mean ... It was just for my number in case ...' Then she realises she's being joshed, gives Lorrie a professional look of appraisal.

'Though I might be able to do something with your hair.'

Dinah leaves with a laugh on her lips and Lorrie, desperate not to misinterpret fun for flirting in her vulnerable state, says that she'll think about it. Then she gives the exterior of the Morning Star a thorough eyeing over. 'Not *that* keen on the colour,' she thinks. But it's only a colour and the rest of the barge has cinched it for her when a big guy, a mass of grey beard and an even bigger mass of grey hair stops her.

'You going to take it?' he says, straight in with the nosing.

'Pardon?'

'The Morning Star. It's been empty long enough. You going to take it?'

'I suppose ... Yes.'

'So we're going to be neighbours. Well, not quite that close.' He motions to the Crystal Lady a couple of berths from the green boat. Then he holds out his hand for the third handshake of Lorrie's morning.

'Ed,' he says and then he's almost leading her by their introductory grip as he adds, 'Come and have a cup of tea. Meet the missus.'

A week later Lorrie's background checks are complete, the Assured Tenancy Agreement signed, the Deposit Protection Scheme activated, and the Morning Star is to be hers for as long as she wants.

The new start begins with the stove lit, a spaghetti Bolognese simmering on the cooker, a glass of wine, her long legs *('Your best features,' Petra had whispered as she stroked softly from ankle to thigh.)* stretched out on the sofa. On the mantelpiece is a trophy of two female boxers squaring up to each other, awarded to Lorrie after an epic four rounder for the Club Championship. Lorrie uses it as a reminder to herself that, 'Tomorrow I'll start to get to fit again. Properly fit.' She'll do a daily run. Find a gym in town. These thoughts, on top of a couple of large glasses of wine, make Lorrie feel like doing something now. This instant. She drops to the cabin floor for twenty sit-ups and turns over for twenty press-ups. She does it, but it's worryingly hard work and Lorrie's breathing heavily. It shows her how far she's fallen since that night – she squints at the trophy – four years ago, just before she met Petra. So Lorrie's laying on the cabin floor of her floating home, staring at the ceiling and she's thinking, remembering, and it's mixed in with the oddness of relief.

'It's my new life, I can do anything I want,' she says to the ceiling. 'I'm free.'

Then she pours herself another glass of wine, lights up what she promises will be her last cigarette – it's not – and switches the telly on. Lorrie settles into the evening. Her evening. Tomorrow she'll have to phone work because she's at the end of sick-leave entitlement. There's no way she can face *that* drive every day. She'll look for a job in Broome. But this night Lorrie sleeps long and deep and, for the first time since the split, she doesn't dream of Petra.

Crystal Lady.
Fifty-foot narrowboat.
At Vixens Mere for the past seventeen years.
Decorated inside and out in New Age Hippie style.
Occupants: Big Ed and Milly, also sometimes referred to as Milly the Mystic. One offspring delivered to them at a week old, named Moses because, as Big Ed laughingly tells the child, they found him in the reeds. Sounds strange, but it's not that far off the truth.

The tenuous trail that brought them to Vixens Mere begins when Big Ed and Milly the Mystic wake up together in his partly, and very roughly, converted Transit van at the Reading Festival in the August of 1978. They're on a lumpy and rather grubby mattress in the back of the vehicle and the sun's already making the steel roof warm to the touch, so it must be about ten o'clock when Big Ed rolls himself over onto his back and encounters the soft prone body of Milly the Mystic. He yawns, looks at her curiously and says, 'You been here all night?'

She says, 'I think so.'

Big Ed studies her a bit more. 'What do they call you then?'

'Milly.'

She sits up, notices that her breasts are bare, lifts the covers, peeps down further at her naked nether regions. She looks at Ed, a question knitting her brow.

'Did we …?' she begins.

'Must have, I suppose.' Big Ed looks appreciatively at her breasts. 'But we could make sure.'

'If you like,' she says. 'Though I must have a piddle first. Have you got a bucket in here?'

Milly the Mystic never does find her clothes, not a stitch. Nothing. She couldn't even divine where she left her knickers so she finishes off the Festival in one of Ed's oversize shirts and little else. But it's really not a problem because the weather's hot in the day and Big Ed keeps her close in the coolness of the night.

After their intimate introduction, Big Ed and Milly the Mystic are never apart. They make a decent living together because, despite their overfondness for alcohol and chemical substances, they're grafters. They work the bars at the festivals together – Milly has a good head for figures and a good figure – and Big Ed's large and strong and always willing to sort out the drama. Milly also sells her merchandise of crystal necklaces, herbs, dried flowers, ankle chains, and the like, from the back of the van. She also pretends to read palms and tell fortunes but she doesn't pretend to take the money, so she does quite nicely in the financial stakes.

With the onset of the snowy winter of '78 the couple pull into an old farmyard, complete with its own deep well, hidden in the Mendips where they meet up with a few more of their own kind. Renovation and gentrification of this kind of disused building is still twenty years into the future. Here there's a stone barn with a many holed roof where a fire can burn brightly and smoke escape without suffocating anyone.

These others of the same ilk gather around the fire at night for a few jars of Special Olde Scrumpy cider – allegedly 12% gravity – and a smoke. There's nothing too outlandish floating around at the mo, the heavier stuff is being saved until the spring, until they're on the move again. It's a rough and ready commune of a dozen gatherers within three large vans, a removal lorry, and a mini-bus. These are of varying ages and even more varying designs; arcs of rainbow, bright flowers, white clouds. Mind they're all spotted with outbreaks of rust.

The Somerset weather's bitterly cold on this high ground and firewood is foraged from the hedges and tumbledown buildings to keep the woodstoves alight, the food pots simmering. Outside, bodily warmth is mostly contained within a common collection of army greatcoats that found their way onto the black market just in time for the first frosts. Discounting the hairy heads and beards, you might be deceived into thinking this could be an army base. Big Ed has two stripes on his arm to Milly's one and he continually pulls rank on her until she blatantly disobeys orders. He says he'll have her court-martialled for insubordination and Milly says she'll serve her sentence in Bluto's van if Ed wants. That shuts him up because Bluto's a muscular lad barely into his twenties and, even on the coldest of morning, he dips a bucket of water from the well and gives his bare torso a good cleanse with soap and flannel. This causes a few curtains to flutter in the residents' windows. For everyone else on site, hygiene is a cat-lick from a bowl inside the shelter of their respective vehicles. This is especially noticeable, and only partially diluted by the Moroccan brand, when backsides are aligned to the evening fire in the barn.

It's a long winter this one and it drags itself well into March before wet weather defrosts the ground. There's talk between them of upcoming gatherings, licenced and unlicenced, and the Summer Solstice at Stonehenge. 'Be thousands there this year. It's going to be a monster.' Talk becomes action and the group begins to disband. Every day the numbers dwindle until there's just Big Ed and Milly left poking the fire. One night they think that they'll take a drive, park up near a pub and have a good drink. They're well on that road when they get into conversation with a fellow traveller. He's called Randy and he walks the walk and talks the talk as the potent cider flows thick and fast. Tales are told, events relived, locations revisited. But their newfound friend talks wistfully of the upcoming season.

'Not for me,' he says. 'I'm calling it a day because,' he pauses, takes a massive swallow of Exmoor Scrumpy, 'because I'm getting married. Settling down.'

The words are delivered as though he's confessing to a mortal sin. It seems he's had a rethink about his life and he's thinking that at twenty-eight years of age it's time for convention. His girlfriend won't live his life and, if he wants her enough, he'll have to live hers. He's been holed up on the canal for the winter on an old barge and now he's putting it on the market. His girlfriend's won not only his heart but the argument too.

Randy says pensively, 'I suppose it'll pay for the reception,' and stares into his glass as though the answer's in his beer.

Big Ed says, 'What's it like?' and Milly, with barely a comma's break between Ed's and her words, continues with, 'Yeah, what's it like?'

Randy says, 'Well, it floats.'

They take a look the next morning, still a little bleary from the consumption of fermented apple juice, but Randy's barge does more than float. This fifty-foot narrowboat, painted every colour of the rainbow and then some, may be pre-war but it's solid and homely and has the steady beating heart of a Lister Marine diesel engine. Without going into too much detail about generating power, 12-volt batteries, inverters, and the like, Randy is open to a reasonable offer. That offer's duly made and a month later Big Ed and Milly have sold the van and are the proud owners of Maid Marion, which Milly promptly changes to Crystal Lady. They leave Randy with a pocketful of cash and a tear in his eye staring forlornly after them as they chug away down the cut.

The summer of '79 is warm and lazy and they slowly explore the liquid highways of the canals. They've a bit of cash put by and it's supplemented by Milly's selling technique and Big

Ed's earning as one the best odd jobbers in the business. Big Ed can labour with the best; he's good on a mixer, a tractor, a digger, and anything mechanical. But for the couple it's mainly days on the warm slow waters and gentle rocking to sleep at night aboard Crystal Lady. The rocking's sometimes more than gentle; they're a lusty pair these two.

For years afterwards Ed and Milly always refer to this first summer on the water as 'the summer,' because it's a time when their adventure was new to them, and they were still new to each other. But summers don't last forever and by October the nights are chilling and they're on the lookout for a winter's mooring. Early one afternoon, after chugging slowly past Broome, they find Vixens Mere. They coast into the basin, tie up the boat. Milly leans over the starboard bow, slowly swings a crystal over the water. With intense concentration, she tracks the crystal's motion and, hardly breathing, she lets it sink slowly into the water. She holds it there, dangling like bait for the fishes, and she thinks that she can feel a gentle rhythmic tug, like a silent ticking, a keeping in time with an aqueous heartbeat. She wonders for minute, fancies it's her imagination, then she straightens up, slowly lifts her line in.

Big Ed, impatient for the ritual to be over asks, 'All right, Milly. Will it do?'

It'll more than do for Milly. She says, 'It's magic, Ed. Magic. A good place to stop.'

If it's good enough for Milly, it's good enough for Big Ed and it becomes their go-to retreat for each succeeding winter. That's until the temporary mooring becomes the permanent mooring 'cos they're getting on a bit and age makes them pull their horns in. They become a part of the floating hamlet of several barges that have settled into the scenery, half above the water and half in it, like they're unsure which world they belong to.

These barges may look untidy, perhaps even scruffy, but they're not neglected. Not dirty. Behind these boats, land-lubber side, Big Ed has cleared a large patch of ground and it's holding his rough-fenced garden, a scrapped vehicle, a decent sized wooden building known as Ed's Shed where there's always a drink on offer. Stacks of bricks, blocks, slates, a rack of timber, ladders, a mixer and a ubiquitous white van are giveaway clues to the trade Big Ed now plies. A pair of goats – animals of Milly's kingdom – wander along the water's edge; as do a band of renegade chickens, led by a cantankerous cockerel, that take free-ranging to another level. There's also an ancient black and white mongrel dog who totters around on uncertain legs. He spends most of his day keeping watch from the roof of Crystal Lady and, in the dusking of this day, he gives a warning bark at the approach of a stranger on the water. This is his last duty as a guard dog. A few days later he topples off his perch, in more ways than one.

CHAPTER TWO

Summer Walker.

Forty-foot broadbeam barge. Scottish blue. Saltire flying from stern.

One occupant, a well-travelled Caledonian. Two, if Mick, his collie, is included.

Makes a living aboard carving figurines, walking-sticks, ornaments, candlesticks, and the like.

Brodie Stewart.

Now you could have cruised slowly by, gone farther up the cut to a modern marina with hot showers, a café, a pub within stepping distance, but there was a compulsion to pull hard on the rudder and steer into Vixens Mere. It looks as though nothing much has changed here. Same barges moored up. Trees dipping into the water. Unkemptness. *Brigadoon*, you laugh to yourself.

But curiosity steered you in because you often wondered how life turned out for some. For one. But these are thoughts that you've forbidden to yourself and you shake them out of your head. You shush Mick, who's raised his hackles to the challenge of the canine aboard Crystal Lady – and tie-up a distance from the other craft. Then it's the lighting of the stove to get some warmth onboard, and there's just enough time to stretch your legs before night falls proper. So, roll-up smouldering between fingers, an inquisitive Mick in tow, you take a slow amble of rediscovery around the perimeter of Vixens Mere. You're right that nothing much has changed here; ramshackle shower and WC leaning further into the wind, unsavoury wafts from the toilet sluice, potholes in the path, bushes need cutting back. Then you stop your walking to pass a few words with Ed – big, bearded, instantly recognisable Ed – who's watching the night start to creep over the water. You give him a 'Good evening,' as he frowns, quizzically tries to place you. Until.

'Brodie,' he says, screwing his face up in the remembering, 'Saw you come in. Thought I recognised the boat. Christ, it must be … thirteen … fourteen years?'

It's actually fifteen but you say, 'Been a while, Ed,' and stay jawing for a bit.

By now night's well on its way and the towpath illuminations, rusty lanterns on rickety poles, are blinking in indecision. Boat lights are flicking on and tables are being set for tea, or dinner, or simply 'Grub's up.' And that 'Grub's up' sentiment is for the dark shadow of a boy, a young man who's strumming a guitar on the deck of Crystal Lady and singing softly to himself. You say, 'Good voice, Ed,' and Ed pauses for an instant, like he's unsure to tell you, 'That's Moses.' His and Milly's boy. Then Ed says for you to call around for a drink and a catch-up at 'About seven if you like, Brodie. Milly'll be glad to see a new face.'

You whistle up Mick to finish your strolling as a cold autumn drizzle begins to fall. The both of you are glad when the exercise is over and you're in the snug cabin of Summer Walker.

Later it's just as snug in Crystal Lady when Ed's asking, 'Lager all right?' and Milly echoing Ed's previous, 'Been a long time, Brodie.' Then she's looking curiously into your face and saying, 'But you haven't changed at all. What's your secret, Brodie?'

Ed sighs that it's no secret because, 'Brodie hasn't had to

put up with a nagging woman 24/7. That's enough to put wrinkles on an eggshell.' Milly mutters that looking after Big Ed all these years hasn't helped her complexion either. Then Milly concentrates on you, wants to know what you've done, where you've been?

You give her place names, quiet backwaters, endless locks, and canal-side stops. She dreams, wishes that she and Ed were a bit younger, "Cos we'd be on your tail, Brodie,' she laughs. But their travelling days are long past. 'Though we still get away for the odd weekend do. Mattress in the back of the van,' Milly laughs, 'Romantic. Like we're on honeymoon, eh Ed?'

Big Ed grunts, says sleeping in the fucking van kills his back. He gets out his tobacco tin to twist one up for him and Milly and she begins to talk about their years at Vixens Mere, all the comings and the goings. Some names you know and some you don't. Milly's good with words and she paints a picture *of a long-ago Christmas night around a red-hot wood burner in the Shed, bottle of beer in one hand, toker in the other, music swallowing the conversation. She recalls the others that shared that night: Mark and Sandra Rawlins, cutting each other blinders: Pigman Pete, someone she can't remember from Morning Star, Ethan and Jenny James, a couple of kids sprawled on hay bales, sleeping under coats. Milly brings back all of these faces from a winter's mooring. But then Karen Jones quietly takes her place in the picture that Milly's painting.*

This Karen Jones is young and touching on the beautiful and you have to let her in because you can't keep her out. Not here, not at the place where it began. And where it ended.

Milly says, 'They're back every winter, aren't they, Ed?'
'Who?'
'Harry and Karen. Should be here soon. Weren't you listening to me?'

Big Ed answers question one with a 'No' and the other, 'In a day or two probably.'

Milly lifts her glass, takes a swallow of Leuven's finest, asks, 'You remember them, Brodie?'

You say that you remember Karen, but her husband, 'Wasn't he in hospital, Milly?'

She says, 'Oh yeah, he was.' She takes a long draw on her roll-up and frowns in the recalling of, 'Karen came to the party on her own.' Milly's silent for a moment, like the sentence is unfinished and she's something to add; a silent inference of *'But she didn't leave on her own, did she?'*

By eleven o'clock you're back on Summer Walker and Vixens Mere is in darkness and a quietness has settled over the water. You take yourself to your warm bed and the weight of Mick on your feet. But before you sleep you add together the countless years that you've been on the cut; all the scorching summers, all the freezing winters, all the budding springs and cascading autumns.

To them you add Karen Jones stroking the softest of all knocks on your door in the middle of the night. And you opening that door to the dreamy moonlight. And you both standing there with a moment of stillness between you. And you taking her hand, drawing her to you, continuing what had begun. Continuing until a guilty dawn colours the sky, until this woman leaves you with your tumbled bed and a mouthful of, 'I'm sorry, Brodie, I'm sorry.'

She might use your name but the words of apology are not for you, they're for her wounded husband bearing a lonely Christmas inside a hospital ward of strangers.

You shake your head but you can't shake her from your mind.

Home Sweet Home.
Permanent mooring close to Crystal Lady. Occupied by owner Jed Rawlins, son of Mark Rawlins (deceased) and Sandra Day (deserter).
Jed and Anna.

There's two bedrooms on Jed's barge and it's the first morning in six months that they've both been occupied. Up until this end time – the half a year ago – Jed would lay abed and listen to his dad's endless coughing. Sometimes he'd find himself joining in as though the cancer was contagious, or that by sharing it he was halving it. But it's neither; its terminal embrace is greedy for one person only. Even weeks afterwards, months afterwards, Jed would be sure he caught the hack of a cough and he would go into his father's room, remembering the day the ambulance came to call and the paramedics stretchered his dad out; the day it was all done. He wanted, and he didn't want, to hear that struggling for breath ever again. But after his dad had gone, Jed slept in his room just to be close to him. Just in case he was needed. In case the ghost of his father woke in the night and wanted a drink to cool his burning mouth.

This lanky, long-haired youth of nineteen has had a lot on his plate in his short life, but that doesn't make him a virtuous victim because you could say he's contributing to others' victimhood. You see Jed deals in drugs. He exchanges popular market products for cold cash. He bargains in crowded nightclubs, dishes out the goods in dark doorways, in gloomy alleys. This good-looking – in a bony sharp-featured sort of way – young man is both problem and solution, depending on your dependency. But Jed's own problem is his growing cocaine intake that's becoming a bit too regular and expensive for comfort.

Last night in Broome – and this is why he's not home alone – Jed had done something that could be described as not his cleverest deed, although it's probably been his most compassionate.

A cold wet street the wrong side of midnight is Jed's last staging post before he takes himself home. Shop signs are dripping, pavements dully borrowing light from shop windows. Jed's standing in the mouth of a dark alley, hood turned up. One hand is inside his coat, finger counting the wraps he's got left. He's shuffling his Nike trainers on the pavement trying to friction some warmth to his damp feet. Business has not been the best on account of it being a flat midweek and the shite weather. And this is when Jed first sees her, when she appears out of the shadows and finds the light. She has a child's face on a woman's body, and she's dressed in the fashion of scruff; long dark skirt, long dark coat, long dark hair, none too clean, but there's an innocence to her. Not a halo of innocence, but it's like she's out of place, unsure of herself; she doesn't thrust herself forward as she sets down her Jumbo plastic carrier; it's overspilling with the giveaways of a rough sleeper. Her blanket, her sleeping bag, is soaking wet and so is she. Wet and shivering.

'Can you fix me up?' she says and her voice is as soft as the drizzle that's swirling in the wind and dimming the streetlamps.

'Thirty a wrap to you,' Jed says as he's putting an age to this girl. Sixteen? Seventeen? He doesn't think eighteen and he's good at guessing ages. He's usually right because he depends on sharpness in his line of work.

'I've got twenty?' she says. There's a hope in the question.

'Thirty,' Jed says. Seems like it's all numbers on this wet night.

He takes a look at this young girl with soggy clothes, a couple of years younger than himself, and adds on, 'Can't do it for less.'

He hears her gulp.

'Please,' she says and the plea is drowning in desperation.

Jed knows why she needs it. It's to make the night bearable. She'll be down some dark alley, in some dark doorway, getting colder and wetter. She'll be watching the sky and praying for the dawn. She fumbles a crumpled banknote, some loose shrapnel, from her pocket and thrusts them into his hand, holds out her own in expectation. But Jed smooths out the note, assesses the coins, shakes his head, thinks she's unlucky because …

'Sorry. Can't do it for that. Look, it's just not enough.'

It's not enough because his cut on this deal would amount to a minus, reduce it to a subsidy. But now he's had a chance to have a decent peep at her, to notice the shivering of her frame. She looks bedraggled. Tired. Ill. Her eyes are large, frightened, in her face. There's a cut on her lip and a bruising to her face; the tell-tale signs of a recent beating.

'Please,' she says, 'Please. I need it.'

She's swaying slightly and Jed is just going to say, again, that it's no can do when she crumples in front of him, begins a sink to the pavement in a slow-motion collapse. She clutches at him, snatches onto his arm. For a moment he takes the weight of her and there's not much of that. Then she manages to straighten up, pulls in a deep breath, apologises with, 'Sorry. I'm sorry.'

And Jed is sorry that this poor disorientated girl is out on the streets on a night like this and, against his better judgement, and because she's vulnerably pretty and must be running from something bad, he says in the generosity of his culture, 'Look you can crash at mine tonight if you want.'

She so desperately needs this offer and she nods an acceptance with such open gratitude that it disconcerts him, and he mumbles that he's a spare room. That's in case she thought there was a cost to his kindness.

So it's here on a cold wet night, with a gusting wind slapping onto their faces, that their story begins. It'll maybe run for a while and there's sure to be happy times and not so happy times in their tale. Like any relationship.

It's a couple of miles back to Home Sweet Home, a slow walk on account of the girl's condition. At the edge of Broome they leave the lighted road and they're into the unlit lanes to Vixens' basin of black water. On this journey he gets the name Anna and not much else. No back story forthcoming. She does say before they step aboard, 'I've never been on a ship before,' and Jed says in the offended tone of a water dweller, 'It's not a ship, it's a barge.' Then they're into the warmth of the cabin and he stokes up the stove. Anna draws herself to the glow, shrugs off her coat, tugs off her boots, takes his offer of a towel and rubdries her hair. Then she arranges her sleeping bag, her blanket, her oddments of clothes around the stove. Those clothes, and herself, gently steam in the warmth. (Not the most fragrant of aromas taints the air). Anna takes Jed's offer of a hot drink, a helping of chocolate biscuits, and she huddles into a chair, mug of coffee in her hand. The raw cold is ebbing from her face.

'Thanks for this. What you're doing,' she says in the way of a stranger thanking a stranger.

'It's all right. No worries.'

He speaks as though this sort of thing happens on a regular basis, when in fact this is the first time he's ever played the Good Samaritan. On this scale anyway. He extends his hospitality further by emptying a wrap on the table. He teases out a line, pulls out a straw and offers her first pull and her snuffling perks her up for a quarter of an hour, brings a brightness to her eyes. But it's only fleeting because then the brightness darkens and those eyes struggle to stay open. It's as though the evening has suddenly dropped its weight on her and she's done for. And then it's to the bedroom where this exhausted young woman pulls off her clothes, leaves them in a not so damp bundle on the floor, and crawls herself under the warm covers of the bed and straight into a deep sleep.

Jed's not so quick at dropping off and, in his father's room, he listens to the moan of the wind, the soft drift of the rain on the windows. He wonders about the girl asleep in his bed, how she's where she is. He thinks that he'll give her a breakfast and then drop her a few quid and send her on her way. But by nine o'clock he's not heard a sound from her room and he taps gently on the door.

'Anna,' he calls softly a couple of times to the silence of a no reply. He calls louder and then pushes the door slowly open. Anna is soundo, snuggled into the duvet like a squirrel, her hair spread over the pillow. Although it might seem a bit pervy, Jed can't help watching her for a minute, studying her pale features, even reaching out and just touching her hair, wondering again how she washed up on the streets, ended up in his bed? It could be the fault of the usual suspects: abuse, drugs, sex, mental … God she could even be on the run, so he leaves her to sleep on. Which she does. And then she stays on because she's nowhere else to go and Jed's heart is too soft to cast her adrift. But it's not for nothing, these board and lodging, she has a part to play in Jed's game. She has to help him in his commerce and she becomes his sales assistant.

A few days later the weather's turned on a sixpence and the temperature's dropped like a stone. It's still falling after dark as they start the rounds and there's a brittle ring to their footfalls on the pavement. But they're well wrapped up and Jed's padded out her boots with an extra pair of socks. He's also dug Anna out one of his old hoodies, 'To hide your pretty face,' he says and she tells him she could get used to his compliments. That's how it is with them tonight, a perkiness to her, an easiness between them. But there's also a trace of nervousness as she scans around herself, glances over her shoulder, as though she might be afraid of seeing something, or someone, she doesn't want to. On this night they visit a few dives, a few suspect pubs, sell a few sweeties in the toilets. From twelve till one they're on his post at the mouth of the dark alley where, several nights ago, Anna tried to buy for under the market price. Then, at an hour past midnight, they walk back to Jed's floating home and in the dark lane, just before the land falls to Vixens Mere, Jed slips his arm around Anna's waist and this child/woman melts to him. And of course there's more to follow, and of course two bedrooms become one.

Jed's up early this next morning; there's business in town. He shifts his lanky frame out of the narrow bed and, Anna sleepy and warm stirs. Sits up. Yawns. Blinks into the light.

'What time is it, Jed?' and he shushes her, tells her that it's early and that he'll be back lunchtime. He'll bring her home a pasty to eat.

Anna says, 'Will you leave me something?'

The something is a fresh wrap on the cabinet top that she'll open out as soon as Jed's on his way. This is Anna's breakfast but Jed's healthier one is a slice of bread under the grill and a smearing of butter. Then Jed, eating his toast on the hoof, leaves his barge and the pretty sleepy-headed Anna to head for town. His walk in the chill fresh air should clear his mind. And his nose. He starts up the rise out of the basin and, out of a habit formed of years, he stops, turns, in a bidding farewell to a ghost who's standing in the fore of the barge watching the leaving.

Jed's twelve years old and he's taking his bike to cycle to Broome.

'Stay on the towpath, Jed.'

'Course I will, Dad.'

He's sixteen years old and he thinks the bus on the road is cooler than the bicycle.

'Got your pass, Jed?'

'Course I have.'

Then he's nineteen years old and there's no Dad to wave goodbye to anymore. But Jed still stops on the track, looks back, raises his hand, mouths a goodbye to his father. Sometimes he adds on a goodbye to his mother, a ghostly shadow beside his father. There are no pictures, no framed photographs of his mother on show aboard Home Sweet Home, and she isn't ever spoken of; it's like she never existed. But Jed knows she did.

So Jed looks back at Vixens Mere for comfort in the memory of images and words. In his scanning of the scene there's the newest arrival; a barge that's moored away from the other craft like it doesn't want company. A gentle shifting of the smoking mist rising from the water seems to blur its lines, subdue its shape. For Jed there might be a slight curiosity – is it vaguely familiar? – towards forty feet of elderly nondescript barge but that's all; comings and goings are part of this wet life. So he doesn't think anymore of it and he heads into town to replenish supplies. But he doesn't get far in his walking because Pigman Pete pulls up alongside him in his work van, emblazoned with *We Bring Home The Bacon* on both flanks, along with a happy smiling pig's head, and says, 'Hop in. I'll give you a lift.'

There's a moment of hesitation from Jed. Past experience reminds him that the interior of the van carries the pungent, sweetly sick aroma of Pete's vocation, but it's colder outside than he expected, so he winds his long frame into the passenger seat.

'Cheers, Pete.'

'No problem,' says Pete. He likes to help people does Pete.

Saddleback.
Permanently moored rent-out. Forty-footer. Twin berth. Lounge/kitchen and usual mod cons. Not the cleanest of barges in the marina.
Tenant: Peter Warman aka Pigman Pete.
At six o'clock of this morning the alarm goes off and Pete's out of bed like a shot. In seconds the kettle's set onto the stove and he's into the WC for his morning relief. Then he lights the ring

under the frying pan and fills it with four slices of thick back bacon. This is one of the perks of his job: a couple of packs of bacon, and best pork sausages, that's added to his wages every week. Pigman Pete, as his nickname implies, works on a pig farm. But it's more than a farm, here the whole process from birthing to butchering is carried out in-house.

Pete's main job is to enable a hundred sows to provide continuous litters in a conveyer belt process of production. He feeds, he cleans, he records, and as long as the supply keeps coming, he's left more or less to himself. And he loves his work. He loves his pigs. He loves the smell of them, the grunts of them (sometimes he even gets a grunting conversation going) their big ears and curly tails, their piggy eyes. He loves sitting in the canteen at lunchtime when a tenderfoot has to hear the tales of rogue swine from the veteran hands. There's talk of children being dragged into sties, losing fingers, arms, legs and feet. But Pete's favourite story always starts with a warning to the newcomer from one of the old hands.

'You want to be wary of these beasts, Nipper. Never turn your back on 'em.'

Then a wide-eyed Nipper is fed the narrative of, 'Bertie Saunders. Disappeared without trace. Mystery that one. They found a tooth. That's all. One tooth left of a whole man.'

According to this rural fable it seems that this Bertie Saunders, recluse and miser, man with a screw loose, tighter than a duck's arse, kept a couple of big sows for company. 'Might have been a bit more than that. Closest thing to a woman they say. Never tried it myself, though.' The old boy always pauses for a laugh here and usually gets a chuckle from his peers. 'Let them run in and out of his cottage he did. Sleep by the fire, sit at the table like they were his family.'

Then Bertie Saunders didn't put in an appearance at the town on a market day. When the same thing happened – or didn't happen – the following week someone went to see if he was all right. But they found no sign of Bertie. 'Not hide nor hair of him. And the house had been ransacked, all the cupboards emptied. Larder cleared out. Pig shit everywhere. Up the stairs. On the bed.'

So it was a mystery until someone realized that the pigs had eaten everything consumable in the house, so logically they must have eaten Bertie. The only trace of him was that undigested tooth. It was reckoned that Bertie must have collapsed – heart attack or something – and the pigs started eating him up. 'Hope poor Bertie was already dead when they started to chobble on his feet. Don't fancy being eaten alive.'

By now Nipper's looking at his lunch and the old boy telling the tale can hardly keep a straight face. He leans across the table, offers Nipper the bottle of tomato sauce, ''Cos this'll go nicely with your bacon and egg.'

Nipper says no thanks; he doesn't feel particularly hungry at the moment.

Pigman Pete loves living in Vixens Mere. And he loves Big Ed and Milly, and Moses, and young Jed the orphan. Well, maybe not really an orphan. His dad hasn't long snuffed it and there's not been hide nor hair of Jed's mum, Sandra, for years. Milly reckoned Sandra had a weakness for anything in trousers and Big Ed observed, 'Well she missed me out,' and Milly said even Sandra had to draw the line somewhere. Pete thinks that he must be in the same club as Ed, what with his body-shape – more than plump – and lack of hair. He hasn't scored in a very long while.

This morning, with the windscreen on his van still defrosting, Pete's barely into the lane when he spots Jed and thinks it'll be nice to have some company on his run in to work.

* * *

Summer Walker.
You.
All this day you've known something was in the air. The dog's caught on your mood, he's watching, he's waiting with you. He's sat on the roof all afternoon, head on his paws, nose pointing like a compass towards the eastern skyline. About three o'clock he gives out a warning bark and, through the starboard window, you watch them come in and wonder if it would be better if you weren't here.

Bombardier.
Broadbeam boat. Union flag fluttering from its stern. Painted red, white and blue. Booked into the mooring at Vixens for the rest of the winter as it has been for the last fifteen years. Harry and Karen Jones.
Twelve months ago, ex-soldier, invalided soldier, Harry could see Karen's features fairly clearly, easily make out the shape to her. Now there's a blurring to the lines of her face, to the boats that pass, the human and animal traffic on the towpath. The sun is dimming for Harry as the wounding from eighteen years ago states its intent onto his brain.

Harry has retained his military bearing; even when he's on the water he holds himself ramrod upright. But the walking isn't good, he drags one foot after the other in a disjointed movement of progress. Karen, engine and tiller girl of the boat, holds the worn look of a carer to her features. There might be a faint forming of crows' feet around her eyes but she's still an attractive woman, and still under forty. Just.

She calls out, 'We're close now, Harry,' and he shades his eyes against the low winter sun and squints into a scene where the edges are vague and unsure. 'Like my life,' Harry thinks and remembers what brought them to their existence on the cut.

* * *

After the detonation of the IED in that far-off country, and two years after the medical discharge from his beloved Company, he'd said to Karen, 'I don't want to settle down yet,' and that was a question to her because they'd rented a place or two, tried the two up two down living. Contemplated the buying of somewhere close to relations.

She'd said, 'What do you want to do?' because it was his shout and it was him that had survived by the skin of his teeth. But the Harry who came back from that survival was not the Harry who'd filled the room with his presence; Harry the joker; the man who'd whispered his love of her in the dark of the night. This is a not-the-same Harry. He's subdued. He's quiet and he needs the quiet. Badly.

'It's here, Karen.' He'd stroked his forehead. 'It's like every sound has an echo.'

So they bought a barge, settled for a spell on the canals, because, 'It's what you said you always wanted, Karen.' And she was right for both of them, because this is the solution, this drifting unhurriedly along the waterways. In this life, they can hide away, because Harry isn't that good with people anymore. Sometimes he'll put his hands over his ears, shut his eyes, and retreat into a world that didn't end with the leaving behind of the bombs and the bullets. One year becomes two, becomes ten, becomes more. Becomes a way of life. Becomes today as they're growing into middle-age and beginning to realise it.

They slip slowly, barely ticking over, into Vixens Mere and the rippling wash of the Bombardier gently rocks the moored boats.

'There's a few in,' says Karen and, without being asked, because she knows that it's a silent question between them, she calls out the names of the boats as they cruise slowly past.

* * *

Saddleback.
Crystal Lady.
Home Sweet Home.
Morning Star.

'All the usual,' Karen thinks. The once-a-year friends for the duration of the worst months of winter. But then suddenly, she sees Summer Walker, and her heart takes a leap into her throat. It can't be, not after all these years?

'Summer Walker?' Harry's not sure he's heard the name before but he digs into the fuzz of his memory like he's going to find it.

Karen says, 'Long time ago, Harry. We – I – stayed here when you were ill that time.' *That dream time of erratic lights, fitful sounds, distant voices, when he'd lost months of his life to a hospital bed. Months that Harry can't forget or remember.*

'Summer Walker, Harry. Scottish bloke on his own. Woodcarver. Young.'

Harry says quietly, 'We were all young then, Karen.'

It's a wistful statement and Karen, lightening it up and wanting the changing of the subject, pushes on with a description of herself. 'Fifteen years ago, Harry. Fifteen pounds ago, Harry. Lots of years and lots of pounds.' But that's an exaggeration because it's barely half that number in weight. Karen Jones has kept herself together, fit and exercised, because she winds the sluice boards, she strains against the lock gates, she drives in the mooring pegs, tethers the barge. She cooks and cleans inside and washes and cleans outside. And she's virtually a fulltime carer to Harry. Unconsciously, she spans her stomach with her hands. She still has her shape; she's one of those women who might grow slightly larger but always keeps the same proportions. There's just a little more of her for the loving she tells herself. Not that there's much of that these days. Or any days. In her mind she starts to count back before she calls a halt to the barren years.

Harry's still trying to make out Summer Walker's uncertain shape, the Saltire hanging limply from its stern, but it shimmers in his gaze and Karen, having given out the boats' names, wonders that soon she might be needing to add a description as well. It's reminders like this that sometimes bear down on her; she's noticing even more his struggling to focus into the distance, the increasing number of times he sits with his head in his hands, the low moaning he doesn't know he's doing. What Karen can't help dwelling on is when this life they're living will become impossible. She steers the boat gently to the bank where a lanky but good-looking boy, watching her in, calls out, 'Throw us the rope, Mrs Jones. I'll tie you up.'

'Thank you, Moses,' she says.

'No trouble, Mrs Jones.'

She so desperately wants to say, 'It's Mum, Moses. It's Mum.' But of course, those words are unlikely to ever come from her mouth. She'll conceal them like she concealed Moses in that summer of deception; hidden under the cover of loose blouses, loose skirts, loose jackets. Her condition secreted in a costume of flowing volume, of cotton and colour, a summer of looking more like Milly than Milly herself.

CHAPTER THREE

Crystal Lady.

Big Ed says to Milly, 'Seeing as it's Friday night, I think I'll fire up the wood burner.'

That's the wood burner in the Shed, the building that's an ample twenty foot by twenty. It's been an extra room to them, and in it there's a long sofa, several easy chairs, a church pew recycled from a renovation job Ed worked on, the wood burner, pot-bellied and ancient, with a cast iron flue that stretches up to the ceiling and pokes its head through the roof. So it's warm and comfortable and ready for the filling, because there's nothing more Ed and Milly like than a bit of a gathering; reminds them of their younger days. There'll be talk, some food, music in the background, and some drinking to excess on the cards. And the invite is for an open house – well, open Shed – to all the ducks on the water; six at the last count.

Milly says, 'Think I'll crack open a can, Ed. Get myself in the mood.'

'Bit early. You'll be legless.'

'Only one position you want my legs in, Ed. Isn't there?'

Milly is rolling up a double jointer and she makes a great show of running her tongue suggestively along its length.

'It'll have to wait, Milly,' Big Ed laughs. 'Need a bit of time for the Viagra to kick in.' He looks at his watch. 'Reckon we should be all right 'bout twelve.'

Milly has a chuckle and says she hopes it'll be worth the

waiting and Ed asks when has he ever let her down? Milly laughs again and says that some nights it's like trying to raise the dead. They sit in the prow of Crystal Lady and Big Ed untabs a beer, offers it to Milly in exchange for a long draw of weed. Then there's a cuddling together, the comfort of their years of loving wrapped around them, as they watch the ending of the light. Into this easiness they bring the talk of the old days, of van and boat, of struggles and laughter.

Ed, an arm around his old lady, says, seriously for him for once, 'You know, I wouldn't change a thing since the day I met you.' Milly says that nor would she and they'll be together for all of time. Ed, Milly, and Moses.

'At least that's what the cards say.' Which isn't cast-iron convincing, because Milly's tarot readings sometimes leave a lot to be desired.

They sit until it's almost dark and frost is starting to slime the metal of the boat, and it's time to step into the warmth of the cabin. But before this, Milly shivers, shivers enough for Big Ed to say, 'Someone walked over your grave?'

The words are in her mouth before she realizes it, 'Not my grave, Ed,' and so she says the words again, more slowly, 'Not my grave, Ed. Not mine.' She wonders exactly whose grave it is and it worries her, because sometimes her premonitions have become truth. Sometimes she's not a charlatan.

Saddleback.
A little later.
Pigman Pete is having a doze after his tea when Milly, preceded by a loud rap, pokes her head through his door, startles him awake.

'What the fu ...?'

'It's only me, Pete. Fancy tonight at the Shed?' She raises her hand to her mouth, mimics drinking.

Pete yawns, 'I've had a long day, Milly. I was going to have an early night.'

Milly kids him: 'What? At your age, Pete?' – he's 45 – 'You have your shower and we'll see you a bit later.' There's an unspoken hint that he's brought the sweet pungency of pig shite home with him. It's soaked into his clothes, crusted on his boots, and it's worse than usual because Pete's had a very long day.

This long day has included the usual feeding and cleaning out of his herd of breeding ladies, but added to this was a session in the butchery department. Mr Long, the Proprietor of Broome Pork Products (We Bring Home The Bacon) likes to involve his workers in every aspect of the business. This includes the laying out of pig carcasses for jointing, boning, and slicing into chops and rashers and the like. Pete's become pretty adept with knife, saw, and cleaver. In fact he's a natural dismemberer, although he much prefers handling the living animals.

Even though he's a bit knackered after all his extra hours, Pete will shave, have that shower Milly's wished onto him, and fit himself into a clean set of clothes. He'll comb his sparse hair over his pate, put a six pack of Premium Lager under his arm and head for the Shed. Actually, he'll probably drink more than his six pack tonight because it's not been the best of weeks for him and this day was the worst.

In all the time he's been working for Broome Pork Products – fourteen years and counting – Pete has kept to the cardinal rule of caring for the animals but not getting too attached to them. Sure he can love them, appreciate their finer points, laugh at their antics, but it's got to be from a step away, as he knows that there's only one place they're heading for. Even so, it's not always been easy; he's had several weaners that he still remembers to this day but there's been none quite like Phyllis.

She'd been a cocky upstart from day one, a right little madam, latching onto her mother's teat and hanging on for grim death despite all the pushing, shoving, and burrowing from her peers. As she grows, Pete's sure she waits for his visits, catches his eye, sees him scrape and brush her quarters. She's alert for him and Pete watches her, knows every line to her clean smooth body, can clearly pick her out among her brethren and, as stupid as it sounds, it seems she's pleased to see him. Her ears definitely twitch, her tail wags. Then, what should never happen happens: she touches his heart and he gives her a name, Phyllis.

But of course she grows, and when she, along with her batch, is nine months old and ninety kilos in weight, she's herded off to slaughter. Phyllis is taken on a shift when Pete's on a day's break and that should be that. Pete turns in for work next day to a depleted but milling mass of weaners who all look the same and squeal beyond loud for their feed. 'Phyllis was just an animal,' he tells himself. Just one out of many that he's helped onto the breakfast plate. He puts that thought into his mind every time his soft heart intrudes on his consciousness. It works for a whole week, until today. This afternoon, in fact, when Pete's taken a turn in the butchery department. He really shouldn't be on this shift but a regular has called in sick and dab-hand Pete is deemed the best man for the replacement. There's several carcasses on the block and Pete and an older colleague, Sam, are slicing, sawing, hacking and chopping the chilled corpses into the primal cuts of shoulder, loin, leg and belly. The radio's playing away and Sam's singing along to the Seventies and telling Pete, 'Now that's what you call a real tune.'

Pete thought it was until Sam renders his version aloud. But he's all right is Sam, and every three quarters of an hour he calls out a fag break. They stand out the back, take a quick warming from the afternoon sun, relieve their chilling from the meat. On this external visit Sam looks at his watch, 'Well, this'll be last for today, Pete, and then we're done.'

Then he says that he'll just pop down to the bog and Pete goes back inside and unhooks the last two carcasses from the rack. Lays them out side by side on the cutting table. One for him and one for Sam.

'Right,' Pete thinks and prepares to make the first draw with his saw. Then he stops suddenly, instantly, in mid stroke. He takes a step back, looks at the headless, footless, open body in front of him, and, as stupid as it sounds, he recognises her. It's Phyllis. He doesn't know how; he just knows. The saw drops to his side and he can't do it, not this one. So he swaps places with Sam, and Phyllis goes to cheery Sam who continues to sing along to the Seventies as he butchers Phyllis, cuts her into pieces. Pete just keeps his head down and works on his nameless carcass until it's done and they're done. It's time to clean the tools of their trade for another day, and for Singer Sam to leave Pete with a cheery goodbye. Pete trails behind his exit, sidling past and trying not to look at Sam's handiwork; bits of Phyllis neatly prepared for consumption. He's never been so relieved to close the door on his work in his life.

Outside in the car park Pete sits behind the wheel of his van, lights up a cigarette that trembles in his fingers. Christ, what the fuck's the matter with him. She was a pig. That's all. A fucking pig. And if that's all it is then why is his head in his hands? Why is he squeezing his eyes shut?

This is what middle-aged matronly Marlene from accounts sees as she's walking to her car; Pete huddled over his steering wheel. She thinks, 'Is something wrong with him?' Her concern echoes Mr Long's ethos of 'We're more than workmates here; we're all one big happy family. All for one and one for all.' Marlene, an ardent subscriber to that sentiment, steps over to

Pete's van, taps on the window and gently opens the passenger door. She puts her head inside.

'You OK, Pete?'

'What? Oh yeah.'

Pete looks over at the intrusion, wipes his hand across his eyes, adds a muttered 'Fine' that doesn't sound fine. Marlene, a soft soul who rescues birds and won't tread on a spider, feels instant compassion for this grown man with tears on his cheeks. She lets herself into the van, slides across to Pete, puts an arm around his shoulder, draws him like a child to her ample bosom, tells him, 'There. There.' and that everything will be all right. Pete settles into the most comfortable of positions.

Marlene, enjoying this spontaneous closeness, thinks that it's a long time since she had a man's head between her breasts. Pete's enjoying the same thing, thinks that it's a long time since he had his head between a woman's breasts. And neither of them seem in any hurry to curtail the situation.

In Ed's shed this evening Pete sits quietly in a corner sipping from a can. He's so quiet that Big Ed says, 'Cheer up, Pete, you look like you've just come back from a funeral,' which, in a way he has. But Pete now has something else on his mind. Well, two things actually, that are warm and soft and extremely comfortable.

Morning Star.

Lorrie's another one, besides Pete, who's had a lot going on today. She's sorted out her present, soon to be ex, employer – Custom Curtains and Fabrics – explaining that she won't be returning when her sick spell expires. On the line to the company's HR she explains a personal emotional trauma (true) and a huge issue with her mental health (untrue). But those magic words, Mental Health, are enough to ensure that Lorrie's employment is terminated with some relief to both parties. The late afternoon of this day finds her in the Factory Gym in Broome. She's slotted in for an intro and assessment with Trainer Tony. He's tall, fair-haired, charming, and his skin is glowing with health. He's in shorts and a T-shirt (Get Factory Fit) and there's not an ounce of excess on his well-proportioned frame. Lorrie slyly compares their respective shapes in the wall mirrors, feels that he's everything she's not. And he's younger.

'God, don't I look fat,' she thinks.

She catches his eye in the mirror and his expression is the same as hers. 'God, doesn't she look fat,' Lorrie silently adds to her previous observation.

Tony says, 'What do you want out of this? What are your goals?'

'To lose weight and get,' she pokes the Fit on his T-shirt and he laughs because they're almost flirting. Sometimes she wishes she was straight; life might be simpler.

It's fairly routine for most of the allocated hour – weights, exercise bench, running machine – but then Tony tosses her a pair of boxing gloves and he puts the pads on.

'We'll give this a go. Now what I want you to do is ...'

He raises his hands and what he's expecting is an amateur approach; arm punches, slaps, misses, confusion of left and right, a tangling of legs. But what he gets, albeit a little rusty, is an unleashed Lorrie who moves and hits, hits and moves. Stings his hands.

'Christ, Lorrie. You've done this before.' There's admiration in his voice.

Oh, and she has and there's a satisfaction in unleashing this cleansing outburst of violence. Imagining. Remembering ... *the goading from Petra. Another pointless blazing row and Petra in her face, 'Come on, Lorrie. Hit me. Show me how hard you are.' Petra's lips are twisted into a sneering dare. This is what Petra wants, this ultimate prize for control in a never-to-be-forgiven act that would lessen Lorrie. Make her the brute forever. And Lorrie had come so so close to fulfilling that desire especially when Petra's cruel slap had scorched her cheek.*

'Now do it. I've hit you, now you hit me.'

Later Lorrie's showered, slicked her wet hair back, and fitted herself into her slightly tight tracksuit. She might be carrying a bit of timber but Lorrie, in a big girl sort of way, is an attractive woman. Tony, catching her on the way out, gives her a low wolf-whistle, which does wonders for Lorrie's confidence. Then he passes her a business card.

'If you're interested, Lorrie?'

She reads '*Broome Boxing Club, Get fit and fight,*' considers it for a moment and says, 'Yeah. Might be. Might see you there.'

Tony, taking this as a yes, gives her a glimpse of his pearly whites and says, 'My number's on the back. Give me a call and I'll intro you.'

There's another dazzling goodbye smile and Lorrie leaves considerably more perky than when she arrived. Yes, her muscles are burning, her legs ache, her arms ache, and her heart still aches. But not as much as it did.

Before she goes back to her houseboat, Lorrie has a good look around Broome town centre. She's enjoying the luxury of her own company, of suiting herself. She finds a café, sits at a pavement table and orders a coffee and a cream doughnut. She justifies the doughnut with the calculation that she must be ahead on the calorie count after her workout and, just to make sure, she promises herself, 'Tomorrow morning I'll go for a run.'

Lorrie sits for a while and watches the world go by: the Friday night shoppers, the early shift into the boozers, the meanderers who wander back and forth, drawn like moths to the brightly lit shop windows. She has another coffee and then thinks she'll go back to her new home, cook up something light and have an early night. These are her intentions but after she's parked her car at Vixens Mere she hears music. It's a floating, cloudy, soft rhythm drifting out of the Shed. Big Ed's framing the doorway, easily located by the glow of his cigarette and a whiff of pot. He calls out, 'Lorrie. We're having a party. You going to join us?'

The new Lorrie says, 'Give me five minutes, I'll get a bottle.'

The Shed.

Party beginning. Most of the residents of the winter moorings are already here: Big Ed, Milly, Lorrie of the Morning Star and Pete (who'll get a clear rebuff from Lorrie later when he tries to put his arm around her. She'll say, 'I'm not *that* sort of girl,' and Pete, bubbling with Premium Lager and several glasses of Milly's sloe-gin, will completely misunderstand what she means; he'll admire her for the wrong reason.) Milly the Mystic's dressed up for the occasion: crystal spangled-earrings and pendant, long, flowery summer dress topped by a full length thick woollen cardigan, 'cos the temperature's well down away from the glowing wood burner.

So it's friendly and comfortable in the Shed. The lighting's subdued, the music's soft and dreamy and the seating is arranged to face the fire. There's no Jed and Anna, they're working tonight and won't be back until the fire's burnt out, and everyone's tucked up in bed.

Karen and Harry Jones.

Karen says, 'Watch the step, Harry,' as they cross the threshold to the Shed.

'I can see it,' he says testily when it's patently obvious that he can't; he's searching for the rise with the toe of his shoe and Karen's practically leading him by the hand.

'Welcome to you two,' greets Big Ed with a flourish of his arm that spills a shower of lager from the bottle he's holding. Then he introduces one to another in a who's who, and settles down to a drink, a smoke, and a chinwag. It's a gathering, 'almost like the old days,' Ed thinks. Mind this isn't the crowd to get off their heads and off with their clothes. Ed remembers a party, 'Now where was it?' So he doesn't quite remember because it was an event that was hazy at the time and even hazier after forty odd years. He thinks he'll ask Milly. Then he thinks perhaps he shouldn't. He takes a deep swig of his drink, a long pull on his roll-up, sighs wistfully for the past, and then settles into an easy chair.

Summer Walker.
You.
You give instructions to Mick, 'Behave yourself. No barking while I'm gone.' The dog pretends not to hear. Now you don't really want to go to this meet-up. You're a loner. Private. Not the mixing type. You've kept your own company for so many years now it's second nature to sit on the sidelines. You'll go for a couple of beers, some minor conversation, and then quietly slip away. But it doesn't quite work out that way.

You see her immediately. Can't help but look. Karen Jones. She's sitting with a thin upright man – got to be her husband – who's warming his bones by the wood burner. When he stands she takes his arm, and guides him outside to the toilet (Or as Big Ed calls it, the Thunderbox.) Then she guides him back. Glances again in your direction, *Glances across fifteen years of time,* briefly raises her hand in recognition of your presence. Gives you a strange sad smile.

You've been talking to Big Ed and Milly, and he's asking what you've done with your life 'thus far,' and he laughs at his own expression. Milly reckons you've still a long way to go and you answer with the usual parries, the usual non-disclosure. Then Big Ed is drawing you over towards Karen Jones and the man who's a constant at her side. Big Ed says to Karen, 'You remember Brodie? Stayed here a long time ago.'

And then she's in front of you and her hand is gently warm in yours and you're seeing into and beyond a woman creeping towards middle age. You're seeing a girl of twenty-five, eyes brimming with tears, who's saying a goodbye that neither of you want but cannot avoid. Tonight that young woman, hiding behind her older self, is looking intently into your face and she's saying, almost in disbelief, 'But you haven't changed at all, Brodie. You look just the same.'

You're thinking that she may be older but she's still as lovely, though it's not words you can utter aloud. Then Big Ed is introducing, 'Harry Jones, Karen's husband' and this tall thin man, whose eyes are out of focus, fumbles for your outstretched hand, latches onto it, says, 'Pleased to meet you, Brodie,' and he says it with such genuine honesty you feel a shadow of guilt flit over you.

Bombardier.
2am on the same night. After the party. Three quarters of the moon showing and the air as still as death. Ice thickening on the water. There's a million stars in an endless sky.

Harry's given up on sleep tonight. He's sitting in the prow of the Bombardier, wrapped up like a mummy against the cold. He has a can of Stella in his hand and a scattering of dog-ends are under his feet. There's the glowing of yet another cigarette in his mouth. His head is playing up and three times Karen's been out to him. 'Come to bed, Harry.'

But he won't just yet because sometimes his head's worse when he lays down, and so he sits out here in the cold and the moonlight and he drinks and smokes. He thinks that if he'd had the choice, if he knew what was coming to him, he would have chosen to die in the blast of the IED.

Iraq. Eighteen years ago. 1100 hours. B company on patrol. They've been bumping along the rutted dusty tracks for a couple of hours and it's broiling hot in the Saladin. The armoured vehicle's so hot – oven hot – that Geordie reckons that he'll soon be thoroughly roasted and ready to serve up with apple sauce. It's the usual banter. It's familiar, as fun as it gets here. Harry's halfway through saying that he's thinking of becoming a veggie when their world erupts and tears them and their repartee into a hundred pieces.

The IED responsible had been dug into the track, laid with especial care into its grave, and wired up for action. The last vehicle in a convoy of four is selected and it only takes a stab of a finger on the detonator and the vehicle is lifted, blown apart. God alone knows how Harry survives this: Hoppy and Geordie meet their maker instantly and Tallyman, blinded and deafened, bloodied and burned raw, crawls into the road to meet an enemy bullet. Head on. But Harry, sitting against the back exit of the transport, is flung twenty feet away and he's shielded by the flaming carcass of the Saladin. Yes, there are gun-shots through the smoke, dust kicked up close to him in more hope than hit, but there's a wanting in their hate to finish off the wounding to Harry's head, the arm hanging limply by his side, the legs that don't seem to belong to him. All of this is in the silent world of burst eardrums and a stunned brain that plays it out in slow motion. So Harry's very close to the end of his twenty-four years of life but Harry's lucky because the rest of the Boys don't give up on him. They regroup, they attack, they exact the ultimate retribution for their dead, and then they lift Harry from the blood-stained sand. Lift him back into this life. To being a cripple in civvy street.

* * *

For Harry the bottle's empty, the cigarettes are finished, and ice is thickening on the water. It's time now to take his freezing self into the warmth of his bed. Harry wants to shut his eyes, shut his mind, to what's gone past and what the future inevitably presents. As he stands there's the clink of a couple of metal washers in his trouser pocket, scuffed by his boot from the floor of the Shed.

'Few more for the pot,' he tells himself.

Although it's not a pot, it's a plastic box in the junk cupboard. These washers will join the hoard of odds and sods of steel bolts, hexagonal nuts, and anything that might come in useful one day.

CHAPTER FOUR

Foxes Farm.
Proper old-fashioned listed farmhouse sitting in a hundred and fifty acres of land of variable usage: wood, pasture, and arable. The house is a large building, circa 1820. Sloping floors, undulating clay-tiled roof and half of a mile walk from Vixens Mere. Home to the James family; Ethan, his daughter Dinah – farm worker and hairdresser – and her boyfriend Barry. There is no wife for Ethan. In his words; 'Lazy cow buggered off with a schoolteacher. Better off without her. Thought he'd have had more sense considering his profession.' Dinah has two horses, an old – older than her – chestnut named Hunter, and Muppet, a Dartmoor pony three years of age, as black as the ace and a little slow on the uptake. Dinah's just finished breaking him in.

Dinah's first up this morning and six o'clock finds the dogs – a pair of collie twins – wolfing down their morning feed and Dinah at the Aga preparing human food. The coffee pot's on and bacon is sizzling in the frying pan. Toast has just popped up in the toaster and all it needs now is for a yawning Barry to complete the breakfast scenario. Himself is twenty-five years young with an effortless attraction that makes Dinah count her blessing every time she looks at him.

'You all ready, Barry?'

'Ready to roll,' he laughs. His case is in the hallway and his van is in the yard.

'Friday?' it's a question for when he'll return to their love nest in the far end of the old house.

'Hopefully,' he says.

Barry's an electrician and works on heavy duty wiring – factories, warehouses, institutions – so invariably there's overruns. Lately, in fact the last quarter of the year, his working days have become more frequent, his weeks longer, and once she didn't see him for nearly a fortnight. 'Pig of a job,' he'd told her on the phone because everything that could go wrong did go wrong. Anyway, this morning she cracks open a couple of eggs to lay on his bacon and toast, pours his coffee for him.

Barry, in a pause between munching and swigging, says, 'You spoil me, Dinah. Don't know what I'd do without you?'

She tells him that she hopes he'll never find out because she can't imagine a life apart. Then it's time for him to go and it's a lingering kiss on the doorstep before Barry drives off into the darkness. She's watching his taillights fade into the distance as she hears her father behind her.

'Barry gone then?' he says.

'Yes, he's gone. Cup of coffee, dad?'

'Tea'll be better.' He loudly sniffs the air. 'A bacon sandwich wouldn't go amiss either, Dinah.'

Barry's on his way and Dinah's first hair visit is at nine, but before that she's on call to her father. There's an hour or so of feeding up the cattle in the yard – pungent squelching of fresh manure beneath her wellies – her work ones, not her fashionable Hunters – a shaking out of rams of hay into the feeders. Ethan wants to take two bullocks to market so they have to be separated from their snorting brethren. It's not an easy task in the slight lighting of dawn but with some pushing, shoving, persuading with an oak staff, and the dogs' help, they load them into the cattle trailer. Then the drawbridge is raised and Ethan's off to the market in Broome and Dinah goes to the stables to check on her horses, promises herself a ride later on. But first must come her work, her job that services her everyday expenses, keeps her car on the road.

Both Dinah and Barry work hard and save hard. Barry has a high interest account that they add to every month. Dinah tots up what expenses she'll need to cover her hairdressing business, living expenses, car, and the like, and then she transfers the left-overs from her account to Barry's high interest one.

'Building our future,' he says.

This future is to be Vixens Mere. Dinah has plans for it, not all at once, but an up-grade enlargement over the next few years: more rental barges, more berths, an up-dated toilet and shower block, electric points, carpark enlarged. Perhaps even a little café.

Ethan says, 'Do what you like, Dinah. It'll be yours one day anyway.'

Although by the look of her hale, hearty, and indestructible father, that day is still a long time away.

Dinah thinks that later this afternoon, and because Ethan will make the market business last all day, that she'll check the sheep and then ride Muppet down to the Marina. She'll have a chat with the Water Gypsies – as Ethan calls the occupants of the basin – make sure there's no issues. Then she'll try and pin Big Ed down on when he's coming to repair the wall that the oil lorry flattened in a reversing manoeuvre. Ed's been promising that, 'You're first on my list. Soon as I've finished this little job in Broome.'

That was six months ago and Dinah wants the wall rebuilt – she's sick of looking at a heap of rubble – and Ethan's saying that he's sure that, 'Ed'll be here any day now.'

Dinah thinks that Ed needs as big a nudge as the wall received and today he'll get it.

* * *

The Dinah that now emerges from Foxes Farmhouse is in complete contrast to the cowgirl who entered with hay in her hair and muck on her boots. This Dinah is fashionably dressed and groomed and could easily have stepped off the pages of a magazine. A little cracker as some would say, or as Ethan tells her, 'You don't scrub up too bad, my girl.' Which is as near a compliment as he's likely to utter. Dinah drives off to the first of her day's appointments, singing to the radio because all is right with the world.

Karen Jones and Moses.

Harry's dosed up on the codeine and he's out for the count this afternoon. He desperately needs this sleep and Karen leaves him with his mouth open and his head on his chest. He looks ten years older than he is; pain has robbed him of his good years, half his hair, and carved its passage across his face. Karen thinks she'll kill time with a walk around the marina, perhaps even up the track as far as Foxes Farm. But then she sees Moses, tackle bag swinging, fishing rod set up, coming towards her on the towpath a hundred yards away and she slows, watches him grow in size, watches his boy's smile form on his face. She thinks he's grown into a handsome lad although his hair is overlong, and his clothes look a little shabby in the style of Big Ed and Milly and … *stop it, Karen. Just stop it.*

She says, 'Hello, Moses.'

'Hello, Mrs Jones.'

'How's school?'

Moses shrugs. 'All right, I suppose.'

'You don't sound too keen,' she laughs.

'I'd rather be helping Dad. Is Mr Jones all right?'

It's a polite regard for Harry's fragile health of body and mind, that everyone here knows about, and there's more in Karen's pause than there is in her words.

He's losing his sight. Losing his mind.

Karen says, 'Not too bad. Could be better, Moses.'

Moses makes a move then, there's things to do in his boys' world. He wants to set his rod up on the shaded side of the water, drop a line in for the monster tench he's sure is lurking in the quietest and deepest part of the basin. He makes his move with a 'Bye, Mrs Jones.'

Hating the indifference of her title, she says, 'Karen. You must call me Karen.'

'OK, Mrs Jone ... Karen.'

Then they both laugh, and he edges past her so closely that she could easily put her arms around him, hold him tightly, stroke his dirty blonde hair. If she was allowed. If she had the courage.

'See you,' he says.

'See you, Moses.' And she will, every day of their winter stay. As she has for the past fourteen years or more.

Niteclub in Broome.
Before midnight.
Anna.

Anna's squeezing, shrugging herself through the crush on the dancefloor. Everyone's up and at it tonight and the music throbs at a deafening volume. She's looking to catch up with Jed who's searching out some custom and this – and the crush – is why she doesn't realise that she's been tracked down. She hasn't seen Carl Thomson, doesn't even know he's in the packed dance, till she feels the warmth of his breath into her ear. He's pushed behind her, against her, and there's no notice for Anna until into her ear is the voice she never wanted to hear again as long as she lived, saying through the frenzy of the music, 'We need to talk, Anna.'

He takes her arm, fingers grasping cruelly into her skin, and escorts her off the floor. She should be able to wrench herself free, scream an escape into his face. But it's as though she has no resistance; he mesmerises her. She's snared into Carl Thomson's spell of terror as he leads the unresisting her outside. In a doorway, thirty yards away from the bright entrance to the Niteclub, he tilts her face to his. His eyes burn with such fury that she's unable to look away.

'I've been watching you, Anna. Watching you and your boyfriend.'

'Look, Carl, I ...' Her voice is trembling.

'Don't you 'Look, Carl' me.' His voice is bitterly angry and the tilting of her face has become a harsh, twisting grip. The pain ignites a reflex of pulling away from him, the words 'Get off me!'

He lets her go, conscious of the curiosity of passers-by, and they stand apart like two people with unfinished business. And that's what it is. Unfinished business.

Carl hisses, 'You owe me, Anna. You stole my fucking money. I want it back.'

'I'll get it for you. Please, Carl. I'll get it for you.'

'When?'

'Give me time. Please Carl. Just give me time.'

It can't be now, this instant, because the money's gone; a thousand pounds has been snorted away in condemned squats, smoked on rancid mattresses, massaged into gums in nighttime alleyways.

Carl Thomson is moving onto Anna now and he sucks in his breath, considers the offer of time, and then says, 'Give me something to go on with, Anna.'

What she gives him is two wraps of Jed's merchandise fumbled from her pocket.

'This for now,' this poor frightened young girl says. 'This for now.'

Carl says, 'And this, Anna,' and they're only a hand's breadth apart and his hand slips under her coat and onto her breast. He squeezes as hard as he squeezed her arm and she gasps in pain.

'You ran when we had a lot going on, Anna, and you're going to have to come back. There's stuff to finish. You're going to bring my money and yourself. Understand?'

'Yes, Carl.'

'A month, Anna. A month or I'll come and find you,' he says with the warning of a terrible retribution to his words. 'He'll get it as well, that fucking pimp of yours.'

Then he steps away from her, saunters his tall skinny frame into the thronging pavement. Disappears from sight but not from mind.

Anna stands for a while in the doorway, soaks up safety time, and then takes herself to find Jed. She's wearing her frightened mind, her shocked body, and Jed asks, 'You all right Anna?'

'I'm not feeling well, Jed. Can we go?'

Jed's considering is an apologetic, 'But it's early, Anna. I still got a lot to shift.'

He's worried about losing revenue, about not meeting targets, but Anna's pale and close to tears and Jed makes the compromise for her to, '... order up a taxi. You go on and I'll catch you later.'

He gets a dumb nod in response and there's an end to it. Not to everything though. That's just beginning.

The taxi stops at the entrance to Vixens Mere. It could take her another couple of hundred yards closer to Home Sweet Home but the trackway is scattered with pot-holes and the driver reckons it's too rough for his springs. He winds down his window, lights up a cigarette, and says, 'This do then, love?' as though there's any option. He tacks on, 'That'll be eight pound ninety then.'

Anna hands him a tenner and he makes a great show of fumbling in his pockets.

'I'm short of change today but I'm sure that somewhere here I've …'

Anna says, 'It's all right.'

'All right?' And then a very quick, 'Oh thank you, my dear.'

Anna, pissed off with men in general mumbles a bitter, 'Yeah, it's all right. You can knock it off the next trip,' and heads towards Home Sweet Home. Her haven. Her safe place with Jed.

Anna lets herself in, puts the kettle on to boil, puts a short line on the worktop, swiftly cleans it up, settles her head before she settles herself for a coffee and a think. She thinks about bad men like Carl and she thinks about good men like Jed, but both in the similar lines of business. She'd dared to dream had Anna, thought that maybe things would work out this time. But now she's going to have to tell Jed her story, her baggage, warn him before she maybe has to pack her belongings, because that Carl is one evil son of a bitch. But she'll wait for the right time, enjoy the feeling of being loved for a little longer. Then she rolls up a special from Jed's secret store and sits out on the prow of the boat under the cold stars. Anna has a little cry and then she has a good sniff, wipes her face with the back of her hand. She's unaware of anyone close by until Milly, stretching her legs on one of her late-night ambles, calls out, 'You OK, Anna?'

And Anna leaves a telling silence until she says, 'No, I'm not, Milly. I'm really not,' and now a sob interrupts her words.

Milly comes aboard, sits with Anna, takes her hand and shares comradely draws of smoke, and then under these cold stars Anna tells her story. Woman to woman. She tells it for the relief of someone who won't judge, who maybe won't look at her with uncertainty smeared on her face. She tells it as a daughter should be able to tell her mother. If she had one.

* * *

Morning Star.
Saturday morning.

Lorrie's Saturday starts with a run out on the lanes. She's marked herself a circular route to the outskirts of Broome and then returning past Foxes Farmhouse and down to the marina. She sets her stopwatch, starts out, and hits her stride. Now a couple of weeks of gym work have worked wonders on Lorrie; that and very little alcohol, proper meals, and these early runs. She's shed weight – her tracksuit is starting to look a little on the baggy side – her body's toned up and there's a healthy bloom to her skin. She looks fresh and wholesome and she feels good. Lorrie's morning exercise clears her lungs, unclouds her mind and today she's floating around her circuit. Then she's at the drive to Foxes Farm and a car's stopped at the entrance and the window's wound down and Dinah's calling out loudly, 'Thought it was you. Don't know how you do it?'

Lorrie pauses for the briefness of a conversation and an invitation of, 'You could always join me, Dinah?'

Dinah thumbs over her shoulder. 'I get enough exercise on the farm. Then she grins and laughs. 'And I could still do something with your hair, Lorrie. If you want?'

Then Dinah takes her teasing, her fun smile, and her attractiveness out to her nine o'clock appointment. Watching, Lorrie unconsciously runs her hand through her hair and imagines what perhaps she shouldn't. And then she thinks of how good she's looking, slimmed down – perhaps that new hair-do in the offing? – and then, without warning, the unbidden and unwanted thought intrudes, slips slyly into, 'If Petra could see me now,' clings on as she tries to outrun this incursion, to leave it trailing behind her in the ether, as she sprints the last quarter of a mile of her circuit. But it keeps nagging, pestering her with the realisation of just how lonely, how frustrating, is the missing of a love affair, of a woman's tender touch. She thinks about it more when she's soaping herself in the shower and again when she's gently towelling her body dry. Then she takes herself off to the boxing gym in Broome to work herself up into a lather all over again.

Lorrie likes coming here, likes the camaraderie of all who have faced exposure in the loneliest, cruellest sport of all. Today it's a middling lunchtime and Trainer Tony says, 'It'll liven up later.' He looks up to the square ring, centre of the gym. Centre of the universe. 'Want a go?' he asks Lorrie. 'Bit of light sparring?'

'Why not?' she says.

Tony's been doing this lately, encouraging her to unhang her gloves. So it's headguards on, mitts velcroid , gumshields fitted, a climb into the ring, automatic timer set, and a readying for action.

It's pretty regular stuff to start with; gentle jabs, slow swings, easy movement of the feet. But it starts slowly, subtly, to change. Tony picks up the pace, starts to crispen his punches. Lorrie responds, raises her game and sticks with him. It must look pretty good because several of the regulars leave banging the bags for the show that's being presented.

'C'mon girl, whack him one.'

'Give him a right-hander from me, Lorrie.'

And the thing is that Lorrie's nearly giving as good as she gets. Of course, Tony's not going all out because Lorrie's meant to be sharpening her tools, practising a variety of moves and punches. Tony's playing a defensive role, blocking, parrying, making her miss. He's laying on the ropes and taking blows on his arms and gloves. But Lorrie's all-action style means that the occasional clout does gets through and is loudly appreciated by the partisan audience.

Tony gives her three rounds to test her mettle, until her arms are sagging and she's slowed to a snail's pace, then he shows her an open palm, 'That's enough for now, Lorrie,' and she's glad of a breather.

They sit on the ring apron, Lorrie's grateful lungs drawing

in rejuvenating oxygen, as she says to her sparring partner, 'Thanks for that, Tony. I think?' and he chuckles and says that she's turning into a lean mean fighting machine. He's so good for her confidence is Tony, that Lorrie reckons if she were straight, he'd be the first man she'd turn to. Tony laughs again and says he'd be at the head of a very long queue. He slips his arm around her sweat-wet torso, tells her she's a damn fine-looking woman who packs a hell of punch, and gives her a quick hug. It's a brotherly hug that carries not an iota of sexual intent. Then he says seriously, 'I've got a proposal for you, Lorrie.'

'I hope it's indecent,' she says unseriously.

'You're handy, Lorrie. You're strong. Controlled. Fit. You'd be good in a tight situation.'

After the second of the compliments Lorrie wonders where this is heading?

She says, 'Just ask me, Tony. I don't need the flannel.'

'All right. Have you ever thought of working the doors?'

'Doors?'

'Being a bouncer?'

'No, I haven't.'

'Well, do you want to?'

'Christsake, Tony. Give me a minute to think about it.'

Then as though he's offering her the inducement of a lifetime, Tony says, 'You can work with me and Marvel.'

Marvel is a huge, shaven-headed, tattooed beast of a man who pounds the heavy bag with a vitriol that makes Lorrie feel sorry for the bag. Only the most slippery of the boys in training will venture into the ring with Marvel, although Tony gives him a few rounds now and again. 'Got to keep testing myself,' he says after presenting a lesson in the art of avoidance and being mightily relieved that he survived the encounter.

The upshot of Tony's proposal is that bad-tempered girls – and women – are becoming ever more a feature of night life in Broome and especially at the Glow Worm, the establishment that Tony and Marvel keep order in. He wants Lorrie to help out.

'Every time there's trouble there's always a complaint about us touching them up. Give us nothing but grief,' he says. 'I mean, how can we get them apart without ...? Well, you know ... touching them.'

'So you want me to do it?'

'It'll be different 'cos you're a woman and ...'

'And what, Tony?'

'And you could call it a perk of the job considering, Lorrie.'

Lorrie surprises herself when she bites sharply, 'I'm not a fucking perv, Tony,' and he's laughing at her because he's kidding, of course he's kidding. Lorrie's hardly the type for furtive fumbling. She gets in a reference to Tony being a 'Twat' before she says, 'I could give it a try, I suppose.'

There's talk then of Lorrie putting in for her doorman's ticket, 'Few training sessions. Nothing to worry about. Piece of piss. If he can get through,' Tony jerks a thumb in Marvel's direction, 'anyone can.'

Lorrie's thinking that she's starting to fill her new life. There are still some pieces missing but she'll find them she tells herself.

CHAPTER FIVE

Bombardier.
Harry and Karen Jones.
Harry might not be seeing her features too well these days but he can still read Karen by the distraction in her voice, by the setting down of the coffee mugs.

'You all right?'

'Yes.' The short answer means no.

'What's the matter?'

She says, 'Nothing,' and she thinks 'Everything.'

His, 'Suit yourself,' is a snappy precursor of what might follow. And now she has to pretend, to keep the peace because it doesn't take much for him to fall into one of his endless moods of black. So Karen brightens her tone in an avoidance of conflict.

'I bought a cake. The one you like. We'll have a slice now. With our coffee.'

The sentences are short stabs of conciliation, and it cuts her to the quick that happiness has to be obtained by cake and appeasement. Sometimes she feels she wants to throw back her head and scream out to the heavens, 'What about me? What about my life? What about ...?'

What about a woman on the fringe of middle-age whose life's secret is entrusted to the guardians at the gate?

Harry says, 'Is it lemon drizzle, Karen? My favourite.'

Now he's trying, poor Harry of the failing eyesight and

the unfailing headaches, to fight the mood. She holds him, this shadow of a man he once was, feels the gauntness of his frame; the effects of a life lived long beyond expectations.

'Together,' Karen thinks, dares the hopeless prayer that, 'Together. We'll beat it. Together.' She hugs him hard.

Harry thinks, 'I wish I'd died that day.'

When she was twenty-one years old Karen Needham became Mrs Karen Jones. Up till then she had lived with her mother and father at a lock-keeper's cottage on a stretch of Abinton canal. Karen was the last of a brood of three – an afterthought by a decade – and all of her life had been spent on the canal's banks. But it wasn't only her life; it was previous lives.

Pictures of the Needham family's canal heritage decorated the walls of the house and they stretched back to the early days of the twentieth century, although the Needhams were on the water over a century before that. There were framed photographs of stern-faced men, neckerchiefs tucked around their throats, pipe smoking women, rough-bonneted girls and barefoot boys, the grinning urchins of the waterways.

Karen's father, Mr Needham – Fred to his friends – can name every person in each photograph up to 1965 when economics and lack of cargo forced his family off the barges and into a house on a council estate. Fred tells Karen that, 'It was death to Mum and Dad, they couldn't live on land.' It sounded romantically tragic, a couple pining away for their old life. Karen thinks that they must have pined for a long time because they were both pushing eighty before their boat finally sank.

After his schooling, a young Fred, clever head sitting on his shoulders, worked hard, and saved hard. By the time he and his wife Iris, of a similar background, had their first child, he could afford to put down a deposit on a run-down lock cottage.

He says, 'If we can't live on the canal, we'll live by it.'

But that wasn't strictly true because his property had its own offshoot of water, and a barge renovation went on alongside the house one. Karen's bedtime stories were the narratives of overloaded barges, of accidental drownings, of being poor amongst the poor, of being iced in – immovable – in the winter of '47. These stories, handed down from one generation to the next, were traced by her young fingers on the pictures on the walls. She followed her line, knew their names, Rubin and Polly, Ebenezer and Nelly, Moses and Edwina. She knew how her family had lived and how they'd died. 'It's in your blood,' her father told her.

Sometimes, on one of the frequent nights she spends on their barge, she dreams of her predecessors, thinks she hears their voices rippling through the waters, snatches of their conversations in the creaking of the barge's timbers. But Karen is also a modern young lady, and a very attractive one, who draws more than her fair share of admirers and one of those is Harry Jones.

He's a twenty-two-year-old soldier and he already has a tour of duty behind him. This weekend he's just begun his leave and he's in his hometown catching up with his old mates. He's already sank a few beers when he bumps into Karen at the Blue Stag. The place is heaving with custom and noise and the bumping is actually done by Karen who, in squeezing past him, spills her drink down his shirt. There's a 'Sorry,' from Karen, an appreciative appraisal from Harry and a joke about it being not an ideal way to start a relationship. But for Karen it's an introduction to a young man who seems older than his years, grown up, mature, tall and smart. And he's irresistible and so is she and it begins; the love of her life and the love of his.

One quiet night they're sitting in a pub garden on a warm summer evening. Harry, thinking that all of the world and all of their lives are before them, asks Karen, 'If you could live anywhere, where would you like to live?' There's not even a split second before Karen's answer of, 'On the cut, Harry. On the water.'

She thinks for a moment and returns the question. 'And you?'

Harry shrugs, 'Wouldn't matter to me as long as we're together.'

The shrug might be casual but his words are not, and Karen doesn't think that she could love anyone as much as she loves him at this moment.

They're engaged before his next Afghan tour and married before his third and final one. Two years after that marriage the army is finished with him and they're living on a barge. On the cut. On the water. Like Karen wanted. Except not.

Flat No. 4 Blackburn Terrace, Broome.
Bedsit. Kitchen area – none too clean. Bed unmade. Tiny shower and toilet. Unpleasant smell of drains. All in all, not enough room to swing the proverbial cat.
Tenant: Carl Thomson, twenty-seven years old, six foot three of skinny meanness mainly due to overuse of crank. Suffers from nosebleeds. To be expected.

Carl Thomson takes his mug of tea over to the window, looks out over dark slate roofs, scores of chimney stacks. To suit the way he's feeling this morning it should be drizzling rain from a dull grey sky. But the sky is clear and frost is retreating into the shadows as the sun inches higher. It's a pure and clean day and the mind inside of a greasy haired cranium should be thinking pure and clean thoughts. But the month's deadline for Anna's return of herself and his money is looming, so his thoughts and his mumbles to himself are: 'Just wait till I get hold of the fuckin' bitch. If she thinks she can get away with this ... I'll fucking show her.'

He still can't really understand why his possession had just upped sticks and left. Took her in he had, took her off the streets into his bedsit, gave her a roof over her head. Only asked her for a bit of gratitude, some help with a few deals, some sweetening up of suppliers. And what was wrong with giving a hand job to ease things along? It's not like they didn't need the money and for fuck's sake, what's five minutes of wrist action? It's not like she had to swallow a load of jizz. Well, maybe occasionally.

He's angry is Carl because that lowlife called time on him, fucked up his business, snuffed him out like a candle, took her sleeping bag, and *his* blanket. Fuckin' thief. He's glad he got a good hiding in before she sneaked away. And by God she'll get another one for the raid on his finances. A thousand fuckin' quid. She'll pay that back, her and her fuckin' pimp. It's not like he can't find out where they live, is it? Right, he's going to lie low for while, wait his time, give the pimp a chance to fill his pocket with readies, and then he'll take what's owed him. And then some, because it's not just about the money.

Carl makes himself a brew, sits on his bed, rolls himself a smoke, sucks a deep satisfying draught of the good stuff, starts to relax, stills the internal rant. That's better. Much better. Now to plan the dish that's best eaten cold if he can keep it that way, which, knowing the effects his lifestyle's had on his cluttered-up brain, might be extremely difficult.

Crystal Lady.
Ten o'clock on a weekday morning.
Milly.
Big Ed's taking the pick-up, Moses, and the roofing ladders, and going to refix some loose slates for a client in Broome.

'You be careful, Ed. Clambering about roofs at your age.' Milly nearly adds, 'and at your weight,' but reckons it might be a bit cruel to say out loud.

'It's all right. Simple little job. I'll send the boy up,' Ed says.

Moses, who really should be into a double geography lesson about now, says, 'Don't worry, Mum, I'll look after the old fella.'

He gives her a big grin, a son to a mother smile, and it fills her heart and she thanks the Spirits for sending her this lovely lad.

'Bring some fish and chips back for tea,' she manages to get to Ed before the truck, ladders rattling and slates sliding, sways and bumps up the track. She thinks she'll have a cup of coffee, a sit down, and then she'll clean her ornaments; her lucky knick-knacks that cover every shelf in her home. Well, not every shelf because there must be a score of framed photographs of young Moses. In these pictures he ranges from cot comfortable to dragging nappy, to boy on a trike, boy on a bike, boy strumming a guitar, to a taller than herself youth. In all of these his smile is there to see, the smile he gave her today.

When she reached forty, Milly had nearly, but not quite, given up hope of ever having a child. She's waited for so long and was so sure, really sure, that one day she'd be rocking her baby, cooing him to sleep. She could almost feel the warmth, the weight, of her babe in her arms. At night she dreamt of him – she knew it would be a him – gripping her finger so tightly she could still feel his grasp after she awoke.

But on her forty-fifth birthday she's lost her optimism. She says to Ed, 'It's just never going to happen now,' and she tries to pack away twenty-five years of hoping and wishing, of false alarms and a dread of dates. But she can't quite pack away the images of her longing, the consolation of the dreaming world where she can touch and taste and smell this promised child. These dreams visit and revisit. They pester her, they nag at her. She reads the cards, she swings the crystal and it always points to a yes. Ed says that she's got to let it go completely, stop pretending, but she tells him that it won't let her go. They do have a few words because he says it's bad for her mind to 'keep going on like this, Milly.' But she carries on with her waiting as Ed learns to live with it.

And then a week before Milly's half century, Karen, eyes red rimmed from lack of sleep, voice subdued by nervous worry, is sitting in the snug lounge of the Crystal Lady and saying to Milly, 'I can't do it to Harry. I just can't. It'll kill him after what he's been through.' Karen's head is in her hands and her baby's sleeping in the carry-cot on the floor. She looks to her child and says, 'I even thought of leaving him in the church porch. Like in the olden days.'

There's a lot of things Karen should have thought of when her husband was hovering between life and death and the latter was expected to win.

To Milly the solution is as clear as the day. She says, 'Give him to me, Karen. I'll look after him.'

Milly, at this time, doesn't think it'll be for that long. Just until Harry's gone. That's all. 'Then you can have him back, Karen.'

But what neither of them can know is that old soldiers don't die, they fade away. Some fade away extremely slowly and the expected months become years. Become much too late for the truth to be told, for lives to be changed.

West street, Broome.
Dinah.

It's Wednesday and Dinah's in Amy Johnson's kitchen, waiting for the colour to soak into her hair. Amy Johnson, ponched in a waterproof cloak, wrong side of sixty, wrong side of thirteen stone, but perky as a budgie, twitters, 'Put the kettle on, Dinah. And there's some ginger biscuits in the cupboard.'

They share a pot of tea and some munching at the table and Dinah turns down the offer of a slice of cake to follow the biscuits. She says, 'I'm taking Hunter out this afternoon. Don't want too much slopping about in my belly.'

Amy reckons, as she takes a mighty mouthful of Victoria sponge, that, 'You don't eat enough to keep a sparrow alive, Dinah.'

Now Dinah might be on the small side, as many woman are in comparison to Amy Johnson, but she's well formed with the curves of a girl who walks on the physical side of life. In her farm work she's always lifting, stretching, and bending, and in the last couple of days she's been itching a bit as well. She blames it on buying a pack of 'Thicker Knicker for Winter' range. There's probably some chafing and although she might be scratching she's certainly warmer in her sensitive parts.

Foxes Farm.
A couple of hours later.
With nothing slopping about in her belly, Dinah's taking a different view of the world from high up on Hunter. He stands at 16.2 hands and his long legs are pounding an outside line around the perimeter of Foxes Farm; a decent stretch of cantering, and a few exhilarating gallops with the cold wind on her face. Then it's back to the stable for Hunter, a de-saddling and a haynet and Dinah's down to the farmyard for the feeding of the bullocks. After which Dinah gets the dinner on as Ethan shuts down the farm for the night. Today that dinner's simple enough – a casserole in the oven – and then there's just time enough for a shower before its serving.

So it's a quick peeling off of her clothes onto the bathroom floor, a blasting of hot water, a quick lather-up, a cleaning douse, and then a rough towelling dry. Now Dinah's a tidy girl and her discarded clothes are going straight into the laundry basket. But when she picks up her knickers the crotch is speckled with pinpricks of red. What the …? God, it must be why she feels sore, itchy.

Dinah stands in front of the mirror, tries to see down there but it's not clear. She takes Barry's shaving mirror and sits on the edge of the bed and gives herself a close examination. Magnified, she sees the cause of her distress; she's spotted with dots. Spotted with pubic lice. She's got the crabs.

When Barry phones at seven o'clock she lets it ring on. Dinah doesn't answer and she doesn't reply to the follow-up text: *Trying to get hold of you. Everything OK? xxx*

No, everything is not OK. I'm crawling with lice and I haven't caught them off the fucking sheep.

Crystal Lady.

Milly the Mystic's sitting with a cup of tea and a roll-up. Through the barge's window she can see a pair of swans gliding across the water. 'Lovely couple. Partner up for life you know, just like me and Ed.'

Big Ed's gone to put some time in on one of his jobs and Moses is making a guest appearance at Broome Academy (Slogan; There's Room at Broome for Everyone.) So Milly's on her own today and she's threading coloured crystals onto bracelets and anklets. She's set up her table with all her materials sorted in chapters for assembly. But first that cup of tea and her roll-up and, to tell the truth, she also wants an easy day, a relaxing day, though she wouldn't mind calling Anna in for some company. She likes Anna, young vulnerable girl that she is, and she texts her to *Call around in a bit if you're not busy.*

She fusses over Moses and still keeps a watchful eye on Jed, and now there's Anna as well. She wonders what a child of hers – really hers – would have turned out like but 'because I was a barren old cow, I never found out.' There had been no baby to grow inside her, no kicking from the inside, none of the stretching and tearing, or blood-soaked sheets. It wasn't through lack of trying though, but Ed's seed had never taken.

They'd tried everything, even dangled a crystal over her belly and tried to read if the time was exactly right. One night, a long time ago, her and Ed had driven out to Cerne Abbas's most famous resident, parked in a gateway, and in the early hours climbed the hillside. There in the moonlight, and right on the tip of the giant's most arresting appendage, they'd taken off all their clothes and did the deed. Milly wanted to do it again to double their chances but Ed said she was lucky he'd managed it at all after climbing all the way up that fucking hill.

There's also something else that's been a bit unsettling for Milly, something that's stayed in her mind today, and that's what she thought she saw on the water last night. Now Milly might occasionally have trouble staying asleep and so she'll slip out of bed, throw a blanket around herself, roll herself a thick cigarette, and take a walk around the basin. She likes the night, the rustling in the trees, the scampering in the under-growth. She'll listen for the hooting of the owls, the squeaking of rats. Or mice. Milly's not too sure. What made her really start one night was the close proximity of a vixen's screaming as it tried to attract a mate. 'Thought someone was being murdered,' she told Ed later. He said if Milly screeched like that there definitely would be a murder.

When Milly had taken her walk last night the moon was peeping through the clouds. There was light on the marina and then there wasn't. She thought she saw something and then there was nothing. But what she thought she saw in a shutter of moonlight was a hand thrusting through the water, clutching at the air like it was expecting Excalibur to land in its grasp. It's just a few moments of seeing as her eyes are trying to focus before an intruding cloud suddenly curtained the scene.

The worrying thing for Milly is that this fleeting vision wasn't alcohol influenced, skunk induced, or even a rare LSD playback. She was stone cold sober and completely unstoned. 'God, it was strange one,' she thinks.

She's still dwelling on it when Anna, white and shaken, invites herself into Crystal Lady, parks herself in front of the stove, gives Milly her unsure news that could be construed as good or not. Depending on perspectives of course.

CHAPTER SIX

Summer Walker.
A long time ago and a long way from Vixens Mere.
You.
In this remembering the sun's warm and bright and the air is clear and fresh in your lungs. Your feet are on a stony path and rearing up all around are high hills, clothed into the shading of gorse and heather. But these colours are subdued, dusty, like age has settled on them. Like the colours that you see in old paintings.

'A sipping of spring,' your nan, your seanmhair, says on this morning.

You're a boy, gawky and thin – 'Stringy as a bean,' you've heard more than once – and you're heading a donkey and cart on a falling track. You're travelling with your seanmhair, an old lady with a lined weather-beaten face, grey hair scraped back. Dressed in clothes of jumble.

She's saying, 'Shios an sin. Sinn sgur shois an sin.'

Seanmhair's slipped into the Gaelic – sometimes she talks nothing else for weeks. But these words instantly translate in your mind, because the English must be learnt, into a meaning of, 'Down there. We'll stop down there.'

She points the way with a thin brown arm along this track that's trailing down into a far valley to a sparkling of running water. You keep moving and the cart, loaded with poles and canvas, lurches onwards. So there's the warming of the sun, the tang of donkey and your own sweat. The crush of gravel under iron-hooped wheels.

You're wanting this journey to be over. You're wanting to be wading in the cool water, sifting the river bed for mussels. Fishing for pearls. Or you want to be laying on a grassy bank by a stick fire while Seanmhair's toasting bread and brewing tea. Or you want both.

You've been on this path since dawn and there's miles behind and you wonder aloud, 'How long have we been walking?'

It's a stopping as this question's asked. You give the donkey a pull-up on his bridle and your seanmhair halts with you. She takes her handkerchief from her pocket, wipes it across her face.

'How long, my boy?' she says, 'How long have we been walking?' like she's pondering the query to herself. Then she looks to the sky, looks at you, and she says in the clearest tone of honesty, 'About a thousand years.'

It seems that's a forever and you try to imagine a thousand Christmases, a thousand winters of snow settled on the mountains, a thousand summers of heat and shade. But you'll remember this moment so clearly, of you and your seanmhair and the donkey, because it's when you first start to realize what she means. But you won't fully understand until the years don't pass as they should.

Morning Star.
Lorrie.

There's two pieces of news in the post. One is confirmation of status as a Security Industry Authority Licenced Security Officer – *fancy name for a bouncer,* Lorrie thinks – upon the completion of her course. This course had been half a dozen sessions, a few hours at a time with a bored trainer, in the Broome Guildhall. It was in an overheated room where men in suits tended to sweat easily and freely and rather rancidly. By going home time Lorrie felt like she had bathed in testosterone. The only consolation was that there was another woman, a little older than Lorrie but considerably heavier, who seemed to have taken a shine to her. Nice enough lady though, who'll take the offer of going out for a drink without misjudging it as come on.

The other letter is from a solicitor who is 'acting on behalf of Ms Petronella Auclair in regards to the property of ...' The upshot of it is that if Lorrie relinquishes her interest in their house Petra will pay her 'in full and final settlement the sum of sixty thousand pounds ...' Lorrie thinks that's not quite enough so later she'll draft a return letter saying that she'll settle for seventy thousand.

She phones Tony with the good news about her bouncer's ticket and he says, 'Why don't you come along tonight, spend a couple of hours with us. I'll show you the ropes.'

'Why not?' she says and at eight o'clock that evening she's standing in the foyer of the Glow Worm with Tony and a Marvel who looks fearsome enough to frighten any would-be punters away. Lorrie's caught sight of herself a few times in the entrance mirror and she thinks that she looks rather fetching in her doorman's uniform of a dark suit, white shirt, and dickie-bow tie. Her hair's brushed flat and she's coloured herself a hint of eye shadow and applied the softest of lipstick. Lorrie knows that she's an attractive package and she's rapidly building back confidence after 'five years of Petra,' she thinks.

Through the doors of the Glow Worm the clientele start populating the venue. They're young and brash, high-spirited, under-dressed, and over-dressed. All the bright sorts. There's banter, 'You're looking fit tonight, Tony. Gonna let us in for nothing?'

'No pay, no way, girls.'

'I see Mr Happy's here,' (directed at Marvel who immediately retaliates with a threat to sit the offender on his arse.)

And then of course the questions, 'Who's this then?' asked of the new face Lorrie.

'Extra help to keep an eye on you lot.'

But there's not really a lot coming into the Glow Worm tonight because there's competition from Broome Rugby Club; they're hosting a cabaret night of local talent and cheap beer. That's how it is for an hour until a familiar twosome to Lorrie, Jed and Anna, are stopped in their tracks by the mighty Marvel. He's planted himself in the doorway.

'You're not coming in.'

'Why not?' says Jed.

'You know why. Trying to sell your shit in here.'

'We're clean. Haven't done anything. Haven't got anything.'

Lorrie can see that Anna has shrunk beside Jed. She looks pale and vulnerable, frightened that things are going to kick off because Jed doesn't seem to want to let go of this. Lorrie looks to Tony who shakes his head at the confrontation.

'Marvel'll spark him out if he keeps arguing,' he says.

Lorrie, not wanting to see her neighbour get a kicking, thinks of her recent training on defusing a situation, the guide of, 'Offer the situation something personal.'

So she does; she sidles alongside Marvel and says to him, 'I know them. Let me sort it.'

For a moment she thinks she's going to get a knock back but Marvel shrugs his mighty shoulders and says, 'You got a minute before I kick the turd into the fucking road.'

There's no doubt at all Marvel means what he says. His eyes have narrowed into slits and Lorrie's sure she can actually feel the antagonism pulsating off him. Marvel, scowling, turns on his heel, gives up his place, and Jed's looking at Lorrie, recognising that his neighbour's stepped inside the spotlight. Lorrie plays it cool; she says a quiet hello, delivered with a warm smile.

'He won't let us in, Lorrie,' Jed complains.

Lorrie, keeping the smile on her face says, 'There's nothing I can do, Jed. If the management say 'No,' that's it. It's not down to me.'

'But Lorrie …'

'This is my first night here, Jed. First night on the job. I can't afford any trouble.'

Lorrie's played it back to him and Jed wavers; he just needs the gentlest of nudges.

Lorrie says, 'Please Jed, will you leave it?' and Jed thinks for a moment, and Anna tugs on his arm, looks into his face, says in a repeat of Lorrie's words, 'Please Jed. Please,' and it's enough to set them wandering back into the night.

Tony says, 'Well done, Lorrie. Handled like a true professional.' He also starts to say something in the line of, 'That's the way to do it,' to Marvel but the words peter out because Marvel doesn't look like he'd take too kindly to advice tonight.

It's been a quiet night by the usual measures and Tony stays to watch the door while Lorrie and Marvel have a sauntering patrol around the dance arena. They have a quick natter with the – tonight at least – underused but rather buxom bar staff. The resident DJ's playing list is not tempting many into the arena, and this DJ is also making frequent trips to the bar to relieve his boredom. Marvel reckons that the DJ won't see the night out, the rate he's tipping them back. The bar ladies are also bored, but at least not drowning themselves like the DJ, and are glad to have a chat. They offer a drink to the Security of Marvel and Lorrie.

'Nothing alcoholic,' Marvel warns Lorrie, 'Remember you're on duty.'

Lorrie has a coke but Marvel has a pint of beer shoved across to him like it's a standing order.

Lorrie says, 'But you said …?'

'I meant you. I'm used to it. A couple of jars don't affect

me.' He drains his pint in two swallows and wipes his mouth with the back of his hand.

The evening passes quietly, there's no more drama at the door, and at one o'clock the shutters come down and the punters move out. It's all very low key and orderly but, 'Don't let tonight fool you,' Tony says to Lorrie. 'It's the lull before the storm.'

Lorrie's picked up her bag and she's fingering her car keys ready for the goodbye.

'When's the storm due, Tony?'

'Tomorrow night. Get here at eight.'

'What?'

'Get here at eight. You're on the payroll now, Lorrie.'

'But ... Really?'

Lorrie had been expecting a gentle breaking-in, a few odd night's work building into the regular. Marvel, finished on a last check around the premises, grunts out to her, 'See you tomorrow, Lorrie. And don't be late.'

Lorrie thinks, 'That's it then, no real discussion. They've decided.' But there's no resentment because these guys have accepted that she's one of them. It's a compliment and it's exciting and she drives back to Vixens Mere tired but buzzing. Everything seems to be going in her direction; her holiday of unemployment ends on Monday – a supermarket recruitment drive has nabbed her organisational skills – there'll soon be, hopefully anyway, seventy K in her bank. All she needs to make her life complete is the love of a good woman. But there's no sign of that on the horizon just yet.

Broome.

A shadowy street in the smallest hour.

Night.

Jed and Anna and Carl Thomson.

Anna sees him. She recognises his tall thin figure, lounging back against a brick panel between the inevitability of two charity outlets. The backdrop of shop-lighting has drawn Carl Thomson in silhouette and there's a featuring to every one of his hated, frightening lines. Anna's hoping that they can walk straight past, not notice him, but she and Jed are abreast when Carl Thomson detaches himself from the wall with a welcome of, 'Hi, you two.'

Jed pauses, stops, gives him a 'Hi,' back. Anna says nothing, looks down at the pavement. She wishes these moments as far away as could be but Carl Thomson is saying to Jed, 'You selling, mate. Thirty bar?' He holds out two notes for the swap.

Jed shuffles out a wrap, drops it into Carl Thomson's outstretched hand. But there's to be no swap because the paper offer is suddenly and swiftly withdrawn, crunched back into Carl Thomson's palm with a, 'Thanks, mate,' and a move to walk away.

Jed, baffled, says, 'You ... Why? ... You forgetting something?'

'Forgetting what? I ain't forgetting nothing.'

Jed laughs nervously, 'But ... the money, mate. The thirty quid.'

Carl Thomson stabs a finger at Anna. 'Take it off what she owes me.' He spits out a sarcastic, 'Mate,' to complete the sentence.

'What?'

'Just fucking ask her.' He gives Anna the evil eye and warns, 'I want what's mine, Anna, else I'm coming to get it.'

Then he's striding away and Jed's looking at Anna with a hundred questions on his face. And Anna's face is showing that her world is crumbling.

'I'm sorry, Jed,' she says in the smallest of voices. 'I didn't mean ...'

But Jed interrupts her, takes her arm. 'It's late,' he says. 'We should be getting back, Anna.'

The unsaid weighs heavily between them all the way home until they're laying side by side in the thick bedroom darkness aboard Home Sweet Home. And then Anna tells Jed the secret story of her life. And then she tells him another secret that can't be hidden any longer, the secret that Milly revealed when she tried her trusted blue crystal – the one beyond age – over Anna's belly and said, 'It's going to be a boy, Anna.'

Vixens Mere.
On an afternoon that's warming with a dashing of March sunshine.
Harry and Karen Jones.
Harry's belted up his heavy army greatcoat. It's rough weight is oversized to his weakening frame but he likes the feel of the coarse material, likes ramming his hands in the deep pockets, pretending that he's still under Her Majesty's orders. Pretending that he's on a patrol in that time before the ambush. Before Karen even.

Karen's saying, 'We'll walk up to the lane. Get some exercise in.'

Harry says that he's plenty thin enough but 'You could do with losing a few pounds, Karen,' and she laughs and calls him a cheeky squaddie. He likes that expression and, for a while the humour's in the air; it's like it used to be between them all those years ago.

They don't walk much these days, Harry doesn't really like her taking his arm in public, guiding him like he's a blind man. Which he nearly is. But Harry doesn't want to go to the lane, he wants to step above the water on the neglected jetty, stand above the submerged world and breathe in the freshness of the air. Try to give the shape to the blur of the feeding swans. He asks, 'How deep is it, Karen?'

She squints down to the water. 'Job to see, Harry. Four, maybe five feet. Bit mucky.'

'And out there?' Harry motions to the middle of the pool. 'Lot deeper, I should think.'

Harry stands silently for a while longer, losing himself in a different horizon of years ago, of bright sharp colours of perfect sight. Perfect sight and perfect body. Then, like a tired old man, he shrugs, says, 'Should be getting back, I suppose,' and when Karen takes his hand he doesn't protest.

She says, 'You seem better today,' and Harry says that he feels more positive and perhaps they should get out a bit more, maybe even go into Broome together soon. Then he says that he knows how hard it is for her when he's 'not right' but she must remember that he always loves her.

'I know you do,' she says. (*She's doubted it a thousand times over in the fury of his onslaughts; the table cleared with a sweep of his arm, plates and cups and a prepared dinner dashed to the floor. Drawers pulled, contents tipped out, in a search for a forgotten something*).

'I haven't been fair to you, Karen.'

'Of course you have, Harry.' (*No you haven't, Harry. You speak to me like shit. You've called me all the names under the sun. You've taken all my best years, Harry.*)

Then he stops on this walk and a glimmer of the old Harry puts his arm around her, his transformation pulls her close to his husk of a body.

'I'll always love you,' he says and for a moment it's a Harry without the lines of pain etched into his face. For a moment he's young and handsome and he's the boy in khaki and they're a couple with a future. The sudden lightening of the mood tempers Karen's bitterness, briefly usurps her discontent, and they walk back to the Bombardier like the pair of young lovers they were once upon a time. For Karen, it's because these moments are rare, they're to be treasured for remembrance when the world becomes bleak again. For Harry, it's because he's made his decision.

* * *

Foxes Farm.
Late Friday afternoon.
Dinah.

Ethan, tilting back a pre-dinner mug of tea in his farmhouse kitchen, says to Dinah, 'What time's Barry back?'

'Shouldn't be long now, Dad.' Dinah checks the clock on the kitchen wall. 'Half an hour if the traffic's been good.'

'Think I'll have a quick swill. Get changed.'

He makes his move towards the door but Dinah interrupts him: 'Can you stay out of the way for a while, Dad? I need to talk to Barry on my own.'

'Oh. Right. OK. I'll make myself scarce.' Which he doesn't immediately because he hovers in the wanting of a little more information. 'Nothing wrong is there, Dinah?' It's his concern in the curiosity that makes her let go of what she's been holding to herself; it's the blurting out of, 'Everything's wrong, Dad. We're splitting up. Me and Barry are splitting up.'

Saying the words aloud makes it real and she thinks that the order of service is back to front; she's telling her father before she tells her boyfriend. Ethan's 'Why?' will remain unanswered because how could she possibly tell him about her unwanted visitors, about massaging the lotion into her hair down there and, anyway, Barry's van, welcomed by the collie twins, is pulling up outside.

Barry's been asking plenty of 'Why's: Why are you not answering? Why are you not phoning me? They were ignored until Dinah texted him, 'You know why, Barry.' That shut him up but now he's at the door, a mask of contrition on his handsome face. But he has to ask, needs to, just in case there's a faint chance of a miraculous escape.

'Look whatever's happened, Dinah, we can talk about it. Sort it out.'

'What do you think has happened, Barry?'

He can't say what they both know, the words won't leave his mouth, snare him in his guilt. But Dinah, angry and hurt beyond measure, can't contain her words,

'You've made me feel so dirty, so unclean. Fucking crabs. You gave me the crabs. You fucking bastard Barry. I had to go to the chemist, ask for ... How could you do it?'

He could do it because he was out with the boys in a strange town, and the drink was flowing. 'Too much, Dinah. I drank too much and there was as a bit of stuff going,' – he sniffs to emphasis his point – 'round as well.' Then there's the hazy recollection of a girl who came onto him and ''Cos I was pissed-up and that, Dinah. That's when it happened. A one off. Didn't mean nothing. Honest it didn't. Never happen again.'

But Dinah's added it to the extended stayaways when his work had overrun, when his phone had been switched off, and once, though she'd ignored it, the scent of a woman was on his underwear. She adds on stripping the bed, cramming the washing machine with bed-clothes, her clothes, hot cycling twice over, checking and rechecking for the mite-sized evidence of his unfaithfulness.

So that's it for them, the end of the affair, and Dinah brings Barry's pre-packed bags of his belongings down the stairs and shows him the door out of their life. From the window she watches him go, the good-looking guy who for the past two years has kept her warm at night, kissed her face, loved her body. Made her laugh. Made her cry. And that's what she does now, she cries.

Dinah's at the table taking her seat in misery row. Her head in is her hands and she's sobbing out her heart and Ethan is knelt beside her. His strong arms are around her, comforting, keeping his precious daughter safe. He's trying to make it better for her. Like he did the last time.

* * *

Foxes Farm.

Another break-up thirteen years ago.

Dinah, Ethan, and Jenny James.

The silences have become longer in these last few weeks. They culminate in snaps of words and short stabs of sentences between her mother and father. Dinah sometimes answers for him and sometimes she answers for her. She goes back and forth, working as a go-between, trying to bring peace to a brooding house. Dinah's been learning about religion at school, how people pray to Jesus Christ, to Allah, to Shiva. She wants to be sure so she prays to all of them at once, asks them to bring back the laughter and fill the hollows of this old house. But none of it seems to work, her father still stomps out early in the morning, her mother still disappears for nights at a time. Then one afternoon, when there's a dusting of snow on the windowsill, suitcases are at the door and a stranger's car is ticking over outside the farmhouse.

Dinah's mother, her face fixed and cold, says, 'I'm going, Ethan,' and he stands there with not a word from his mouth.

Dinah says, 'Where are you going, Mum?' and her Mother spits a look at Ethan and says, 'Anywhere away from him.'

Then there's swiftness of a soft kiss, a mother's hug, and she hefts her cases out to the car where a stranger stows them in the boot. Dinah watches the going, trying to understand the enormity of what's happening in her life.

Then her father's arms are around Dinah and he's holding her, comforting her, telling her that it'll be all right, that they'll manage. Just like he'll be doing again when a loved one leaves by the same door thirteen years later.

In those thirteen years Jenny James raises a new family and Dinah's visits start to seem more like intrusions; things happen that she's not a part of in this family's life. She's on

*the outside and she's always glad to return home to Foxes
Farm and the familiar.*

Today Ethan's holding the preciousness of his daughter and
wanting to take his 12-bore shotgun and blow Barry – the
Barry he treated like a son – to smithereens. Dinah's breathing
in the scent of her father, the warm familiar smell of the farm,
of bullocks and heifers, of shaken straw and sweet hay, and
of the ever-clinging manure.

Later, before it's dark, Dinah calls up the collie twins and
she walks out to the horses. At the sight of her Muppet comes
cantering across the field to nose her pocket for a handful of
pony nuts.

'At least someone's glad to see me,' Dinah thinks but the
horse's welcome softens the bitterness of the expression.

Next morning.

It's not been a good night for Dinah and this Saturday finds
her up even earlier than usual. Dinah starts to fill her day with
things to do and the first thing, after letting the dogs out, is
to cook Ethan a hearty English breakfast. She shouts up the
stairs and he comes down rubbing the sleep out of his eyes.
He does a double take on the kitchen clock.

'Christ, it's only half past six.' He starts a moan about it
being the weekend and then he remembers what Dinah would
like to forget. To fill her mind she'll do the usual chores then
ride out Hunter for a long hack across the fields. She wants
freshness of a new day on her face and the breeze streaming
through her hair, then she'll take a walk down to Vixens Mere
and rethink her ambitions and her plans. She'll also text Barry
for the transfer of her money back into her account. But Dinah
stops there because she realises that she's seen no statements
since …? She counts back on her finger. Three months at least.
There's a jolting to her stomach. He wouldn't touch it, would

he? And then she thinks he just might because he's fucking lied about everything else. Dinah wonders if she's been made a fool of two times over?

Dinah's done her morning rounds on the farm, given Hunter a harder than expected – for him anyway – work-out and it's half past nine before Barry answers his phone with a cheerful like nothing has happened greeting, 'Hi Dinah. I was just thinking about you.'

But Dinah's reply is a cold and distant and straight to the point of, 'I want my money back, Barry.'

There a silence that lasts a second too long before he says, 'I'll do it in the week, Dinah.'

'Now, Barry. I want you to transfer it now.'

The silence is longer this time before he says, 'I can't do it, Dinah. Not all of it.'

In fact it's not much of it at all, it's a couple of grand with the rest to follow because Barry's been hit with a monster tax bill, and there's, 'been a lot of expense with the motors and that.' Barry runs a nice flashy car as well as his work van. But it's the 'and that' that gets Dinah's goat because, fucking 'and that' includes the cow who gave him the crabs who then gave them to her. Just the thought of it gives Dinah an almost irresistible urge to have a good scratch.

Barry's saying, 'Look, I will pay you back. I promise, Dinah. Let's meet up and I could …'

But the phone's been stabbed to the off and Dinah wants to go and sit in the womb of the farmhouse, in front of the Aga, and have a mug of strong tea and snaffle one of her Dad's cigarettes. Then, ever the pragmatist, she'll call out the dogs and walk down to Vixens Mere, to where her tattered dreams have parked themselves.

CHAPTER SEVEN

Morning Star.

Lorrie could have sworn that a few seconds ago when she looked at her bedroom clock it was nine o'clock. She'd thought she'd snuggle down for five minutes and now it's suddenly 'Half past ten?' She swings her legs out of the bed, takes a peep in the mirror at her sleep-smudged eyes, 'Jesus!' and pads into the kitchen to stick the kettle on. Now Lorrie was going to rise early, give Morning Star a good clean through, and then go into town for the week's groceries. Shopping is one chore she's never been fond of and Petra had always laughed and said, 'I'll buy it, Lorrie. You cook it,' but that hadn't worked either because a Nigella Lawson Lorrie wasn't; she struggled to fry an egg without breaking the yolk. Petra had laughed again in the time when it was all sweetness and loving. And pretence.

Lorrie thinks she'll have a breakfast of – checks for bread, bacon, and, she can't help a wry smile – a badly fried egg, although first she'll take her mug of tea up-deck and watch the wildlife on the water. But what catches her eye is the slight figure of Dinah and the dogs on the jetty.

Dinah's standing on the edge of the pier, staring across the marina and she's as still as a heron. Lorrie watches her for perhaps five minutes and Dinah doesn't come to life until the collie twins decide to have a set to. They have a scrabbling, noisy argument and settle it with a race along the towpath. Dinah's following and when she's alongside Morning Star

Lorrie calls out a cheery, 'Good morning, Dinah.' She actually calls it out twice because Dinah, head down into deep thoughts, doesn't seem to hear the first greeting but then it's a subdued, 'Oh hello, Lorrie. Sorry. I was miles away.' She looks up and Lorrie, from a fathom distance, can see Dinah's eyes are rimmed with red.

'Are you all right, Dinah?'

Dinah starts to say 'Yes' but then halts with a catch in her voice before she says, 'No. Not really, Lorrie.'

There's a sad honesty in this answer and Lorrie's saying to her that the kettle's on the boil and if Dinah wants a sit down and a cup of tea?

Dinah says, 'And a fag?'

A nod back from Lorrie in agreement. 'And a fag, Dinah,' she says, 'but it's a bit early for gin,' and Dinah steps aboard.

Up ahead the dogs are investigating Milly's sweet-smelling goat who's lowered his head and is up for a game of head butting. It'll be fine for a while until Milly decides that the excited yapping is getting on her bloody nerves and chases them off with curses and a broom.

It's during that cup of tea and fag later and Dinah's not spilt all of the beans – no mention of mites – but she's given out enough for Lorrie to form a picture of a cheating robbing boyfriend. Dinah's perked up a little as though some of weight's been lifted with the telling, but she did take up the offer of Lorrie's handkerchief to dab at her eyes occasionally.

'We'd been saving up to get stuff done.' Dinah shrugs. 'Or at least I was. We were going to do things here. Together. A business. This was our future. Mine and Barry's, Lorrie.'

Lorrie's thinking, 'How could, why would, anyone hurt her like this?' She's angry at that someone she's never met.

Aloud she says, 'You know I thought there was something wrong when I saw you on the jetty.'

Dinah says with a blackness of humour, 'I was thinking about throwing myself in.'

Lorrie, with open humour, touches her head and scolds, 'Not before you've done my hair, you won't.' This brings the reward of a smile for Lorrie and then Dinah says, 'I'm sorry for unloading this on you, Lorrie.' But Lorrie's not sorry, she feels that it's been a privilege to be taken into Dinah's confidence, to be treated as a friend.

Dinah makes to take her leave but before she does, she offers an embrace, slips her slender arms around Lorrie, thanks Lorrie again for her listening. For the first time in months Lorrie feels the closeness of a woman, her warmth of body. There's the dizziness of desire in Lorrie's body, a jolt of her heart. What she'd give to hold Dinah even closer, meld them together, stroke the worrying lines of unhappiness from that face. Kiss her tenderly on her soft lips, breathe in the scent of her hair. But her mind has a strength that overrides desire.

'Don't. Don't spoil this, Lorrie. Don't embarrass us both.'

So Lorrie lets her go, watches Dinah leave as she watched her come. But she's shaken is Lorrie because she's feeling the beginning of something more than physical attraction, more than sexual frustration, and she's doesn't want to go through that again.

'Better keep my distance,' she promises herself and then she catches sight of Dinah's business card on her shelf, turns herself to the mirror and thinks that maybe a spruce-up in a few days wouldn't hurt. A harmless trim and shape. What could possibly be wrong with that?

Big Ed, Milly and Moses.
Ed and Moses have been to the wood merchants and brought back up enough staves to build a picket fence around Milly's little patch of vegetables.

'It'll keep the goat off my beans,' she says.

Big Ed reminds Milly that it's her goat and says, rather sarcastically, to Moses that Milly'll probably want the fence painting fucking white as well. Milly says that's a good idea and it'll be really purty to look at with roses growing up it, 'Like in those old American films.' Ed says that Moses can have a few days off school to help, seeing as he'll be eating most of the produce anyway. Moses's appetite is a source of amazement to his mother and father; they just can't believe how much he can put away in a single sitting and still be hungry five minutes later. But for now the lengths of three inches by one inch by four feet are stacked by the side of the towpath until, sometime in a hazy future, Big Ed'll find time to set it all up. Until then the timber stack will be an eyesore and something to trip up on a dark night.

'Well at least they're here, and that's a start,' Milly thinks, even if that start might be several months away. Then she asks if they want a cup of tea and Moses says could he have a sandwich as well because it's a long time till tea?

After the unloading Moses says he's going to cut into town for an hour. He's been doing this a lot lately, cycling into Broome. It usually coincides with a mobile call and Big Ed wonders if Moses has a young lady in tow. He's talked with Milly about offering Moses some contraceptive advice but Milly scoffs that the only advice Ed could forward is, 'to keep your thumb on the end' which she thinks is hilariously funny and makes Ed think that it's no good trying to be serious when she's in this fucking mood.

Milly thinks she'll give Moses's room the once over while he's out. He's not an untidy boy but he is a boy and his room smells of teenager. Milly strips Moses's bed, tugs off the sheets, thrusts them quickly into the wash basket; she doesn't want to encounter any damp patches on her boy's bedding. Despite joking with Big Ed she doesn't really want to think about her boy doing things boys his age do at night.

Milly finds three odd socks and a pair of underpants, coated with fine fluff, under the bed. She tidies up his desk, gives the computer keyboard and screen a quick wipe-over with a damp cloth. But there's two things that she doesn't need to move, that are always in their sacred places. Moses's two passions (she might have to count up to three if he's meeting a girl in town) are his fishing and his guitar, his music. Milly runs her fingers across the strings, thinks of Moses sitting quietly canal-side, loving his guitar as a melody floats across the Marina.

The years in between then and now.
Moses and his guitar.

Although Moses doesn't really remember, he's sure he has impressions of early times at summer festivals, of bright lights and smoky fires, of being held aloft in an ocean of hands to see a band performing on a rickety stage. The way Milly describes these scenes to him is how Moses sees them, whether he actually did or not. She's also told him countless times that Sloping Joe, of alternative folk-rock group the Razor Slashers, laid Moses's chubby little fingers on the fret of his guitar, drew them gently across the strings and swore blind that Moses had strummed a tune.

'He said you were a natural,' says Milly proudly. She ignored the fact that Sloping Joe's judgement might be a little skewed; after all he was badly coked-up and at the wrong venue entirely. But it seems that Sloping Joe might well be right about Moses because at nine years old Moses picked up a Spanish six string that Big Ed brought back to Vixens from a house clearance, and started plucking at the chords. Milly thought it sounded like a tune and promptly arranged lessons with a tutor acquaintance in Broome – preferred payment in cash with a weed supplement – and soon Moses had confirmed Sloping Joe's hazy opinion of him; he actually was a natural. Moses can accompany his guitar with a very pleasant singing voice. By the time Moses is twelve that voice will be raggedly attractive with the breaking.

At the Shed on some evenings Moses will sit himself in the corner and provide a melodic background to the chatter of several different conversations. If the talk is loud he'll give the strings that extra depth of twang. If the talk is quietly low, and on the nostalgic side, he will stroke a tune that fits the mood. It seems that Moses has only to hear a piece of music the once and it's in his head forever. Sometimes he'll be quietly strumming away and a melody will form in his mind, and snake into his fingers. He'll stop then and, in Big Ed's vocabulary, wonder, 'Where the fuck's that come from?' before letting it play out. When Moses was pushing eleven, an elderly Scottish couple, into a month's retirement touring on the canals, moored for a few days in Vixens Mere. Big Ed gave them the invite to join in with a few drinks at the Shed and by the latter part of the evening everyone was four sheets to the wind; glasses of beer were chasing large drams of whisky. The elderly Scottish gentleman observed tartly at his depleting resources, 'Och, it's a good job we brought in two bottles.' (No one agreed with that sentiment come morning.) While everyone became increasingly tanked-up, Milly had her Tarot cards spread out on the table and made no sense at all to anyone; Pete talked about his beloved pigs, explaining in great detail the life cycle of his charges to an entranced listener; Moses was in the corner, not playing anything in particular, just a bit of this and that. But Mrs Elderly Scottish lady had cocked an ear and called over to him, 'Hey, Laddie. Can you play that again?'

Moses, well into the escapism of his musical world, couldn't think what 'that' she meant and the lady came over, sat down beside him, mighty amount of a wee dram clutched tightly in her hand, 'This,' she said, and in a sweetly tremulous voice started the old Scottish Skye Boat song. She's straight into it with, 'Fly bonny boat like a bird on the wing, harken the sailor's cry,' and Moses picked it up alongside her as she sang it from beginning to end. And they had an audience. Glasses nursed, attention turned to them, while this unusual duo put together a performance; there was even a clapping of hands as the last note faded.

'Where did you learn to play that?' Moses's partner asked him.

'Dunno. Just sort of picked it up, I suppose,' said Moses because he can't really describe how he hears the tune in his head and how his fingers seems to know to pluck it out.

She studied him for a moment, this grey-haired grandmother listing slightly with her whisky intake. She laughed, 'Well, all I can say is that you must have a good dash of the Scottish blood in your veins, young man.'

This said loud enough for Big Ed and Milly to hear and within the briefest exchange of looks there's a knowingness that passes between them.

The top of the track down to Vixens Mere.
Daytime.
Carl Thomson parked with an unsavoury acquaintance in an untaxed vehicle.
Carl Thomson's looking down to the marina and he's thinking, 'So this is her hideout; her and her fucking boyfriend.' He's also thinking that he's been done over twice; once when Anna stole his money and again when Jed stole Anna. Now that's the two things he has to do; get Anna back, get his money back and – OK so it's going to be three – give that lanky streak of piss a fucking good hiding. He's looking forward to that part, it's been feeding his paranoia ever since he saw the happy

couple. Well, he warned them, didn't he? He's given them plenty of time, plenty of warning, and what have they done? Shit on him, that's what they've done. Shit on him. That's why he's here on this afternoon, casing the joint, wanting to put a proper plan together to even the score.

There's a boy wheeling his bike up past them and Carl Thomson calls out, 'Wonder if you could help me, mate?'

The boy is Moses and he stops, looks up.

'I'm looking for a friend of mine. Jed Rawlins. You know him?'

The boy nods, points down the hill at the moored boats. 'Home Sweet Home,' he says. 'But he's not there. They went out earlier. Don't know when they'll be back.'

He's mounting his bike and Carl Thomson says, 'Thanks for that, mate,' and gets back into the car where his acquaintance says, 'All right?'

'All I need to know, mate.'

And it is, because forming in Carl Thomson's fermenting brain is a plan to break into Home Sweet Home one dark night, take what's his in money and kind, and then later apply the physical revenge and reclaim ownership on his property. By God she'll get what for and Jed'll get what's coming to him.

The acquaintance fires up the motor. 'Where to now?' This acting chauffeur is working off a rock debt and there's still a few miles left on the clock.

Carl Thomson says, 'Just drive around for a while, mate, I need to think some more.'

'Or a drink somewhere?'

'Why not?'

So he'll sit and drink and think. Later he'll have a snuffle and a smoke and all the time his plan will niggle at him, it'll grow, fill all of his head. It'll sit there, pecking away at him, until the moment he's actually squeezing his sweet revenge between his grubby fingers.

'Won't be long,' he tells the beast inside himself. 'It won't be long now.'

And the beast says that it better not be because he can't wait for much longer.

CHAPTER EIGHT

Vixens Marina.

Fifteen years ago.

In the Christmas time of this year, the barges of this floating hamlet are lining the bank in their usual winter mooring. There's the colourful Crystal Lady – lit up from prow to stern with twinkling fairy lights – where Big Ed and Milly are already qualified as long term residents. Summer Walker, with the quiet Scotsman who mostly keeps himself to himself. Morning Star, holding a temporary renter whose name no one will ever remember. Bombardier, occupied by Karen Jones alone because Harry's in hospital – has been for a week now – awaiting an operation for the continuing after-effects of the IED. Home Sweet Home with a full family; four-year-old Jed and a mother – recently returned from another contentious excursion – and father that are vaguely on speaking terms. Uneasily and occasionally. End of the line is Saddleback, crewed by Pete who has only just started working with swine and has begun to earn his sobriquet of Pigman Pete.

Just up the track from Vixens Mere, at Foxes Farm, Dinah's mother is on countdown until circumstances allow her to pack her bags. Much further away, Carl Thomson has had a couple of good hidings from his father to keep him in line. They don't. Lorrie Smith, thirteen years old, has a new best friend that she can't stop thinking about. She's been trying to persuade her mother to allow a sleepover but her mother's on a no. Anna, into the third year of her life, is already matching that number with her foster-homes.

So at Vixens Mere in this winter of fifteen years ago the future dead are still living and all the leavings have yet to occur, and the birthing of Moses is a fraction over nine months away. The seed hasn't been planted just yet.

Crystal Lady.

That same time.

Milly the Mystic and Big Ed.

Milly says, 'Christmas night is the most boring night of the year.'

Ed, snoozing by the wood burner, grunts that she's probably right but it's comfortably boring.

'Come on, let's open up the Shed. Get some music going.' Milly has had a little sniff and she's raring to go.

'It's dark. It's late.'

'It's six o'fucking clock. Get off your fat arse and turn the lights on. Fire up the stove. We're going to have a party.'

'OK, OK, Milly.' Ed eases himself up, laces his boots, warns ,'But it's not going to be a late one.' These words will come back to haunt him at approximately 1AM when he slips over on a visit to the outside loo and finishes hands down in a pool of cold wet, and pungent, mud created by mis-aimed pissing.

Milly says, 'You get things ready and I'll go round. See who's up for it.'

Because the clientele are mostly young – well youngish – and share the sentiment that Christmas evenings are boring, Milly collects a full house: Sandra and Mark Rawlins with their four-year-old Jed, who's going to be stretched out on a couple of hay bales and blanketed in coats before ten o'clock, Brodie the quiet Scotsman who'll share a wee dram or two with everyone and always attracts the curiosity of the ladies, the tenant of the Morning Star whose name no one will ever remember, and Pete, the man with the whiff of swine about him.

Milly also knocks gently on Karen's door. 'Thought I'd ask, seeing as we're having a do and you're on your own.'

Karen politely says that she might look in later, if that's all right? Milly tells her that any time's OK and to 'Just bring a bottle with you.'

Then Karen sits in her lonely floating home trying to settle down and watch Wonderful Life *on the telly when hers is anything but. Harry's hospital, specialising in combat inflicted wounds, is in Manchester; a good train ride away from Vixens Mere. Or it would be if the Rail Union hadn't decided to stage a strike of maximum disruption over the holiday period. So there'll be no Christmas visit until Christmas is over. Man and wife have managed a half hour on the phone – in a bitterly cold telephone box halfway to Broome – and Harry's said that his stay might be a bit longer than what they thought.*

'Few things showed up on the scan. Know more later.'

This disclosure didn't bring any season's cheer to Karen and after brooding for a spell she decides at nine o'clock that, desperate for some company to take her mind off things, she'll go and join the venue in the shed.

The Shed.

Same night. About 10:30.

Brodie Stewart.

You like this crowd, they're pleasant enough, and Big Ed always keeps the fire stoked up and a beer at hand. Milly has sausages and onions simmering in a huge frying pan on top of the wood burner and she's singing along to Umbrella *with a thick joint glued to her bottom lip. A tiara of tinsel is threaded into her hair and the hem of her long skirt sparkles with stitched-in sequins. A quick glance around the shed shows you the familiar faces of the usual winter's quartering. Except for one.*

You're looking at an attractive woman who's leaning back in an armchair with a drink in one hand, cigarette in the other. She seems a little remote, like she's lonely in a crowd.

Big Ed's saying in your ear, 'Bit of all right there, Brodie,' Then he checks himself and mutters guiltily, 'Shame about her old man though,' and sketches a husband who carries the scars of the battlefield wherever he goes. 'Blown-up,' he says. 'He'll never be right. In hospital now, you know.'

You can't help watching this woman taking her nervous swallows of whatever Milly's been feeding her. When she upends her glass completely, sits it between her knees, you go over, offer her a refill and some company. She says that she really shouldn't have any more because she's not used to drinking, but she takes the offer and then you sit beside her. She starts to talk and her eyes are bright and her words tumble over each other as she tells you that she couldn't face Christmas night on her own. You say that you were thinking the same, and to you it's a recalling of empty nights at some remote mooring with rain tapping on the roof.

You get her name. 'Karen Jones,' she says and holds out her hand like it's a formal introduction at a party.

'Brodie,' you say. 'I'm a Scot in exile,' and she laughs.

So the both of you sit in the warmth of fire and company and she asks you how long you've been on the water and you tell her it seems like a forever, well a long long time. She says that it's their third year and money's tight and Harry – my husband – can't settle. Then of course you get the rest of the tale because this lonely woman needs to tell it. She pulls you into the story of her life, unassumingly sadly, while around you the background of music and conversation ebbs and flows. That's until Milly kills the tunes, centres herself, tells everyone that it's twelve o'clock and that Christmas is officially over.

'But not for us.' She raises her glass, takes a long pull on her roll-up and then her drink. 'To the Christmas past and the Christmas future. May there be many more.' Then the music starts up again and the party resumes its merry way till God knows what time.

You'll remember this Christmas night; Milly swirling around with tinsel in her hair, Big Ed, St Nicholas hat askew on his head, reliving a summer festival, Pete snoring gently in the corner, little Jed sleeping like a baby on his bed of straw bales while his mother and father hiss daggers at each other, Ethan and Jenny Jones and a bright-eyed Dinah relishing this attention in this grown-up world. But most of all you'll remember it because of Karen Jones, because of what starts here and what ends here.

The starting is of the taking of her arm, walking her back to Bombardier, conscious of the closeness of her. The marina's floating with stars and these early hours belong to the hoot of the owl and a woman's scent colouring the night air. Outside of the Bombardier you stop and tell her that you've enjoyed talking to her and if she wants a coffee sometime?

'I'd like that,' she says and you stand in the awkwardness of what to do now. What you intend is perhaps a friendly hug and a peck on the cheek as a way of thanks for a pleasant evening. You slip your arms around her in a loose embrace and offer a soft touch to her cheek. But she surprises you because she holds on, draws you to her, offers her mouth in a searching question that you only begin to answer because it's a very brief tasting of honey. Then she's suddenly pushing against you, pushing you away, and apologising, 'I'm sorry. I'm sorry. I never meant … It's the drink and that.' She's punctuating her words with a break in her voice.

You tell her that it's all right, that you understand. So it's left there with her walking the short plank onto the Bombardier *and you going back to your dog's wagging tail and the warmth of the cabin. In bed you lie awake and dream a little, can't help thinking how long it is since you tasted the sweet delight of a woman in the class of Karen Jones. That's the trouble with your drifting existence; restlessness and relationships rarely travel hand in hand. That's how it should be because it can only be a good thing for you. Can't it?*

Same Christmas night.

Karen Jones.

She's playing tonight back to herself, re-running it through her mind. It's been a different time for her; she's been with people, sitting at the Christmas party, listening to the music, having a drink, being paid some attention by a rather handsome young Scotsman. At least she thinks he's young, but he's one of those lucky people who always appear to be ageless. He'll look almost exactly the same fifteen years from now when their paths coincide again at Vixens. So Karen's sipping a very strong wine of indeterminate origin, enjoying a puff and the sound of Brodie Stewart's soft Scottish accent. In fact, she's like a normal person in a normal existence. For once she doesn't need to hurry home. She's no Harry waiting to clock her in; he's safe and warm in his hospital bed. So Karen Jones has stepped away from her unasked-for career of full-time carer; she's in the place where a good smoke and a good drink has lifted her; the land where inhibition and convention sometimes take second place. She has had a good night. She might have been a little giggly, lightheaded, but when Brodie walked her home, leaned in close to her, she didn't expect her own reaction. It unnerved her with a sudden intensity of feeling that was almost immediately usurped by embarrassment and guilt and the bolting for safety.

'*My God, what must he think of me?*'

But afterwards, lying in her bed, she remembers the burn

of his mouth on hers, the closeness of embrace, and she can't sleep because she feels so alive, so hungry. She knows that its name is Desire, and that's what she's had to suppress for so long now, this yearning for the carnal. She's tied to a loving marriage without any of the loving. She knows that she's not going to sleep now and so she wraps her dressing coat around herself, goes out on deck to watch over the star-strewn water. The night's cold and silent and everyone's abed.

'The party's over, Karen,' she tells herself and she doesn't think she ever felt so desolate and more in need of human touch in the whole of her life. It's Christmas. 'Fucking Christmas.' And she hasn't got a soul in the world to share it with. Then she thinks about Brodie again and acknowledges that it wasn't him who pulled away from consequence. Right now she needs a cigarette and she needs a walk, even though it's the middle of the night. So she takes that duo along the path, past the sleeping barges, to the mouth of the marina and back again. Well, not quite back again because she stops at Summer Walker, steps onto the gangplank, feels the slight give under her feet as she carries that step to the door and softly raps her knuckles on it. She wants him to answer and she doesn't want him to answer and if he hadn't opened his door, taken her hand, pulled her gently inside, her love would have been wasted and a life wouldn't have been created.

Bombardier.

Morning after the night with Brodie.

Karen Jones busies herself tidying up when the barge really doesn't need to be any more spick and span. She has a long shower, thinks she'll wash away the guilt of the night. But it doesn't happen because she can't find any sins to sluice away. She feels so alive, glowing; she knows that she ought to be sitting with regrets for company, and she knows that they're hovering in the background waiting to swoop, but for these few hours she wants to relive the night where Somebody wanted her. Somebody needed her. Somebody loved her as a woman. After so long. Karen Jones might be apologising, 'I'm so sorry, Harry. So sorry.' But he's never going to hear these words as she tells herself that it's a one off, that it must never happen again. It's to be a delicious memory, a reminder that she's still an attractive woman, a wanton woman. It'll be a confirmation in her memory when her marriage will only ever consist of a kiss, an embrace. Nothing more. Nothing like a perfect fitting of mood and desire and heady, illicit, thrilling passion in the bedroom of Summer Walker with a stranger.

God, she needs a cigarette just thinking about it.

Broome railway station.
Four o'clock in the afternoon a few days later.
Karen Jones, returning from the long journey after seeing Harry in hospital.
This hasn't been the best of visits. Harry was in a morose mood. He used the expression 'Pissed off' because his consultant surgeon has given Harry a blow-by-blow account of the screwing and pinning his bones need to stop them twisting further out of shape.

'It'll take two, maybe three ops,' Harry says to Karen and then his face darkens and it's a sudden anger that blurts out through clenched teeth, 'I wish that fucking bomb had ...'

Before he can say it she stops him with, 'Don't say that, Harry. Never say that. Please.'

She's shaking her head, grasping his hand, and she's close to tears. Her handsome wounded soldier shakes off his feelings for her feelings, apologises. 'Sorry Karen. Karen, sorry. It's just that I want to be a normal man again.'

Then they talk about how the operations may help, may make like easier for him, for them. But his body will never be right, and there's no cure for the creeping loss of his senses.

They both know that. Move on. Move on. No miracles to see here.

All of these thoughts make for a quietly brooding home journey for Karen Jones and, by the time the train pulls into Broome station, she's several pegs down in the depression charts. She's thinking of a lonely cabin, a dinner for one, the buzz of silence in her head. But when she steps out onto the platform there's someone waiting for her, taking her hand, ready with a greeting on his handsome face. Karen Jones can't stop her heart from leaping.

'Oh, no,' she thinks. 'Oh, no,' and then almost immediately, 'Oh, yes.'

Yes, please. And it's yes please right up to the week that Harry's due home.

Home Sweet Home.
Still in the Christmas week of fifteen years ago.
Mark Rawlins and Sandra Day.
The argument that began two days before Christmas eve, and after a week with no sight of hide nor hair of her – usual pattern of her behaviour – Sandra Day turns up as bold as brass. She says that she's done with Mark and that she's going to take Jed – her Jed she calls him – and leave this shithole behind. But that won't be just yet because she's some loose ends to tie up. Mark Rawlins just shrugs; he's heard it all a thousand times before.

There's two things that twenty-one-year-old Sandra Day is lying about; Home Sweet Home isn't a shithole because thirty-six-year-old Mark Rawlins is fastidiously clean. The barge is spotless from stern to bow, inside and out. The second thing is that 'her Jed' isn't really hers. Yes, she did birth him but from the moment Jed was separated from her, Mark bottle-fed him; 'Don't want my tits sucked dry, shrivelled-up like an old lady's,' *changed him;* 'Yuk. I can't stand that mess. The smell!' *went to him in the night;* 'How much longer you going to let him cry?'

So Jed is his father's son, became more of his father's son as each year passed, as Sandra Day came and went in her fashion. Milly called her a boat-hopper, 'Arrive on one, leave on another,' which was a good analogy for Sandra's lifestyle. And that's because she'd turned up at Vixens Mere aboard an overcrowded rented cruiser, the Pleasuredome, a floating venue for an all-night all-bright party of laughter, drinking, and extremely loud music echoing around their stretch of water. Big Ed's polite early hours request to 'Shut the fuck up,' was met with an equally polite response to 'Mind your own fucking business,' which left Ed with dark thoughts of holing the Pleasuredome below the waterline. The party left the next morning, creeping out in grey wet dawn, very subdued and hungover. They also left Sandra Day sitting astride her suitcase on the towpath with the rain forming a puddle around her. What her hedonistic erstwhile friends didn't realise was that an array of credit cards, cold cash, and a magpie's hoard of shiny things, were tucked away in the pocket of that suitcase. Sandra's long blonde hair is curling in the rain, her mascara is smudging her face, and she is drawing on a very soggy cigarette.

This is the image that meets Mark Rawlins as he steps off Home Sweet Home to buy his morning paper. He says to this soggy angel, 'You all right?'

'No' she says. 'Just been fucking dumped.' She waves across the water, adds the description of a vehement 'Cunts' to the occasion. Seems she's not a one for holy language.

Mark Rawlins, good Samaritan that he is, asks if she wants a cup of tea and a chance to dry out and she's aboard Home Sweet Home like a cannon shot.

The tea's brewing and Sandra Day's eyes are darting around the clean warmth of Home Sweet Home; the flickering stove, the comfortable furniture. She spills out that she's nowhere to live, nowhere to go to, swallows a sob, plants a question. 'Don't suppose you've a spare room I could rent?' and Mark Rawlins melts, softie that he is. Takes her in all her bedraggledness into Home Sweet Home. 'I'll pay rent every week. Keep the place clean. Cook for you even,' she told him but proceeded to do none of those things. But it didn't matter, not in this beginning, because Mark Rawlins, double her age, had fallen hopelessly in love with her thick Liverpool accent, her sluttish attractiveness. He was blind to the sowing of the seeds of discord: the laying in bed till midday, the drinking, the disappearing into Broome and coming back bright-eyed and bushy-tailed in the early morning. She would sunbathe on the roof of Home Sweet Home in the minutest of bikinis and Big Ed, casting a sly eye over her tender young body, thinks, to himself of course, that she looks like she could be really really dirty. Milly recognises that look, tells Ed that if he's not careful, 'he'll go fucking blind.'

So Sandra Day turns up at Vixens Mere, tries to tap Mark Rawlins for a few quid, announces she's staying a day or two and then she's going to steal Jed away. But meantime she quite fancies going to the Christmas party in the Shed. They do go, sharing barely two civil words and plenty of evil looks, because big soft Mark will never refuse her anything. And then the ongoing row, fuelled by heavy drinking and God knows what else, gains in festering and finally explodes in the night. In the season of goodwill to all men.

Crystal Lady.
In the small hours of Boxing night.
Milly's been on her after-midnight prowl around Hunters Woods, bathed herself in the moonlight, wished upon a star,

whispered to the woodland spirits. Seen what she's seen. When she slides back into bed beside Ed, he starts and moans, 'You're like a fucking iceberg, Milly.'

She says, 'Guess what, Ed?'

Ed knows she won't give him any rest until she's told her story, asks wearily, 'Guess what, Milly?'

'They're at it again.'

'Who? At what again?'

'Summer Walker. It's rocking like fuck'

Ed, sure it wasn't rocking like fuck, but just wanting to get back to sleep tries to kill the nocturnal chat with. 'It's not our business, Milly.'

'I know, Ed but …'

'But what Milly?'

'Well the thought of it going on has made me feel a bit like … you know.'

'Milly, I've got a ceiling to plaster in the morning; I need some rest.'

'A quickie, Ed. That's all.'

A problem for Ed is that Milly isn't only talking, her hands are beneath the covers and her ministrations are starting to raise Ed's interest. Ed also knows that he won't have any peace until the deed is accomplished. So a quickie it is and afterwards Milly says, 'Is that it, Ed?'

'You said a quickie.'

'I know but there's quick and quick, Ed.'

The now not quite so Big Ed tells Milly that's her lot for tonight and so she cuddles to him and says that she'll wait for the morning glory. Ed asks God to shut her the fuck up so he can get some sleep. Milly says that he shouldn't take the Lord's name in vain. But she does shut up and she's asleep in minutes and loudly snoring her head off. Ed can't join her in the Land of Nod because Milly sounds 'like a fucking express train.' He gets up to have a fag and to a falling asleep on the sofa.

* * *

At a quarter past seven Milly wakes him with a cup of tea and a bacon sandwich, and all is forgiven. He tells her that she's not such a bad old bird after all, and she says that if he can pop back at lunchtime maybe she can finish off from last night? Ed says the only thing he's getting up today is the ladder to plaster the ceiling.

But Ed's not going to do any plastering because a nail-raked, ashen-faced Mark Rawlins is standing at the door with a red-eyed Jed in tow.

He says, 'Something's happened Ed. I've done something bad.'

That something bad has lain still and cold aboard Home Sweet Home for nearly thirty hours.

Summer Walker.

Early March.

Weather cool in the day but, more often than not, a shared body warmth at night.

Harry Jones is due home – at last – after repairs to his bomb-blasted bones. A love affair is taking its last breath.

Brodie Stewart.

There isn't much preparation before you're shipshape and ready to cast off; there's only the goodbyes to Big Ed and Milly, Pete, and the rest, with a talk of mooring-up again in the Autumn. So you do the rounds, say the goodbyes, until there's just the one left. Karen Jones.

She's aboard Summer Walker sitting at your table, a sparkling of tears in her eyes, not really sipping at her coffee but certainly drawing heavily on her cigarette. You're feeling a bit choked yourself, you've never let anyone get this close in a long time, but there's something about Karen Jones that's touched the heart of you. You reach out to her, stroke the softness of her skin, taste the salt of her tears, hold her close until the clock has moved on to the ending.

You hand her your present, a carved figurine, a keepsake eight inches high that'll give nothing away and can sit on a shelf and gather dust. Or it can be lovingly held in a remembrance for the secretly loved.

She's a little taken aback and a tremor is in her voice. 'It's beautiful, Brodie. It's just beautiful.'

You've spent time on this piece, you've worked slowly and patiently, gently carving, subtracting, smoothing, until there's this boy, his face slightly up-turned, smile forming on his mouth, and looking to you as though you're not a stranger in his life. Like he recognises you. Karen Jones holds this child, wondrously, tenderly to herself.

'Who is it, Brodie?'

You don't know who he is, whether he's been plucked from a recollection, or whether he's ever existed in past or present. But he's familiar, you felt it as he formed through mallet and sculpting chisel. Each shaving brought him closer to creation. Who is it? With no hint of forethought the words are out of your mouth.

You say, 'He's ours, Karen. Mine and yours.'

Then it's like the ritual of parting has been fulfilled and everything has been said except for Karen Jones's very softly delivered, 'Goodbye Brodie,' and she's gone and you don't know if you ever will see her again.

CHAPTER NINE

Vixens Mere.
The Shed.
Christmas Eve. Present day.
Pigman Pete, Milly, and Big Ed sitting around the wood burner.

Big Ed says that it's a shame that Pete doesn't work at a turkey farm because he could have brought a bird home for their Christmas dinner. Milly says to Pete take no notice of Old Misery Guts and reckons that you can't beat a pork joint with all the trimmings, 'and the crackling, Pete.' She cuts Big Ed a blinder. 'And don't forget that's it's me who'll be slaving away at the stove, cooking it all.'

Big Ed, like he always does, reminds Milly of the Christmas morning when she'd swallowed too much of her own home-brewed wine. He laughs, 'Didn't cook much that day, did she, Pete? Being sick as a dog and sitting on the bog all day, weren't you Milly?'

Neither of them wants to answer Big Ed, and Pigman Pete, seeing the way this is going, suggests he pulls the tabs on a can apiece and makes up a couple of roll-ups to share. He's sitting comfortably here in this company is Pete. He's warm, he's a drink in one hand, a smoke in the other, and the companionship of the family who took a no-hoper under their wing. He doesn't ask for much in life and Milly and Ed are brother and sister to him. He'd do anything for them. And Moses.

Anything at all. He often thinks that he'd feel grateful if he were to stop a bullet for any of them.

At one time Pete had been a well-known waster around Broome. He'd drifted down from the north in the early part of the century and made the pubs his home. Work to drink had been his motto until the work dried up because of the drink. One sunny morning, desperate for cash, he'd spotted Big Ed's Transit parked outside a roofing job, climbed up the ladder, poked his head over the eaves, and asked a very surprised Ed, 'You haven't got a couple of days for me, mate, have you?'

Big Ed, who was contemplating the hard graft of hefting slates and battens onto the roof by himself, thought briefly – about one second because the temperature was rapidly climbing – and gives Pete a try out, shares his sandwiches and tea with him, pays him at the end of day, and drops Pete at his abode on the way home. Pete's abode is the sheltering of a half derelict house. There's no glass in the windows and the front door is permanently open.

Big Ed, taking in the condition of the house and the fairly ripe aroma of Pete says, 'Tomorrow? Morning? See you on the job?'

'Yeah, sure. Thanks, mate. See you tomorrow.'

Big Ed drives thoughtfully away from that unsure sure.

By eleven that night Pete had drunk himself nearly insensible. He's had a ruckus in the Greyhound, another in the Phoenix, and been refused service at the Lucky Card. He's managed to weave his way home and fall onto his mattress fully dressed, boots and all. And there he would have stayed to midday if, at eight o'clock, he hadn't been woken by Big Ed's imposing figure looming over him and wishing him a 'Good morning, Pete.'

'What the fuck?' ends in a groan.

'Time to get up. We've got work to do.'

Big Ed offers his hand, pulls Pete to his feet, gets him in the Transit, feeds him a Milly bacon doorstep and a cup of sweet tea from his flask. Then Ed works Pete hard until he's sweated all the night's excesses from every pore in his body. Every time he'd flagged, Ed was on his case and Pete was really looking forward to labour's end. He can't wait, he's counting down for the evening when his raging thirst will be cooled by a pint of draught pouring down his throat.

'It won't touch the sides,' he promises himself.

It's a scorcher this day, the slates are hot to the touch and the roofing felt is sticky in the heat. Pete's mightily relieved when Ed blows the finishing whistle and he's in the cab for his ride home. Ed doesn't start the vehicle straight away, he rolls two cigarettes, passes one over to Pete and says, 'Can't be safe keeping stuff at your place?'

Pete reckons that he doesn't have much worth stealing. He has, he says, 'Just a few old clothes and things.'

Considering the state of Pete's present dress Ed wonders what he means by old clothes.

Ed says, 'Look, I need someone reliable for the next few weeks,' and Pete's sure he's getting the big E from Big Ed but his new employer adds, 'Do you think you can do it?'

With less confidence that it sounds, Pete thinks he can and when they're outside of Pete's town house residence Big Ed says, 'Right. Get your gear.'

'What?'

'You're coming back with me.'

And that's it. That's how it's done, and waif and stray Pete is allocated the sofa in the shed for his dreaming time. Milly, used to adopting lame dogs, thinks that it's good to help someone for a couple of weeks.

'Christian thing to do,' she says, even though her Gods belong to another religion. 'Just to give him a chance to get back on his feet,' she agrees with Ed. Mind she baulks at washing Pete's clothes. 'And I'm definitely not going anywhere near his underpants.'

In the way of things, a couple of weeks become a couple of months and then Saddleback loses its lodger to a moonlit flit and Ethan James says that Pete can have it as long as the rent's paid every week.

It's not all plain sailing. A number of times Big Ed gets a phone call from a local hostelry to rescue Pete before the law's notified. One time Ed, totally pissed off, dragged a muppet floppy, near senseless Pete out of the King's Head and with great difficulty heaved him into the back of the Transit, drove back to Vixens with his live cargo. Ed was going to leave him in there sleeping it off but, because the night was a chilly one, Milly sent Ed on a guilt trip.

'What if he's frozen to death in the morning?'

Ed reckoned that if Pete's as stiff as a board he'll be a lot easier to handle. This earns another rebuke from Milly. So Ed, not in the best of moods at this late hour, then hauled floppy Pete none too carefully into Saddleback, stoked the stove up and left him to it. He also left him with a few extra bruises as compensation for all the drama.

Although it does become much better with Pete, it'll never be completely right. It's a slow process weaning down Pete's problems to manageable – evenings and weekends to start with – but after a couple of years Pete is almost a proper person. He starts a permanent job on the pig farm and working with the animals helps him to keep his lid on.

'My girls,' he calls the farrowing sows and he knows them all by name and Ed says that he moithers like an expectant father when a sow's due to litter.

'For all we know he might be the daddy,' Ed says. 'He doesn't seem to get any action anywhere else.'

'Bit like you,' Milly says. 'When did we last see any action?'

Ed says that when you spend half the week perched on a ladder it affects your goolies, all that straining, but the weekend's coming and she'd better watch out when she's bent over the sink. Milly reckons if she's doing the washing-up she probably wouldn't even notice.

'Just pull my dress down when you've finished, Ed,' she says and they both have a chuckle in the easiness of their loving.

So Pete will go about his business. He'll still have a drink, still get merry, maybe get lairy occasionally, but nothing like he did and he knows that Big Ed and Milly have probably saved his life. And he loves them and can't imagine being anywhere other than where he is now.

Scotland.
Many miles from Vixens Mere.
Night.
Casualty Ward, Raigmore Hospital.
Dr Callum Macgregor, Nurse Sally Small, and Seanmhair.

It's two days now since the old lady was brought in, and for those two days she's hung impossibly onto survival. Ward nurse Sally Small says the old lady was hit by a van near Dores. The van driver, shaken up by the accident, had stuttered to the ambulance crew, 'I didn't see her in the mist. Just didn't see her.' A few of the nearby residents gathered to the scene had told the police that she was Mary Stewart, one of the Tinks, who'd been travelling these roads for a long, long time. 'Shame it's ended like this,' one of them said like she was already dead. But she wasn't, not yet.

Dr. Callum Macgregor has a razor-sharp mind and an even sharper memory and the name of Mary Stewart conjures up a hot highland day, a picture of an elderly woman, a donkey and cart, a young man, and a ranging lurcher dog. He'd watched them pass from the gateway of his grandmother's house – an August holiday respite from the Glasgow streets – and he'd asked his grandmother, 'Who's that?'

She'd made the sign of the cross – a rare Catholic in these highlands of Scotland – and said, 'They're a strange people, Callum. They're Tinks. Summer Walkers. Never have anything to do with them. Ever.'

Later, from a village lad, he found a name and some history of these people who appeared every summer to sell or mend pots and pans, sharpen knives and clippers, sell wood carvings of birds and animals, along with an offering of labour for a few days. These people would hole up in a shed, barn, or half-ruined croft for the winter and then, when the warming sun of spring began to creep down into the valleys, they would take to the road.

Over his school holidays of three summers, he saw the Tinks pass and on the last of those passings the old lady stopped, called him over, pressed a silver half a crown into his hand, wished him luck, and told him that one day they'd meet again. As she's speaking, she's fixing him with the clearest blue eyes he's ever going to see in his life.

He'd kept the half a crown, put it in his coin collection, and, when he bought his first car, he had drilled a hole in it and threaded it to his key ring. Dr Callum Macgregor thinks he's not a superstitious man but this silver coin of 1954, his birth year, has been with him so long that it's become his lucky charm. It accompanied him to Edinburgh University, sat under his table lamp when he was studying his medical finals, was in his pocket when he walked down the aisle. It's in his pocket now as he's remembering that summer's day of fifty-eight years ago. And he's remembering the name of Mary Stewart and thinking that this old lady, laying quietly in the critical ward, must be the daughter of that Tink.

Later he's nursing an early hour's cup of tea in the nurses' station. It's been a quiet night so far except for the occasional low moaning or groaning that heralds expiring mortality. Dr Callum Macgregor has always tried to make the dying as comfortable as possible. This caring man has made a rule that no one, if it could possibly be avoided, should take the final journey alone. That's if he has any say in the matter. He's lost count of the number of times that he's held together a clasping of hands in the ending spasm of a life. 'Least any human being can do for another.' Then there's an interruption to his maudlin thoughts, a tap on the door and Nurse Sally Small, back from her rounds, says, 'I think that maybe you should come, Dr Macgregor. It's Mary Stewart.'

Mary Stewart has been placed in a side ward and the pale light of the pre-dawn is stealing softly over her. Her laboured breathing sucks at the air. He looks across to Nurse Small, motions her to go, but she shakes her head and pulls a chair to the other side of the bed.

'I'll sit here awhile,' she says. 'Keep you both company.'

There's not much sitting awhile because Mary Stewart is letting go fairly quickly, unclinging herself from the world. But in the moments before that letting go, her eyes, startingly blue in the growing light, snap open and she looks directly at Dr Callum Macgregor. Her dry mouth slowly rasps out the words, 'You'll still have the half a crown?'

It's not really a question, it's like she knows he has. So the answer can't be anything but a confirmation and with that her eyes shut as suddenly as they opened. There's not a whisper of movement from her again and her lips, clamped tightly together, fade slowly to blue. And she's gone.

Nurse Sally Small goes over to the window, unlatches it, opens it wide. Lets the cold in and the warmth out.

'I'll let her soul free,' she says of the old custom. Then she asks, 'What did she mean about a half a crown?' and unable to explain, or understand, Dr Callum Macgregor says, 'Confusion, I suppose,' but it's him that's confused because it would be an impossibility for it to be the same woman. But how would she know about ...? He thinks he'll have something to ponder on in the dark Scottish evenings.

Summer Walker.
Brodie Stewart.
A brazier, a ten gallon can with holes punched into it, is glowing hot with burning logs on the verge of the towpath. Metal teapot sitting on a brick. Mug and milk and sugar to hand. Mick the collie is hogging the heat.

You always work outside as much as the weather will allow and today you're sharing the warmth of the fire with Mick, working on a figurine of a naked lady. You're giving it a final, very thorough buffing, bringing up the colour to a light finish, a showing of her lines. You study your work. She's a slender beauty; her arms are behind her head and she's bending slightly backwards. You steadily polish on because this is it; you're nearly there. All of the intricate crafting of the last week or so has brought you here to the earlyness of a frosted morning. And you know this one's special; it seemed to flow more easily from your imagination, through your fingers. Almost carved itself. You're concentrating hard, holding this foot-high model of feminine form at arm's length. Turning it around. Looking for any blemish of distraction. Then Mick's head goes up and you know someone's coming.

That someone is Karen Jones and she's hunched into a long thick coat, red woollen hat on her head, face brightened from the cold. You give her a 'Good morning' and she pauses in her 'Hello' and you think she's going to walk on by but she stops, looks at what you're doing.

'That's lovely,' she says, and you would let her hold it, 'But the polish. You know ...'

She joins in the crowded warmth of your fire and asks if you've a cigarette to spare. You light her one from the brazier, pass it to her. Your fingers touch and her hand is trembling. She takes a deep pull, looks over the marina at the sheen of ice on the water, the frozen trees. You sit without words for a while until you say, 'Harry? How is he?'

'Good days, bad days. Nothing changes.' She shrugs, flicks her cigarette stub into the fire. 'Sorry,' she says, 'Didn't mean to sound bitter. Still. I better get on.' But she pauses like she's going to say something else, *speak of the unspoken.* She shrugs again, pats Mick on his head again, and leaves you to your work. You watch her going, this attractive woman who's taking her air of sad discontent with her. Karen Jones. And that's the name that was in your head as a block of wood was shaped into a long-ago memory.

You go back to your polishing, take another look at what you've carved, created through your hands and eye. You'll go into town later, box up the lovely lady very carefully and she should arrive at Arts and Craft by tomorrow's delivery. In a day or so Art will transfer your money over and then he'll be asking what to expect next. He has a few spaces in the shop window? You'll promise that you've something in the offing even if you haven't.

You take some time for yourself, settle your eyes on the stillness of the water, the rushes cut back by the frosts of winter. There's another cigarette in your mouth, a mug of stewed tea in your hand, the dog at your feet. And then suddenly there's a moment when every sound of this morning seems to have paused for breath, an immeasurable interlude of sheer silence, to allow access to the shrill demand of your mobile.

You know the voice, a cousin of a cousin, even though it's

been a long time over decades of distance. The message is delivered in an undiluted highland accent.

'I'm sorry Brodie, it's your seanmhair. She's gone. An accident. I only got word a few hours ago.'

Then there's talk of the details, the arrangements to be made and you say that you're coming up today, first train caught. Then you sit and stare across the water. Remember. Conjure her up. And then it seems for the briefest of time that she's here beside you and she's whispering within a cool breath that's fanning your face, 'Beannachd leibh.'

It's a day long ago and you're sitting on the bank of a falling highland brook somewhere above Inverness. You're saying a goodbye and you're eighteen years old and the tools of your trade, the chisels of carving, are in your backpack. You and your seanmhair are watching the flow of the stream as she talks about the days past, and the days to come for you. You tell her that you worry about leaving her and she says that there's been many years in her life when the only company has been her own. 'You have to go,' she says. 'The time is right for you.' So there's the leaving; an embrace, a soft kiss, and you start on the path to the rest of your life. You know she'll be watching you until you're out of her sight and you can still hear her words even though, when you look back, she's a speck on the hillside.

'Beannachd leibh. Beannachd leibh.'

You pack a few things you'll be needing, turn off the gas, electric, go to Crystal Lady, ask Big Ed to keep an eye on Summer Walker for a while, ask for a lift to Broome station. Then you and Mick will take the high road for a gathering in a frosted country churchyard. You don't think there will be too many there because there's not too many left. You belong to a dying breed.

* * *

You imagine an ice-cold chapel, a plain wooden box on a bier, a sparse scattering of Tinkers throughout the pews, a eulogy from the man of the cloth, an echoing of hymns, a following to a deep dark hole into the earth.

That'll be it except for a few words of condolences, a few recovered memories about the old days, a few drinks in the local hotel bar, a parting from your own kind who say their goodbyes, leave you with the thoughts of so many years that they can never have but they know that you have.

That's how you imagine it and that's how it is.

Bombardier.
Harry Jones.
Harry watches Karen for as long as he can see her, until she becomes a blur and there's only her bright red woollen hat to confirm her identity. He follows her past Morning Star, Crystal Lady, and for another twenty yards until she stops at Summer Walker. He can make out Brodie Stewart and, he thinks, his dog. But he can clearly smell the sharp tang of the burning fire and it seems to Harry that his nose has become more sensitive as his vision decreases. Some mornings when he steps onto the deck, he sees through the feel of the freshness of the air, the splashing of squabbling ducks, the warmth of the sun's first rays, the arguments of wheeling crows. 'Compensation,' he tells himself, 'for what I'm losing.'

He wonders what Karen and Brodie are talking about and it seems he's always wondering something. He knows it gets on Karen's nerves having to repeat every word of every conversation she has.

'For God's sake Harry, do you want me to record it all for you?' she says, impatience edging in. But he doesn't want that, what he wants is to be a part of life like he was before. He wants to be involved. And she knows that and she'll apologise and he'll say she should have a medal for what she puts up with. Sometimes he's so angry with himself for the existence he's created, for getting blown up, for his increasing dependence. For his surviving. He knows that the future is winding down, shutting down.

'What I can tell you, Mr Jones, is that your condition will never improve. It will worsen with time and you should prepare yourself. Make things easier for you both. Perhaps change your lifestyle?'

He thinks that while Karen is out he'll take a walk as far as the jetty, feel the timber planks beneath his feet. Know that the water is below him.

On his shuffling, careful journey he scuffs a stone – it nearly trips him – and then slowly, painfully, lowers himself to pick it up. He holds it close to his failing vision. Squints. It's a rough two-inch square and heavy for its size. 'Ironstone,' he thinks. He hefts it, considers it. 'You'll do,' he says in the passing of his selection. Now it'll settle in the plastic box in the junk cupboard, added to twenty-eight pounds of odds and sods that might come in useful one day. In fact, this might be the one that signifies the completion of the collection. It might be enough.

Back on the Bombardier Harry fills the kettle, checks the level with his finger, sets it on the stove, and waits for Karen to return.

Broome County Hospital.
Three miles from Vixens Mere.
Maternity wing. Ultrasound room.
Anna, Jed and Nurse Richards.
Anna's had her belly greased up – that's what Jed calls it. Nurse Richards calls it an ultrasound gelling – and the probe slides smoothly over her 'lump'. 'Her expanding stomach,' the nurse corrects him again.

Jed and Anna study the picture formed on the screen, slightly bewildered that the twelve-week vision of alien life on the monitor is down to them. They've talked about what's going to happen now; all drugs and selling are being kicked into the dustbin, Jed's been to see if Big Ed can offer him enough work till he finds something permanent, and got an aye as an answer. 'Not another lame dog, Ed,' protests Milly. 'We've taken in more animals than Battersea Dogs' Home.' In the euphoria of good intentions Jed and Anna have decided that they're going to become proper people. But it's not going to be easy. This is the real world where a ticket to fulfilling a habit is only a thirty quid wrap away. When that temptation leaves a film of sweat over her body Anna puts her palm onto her stomach, imagines what's growing there. And Jed's made all this possible; he took her in, offered her a life. She thinks that sometimes her beating heart might burst with love and gratitude for him.

Nurse Richards is saying, 'We can't tell the sex just yet, not until you're back for the twenty-week scan.'

'It's a boy,' says Anna, thinking of Milly and the gentle swaying of her crystal pendulum. Right to left. Or was it left to right? Milly had said, 'Male. Best choice of two. Better behaved. Easier to bring up.' She laughs 'And he can't get pregnant.'

There's a knowing smile from Nurse Richards, 'All our mothers think they know, so be prepared to be surprised, Anna.'

But Anna's also sure because all of her dreams are coming true. Things that she never imagined having are ticking themselves off one by one: somewhere to live, someone who loves her, kicking the coke. A still-can't-believe-it baby. And that piece of shit, Carl Thomson, has disappeared. There's been no sign of him; his face hasn't shown on the streets for – Anna thinks – weeks and weeks. The Word is he's crossed the wrong person and paid the ultimate price. 'Just let it be true. I hope he's rotting in the ground somewhere.' But the thought of Carl Thomson, even just the thinking of his name, shivers her spine.

CHAPTER TEN

Westcliff House in the country town of Endhurst.
One hundred and fifty miles from Vixens Mere.
Purpose built flats for disabled people who can almost manage independent living.
One flat, two storeys up, is being used for a County Lines project.
Mike Douglas is the legal occupier; he's a forty-year-old male who lost a good portion of his reasoning, and several of his physical faculties, in a motorbike accident twelve years ago.
Carl Thomson and Mike Douglas.

Carl Thomson is here for a two-month stint on a job that he couldn't turn down if he wanted to keep his legs intact. Like virtually everyone in his game, and being in the lower echelons of the food chain, he has had to repay a favour and obey a request. A request that's not a request. It's good pay but shit conditions and it's not a pleasant break for Carl Thomson. 'Playing fucking cuckoo in a stinking flat with some half-wit,' is how he describes it on a phone call to one of his Broome mates. The stench of stale piss is soaked into the furnishing, stained into the carpet. The bathroom is in an even worse mess and Carl Thomson has never seen a toilet bowl in this state and he's seen some. Mike Douglas, the tenant of this DHSS flat, is middle-aged and muddle-minded. So Carl Thomson's first task, before the merchandise for his real job arrives, is to grit his teeth, peg his nose, and give the place a thorough clean through. Later, Mike's social worker, on her monthly visit and totally unaware of his illegal lodger, comments on the cleanliness of the flat. She writes in her report that it seems Mike's turned a corner.

'He's tidied up the flat and himself too. He's using the washing machine at long last and he's even made a friend. Although he didn't seem to want to say much about him, but I'm sure I'll find out more on my next visit.'

The nest is made comfortable, the deliveries begin, and Carl Thomson's job starts proper. He's here to watch over the stocks, to protect, and to prepare for distribution. He cuts and rolls and packages on Mike's kitchen table and worktops. Stuff comes up the stairs and stuff goes down the stairs to youngsters of school age, to the hoodies on wheels. Business is brisk, good, spread all over town and beyond to the villages and hamlets in the area. Mike Douglas's spare room holds a strongbox that's crammed with a fortnight's pick-up revenue. There's a lock on the door to keep Mike out but it's not a problem because he's perfectly content to stay in his comfy chair watching television. Very occasionally he'll see something on the flickering screen that activates a glimpse of memory and, for a fleeting ungraspable moment, there's the glitter of headlights on a shining wet road and he's the man he was before his head smacked on to the kerbstones. In the mirror he might stare at the strangeness of his reflection, stroke the furrow that cleaves from his crown to his eye socket, wonder why he's hunched to one side. Sometimes, head in his hands, he'll sob away to himself and although he knows there's a reason, he can't think what it is.

But Mike likes having someone else for company. He likes it that Carl's here, that the young lads knock on the door, burst in with a 'Wotcha, Mike,' and ripple raw energy through the flat. He likes the takeaways that his friend Carl orders in.

He likes Carl pouring him a lager, lighting him a cigarette, telling him to, 'Shut the fuck up, you're doing my head in.' He doesn't know how long Carl's been here because time is confusing. And who was staying before Carl? Was it Dave, or was it Andy the black guy?

Anyway today Carl tells him that he's off, he has to pack his bags and go home, that his holiday's over, although not to worry because someone else is coming to keep him company.

'A young lady,' Carl Thomson says, 'but it's no good thinking that you're going to get your leg over; she's more man than me.'

That's his last words on changeover day as he heads out of the door with his hold-all over his shoulder.

Carl Thomson sits in the window seat of his train carriage and watches the distance wind down on his return journey to Broome. He stares out of the window but doesn't really see the passing countryside, only vaguely hears the murmur of conversation from the other passengers. In the forefront of his mind is the unfinished business, interrupted by the call of the cuckoo, and in his heart is the unbridled desire for a black revenge. It's now within reach, getting closer with each passing mile.

'Make a fool of me, would they? Laugh at me, that tart and her pimp. Well, I'll show them. I'll fucking show them. Fucking show them. Fucking show them.'

It's a moment or two before he realises that he's thumping the train's window in rhythm to his words, and that the rest of the carriage is silently watching him. Most people would have been embarrassed by this loss of control but not Carl Thomson. He sweeps his eyes over the shock of his fellow travellers and nobody will hold his gaze. Now he doesn't give a fuck about any of them but, all the same, he straightens his head out and refrains from drawing any more attention to himself. He can't afford a tug, not with what he's carrying inside his shirt. He checks the time on his mobile. Two o'clock. Another half an hour and then he'll be back in Broome and onto the revenge trail. Carl Thomson settles back into his seat, closes his eyes, and savours the taste of expectation.

Broome Academy.
3.00 p.m.
Sunshine streaming through the windows of Ms Edwards's year nine class.
Moses and Ms Edwards.

Ms Edwards is setting some homework for family history. Tracing your roots, she calls it and it's been her pet subject ever since she joined Ancestors R Us. Handouts have been issued.

Ms Edwards is a slender forty-nine-year-old spinster of Broome parish. She explains the handout. It's a simple family tree chart going back four generations and 'If you can add occupations it'll make a clearer picture of what life was like in times gone by.' She scans the class as she's talking and the subject seems to have raised most students' interest. Suzy Carter is already bent over her desk. As usual.

'Talk to your parents, your grandparents, and write a short piece about how different their lives were when they were your age. And old photos, bring in any old photos.'

Ms Edwards's scanning stops at Moses sitting at the back of the room. She thinks that if anyone can convey disinterest, it's him. Unless it's music. He's lounged back in his seat, looking out of the window, and she wonders if he's heard a word that she's said. Ms Edwards, if she had to describe Moses would say, a little flowery perhaps because she has designs of being a writer, that he sits there with the careless abandon of the unconventional. His hair is long, curly, dirty blonde. He's not wearing a stitch of school uniform as usual, his shirt is a middle blue, his trousers are a baggy black, and his jacket is a summer fawn. All this sits atop of a pair of scuffed trainers. Ms Edwards is quite pleased with her mental description of him and she'll scribe it into her Author's notebook when she gets home.

The bell goes for the end of lessons, for the scraping of chairs, and the ignored appeal of, 'Quietly, please.' The teaching day's over and thirty fourteen-year-olds will be heading home to question their parents about their parentage. And that will include Moses.

Crystal Lady.

Tea time. Cabbage leaves and potato peelings on the draining board. Plates on the table. Milly's checking the cottage pie in the oven. Big Ed's laying back in his comfy chair untabbing a can of cider. Moses is at the table studying the handout from school.

Big Ed says, 'What's that then, Moses?'

'Homework, Dad.'

Milly echoes, 'Homework?' She laughs, 'That'll be a first for you, Moses.'

Big Ed asks for a showing and Moses passes over his assignment and Milly, poking her nose in, says, 'If it's maths, you better let me have a look, Ed.'

Ed says, 'It's not maths, it's …' He stops and Milly, waiting for rest of the sentence, instead gets the handout passed to her. Then Milly, smile freezing on her face, thrusts a handful of cabbage leaves at Moses.

'Take these down to the Billy the Kid please, Moses.'

Billy the Kid is a young goat that Milly's taken on to replace Billy-goat Gruff who just last month succumbed to his advanced years and keeled over on the dung heap.

Moses says he will for a Bounty bar and he's given it from the sweet drawer without the usual lecture of it being too close to tea-time and that he'll ruin his appetite. He tears out of the kitchen and leaps from the barge.

Ed grunts, 'You spoil that boy, Milly.'

Milly says sharply, 'It's not *that* boy, Ed, it's our boy.'

Ed briefly stalls his speech until he infers, 'He'll have to know one day, Milly.'

'It's too soon,' Milly says. 'It's still too soon, Ed. The time's not right.'

Big Ed wonders if there'll ever be a right time and Milly knows that when the story's properly told Moses won't belong to just them anymore. But Big Ed and Milly have never made it a secret to Moses that they took him in when he was, as Milly says, 'Given to us at seven days old and mewing like a cat.'

Big Ed says, 'And his nappy stinking like a polecat,' which Milly doesn't think is a very nice thing to say about her boy. Ed says, adding a little poetic licence, that it's apt that Moses is called Moses because he came in a basket.

'It was a carry-cot, Ed. A carry-cot.'

'Same difference,' sniffs Ed.

So Moses, although he is becoming more curious, has never asked too many questions. Ed and Milly – Mum and Dad – have made him their own.

Moses, five minutes of Billy feeding over, leaps across the gangplank of Crystal Lady, bursts into the kitchen, seats himself at the table, picks up his Biro, flattens his worksheet, and in capital letters, writes Edward in the Father compartment and Milly in the Mother's.

Milly's name belongs there because she's the one who changed Moses, 'those polecat nappies,' fed him from the first day of possession, watched him crawl, walk, start school, ride his bike. Everything that a mother would do.

Later, when Moses is bunked up, Milly and Ed talk about that time, retrace the events of over fifteen years ago, the fortune that brought Moses to them. The day when Karen Jones was losing her mind.

'*What am I going to do, Milly? It'll kill Harry if he knows.*'

The despair of a decision is rearing its head and Milly's quiet for a moment, thinking, and then she simply says, 'I'll take the child, Karen. We'll look after him. But he's no name, what'll we call him?'

Now Karen had thought that one day she would be holding a baby Harry, Harry's baby, but that was in the briefness of a normal life. So she's held off in the naming of her baby out loud, although she's whispered to the sleeping child, 'I know what I'll call you,' because in her mind is her heritage; her parents' house, the gallery wall of her predecessors; an old black and white framed photograph of two of her ancient relatives, Moses and Edwina Needham sitting at the stern of a smoke-belching barge, their unsure gaze caught by the camera.

'Moses,' she says to Milly and Moses he becomes.

Every year from this time Bombardier makes a pilgrimage to Vixens Mere for a stay throughout the cold weather. And Karen is a mother of distance and Brodie is an unknowing father. And Moses will know it all one day.

CHAPTER ELEVEN

Broome.
The Glow Worm.
Saturday night.
Langley Ladies' Rugby Team, positional numbers on their tops.
Reserves, coaches and supporter, have been celebrating a loss to Broome Ladies in the County Cup.
Lorrie, Tony, and Marvel.
Tony says, 'Soon be time to get them out and then the fun'll start.'

Marvel says, 'Nothing but trouble. I fucking hate pissed-up women,' and Lorrie thinks that it's not just women Marvel hates, it's everyone, and pissed-up isn't a requisite for his feelings. But it's probably women more because he can't whack them like he does the guys.

Langley Ladies' RFC have virtually taken over the Glow Worm and there's been high spirits all night; drinking competitions, singing loud enough to drown the music, a conga around the club, an impromptu striptease in front of the DJ – who's now only supplying a minimum of drum and bass to the ambience – whistles and catcalls every time Tony and Lorrie do the rounds. Several of the Langley pack – numbers 1, 2, 4, 6, and 8 – lift up their tops in unison with a 'Cop a look at these, Handsome,' directed at Tony. It's not a pretty sight; multi-coloured bras and a massive amount of spare flesh on display. More wobble than ripple, Lorrie thinks. Tony, cupping his hand to Lorrie's ear, says, 'That's not doing anything for me.'

Lorrie says, 'Me neither,' and he laughs.

Someone else who's here tonight, with a couple of her friends and having an unquiet drink, is Dinah. Lorrie's has a snatch of conversation with her and Dinah says how good Lorrie's looking, how toned up she is. This gives Lorrie a warmer glow than perhaps it should. She says that next time Dinah's at the marina to call aboard the Morning Star for a cup of tea and a ciggy. Dinah promises. Then she throws herself into the frenzy of fun on the dance floor. Watching her for a minute, Lorrie thinks, 'Putting herself out there again. That's what I should be doing.'

But she hasn't the stomach for it just yet. The bruises are still healing.

Half an hour before the Glow Worm's official closing time the coach driver for the Langley Ladies and entourage parks the bus outside the club. He comes in for a chat with Lorrie and Marvel – Tony is doing the rounds, gracing his fan club with another guest appearance – and a hope that the boarding won't be an all-night business.

'Like herding cats, getting this lot onto the bus,' he says and he's not far wrong. The shutters come down on the bar, the DJ gives up the ghost, the lights go on and Langley Ladies very slowly, in fits and false starts, congregate around the exit. They're full of good spirits, laughing and joking, trying to get a snog off Tony. Even Lorrie gets an offer.

'She's just your type, Avril,' someone calls out.

Avril shouts back that Lorrie could soap her back in the shower anytime she wants. Even Marvel gets an invitation to a ride home with the ladies and he smiles for the first time this evening. So it's all good-natured, well nearly, and that's a nearly because Langley Ladies' tighthead prop – number 3 on her shirt – has spent the whole evening drinking herself into the nasty side of inebriation. She's looking for a blow-up to salvage her dented reputation as a brutally hard daughter of a bitch.

This 3, Ellie Davis, had been given a torrid time at the scrums all of the afternoon's game by her opposite number, Broome Ladies' Abby Hill. Now Ellie Davis is a perfect prop shape, short, stocky, possessed of enormous upper body strength but Abby Hill, taller and lighter framed, had twisted and turned and forced Ellie down from the first scrum. No matter what Ellie Davis tried Abby Hill had the answer to it, though the Langley Lady still played the rest of her game of niggle, sly digs, and thunderous charges into the opposition. And so to the last scrum of the game with Langley's put-in, ten meters out from Broome's try line and with a minute left on the clock. Langley are also two points behind so they desperately need to hang onto possession and come away with a score. The second row behind Ellie kneels into position, her shoulder drives hard into Ellie's ample posterior on the 'set' and she just has a couple of seconds to mutter, 'Give it all you've got, Ellie,' and Ellie does and she holds her side of the front row. It seems that it might just be enough to do the job but then Abby Hill, with a mighty shove up her more shapely bottom from the Broome second row, picks up where she left off and Ellie's on the retreat again. The ball's stolen, comes back on the Broome side and the scrum breaks up with a few tussles going on. One of them is Ellie swinging a mighty haymaker at Abby Hill but what Ellie doesn't know is that Abby is a keen and classy amateur boxer – sometimes she trains alongside Lorrie – and the punch skids across the top of Abby's ducking head. What comes back in a reflex action is a cracking right hander that sits Ellie on that ample posterior. All of this is missed by the referee because he's following the ball along the three quarters until it reaches the trusty boot of Broome's outside centre. Then it's a massive kick up-field and a bounce into touch to virtually end the game.

This is why Ellie Davis sits and drinks, and broods in the corner of the Glow Worm while the rest of her team, having left the game and their differences on the field, have a night's fun. Ellie Davis is looking to do something, something brutal, to restore her reputation as the baddest girl in her team, and to restore her faith in herself. Her chance comes at last when in the leaving of the Glow Worm there's a spell of high jinx in the foyer of the club. A bit of harmless shoving and pushing.

Marvel grunts, 'Sort it, Lorrie. Get 'em fucking out of here.'

Lorrie ushers, with a few pleases and a few gentle propulsions, and herds – like cats – the half a dozen remnants of Langley Ladies' Rugby Club towards the exit. There's no real opposition to Lorrie's gentle approach until she puts a guiding hand on the broad shoulder of Ellie Davis. This number 3, whom no one would want to meet in a dark alley, seizes her distorted chance of redemption, whirls around and grunts loudly, 'Take your hands off me, you fucking dyke,' as she aims her second right-handed haymaker of the day at the wrong person.

This shot is only slightly more successful than the afternoon's previous one because, unexpected as it was, Lorrie picks it out in mid delivery. She has a millisecond in which to ride back with the blow, and so its power is nullified somewhat as it glances off the brow of her left eye. Ellie Davis, untrained fighter that she is, continues her bodily momentum, following through on her wild swing. Lorrie, trained fighter that she is – like her stablemate Abby Hill – strikes her own counter right into the exposed face of Ellie Davis. It's solid and extremely fast and the self-proclaimed baddie is sat on her arse for the second time this day. Then she's helped to her feet by a couple of her teammates – one who is also a 'fucking dyke' – and deposited heavily onto the coach where the driver, seeing two runnels of claret pouring from Ellie Davis's mashed nose, asks her 'not to bleed on the fucking upholstery 'cos he's got a trip to Ironbridge in the morning and he don't want blood and snot all over the place.' He also won't be wanting the aisle awash with puke but by the amount of cider, beer, and lager his passengers have consumed that's already a given.

Lorrie's excursion into the violent side of her Doorman's job has left her with an upcoming black eye and gash above her socket that's forming a tricklet of blood. Lorrie takes herself into the cloakroom and wets a tissue, dabs at her eye in the mirror. Tony comes in, catches her attention in the reflection.

'You OK, Lorrie?' He pauses to add, 'Better check the CCTV. Make sure we're in the clear. You sure you're OK?'

Lorrie nods. She's more than OK, she's cool, she's calm. Not a tremble to her fingers. She doesn't know what it is but what happened in the foyer feels like a victory, like an achievement. And then she realises she hasn't felt like this since she won the club championship. Not since before Petra.

'I could do this for real. I could get a licence again.' In her mind the 'I could' becomes an 'I will' and she relishes the moment of sheer autonomy, of being her own mistress of choices.

Tony, back in the picture, says that the CCTV didn't show anything incriminating. 'Too much of a melee. Bit unsighted thank fuck. Don't want any comebacks, do we?'

Marvel says that Tony's been checking that he wasn't captured out the back with that pretty little scrum half who has the number 9 on her back. Tony says it was only a fag and a chat and Marvel says that Tony's flies are still undone and Tony has to check and Marvel's normal scowl transforms into a broad smile, warms up his face.

'Got you there,' he almost laughs. There's a slight tremor to his massive shoulders. Then to Lorrie he says, 'You get yourself home. We'll close up. And Lorrie …'

'Yes.'

'You did well tonight, Lorrie. You did well.'

Lorrie glows a little again tonight. A compliment off Marvel isn't given out in a box of cornflakes. Tony agrees with Marvel and gives her a quick goodnight hug and Lorrie, up close to him, sniffs loudly. 'You smell nice, Tony.'

'You like it, Lorrie?' He's pleased. 'It's my new aftershave.'

Lorrie says, 'It smells like Chanel ...' she sniffs loudly again, 'number 9, Tony.'

Marvel's grin turns into a chuckle and Tony says, 'Fuck off, Lorrie. And to think I was going to set you up with my sister.'

Then it really is goodbyes all around and Lorrie steps out into the empty street. But it's not quite empty because there's a couple of benches down the road from the Glow Worm where the late-night taxis pick up. On one, huddled up against the cold of this earliest hour, are Dinah and her companions, Amy and Mandy, from the club. They've been waiting for half an hour and as Amy, decidedly the worse for drink, succinctly puts it, 'I'm freezing my tits off.'

Lorrie says, 'I'll give you a lift, if you want?'

Lorrie doesn't have to offer twice and the trio are soon in the car asking for the heater on full blast. Dinah's mates – Lorrie's dropping them on the other side of Broome – have settled themselves in the back seat and are having a non-stop discussion on frostbite.

'Apparently your fingers go black then they have to cut them off,' says Mandy.

'Really?' says Amy.

'And your toes.'

'What else?'

'Anything that goes black.'

'Christ, what about my nipples?' This from Amy who's now worried about really having her tits frozen off. 'I'm going to have to have a look.'

There's a few moments of giggling and fumbling and then the flash of a mobile's torch.

'What do you reckon?' she asks Mandy.

'They look all right to me.'

'You sure?'

'Yeah.'

'What do you think, Dinah?'

There's a leaning over the top of the front seat and lit up by the torch, and completely obliterating Lorrie's rear view mirror, are a pair of firm, pink-nippled young breasts.

Dinah, laughing, says, 'I think you should put them away.'

Then the girl asks Lorrie, 'What do you think?' and Lorrie risks a sidelong glance and says that they're a very nice pair but she really needs to concentrate on the road. Then there's a noisy unloading on a housing estate where the goodbyes and shushes are enough to set a few dogs barking and for a few lights to flick on.

So Dinah's mates are dropped off and ten minutes later Lorrie pulls up outside Foxes Farmhouse.

'Quick coffee?' Lorrie hesitates and Dinah adds, 'Reward for the lift home, Lorrie.'

They go into the warmth of the Aga heated kitchen and the twin collies, deep in slumber in front of the stove, don't even stir.

'Good watchdogs,' says Lorrie and Dinah says that they don't bark at friends, 'and … you're bleeding, Lorrie.' Dinah's peering at Lorrie's face where the swinging cut from Ellie Davis has opened up. Lorrie touches her face, inspects the blood on her fingers.

'It's all right, Dinah. I'll sort it out when I get home.'

'No, no. I'll clean it up for you. Put a dressing on.'

Lorrie's, 'It really isn't …' is wasted; Dinah's already into the cupboard above the sink for a rummage around, prising the lid off the first aid box.

* * *

At two o'clock in the morning Lorrie sits in front of the Aga, her damaged eye swelling and bruising. (The discomfort is nearly worth it for the ministrations of this pretty young woman.)

Dinah giggles. She's still more than tipsy, 'I should have my nurse's uniform on.'

Lorrie thinks, *'Oh yes please, Dinah. Yes please.'*

There's a cool touch to her skin, a closeness of warmth leaning into her, a fan of breath on her face. It's not exactly fragrant, because of the taint of alcohol, but it's sweetly bearable. It would be so tempting to slip an arm around that slim waist and pull Dinah close. So tempting but so not the right thing to do. Definitely not.

Lorrie gets patched up; a square of antiseptic gauze taped over her eyebrow.

'You look like a pirate, Lorrie.' Dinah's still giggly but she's also yawning now, and it's very late and the coffee seems to have been forgotten.

Lorrie says, 'I must get going,' and there's a quick thank you hug – a two-way gratitude for a lift home and the medical attention – and then Lorrie takes the farm track down to Vixens.

She keeps glancing in the rear mirror – even though there can't possibly be anything behind her – and reimagines those two delectable breasts filling the view.

'Christ,' she shakes her head, mutters to herself, 'I'm really going to have to get laid.'

Foxes Farmhouse.
3 o'clock.
Dinah.

It's not been the easiest of evenings for Dinah even though she's had a laugh, and too much to drink, at the Glow Worm.

She'd naively thought that Barry's betrayal would wipe out his existence in her heart, but when she thought she caught a glimpse of him – it wasn't – tonight her heart leapt. She's lying in bed now and the moon's beaming down onto a lawn that's twinkling with frost. It's shining into her room for one, across the double bed for one, where the loving used to be shared. Dinah's in that place of being not awake and not asleep and that loving is in her mind, in her body. She's thinking of how Barry would sometimes call her when he was on the way home.

'I'm seeing you in stockings,' he says, 'with that sexy underwear I bought for your birthday.' The desire's in his voice, in his anticipation of her body. And Dinah loves it, loves being wanted so badly by someone she adores.

Now these thoughts are in her mind, in her flesh. It's like when she had the needing for midweek relief and Friday, and Barry, were too far away. She imagines that these hands, these fingers tonight, are Barry's. She dreams of his mouth, his tongue, and then she's almost there. Just one more wave, one more shudder and ... and then it's not Barry's face she sees at this moment, it's Lorrie's. And it's too late to stop, she's passed the point of no return.

Dinah sits up in bed. She's bemused and she hugs the covers around herself. 'Christ. Where the fuck did that come from?'

CHAPTER TWELVE

Crystal Lady.
Late afternoon. Tea time.
Big Ed and Milly.
Milly's taking a tray out of the oven. She says, 'Something special for you tonight, Lover Boy.'

Big Ed, without taking his eyes off the television, says hopefully, 'Hash cakes?'

'Sausages, Ed. Sausages. It's only Wednesday night.'

In a random change of subject and still without taking his eyes off the television, Ed says that Brodie has given him the keys to Summer Walker and left with a backpack and his dog.

'Where's he gone?'

'Dunno. Said he'd be a few days. Get us a lager out the fridge.'

Milly, her curiosity piqued say, 'He must have said something?'

'I'll probably remember a bit more with a Stella in my hand.'

Milly says that if he wants to play that game he'll remember a damn sight quicker with a hot sausage up his jacksie.

Big Ed sighs, says that some relative in the Highlands has snuffed it and Brodie's catching the train up there. Funeral and things.

'He has taken the dog?' Milly has visions of yet another lame dog – but this time a real canine – residing in their shed for the forseeable.

'Course. You know Mick's always with him. Never leaves his side.' Ed chuckles, 'Bit like me and you, eh Milly. Can't bear to be apart.'

Milly supposes it's a good comparison, because she's tied to a smelly old dog that she's never going to get rid of. Big Ed says he prefers to think of himself as a thoroughbred, a well-proportioned pedigree. Milly reckons that well-proportioned doesn't mean fat as a pig. Ed says that he's fifteen stone of dynamite and she says he might well be but he's only got a two inch fuse. Ed says that if she's finished burning the dinner, he'll give Moses a shout to come and eat. Doesn't see why he should be the only one to suffer.

The Bombardier.
Sunday.
One o'clock in the morning.
Vixens Mere dark and silent.
Harry Jones.

This waiting, the preparing of himself reminds Harry of the eternity of watching the clock and sharing cigarettes until the order came to embark into their armoured vehicle. He remembers the scorching sun, the raising of dust, sharp and bitter in his throat, then the growl of the engines as they took line formation for the patrol into hostile territory. This day they're fourth, last in that line. The most vulnerable.

'Back fucking marker again,' moans Hoppy and Geordie snaps that it's bad enough without Hoppy stating the fucking obvious.

Harry thinks that it's always like this on set-off; always edgy, snappy. But, after a few bumping, grinding miles together, they'll have slipped into the contradictory zone of high alert and flippant asides. Jason has a tale to tell of the extraordinary size of a brothel girl in Kabul. He hands his rifle to Tallyman, stands up in the swaying vehicle, holds his arms out wide, mimes the occasion with rabbit thrusts of his hips, says, 'Acres of wobbly flesh, lads. Acres. Lost meself there. Never knew if I even got it in the right wrinkle.'

Harry, on this still dark night, relives these moments on the last day of his *real* life – when he was whole in mind and body – to this last actual day of his half life.

It's time now; time to drain his can of strong lager, flick his cigarette stub into the waters of Vixens Mere, stand as upright as he can muster, and salute the world. It's his time to take a slow walk towards a noble deed, a dual release.

This is it: affairs are in order, goodbyes have been written and Harry Jones – ex-soldier in his betrayed body and mind – takes his first dragging steps on his journey towards oblivion.

Crystal Lady.
Early morning.
It's close to waking up time but Milly's rooted inside a last-minute dream. She's watching a man walking into the black waters of Vixens Mere. He's draped in a heavy overcoat and he's moving slowly forwards, slowly deeper, and a shaft of moonbeam is putting him in the spotlight. Milly wants to call out but there's no sound to her voice, no movement to her limbs. So she's waiting for this dream to end in a swallowing of the man, until there's a glimpse of just an arm, a fist, raised above the water. That's how it ended before. But it doesn't this time because this man pauses, chest deep in the mere, and turns to Milly. He seems aware that she's there. Like he wants to be seen. And from Milly there's an instant recognition of a man illuminated in the moonlight. A gaunt man. A thin featured man. A damaged man.

'Harry Jones. It's Harry Jones.'

Milly's voice is loud enough to wake her, and she's in the warm cabin, the double bed, of Crystal Lady. Big Ed, jolted out of deep slumber, has exploded into a 'What the fuck, Milly? Shouting like that.'

Milly sits up, says quietly, 'I had a dream. It was so real. So real,' and Ed, seeing that Milly's really shaken says that he'll put the kettle on and, when he's recovered from his heart attack, he'll make the tea and she can tell him all about it.

But as Big Ed's in the kitchen rattling the cups there's such a frenzied knocking on the door it raises his heart rate dangerously high for the second time this morning.

Bombardier.
A little earlier in the day. Pre-dawn.
Hedge-sparrows, feathers puffed up for warmth, are contributing to a half-hearted chorus to greet the advancing day. Fine snow has fallen during the night and the residents' barges are dusted with icing sugar.
Karen.

It's still dark when she wakes and listens and then, intent on letting Harry sleep a little longer, she slips out of her bed. Soft footed, like a cat, she pads to the kitchen, quietly lifts the kettle onto the gas. Then it's an ear to Harry's bedroom door for the sound of a cough, a heavy breath, but it's as silent as the grave. Good. She should be able to make breakfast: pot of tea, toast, butter, marmalade. Karen wants to set it out in an act of caring; just lately she may have been sharper to him than intended but it's sometimes, even now, difficult to judge Harry, not to make allowances for his restrictions. Lately Karen's becoming more worried about him, about his failing eyesight, more weight dropping from his skinny frame, his sitting on the front deck well into the dark night. Sometimes he tells her what's in his head, his memories. 'But,' he says, 'it's like I'm remembering for someone else. Like they don't really belong to me anymore.' Karen will hold him and say that she'll look after their memories, keep them safe, 'So that we'll always have them, Harry. Always.' She holds him like a mother holds a child.

Karen's set the table, poured Harry a mug of tea, and now she knocks on Harry's bedroom door. 'Harry. Breakfast.' There's no acknowledgment and Karen knocks again. Louder.

'C'mon, Harry. Rise and shine.' Still nothing, so she opens the door as she's still talking, 'Right. I'm coming in, Harr ...' She doesn't complete the rest of his name because she's walked into a room that carries no human warmth or heartbeat. It's silent and cold and the pillow on the bed carries an envelope with her name on it and love and sorrow tucked inside.

'Forgive me, Karen.'

'Oh God. Oh no, Harry. No. Not this. Please not this.' Her voice is fractured and her words are already mortally wounded. Then it's like she's outside of herself, watching her fingers stabbing at her phone, hearing her voice, like a recording, asking for police, for an ambulance. And then, slipper-footed, a coat draped around her shoulders, she runs to the Crystal Lady to frantically bang on the door loud enough to wake the dead.

Crystal Lady.
Milly, rudely awakened, takes her half-dressed self out of the bedroom and into the kitchen to catch a white-faced Karen telling Ed, 'He's gone. Harry's gone. I went to wake him and he wasn't there. He's gone, Ed.'

Milly sits Karen down, pours her a mug of sweet tea, gives her a cigarette. She asks no questions; she waits until the words start to tremble from Karen's mouth.

'I thought he was in bed, Milly, but he was gone. He left a note, Milly. He left a note. I've got to look for him. Just in case he's ...'

Just in case he's what? Alive? Wandered into the woods. Gone walkabout down the lanes? Sitting under a tree somewhere? But Karen knows, she read the finality in his written words, that Harry is never going to set foot on Bombardier again. But she'll look for him, join in the search, feel the onset of reality gradually usurp her impossible hopes.

Big Ed's pulled Moses out of his slumber, says they'll search through the top-end of Hunters Woods. In Ed's mind is a long ago search for Paranoid Paul, who should have really been in a mental institution, not living in a camp of vans and buses outside of Glastonbury. It hadn't ended well, that one. In fact it ended with a rope and a hanging body on a hillside with a corpse in a copse. Ed still shudders when he remembers the blackened face and rolled eyes of poor Paul. So Ed's going to keep Moses close; he doesn't want him finding anything like that on his own.

Now there's banging on the barges' roofs and an early morning awakening for Jed – What the fuck's going on? – and Anna, and for Lorrie, for a sparse search party of half a dozen souls.

Milly says, 'You should stay here, Karen. For when the police come.' But Karen can't sit still and she can't stand still and the only thing she can be sure of is that Harry's wasted body couldn't have carried him very far.

'I've got to look. I've got to find him,' and it's Milly who's going to stand on guard while Harry's name echoes all around Vixens Mere and beyond. So Milly, keeping a weather eye open for the law, climbs a little way into the woods. She stops, fishes out half a cigarette from her pocket, strikes up her lighter and takes a long calming drag. From this vantage point she can see the marina, the barges, and where there'll soon be the men in uniform and the flashing of blue lights.

* * *

Milly looks across to the water, and fits together a dream and a reality in the vision of Harry Jones turning to her in the saying of his goodbye to the world. Milly's knuckles go to her mouth. He's in there, Harry's in there. He's under the water, weed in his hair, lifeless, sightless, soulless. Milly knows he's in there but she hopes he's not.

Then the blue lights are here and it's time for the professionals to take over.

Vixens Mere.
Towards the end of the afternoon.
Temperature on the way down. Orange inflatable on the water.
Two policemen prodding and probing with poles. A black-suited diver peering over the side of the boat. Barge dwellers watching from craft and path.
Karen and the police.

It's cold and Karen's standing on the jetty watching the bright orange boat on the darkening water. Her feet are numb but not as numb as her heart. There's a WPC keeping Karen company, who puts an arm around her and says, 'You don't have to be here, Karen. Let's go and get you a hot cuppa.' But there's another reason for the WPC's offer and that's because the poling, the probing, of the water has stopped a dozen meters out from where they stand. But Karen's also noticed the slowing down of activity, the much gentler thrust of the pole in its blind search.

She says to the WPC, 'They've found something, haven't they?'

'I'm afraid it looks like it,' and then compassionately, 'You don't need to see this, Karen.'

But Karen's going to watch for as long as she dares and what she sees is the black-suited diver slip over the side of the boat, disappear for barely a minute, resurface, give the thumbs up. She sees the sling lines go in and the two-man crew hauling away like fishermen pulling in their nets. But this catch is an invalid soldier, a man whose pockets are spilling out nuts, bolts, washers, and pieces of iron, and who won't be a burden to anyone ever again. All the years of caring and loving are being salvaged into an indignity, into an orange inflatable boat. Then it's enough for Karen; she can't watch for another moment and she walks away, seeks the shelter of the Crystal Lady where she shivers in the warmth of the stove and the company of Milly.

In the confines of the Crystal Lady, Karen Jones won't see Harry strapped to a stretcher, brought ashore, loaded into an ambulance, taken to the morgue. She won't see him cut open, his blood tested for drugs, his lungs squeezed for the verdict of drowning. Suicide by drowning. She won't see his pockets emptied of the shrapnel that tethered him to the silt of Vixens marina. But she will see his face just the once more, kiss his cold cheek, tell him that she loves him, and wish him the peace that deserted him for all these long years.

RIP Harry Jones, a casualty of war. He was a long time dying.

CHAPTER THIRTEEN

Crystal Lady.
Evening.
Milly and Karen.

Karen's sat by the stove with a blanket wrapped around her. She's a glass in one hand and a cigarette in the other. Milly's frying up chips for Ed and Moses who are finishing up the outside chores.

Milly offers, 'You really should try and eat something, Karen. There's plenty here.' And there's going to be plenty more because the deep-fat fryer that Milly's using is the one Ed rescued from a takeaway he was helping to renovate. 'Shame to dump it. You can get a bucket of chips in there.' Karen says thanks, but that she really can't face food.

'Another drink?'

Karen's, 'Why not?' is a bleak answer filled with, 'What does it matter now?'

Milly, who has her own glass on the worktop, deals out two generous slugs of brandy and lights herself a roll-up.

'I'll give the boys a shout for their tea in a minute,' and Karen says that she'll finish her drink and leave them to it, she'll go home. But Milly says Karen shouldn't go back there tonight, not on her own.

'Leave it till the morning. I'll come with you.'

'But …'

'No buts. You can have Moses's bed tonight. He can doss down on the sofa.'

That's how it is for Karen, this first night of widowhood, and for the first time in over fourteen years she sleeps in the same bed as her son. Her head might feel a little on the light side – courtesy of Courvousier brandy – but Moses is here. She can smell him on the sheets, on the pillow, and she falls asleep with the scent of her son wrapped around her. But the last words in her mouth are, 'I'm sorry, Harry. I'm sorry,' and they'll be the first words on her lips in the morning.

Crystal Lady.
Same night.
Big Ed and Milly's bedroom.
Ed whispers, 'What a day, Milly. What a day,' and Milly says that they'll help poor Karen as much as they can. 'We can take her into town, help her sort stuff out.' They lie in the dark for a while carrying on their whispered conversation and then Milly says, 'You know what this means, Ed.'

'Know what what means?'

Milly takes a deep breath and it's a sad voice she uses. 'Moses, Ed. With Harry gone there's nothing to hide anymore.'

Ed's silent, thinking for a while, and then he says, 'Well, except for Brodie, I suppose.'

He gets up to pull the curtains across because the police lights on Vixens Mere are playing into their bedroom window. Then he pauses, squints at the scene through the glass.

'Thought they'd be finished now they've got poor Harry out.' Then in an unspoken realisation that had been gradually worming its way into both of their minds, 'Christ, Milly you don't think …?'

But Milly does think that they won't be finished until the earthly – and very saturated – remains of Sandra Day are carefully removed from her fifteen years of slumber, unwrapped from her tarpaulin shroud, laid out on the slab, and the dent in her skull established as the probable cause of her demise.

And then there'll be plenty more questions to ask, in fact a different set for each corpse. It might be an additional headache for the local constabulary but it can't be as deadly as Sandra Day's headache was.

Milly says, 'Fucking Harry Jones if he hadn't …' as though all of this is his fault.

Moses.
Stretched out on the sofa Moses is in the oddest of dreams. In this dreaming he's walking in warm sunshine down a stony track with an old lady who firmly, almost painfully grips his arm, stops him in his stride, looks into his face. And he looks into hers; familiar but ancient, leathery and weather-beaten. Except for the startling blue of her eyes. Then she speaks to him and although Moses doesn't recognise a word, he understands exactly what she's saying. She's pointing at a figure, a woman, climbing up the hill towards them. This woman gets closer, becomes clearer. Becomes touchable. Becomes Karen Jones.

'Hello, Moses,' she says. 'I've waited a long time to be able to do this,' and Karen Jones wraps her arms around him, squeezes him so tightly that she suffocates his movements. And that's what he's doing as he wakes in the pitch black of this night, struggling against suffocation because his quilt is as restricting as a straitjacket around him.

On his awakening, and unlike most of his dreams, this one stays fresh in his mind; it's taken a lodging in his head. When there's a moment for them, he thinks he'll tell Milly. See what she makes of it. She's the expert on dreams. He stretches to pull his socks on and there's a tingle in his arm like the residue of an electric shock. He examines that arm – the one the old lady clutched – and there's a tenderness in the markings of a pale blue thumb and fingers bruising to his flesh.

* * *

Home Sweet Home.
Anna.

Usual morning sickness for Anna, the mother-to-be, and still a sense of unreality for Jed, the father-to-be. Jed's gone off to work with Big Ed to supplement their Family Credit Benefits. Anna's lying in bed and feeling rather bilious and sorry for herself.

Now that she's well on the way to becoming a mother Anna's thinking of her own mother. She's no idea who her father was and her mother hadn't either. From what Anna knows her mother was a lost soul who spent her money, and her love, on as much drink and drugs and men that her body could handle. But as it turns out couldn't handle, because in the awfulness of cliché, she choked on her own vomit after a deadly combination of two of her vices. So poor little Anna, still a toddler, is shared between Children's home and Foster home. She does the rounds because she's an awkward child, silent and withdrawn, and as she grows into her teens, she does the first of many runaways. It's like she's searching for something, but she doesn't know what because she's never tasted it. When she's fifteen she runs away and no-one bothers to fetch her back anymore. No one's concerned about her because she has, in a crudity of past expression, shit her nest; she's left to her own devices to follow in her mother's ghostly footsteps. So the path Anna was walking was only going one way – bad choices, bad men – until, on a cold wet night in Broome, she met her saviour,

Jed, and now she's into a fairy-tale ending, or very close to it, because no one's ever loved this waif of a girl before. Oh, they've been attracted by her pretty face, wanted her for her pliability, her sexual availability.

This is what she's thinking as she lays abed a while longer, that and the promise she makes that her child is never going to endure a life like she did. But of course these thoughts are interspersed with the awfulness of what's happened with Harry Jones. Anna can't help shivering when she looks across the water, imagines what was under that water, but she still looks because it draws her eyes, makes her clutch Jed more closely at night.

'If anything was to happen to you ...'

'It won't, Anna. Don't worry. What could possibly happen to me?'

But she does worry because she thinks that no one's really loved her before, treated her like Jed has, and now with the baby and everything it just seems too good to be true.

At the beginning of this too-good-to-be-true period, just after the pregnancy verdict, Jed went into town, sold his stock of enhancers, and then came back and gave his own dope and tobacco to a surprised, but grateful Milly who uttered an unlikely 'I'll keep some back for you, Jed.'

But there was no need. Jed and Anna swore they were done. They shut the door of their boat for the best part of a week, kept away from the world, lived on coffee and cereal, and then paler but considerably healthier, emerged blinking into the light on a Sunday lunchtime. But keeping a promise like this is not the easiest thing to do.

Still Home Sweet Home.
Afternoon.
About five o'clock.
Jed and Anna.
Anna, feeling much better than this morning, has sausages – courtesy of Pigman Pete – frying on one ring of the cooker and a pot of potatoes ready for the mashing on the other. There's a basin of baked beans in the microwave all ready for the ping. She takes the weight off her feet for a moment, gives

her swelling belly a quick hug, raises herself on thickening ankles, and starts to set the table. Then she thinks of poor Karen Jones who'll be laying a table for one from now on.

Jed's on the quiet side this tea-time. In fact he hardly says a word, just sits down at the table and starts on his food. Jed's one of those whose face is always a giveaway to his emotions and this face is a worried one. Anna waits, watching him, waiting for it to come out.

Jed stops eating, puts down his fork. Looks over to her. 'Anna?' he says. She gives him the 'Yes,' and then she gets the 'Anna' again only this time Jed adds, 'He's back.'

She answers, 'Who's back?' when she knows very well that it can only mean one person.

'Someone saw him, Anna.'

And Anna's satisfaction with her lot instantly evaporates with just those few words.

'What are we going to do, Jed? We haven't any money or ...'

Jed says that perhaps he can make an offer to Carl Thomson? If he can work with Ed in the day, go back to selling at night, and ... and Anna's crying and saying that it's all her fault. She's ruined it and then Jed's arms are around her and now the dinner's fucked up as well. It's like there's another person in this room with them and the trouble with this person is that it's not just about the money. It never is with someone like Carl Thomson.

Jed says, 'We'll keep out of the way. I'll try and sort it, Anna.' But they both know that if the debt was repaid today there would still be retribution tomorrow. He wishes his father were still here. Calm, collected Mark Rawlins – who Milly said was a cuddly bear of a man; a perfect cliché of a gentle giant. A man who always sorted out Jed's problems with cash and a quiet word. A lone parent who'd dedicated his life to the son he loved above everything. Loved enough to kill for.

* * *

Broome Police Station.
Superintendent Jane Kirby and team.
A morning meeting after post-mortem results and prelimi-
nary investigation on the two bodies/remains removed from
Vixens Mere. Investigations are running concurrently as there
may – although very unlikely – be a link between the recent
and the historical deaths.

Investigating officer Superintendent Jane Kirby addressing her
team has had several long days and short nights to contend
with and it shows on her face, the throbbing in her head, her
suppressed yawn. She's thinking, with more than a touch of
resentment this morning, 'For fuck's sake, it's not as though
we don't have enough on our plates? A simple suicide we
can easily handle, but a suicide and a murder a few feet from
each other?' There's another 'For fuck's sake,' directed to the
Gods who have ordained this log jam. But Jane Kirby is a
professional and that mindset kicks in with a positive, 'Right
team. Let's pool our updates.'

There's no need for updates on Harry Jones, he's a straight-
forward suicide. All the attention is on the suspected victim
of murder.

'Post mortem confirms a young woman. Mother. Twenty
to twenty-five, Super.'

'Any identification yet?'

'Awaiting DNA results, Super.'

'Missing persons?'

'One which might suit, Super.'

From Missing Persons list of Possible People Sandra Day's
name has reared up.

Reported missing by her partner. Twenty-one years old.
Mother to a young child. Had form for disappearing. Fondness
for drink and drugs. And men. Lived in a barge on the marina
fifty yards from where her body was recovered.

'When did she go missing?'

'Fifteen years ago, Super.'

Superintendent Jane Kirby's mood suddenly lifts; her head clears. Something is going right here, you just know it is. This Sandra Day fits the bill to a T.

Now very soon there's going to be a knock on the door of Home Sweet Home and some important questions will be put to Jed Rawlins: 'I know it's a long time ago but can you remember anything about your mother? Anything you saw or heard? Anything at all?' To which the answer has to be a 'No'. And then another question of 'Do you mind giving us a DNA sample?' to which the answer has to be another no.

And then living and dead DNA will match, expose a secret that has lain for so many years in the murky waters of Vixens Mere. It will be identified, dragged into the light. A part of it anyway, because suspect number one is no longer on God's earth to provide any details of Sandra Day's last moments. But it may seem that poor Jed Rawlins will have some consolation, or at the least a reason, as to why his mother didn't actually desert him, couldn't come back to him. That's what everyone will think but not necessarily Jed Rawlins because he knows the truth. Well, some of it.

Home Sweet Home.

Fifteen years ago.

Early hours of the morning after Christmas party.

Jed Rawlins.

After an extremely late night for a four-year-old, Jed is in an exhausted sleep that a parent's usual argument might not normally intrude into. But it's not only the sound that filters into Jed's bedroom this night; the atmosphere, charged with expectancy, seeps under the door, settles on his pillow, tugs at his ears, causes him to sit up, listen, slide out of bed, open the door just enough to see his parents hissing hate at each other.

That's until the violence of words grow to become irresistibly loud, irresistibly contagious. Until his mother's head slams against the door-lining. Jed's bladder activates and a trickle of warm urine drips to the floor, pools around his bare feet. He watches for bare seconds – but for long enough – and then he takes himself back to his bed, squeezes his eyes shut, covers his ears. Silently cries himself to sleep. Begins to stow a memory that'll flicker to the surface in unguarded moments.

Mark Rawlins and Sandra Day.
Mark Rawlins is tired, exhausted. His mind is blurred and he's still half-pissed. He wonders just how much longer Sandra can keep up this relentless tirade at him. She's not tired, still well-pissed, and has enough speed lurking in her system to add to the count. Sandra won't let go of the bone until she's gnawed it to pieces. Had her full say. Which will be never.

The crux of it all is that she wants, really wants, Jed this time. 'No fucking about.' Needs Jed because 'then the council would give me a proper home, not a floating shithole like this fucking boat in this poxy marina. And I'll get Jed. I'll go to a solicitor, go to court and … fuck you, Mark. That's what I'm going to do. First thing in the morning, I'll take him and there's sod all you can do about it. In fact, I'm going to pack my things now and it's no good you grabbing my arm. You're not going to stop me.'

Perhaps he wouldn't have stopped her, perhaps gentle giant Mark would have let her walk away holding the hand of his boy, his only constant in this storm of a relationship. So if he hadn't grabbed her arm, lit the touch-paper, she wouldn't have scratched at his eyes, raked his face like a she-cat, drawn blood and pain. And Mark Rawlins, judgement impeded by days of alcohol, carrying the frustrations of the years, the thought of losing his boy, unleashed the tremendous latent strength of himself from dormancy. So his hands wouldn't have pinioned her shoulders, lifted her to tiptoe, shook her like a rag doll, thudding her pretty head several times onto the sharp-edged door-lining, causing her 'You fucking bastard' to be loud enough to penetrate his temporary insanity.

He lets her go, takes a step back, can't quite believe what he's done. Looks at his hands like they don't belong to him. She's a little groggy on her feet and her hand is to the side of her head. Mark Rawlins is back to his normal apologetic self with an aghast, 'I didn't mean to, Sandra. I didn't mean to.' A sob of emotion is colouring his words. Contrition is stooping this bear of a man who's hardly raised a fist in anger in all of his life. His problem now is that he's given her a reason to add something else to her morning plans. And that's the Bizzies.

'You'll pay for this.' She touches her head again, looks at her fingers expecting a flush of blood, looks disappointed that there's none. She tells him, 'I'm going to the police. You'll be fucking locked up for this, you bastard.'

Sandra Day has the beginning of a headache and she's suddenly so tired that all she wants is sleep. She slams the door on him, doesn't bother to undress, settles herself between the covers of her bed and, still cursing him, she falls into a deep, deep sleep. And she never wakes from that sleep because the edge of that door-frame was sharp enough to crease her skull, push a bone ridge into her brain, cause a cerebral haemorrhage. Her slumber becomes a coma of no return.

Broome Police Headquarters.
Interview Room Number Two.
Interview led by go-getting Sergeant Joyce Taylor and her sidekick – and admirer – DC April Showering.
Big Ed and Milly, looking like a couple of old hippies – which they are – have been invited in for an informal chat. 'Just to fill in a bit of background to Mark Rawlins and Sandra Day.' It's a solo interview for them both. Milly's first in.

Sergeant Joyce Taylor asks, 'So, Milly – don't mind me calling you Milly? – I know it's a long time ago but can you remember when you last actually saw Sandra Day?'

Milly screws up her face. 'Around Christmas time, I reckon. We had a party.'

'And how did she seem?'

'OK.'

'What's OK?'

'It was a party. We'd all had a few.'

'And she was with Mark Rawlins.'

'Yeah.'

'How did they seem? Like, together, I mean. Was there an atmosphere? Like they'd had a row?'

'They were always having a row. She'd only just come back. Again.'

'Where had she been?'

Milly shrugs. 'God knows. She was always on an away ticket.'

'And she left with Mark Rawlins?'

'Think so. Didn't see them go exactly.'

'And you're sure that's the last time you saw her.'

Milly makes a show of screwing up her face even more in pretence of the remembering. 'Yeah. I'm sure,' she says.

But this lie began its life on a cold morning in a bleak midwinter on Vixens Mere.

Crystal Lady.

Mark and Jed Rawlins, Big Ed and Milly.

Four-year-old Jed has been given some crayons and paper and shunted into a bedroom out of hearing distance.

Mark Rawlins, his outsize hand wrapped around a mug of tea laced with whisky – half and half – says, in barely above a whisper, 'I've done her, Milly. I didn't mean to, but I have.' Resignation and despair are bitterly coupled together on his drawn face.

155

Big Ed says, 'You sure she's …?'

Milly says, 'Me and Ed'll take a look. Just in case.'

But there's no 'just in case' to be had here, Mark Rawlins knows this; he's checked every hour since before dawn of this day. He's opened the door on a cold room and willed a miracle of Sandra sitting up and spilling hate onto him. He's hoped until he's given up hope.

Big Ed and Milly's lookabout shows them that aboard Home Sweet Home Sandra Day is laying in her bed, in her party clothes, pretty face grey under her masking of make-up. But this doesn't hide a bruise, the size of and colour of a plum, on her forehead. Milly touches Sandra Day's face, strokes her cheek, feels the warmth being sucked out of her fingers by the chilled flesh of the dead. There's absolutely no doubt that 'She's gone, Ed.' Hours gone.

Big Ed shakes his hairy head at Milly. 'Christ. What the fuck's going to happen now?'

They talk about what's going to happen as night deepens over Vixens Mere and young Jed falls asleep on Ed and Milly's bed. And long after Karen Jones has slipped into slumber on Summer Walker in the arms of her highland lover.

The upshot is that if the police (Sandra Day would use the Liverpudlian term 'Bizzies' if she could still speak) are notified, then gentle giant Mark Rawlins will be looking at a ten to fifteen stretch, Jed will become an orphan, an inmate of a children's home, as the social would never let a couple of old hippies bring up a child. All this suffering for a disclosure that won't help anyone with its telling. Milly counts up to the seventh magpie, purses her lips, says what's the worst that could happen now? On balance she reckons that the deceit plan is worth a punt.

'She's always coming and going. No-one'll miss her for months.'

Truth is no-one will really miss her at all. Mark Rawlins might for a while but that's coloured with a relief to the ending

*of drama, money-taking, mickey-taking, and downright nasti-
ness. Jed will have only tattered erratic memories that will
fade to vagueness. Mostly.*

'Yes, I'm sure,' Milly the Mystic says to Sergeant Joyce
Taylor and then she takes her leave.

Same interview room.
Same police officers.
Half an hour later.

Big Ed under the spotlight for a more intense questioning
than Milly received.

'You knew Mark Rawlins, Ed?'

'Yes.'

'Did you know him well?'

'Pretty well.'

'Do you think he was the sort of man who could have
killed Sandra Day?'

'No. No way.'

'Can you think of anyone who would have wished Sandra
Day dead?'

'No. Can't.'

Then a softly delivered, 'Did you kill Sandra Day, Ed?

'Christ. Me? No.'

'She was wrapped in tarpaulin. Like builders use. Weighted
down with concrete blocks. Like builders use. You're a
builder, Ed?'

'Was. Don't do much now.'

'Did you notice any of these – your – materials missing
around the time Sandra was last seen?

'Don't think so. Job to keep tabs on everything.'

'So they could have been yours? Someone could have
sneaked them away?'

'Suppose so.'

Sergeant Joyce's selection of conjecture is just about

exhausted and, as she gives DC April Showering the nod, she says, 'Ok, Ed. There's just another couple of questions then you'll be on your way. OK?

'OK.'

DC April Showering has been internally reciting her lines and she's straight onto Ed with, 'Don't you think it's strange Sandra Day wasn't reported missing earlier?'

'She was always coming and going. Used to disappear for weeks on end.'

'Other men? Drink? Drugs?'

'Maybe. Couldn't say. Not my business what people do.'

'And you say the last time you saw her was …' The DC makes a pretence of looking down at her notes, 'was when she was at the Christmas party.'

'Yeah.'

'Are you sure, Ed?' She frowns as she asks, like she knows something different but Ed says that he's sure and adds to Milly's lie by the not telling that…

Vixens Mere.

Sable breeze in the willows.

Water still and dark and expectant.

It's three am and as black as pitch and Sandra Day has been carried from her death bed and wrapped in her funeral shroud that two days ago was protecting a newly built brick pier from the elements of winter. She's quite easy to handle because she's not a big woman and she's stiffened – doesn't fold up like a deckchair – as, Big Ed at her head, Mark Rawlins at her feet, she's carefully stowed aboard a leaky rowing craft. Her final journey ends, weighted with concrete blocks, into a lowering beneath the freezing waters of Vixens Mere. The body of Sandra Day sinks from sight; a short life ended with no priest. No service. No hymns. There's a few tears and a series of 'I'm sorry' from half

the attendees. The other half just wants it over asap. He's
gasping for a fag.

And that's it, a consignment to the deep that's lain undis-
turbed all these years – and still would be – if Harry Jones
hadn't decided to take a night-time plunge.

DC April Showering looks to Sergeant Joyce Taylor, gets the
assent, stands up, gathers her papers, gives a thank you to
Big Ed. Lets him out of the Interview room. She says to her
superior, 'What do you think, Sarge?'

'Probably the boyfriend but we can't bring him in, can we?'

This is delivered with the slightest of chuckles and it's met
with, 'No, Sarge,' and an unsure smile that Joyce Taylor thinks
makes April look even more attractive than usual.

Outside the station Big Ed mutters to Milly that he didn't
realize that it was going to get so fucking crowded at the
bottom of Vixens Mere.

Milly passes him a fag, shushes him up.

CHAPTER FOURTEEN

St Michael's graveyard at Danelow.
Midday.
Bitterly cold. Not enough of a shy sun to lift the temperature by more than a degree.
Harry Jones's funeral.
Another interment – in the earth this time – separated by fifteen years of time and eighty miles – by canal passage – from Vixens Mere.
Three miles by road from Fred and Iris Needham's Lock Keeper's cottage.
Karen Jones.

It's a chill wet day, late in the morning, with an icy wind that could cut right through anyone. Harry Jones's coffin, draped with the union flag, has been carried out of St. Michael's Church by six bearers – courtesy of Danelow British Legion. These bearers are grizzled army veterans, cap and badge identifying regiment. 'Least we can do. He was one of our own.' It seems Harry Jones is back in the bosom of his family. Soldier to soldier. Warrior to warrior.

There's a brief ceremony at the graveside by a softly spoken priest whose words the cruel wind tries to snatch away. At 'ashes to ashes, dust to dust,' the veterans, three to each flank, raise a salute as the undertakers slowly lower Harry Jones to eternal rest. 'He would have appreciated this,' Karen thinks of the service, this ceremony. She tries not to imagine Harry, stiff and cold and all alone in the pitch blackness of his box, doesn't want him to hear the hollow scattering of earth onto his wooden roof.

It's a small gathering here; Karen's Dad and her Mum, with a wandering mind that's perplexed, trying to gather in the scene. Harry's Dad and stepmother were rarely visited by Mr and Mrs Jones because there was a truth in the prefix wicked. The stepmother was the main reason Harry joined up as a boy soldier. He'd gone from losing his real mother, whom he hardly knew, to one who didn't want to know him. Who was glad to see the back of him so her own brood could have rooms of their own. There's also half a dozen of Harry's old acquaintances, who've heard the word and turned up at the church, offered their condolences and stated their respect. Karen takes twenty years off their faces, takes the rain out of their hair, weight off their bodies, puts them into a wedding venue, colours it with a warm summer day, Harry looking so handsome in his army uniform.

But this is today and there's to be no congratulations. Instead it's a clasping of her hands, a 'I'm sorry for your loss, Karen,' and Karen's 'Thank you.' 'Thank you.' 'Thank you.' until it's time for her father to say, 'You better come on, girl. Get yerself into the warm.' Fred Needham's arm is around his daughter, and getting into the warm means tea, coffee, maybe a tot of whisky, a pint for some, a helping from a small buffet, in the backroom of the Drayman Arms. But Karen's not ready just yet.

'You go on, Dad. I'm going to stay a while.'

'You sure, Karen?'

'I'm sure, Dad.'

He hesitates in his leaving but Fred Needham is pushing eighty and the wet is soaking through his clothes and he says, 'I better get your Mum out of this, Karen.'

Iris Needham, rain dripping off her nose, is looking vacantly around, looses a wavery, 'Where are we, Fred? What's going on? I'm cold, Fred. I'm cold, Fred. I'm cold.'

Karen's cold as well, and wet, and now she's the last person left standing in this desolate churchyard. By the open grave Karen makes her confession, tells Harry all there is to tell. Wishes that her son could have been their son.

'I'm so sorry, Harry. So sorry.'

She wipes her handkerchief over her face, blows her nose, flicks the rain from her hair. The bedraggled, but still more than pretty – tragically pretty in fact – Karen Jones stands inside of this stormy day on soddened cemetery grass in damp shoes, damp coat. She says her goodbyes to Harry Jones.

She says goodbye to endless worrying, endless caring, to bad-tempered depression, to glimpses of the old Harry and incursions into hope and laughter. A goodbye to all she loves. She knows she could not have done more, but she knows she could have done less. Then she walks away.

In a year from now there will be a headstone to Harry Jones dating his time on earth. Harry Jones, soldier, hero, and warrior, who spent half of his life living and half of it dying.

Crystal Lady.
Sunday morning.
Two weeks after Harry Jones's suicide.
Big Ed and Milly – who's becoming increasingly concerned that she may be more of a mystic that she thought, what with the foreseeing of poor Harry Jones's curtailment and all.

Milly yawns, sits up in bed and draws back the curtain on the waterside window, takes a peek over the marina. There's still blue and white plastic tape along the jetty and to the water's edge, marking out a 'Do Not Cross' area. Ed had to tell Moses it meant no fishing there and Moses was a little miffed 'cos the best fish swam in that patch. But he's taken notice because Milly spots the boy casting out his line on the far side of the water. She thinks, 'Give him an hour and he'll be starving and shouting for his breakfast.'

But in the meantime, Big Ed throws the covers back, says he'll leave their warm bed and put the kettle on. Milly takes a good look at Ed, has a rush of love for this large amble of a man. His once golden hair now streaked with grey, and his age and waistline are very near to coinciding in numbers. Milly has a sudden yen for a bit of action to relieve the tensions of the past weeks, all the running back and forth for the newly widowed Karen Jones. The lies told on behalf of a dead man. She snuggles up to him and says there's no hurry and, 'It is Sunday morning, Ed.'

Big Ed acting dumb says, 'Sunday morning?'

Milly says coyly, 'You know. Sunday morning. What usually happens on Sunday morning?'

'Oh, me getting up to make the tea you mean?'

Milly says, 'Maybe getting up to something else, Ed.'

Big Ed, thinking that Milly's certainly changed her tune since his last attempt at conjugal rights, says in resignation, 'Well if I have to. I suppose we'd better get started.'

He wraps her in his big arms and she whispers in his ear that some dirty talk might spice things up so Ed says that the goat-shed's a mess and could do with a good clean out. Milly says he'll need a decent prong for that, not that rusty old tool that's seen much better days. Ed says she'll be surprised at how well it polishes up and then, running out of innuendos, they get down and dirty as quickly as their ageing bones will allow.

It's ten minutes after what Big Ed calls his vinegar stroke and they're sitting up in the bed sipping the promised tea. Milly has also promised a huge fry-up as soon as 'I've got my breath back, Ed.' Her breath recovery isn't helped by the lighting up of the first roll-up of the day. They've just settled into their luxurious lie-in of tea and tobacco when Ed's mobile loudly notifies him that he's a wanted man. He squints at the screen.

'Brodie,' he says and then it's some listening and nodding and a goodbye.

'Well?' asks Milly.

'He says he'll be back later today.'

It's the same day as Karen's due into Broome railway station and Milly's thinking that all of Moses's parents will be in touching distance of each other; the three that know and the one that doesn't. Yet. There's a minute or so while Ed and Milly think their thoughts. The same thoughts.

Milly says, 'This is going to be the time, Ed.' There's a trickle of a tear on her cheek for a day that she desperately never wanted to arrive.

'Moses will still be ours, Milly. It won't make a difference.'

But they both know that things will never quite be the same again.

'He was mine, Ed. For all of these years he was all mine. I don't want to share him now.'

Then Ed holds Milly tightly to him as she sobs her heart out. She's still crying as there's a clump of boots and the unloading of fishing gear onto the kitchen floor and a voice shouting through the bedroom door, 'What's for breakfast Mum? I'm starving.' Without waiting for an answer, he tags on, 'And the police are at Jed's again.'

Big Ed hopes the police will give Crystal Lady a miss this time. Christ, he can barely remember last week, let alone all those years ago.

Home Sweet Home.
Police visiting.
Jed knows that the young and earnest WPC Angela Woods, Family Liaison Officer, is only – though very caringly – doing her job. But to Jed it seems like she's pushing for a bonus,

picking up points on the offers of provision. She pesters, like she wants to be saleswoman of the month.

Have you thought about bereavement counselling, Jed?

Have the undertakers given you a cremation date?

He almost expects her to whip out a selection of urns for Sandra Day's ashes. 'Top of the range this one, Jed. Just look at the detail. Be perfect on the mantelpiece.'

Jed wearily nods acceptance to every suggestion. He needs it to be over with and he doesn't want the subtle questioning occasionally dropped into the conversation. 'Anything come back to you, Jed?' 'Do you remember her in that photo?' A pointing to a picture from his father's drawer that Jed's propped up on the shelf. It's of Jed's family of three, taken against the backdrop of Vixens Mere. Jed's flanked by his mother and father and it might look like he's keeping them together. Or keeping them apart.

So Jed gives a no to every line of enquiry, lets it hit the buffers, but if he concentrates his mind, peers into the fog of the past, he can remember pressing his hands over his ears, peeping through the gap of his bedroom door. He can remember the last time he saw his father and mother together. Violently together. Now that the can's been opened and the worms are crawling out, there's only the one person he can possibly tell. Jed needs to share; it's too heavy to hold in just his hands.

'I know what happened, Anna. That last time I saw her.' *Shook like a terrier shakes a rat. Puddle of piss between his feet. Seeing something that can never be unseen.*

Anna takes Jed's secret, buries it with her own secrets, cradles Jed's head in her lap, against their child listening in her belly, adds to a bonding that should never be broken or betrayed. But for Anna there's a bitter fleeting thought of 'at least you knew your Mum and Dad, Jed' that is instantly swallowed by the fierce promise that her child, their child, will have a life that she or Jed have never known. With both of his parents.

Foxes Farmhouse.
The weekend. Should be a time of relaxation.
Dinah and Lorrie.

In the freshness of this Sunday morning the sun's flickering through the trees and Dinah's rising to the trot on Hunter. She gives a little laugh to herself; she thinks that it's been a while since she's been in a regular rhythm like this with another living being. With anyone in fact. With anyone like Barry. And that's a name that's barely mentioned at Foxes Farmhouse now. Ethan has gone past the ranting stage of, 'Never liked him anyway,' and 'He's probably plugging into someone else's socket by now,' which is probably true but Dinah doesn't want that picture in her head. She concentrates on her riding, a regular circuit of four miles using Ethan's fields and the quiet run of bordering lanes. She's building up to a fast canter, Hunter's long legs eating up the furlongs. Then, because she's still on grass, she gives Hunter a hard slap on his flank. 'Let's go, boy,' and Hunter, hardly in need of encouragement goes through the gears to an exhilarating gallop. Dinah's flying and the hedges and trees are flashing by and ahead of her is a dropped fence into Foxes lowest field. They soar over and, although Dinah wants this ride to last forever, she pulls Hunter down into a more sedate walk. They're only a cockstride away from Vixens Mere and she thinks she'll go on a passing visit.

She stops outside of Crystal Lady where Big Ed is cleaning out Billy the Kid's stable. The goat wanders over to Dinah, has a good sniff around a nonchalant Hunter, even takes a nibble on his tail. Dinah calls down from her high horse, 'You're busy, Ed.'

Ed pauses in his labours, stabs his prong into the bed of manure. He looks glad of a break.

'Thought I'd better catch up, Dinah. Bit to do next week.'

'You haven't forgotten you're repairing our wall?'

'Next on my list, Dinah. Next on my list. Me and Moses'll be on it soon as.'

Dinah thinks, 'Soon as what?' but leaves it unsaid.

Dinah's next stop, a couple of moorings along, is a chat to the tenant of Morning Star, who's rubbing her eyes and covering a yawn with her hands.

'Late night, Lorrie?'

'No one wanted to go home; they'd dance all night if they could. Didn't see you about, Dinah?'

Didn't see you about, Dinah. Even though I kept looking out for you.

'There was a twenty-first on at the town hall, Lorrie.' She adds with a touch of ruefulness, 'Seems everyone brought a partner except me. Felt like a gooseberry.'

'Nothing floating then, Dinah?'

'Nothing. Wouldn't have bothered anyway. Men are nothing but trouble.'

Lorrie's starts to say, 'I wouldn't kno ...' when she's interrupted by a long rumble of stomach wind from Hunter's rear end. There's a look, a giggle, between Dinah and Lorrie and then Dinah says, dead pan, 'I hope you didn't think that was me?'

Lorrie lets go a laugh, thinks how down to earth this farmer's daughter is, then Dinah says, 'If you're doing nothing tonight, pop up for a drink,' and Lorrie says. 'Not if you're going to do that again, Dinah,' and Dinah, having her own laugh now and urging Hunter on calls over her shoulder, 'about seven if you like.'

Oh I do like. I do like.

Foxes Farm stables.
Later that morning.
Dinah's unsaddled Hunter, tethered him with his halter, and

given him a good brush down. He's munching away on a bowl of horse nuts and Dinah's still exhilarated by her cross-country ride. But that's only until a familiar white van pulls into the yard. Stops. Stops her heart. Barry's van. Barry the ex-boyfriend who'd taken her money, given her an unwanted present. Lots of them, in fact. Humiliated her. But he's standing here as bold as brass on this beautiful Sunday morning and he's saying, 'Can we talk, Dinah?' and her mouth, not under her control, answers a 'Yes' for her.

It's the same old Barry, soft voice, charming smile. Muscular arms. Muscular body under his shirt.

'Talk while I work, Barry. But I don't know what you can say.'

So she works, scatters bedding inside the stable, dips a bucket of water for Hunter's trough, listens over her shoulder. But she's so aware of his closeness that she's trembling.

'I'm sorry for what I did, Dinah. Give me a chance to prove it. Let me …'

'Let you what, Barry?'

'Make amends. We can start again.'

'I don't want to,' is accompanied by a vigorous shake of Dinah's head.

'I'll get another job close to home.'

'I don't want to, Barry.'

'Look if it's about the money, I'm getting it together.'

Dinah starts to tell him that although the money does matter there's no buying back into her life. As he's been talking, Barry's been edging closer to her; she's aware of him behind her, aware of his arms drawing her around to face him, his hands cupping her face, and then his way of kissing her; softly and gently, melting her. Dinah almost gives way.

There's the hardness of his body against her, the tempting of unfettered loving. There's straw bales for a bed, the sweetness of hay in the air, the gloom of the stable, his finger's unbuttoning her shirt, sliding under her bra. It's like she's watching a film of herself being seduced and any second now it'll be too late for a no. But then the ticking of alarm explodes and she's remembering the betrayal that can never be washed away; the hurt, the nights of crying in her pillow, the spotting on her underwear, the thought of another girl's body twisting beneath him, twining with him. Another girl's body sharing his lies. All of this can't count for nothing and it's, 'Fuck off Barry. Just fuck off,' and Dinah's wrenched herself violently away from him. She's on the verge of hysteria, screaming into his face like a wild animal, 'Fuck off, Barry. Fuck off. Fuck off. Fuck off.'

He lets go of her, steps back in shock at the vehemence of her delivery, the prize being snatched away from him.

'Dinah, I ...'

'No Barry. Never again. Never.'

There's a resolve in her that doesn't crumble until his van has wheel-spun its exit out of the yard and out of her life. Dinah needs a sit down on a straw bale, a tugging out of her cigarettes, her lighter, and a deep pull of nicotine to calm her racing heart.

'Christ, Hunter,' she says and the horse pricks up his ears at the mention of his name linked to blasphemy, halts the nonchalant munching of his feed to turn a quizzical look to Dinah's, 'Whatever's happening to me?'

If a horse could shrug at human behaviour Hunter would do just that before turning his attention back to what's important, namely his meal. Dinah sits and smokes and waits for the desire in her flesh to cool down as she finishes her cigarette, douses it in the water bucket, thinks that accidently setting the stables on fire would just about cap her day off. But there's also the relief that things hadn't gone Barry's way, he hadn't got his foot in the door again. Dinah allows herself the luxury of a chuckle, 'Well, not exactly foot and not exactly door but the meaning's the same.' She sits a little longer and wishes she had someone to share the joke with. She laughs so hard that there're tears running down her face. And then the laugh stops but the tears don't.

CHAPTER FIFTEEN

Vixens Marina.
Sunday lunchtime.
Brodie and Mick.

You're back here again and you're thinner, lightened by the pilgrimage of walking the highland lanes and tracks, of sleeping in rough shelters; you and the dog. You've nestled on bitter hillsides, shared the sleeping bag with your best friend, lit a fire in the mouth of an ancient cave and portioned out toasted bread and a can of sardines. You've covered the old paths in homage to your seanmhair, and to a way of life that's a step nearer to the death. One dark night you watched the northern lights dancing in the sky and her breath was on your face, and her whisper was in your ear. She was never far away in these remote places and you promise to return, to walk these lonely paths. To visit again.

First stop is Big Ed's to pick up the key to Summer Walker. Milly insists on making you a cup of tea, giving the dog a biscuit, 'And a sandwich, if you want?' but you don't want; your appetite has shrunk with your belly. You can't help noticing that Milly and Ed are not their usual selves, their words are the usual ones but they're subdued, like they've had some bad news. And then they tell you about Harry.

'Didn't see it coming,' says Ed.

Milly says, 'Imagine that, Brodie. Imagine wading out there with all that weight in your pockets in the middle of the night.' Her tone adds a description to her words as though she's seeing it as she speaks.

You ask, 'And how's Karen?' and Ed shrugs and says that she's back now. Harry's funeral is over and done with. Ed says. 'No fuss. Small and private was what she wanted. Only right considering what happened, I suppose.'

You say that you'd better go, light the stove, get Summer Walker warmed up a bit. Milly reckons that they'll have an hour or two in the Shed later and, 'if you want to bring a couple a cans?' They'll try and get Karen over, need to cheer her up a bit. You half promise that you'll be there and then you walk on towards your boat. You walk past Bombardier where all the curtains are drawn and there's smoke curling from its chimney. You slow, almost stop, can't help but notice there's a stillness to Bombardier, like it's in mourning.

You walk on.

Broome.
Late Sunday lunchtime.
The Packhorse Inn.
Last shift at the Carvery.
Pigman Pete and Marlene.

Pete, Marlene in tow and large plate in his hand, is leading the way along the counter of displayed dishes. It's a very warm chef carving meat, and dripping sweat, at the first port of call. This chef draws his sleeve across his brow and asks, 'Pork? Beef? Turkey?'

Pete gives a 'Yes, please,' to each question and then moves onto the trays of steaming vegetables where another flushily warmed person is waiting to dole out 'Roast potatoes? Cabbage? Carrots? Peas? Cauliflower cheese? Beans?'

'Yes, please.'

This continues down the line until Pete's plate is piled as high as structurally possible and washed with thick gravy.

Marlene, following on from Pete, says to the servers, 'Same as him, please.'

Then Pete and Marlene sit themselves down and quietly demolish their monster meals from the top down.

After twenty minutes of steady eating Pete leans back in his chair, smacks his lips together.

'Pint to wash it down?'

'Yes, dear.'

The 'dear' is a familiarity now because they've entered another month of a very satisfactory relationship. Marlene, large lady that she is, can match Pete pint for pint and, like today, meal for meal. The size of their takeaway fodder is legendary in the Chinese and Indian communities of Broome. They're happy these two, see each other most days, and Pete stays over in Marlene's little terraced house a couple of times a week.

When she's downed her glass of lager Marlene stretches her hand across the table, grasps Pete's fingers.

'Thanks for this, Pete.'

'It's nothing, Marlene,' but she says it means a lot because Pete's good to her and she's bitten into a few bad apples in her time.

Pete says, 'Shall we have one more?'

'Just the one, Pete, and then we'd best get back.' She leans forward, deliberately overspilling her very ample cleavage. She feigns a yawn, flutters her eyes at him. 'I got plans for you this afternoon.'

Pete, sizing up her prize assets, thinks for a moment and then says, 'Sod the drink, Marlene, let's go now.' He feels that he suddenly needs somewhere comfortable to rest his head.

Vixens Mere.
Afternoon.
Brodie Stewart and Moses.

Moses has taken himself to a few hours fishing before the day pulls in too much. Several small roach, live bait, are in his keep net awaiting their turn on a treble hook. Moses is sure that there's a good-sized pike lurking in the deeper water.

You wouldn't have thought that you'd need to stretch your legs today after all the miles put under your belt recently, but you do. You've sat for a while in Summer Walker and it seemed so restricting after all those days in the mountains, all the chilled salt-laden winds sweeping across deserted stony beaches. You call up Mick who drags his heels, looks back longingly at the stove. 'Just five minutes,' you lie to him and you take the path through Hunters Woods and out onto Ethan James's ground. The five minutes is half an hour and you cut back to the top end of Vixens and here Moses is sitting on an upturned bucket, holding his rod, eyes glued to the big yellow blob of his piking float.

You say, 'Good spot?'

Moses shrugs, laughs, 'I'll let you know.' There's a moment or two of silence and Moses adds, 'Usually fish off of there.' He motions to the jetty. 'But, you know …' His eyes haven't left the water.

You're looking to this boy as he's studying his float and you wonder about him, this fourteen-year-old whose voice is deepening to adult. You know Big Ed and Milly are at the wrong end of their sixties and you don't need fingers to count that they're too old to be his real parents. Well, Milly is. So what's the story attached to this boy? Where did he come from?

You give it a little thought but not too much because it's other people's business, not yours, and you've learnt over the years to be as unnoticed as possible.

But you can't help thinking of yourself as a boy, of the refresh of the highland river washing over you; the searching for clasped mussels, cold fingers fumbling in the depths of a chill torrent. You're good at locating the pearl-mothers,

*picking them out of the colonies anchored to the riverbed.
'You have the gift of finding,' says your seanmhair but you
don't really think like that. All you want to do is get in and
out as quickly as you can. So you pluck the rough, hand-sized
shells from their gravel mattress and tip them onto the bank.*

*Seanmhair's lit a stick fire and you warm your skinny frame
as you dress. Then you sit together, mug of black tea in your
grasp and a short broad bladed knife in hers. She prises open
each mussel, examines the inside flesh for the whiteness of a
pearl. This day is a good day and your seanmhair holds up the
largest of the gemstones between her thumb and forefinger,
shows you its beauty.*

*In the selling of the pearls, a month from now, it'll be held
up again and inspected by the dealer in Perth.*

*'Very nice, Mrs Stewart. Very nice,' and he'll want this
one, offer top money for it, but it's not for sale because this
is for you.*

'It's yours, Brodie. Look after it forever.'

*And that's what you do, and today that same pearl sits in a
drawer in Summer Walker with a handful of its compatriots.
Occasionally you'll take it out, polish the age on its surface.
Rub away the years. Think about the swirl of water over
your head.*

Just like Harry Jones.

Foxes Farm.
Early evening.
Dinah and Lorrie.

Ethan has gone for his Sunday night meet with his pals; a
game of euchre, some serious pints, and putting the world
to rights. He shouldn't be home till past midnight, and he'll
be full of cider and deluding himself that he has the voice of
Elvis Presley. He'll also be extremely delicate the next morning
and he'll sit with his head in his hands at the breakfast table

and swear that he'll never drink again, a promise that will last until the next time.

Dinah's opened a bottle of red wine for the breathing and, in case white is more to Lorrie's taste, there's a bottle of that cooling in the fridge. Lorrie, also unsure what Dinah drinks, turns up on the doorstep with a red and a white. That's just in case as well. She looks smart does Lorrie, trousers, blouse, jacket, brush of eyeshadow, pale pink lips. She's walked in on flat shoes – she doesn't want to tower over Dinah – and her hair is gelled to spiky. Lorrie is a handsome woman.

After the briefest of hugs, and a re-introduction to the collie twins, there's a decision on the red, glasses on the table, and Dinah offering, 'Shall I be mother?' and Lorrie, deadpan, saying 'You've more chance of that than me.' Dinah grins, 'You never know. That Tony's a bit of all right. He might turn you.'

Tony is a bit of all right, he's a friend, a trainer, a mentor to Lorrie. He wants her to take a medical, step into the ring again. Properly.

'Been a long time since I've done it for real. I'm not your Million Dollar Baby, Tony.'

'And I'm not Clint Eastwood. But you're good, Lorrie, and if you don't give it your best shot …?'

Lorrie thinks about this sometimes because she doesn't want to look back and regret wasted time.

Like the four wasted years with Petra; her best years drunk on love and lust with the erratic, erotic, and exotic Petra. But going nowhere. Going backwards. Slowly falling apart. Crumbling between her fingers. Her anger at a dear friend's warning, 'Get out, Lorrie. She's poison, that Petra.' She was right though because …

'Penny for them, Lorrie.'

Dinah's holding up her glass for a toast in the kitchen of

Foxes Farmhouse; Lorrie's past life on a smart estate fades from her thoughts.

'Sorry, Dinah. I ...'

'Didn't know I was such boring company, Lorrie,' Dinah's laughing, kidding her.

'Oh you're not, Dinah, you're not. It's just that I've got a few things going on.' Her protest sounds stronger that she intended and Lorrie thinks that she should explain her excuse. She tells Dinah that she's tidying up an ending and it's not been easy.

'Can't seem to get it out of my head,' she says.

'This'll help.' Dinah tops up their rather large glasses with two more tilts of wine. 'At least it helps me.' Then she takes a huge swallow, raises her glass in another toast and says, 'To partners. Who the fuck needs them?'

Lorrie, aware that the wine is flowing rather quickly but totally in agreement with Dinah's sentiment, says, 'Yeah. Who needs them?'

Dinah, in what is developing into a drinking game, lifts her glass to 'Barry the Knobhead.'

Lorrie echoes, 'Barry the Knobhead.'

There's two very quick deep slurps of red and Dinah's on with, 'And to? Who's your ex, Lorrie?'

'Petra.'

'Petra?' Dinah thinks for a moment and then it's, 'To Petra the Extra,' which she delivers with a snatch of contagious humour.

By nine o'clock there are two empties in the bin, an ongoing devouring of cheese and biscuits, and stubbed cigarettes in the ashtray. At the latest lighting-up Dinah asks, 'I thought you were in training, Lorrie?'

'Not tonight, Dinah. It's my day off.'

Lorrie says that she'll have to put herself though an additional session at the gym to atone for this decadent evening. 'Sweating away your sins, Tony calls it.'

Dinah says that she'll sweat her sins off with the early morning round of seeing to the animals, 'I'll be smelling of BO and cattle shit before breakfast, Lorrie.'

Lorrie can't help but laugh at this farmer's daughter as she's thinking, 'But you'd still look gorgeous, Dinah.'

Like she does now, this petite young woman in jeans and jumper, bare-footed and tousle-haired, and creeping onto the wrong side of tipsy.

So the night's pushing on and two wronged ladies are enjoying each other's company in light relief. They're now well into the third bottle – the bottle of disclosure. Lorrie, glass in hand, cigarette in the other, bum against the Rayburn sighs, 'I love these big old rambling places,' and Dinah says, 'Would you like a look around?'

So Lorrie's shown a house of sloping floors, tilting ceilings, creaking stairs, an abundance of fireplaces. The grand tour ends in Dinah's room. On her bed is a half-packed suitcase flanked by a robble of clothes.

'Going somewhere, Dinah?'

'What? Oh no, it's the last of Barry's stuff. I keep finding bits of him. Well, not him but you know.'

Dinah gathers up Barry's flotsam, rams it into the case, zips it shut, lifts it off the bed.

She says, 'Goodbye Barry Knobhead,' but her voice is tight, strangled, and she stands as still as a statue staring at the suitcase and Lorrie gently asks, 'You all right, Dinah?'

Dinah turns to her, says, 'No, I'm not, Lorrie. I don't want to feel like this. Not over him.' She takes a deep breath, sits herself onto the bed, touches Lorrie's hand.

'Look, I don't want to spoil tonight, Lorrie.'

'You won't. You can tell me if you want? Only if you want though, Dinah?'

Then Lorrie sits beside her, waiting to see if the words come. And they do, they tumble out as Dinah tells the story of the farmer's daughter and the electrician who fell in love when Ethan James needed his workshop rewired.

It's hot this afternoon when an eighteen-year-old Dinah, brief shorts, cutaway top, sandals, and a floppy hat on her head, drives the tractor into the yard for refuelling. She's been turning hay and the grass seeds have really been getting but everywhere; hair, in her bra, inside her shorts. Dinah's in a hurry. She wants to fill up with diesel, get back out to the field, and finish the job. She's had a long day already and it's only five o'clock and she wants to go out tonight. But why of all the space in the yard does someone have to park their van right in front of the fuel tank? Dinah leaps down from the tractor, storms into Ethan's workshop and, while her eyes are still adjusting to the gloom, kicks off with, 'For fuck's sake, I'm in a hurry and some prat's parked in ...' Her words run out then because this guy, this gorgeous guy with muscular arms, puts down his screwdriver, holds out his hand and says, 'Barry. I'm Barry. And you must be Dinah?' Dinah's suddenly conscious of her sweat-stained top – least she hopes it's just her top – her muddle of hair, her armpit smell. 'Yes. Dinah,' she mumbles in a brief confirmation. Then she says it's very hot and she lies that she was going into the house to get a cold coke and did he want one? And that's how it starts, and it continues for three happy years until a flock of hungry little bloodsuckers make a guest appearance in Dinah's underwear.

'He made me feel so dirty. So dirty, Lorrie. And to think I'd have trusted him with my life.' Then there's a dash of bitterness with, 'And with my money.' Dinah adds with a flash of anger at herself for what nearly happened half a day ago, 'But after all he'd done, I still wanted him. I almost let him have it, Lorrie.'

The anger has dried up Dinah's tears, resolved her it seems. She stands up abruptly and Lorrie's arm falls away from her.

'Sorry, Lorrie. Shouldn't have unloaded all that on you,' and Lorrie says that it's OK, she understands. And Lorrie does understand because she's stood at a similar door on a hundred different nights. But this is Dinah's time, not an outdoing of miseries over several large glasses of potent alcohol. All the same, for Lorrie there's a stab of Petra, a woman who could probably tempt the devil if she had the mind.

The social evening has come to a close. It's nearly midnight and there's been an inadvisable inroad into the fourth bottle. 'Last one and then I really must go, Dinah,' and Ethan'll soon be wandering home. So it's a tipsy goodbye in the open threshold where the kitchen light spills out into the night. There might be just a moment of awkwardness in an unsure move to an innocent embrace, a fleeting touch of soft lips on soft lips, and then a stepping back, and maybe a second of awareness before Lorrie says, 'You come to me next time, Dinah. I'll cook us a meal.'

Dinah says, 'I'll bring the wine, Lorrie. Plenty of it.' She's more like her old self now as though the telling of Barry has lifted some of the weight off her.

Lorrie's gone and Dinah leans against the door. She stays there for a minute because the kitchen's swaying a little and she needs to catch her balance, and gain command of her thoughts. And in this time she thinks of Lorrie. 'What is this?' It must be that she's lonely, wants company, that she's mixed up after Barry, and that she'll be all right when she gets herself another boyfriend. Then she gently strokes the softness of Lorrie from her lips.

* * *

Morning Star.
After midnight.
Lorrie.

There're ten wooden steps up to the roof of Morning Star and sometimes Lorrie sits up there when she has things on her mind. And she does tonight, a fathom above the water and drawing on the last cigarette of this day. She looks across the stillness, the dark woods, the sleeping barges and then she whispers into the night, tells her secret to the marina.

'I think I'm falling in love with you, Dinah James.'

Lorrie flicks away her cigarette butt, follows its arc, hears its hiss of extinction. Time for bed now. She's a full shift at the supermarket tomorrow. 'Today,' she corrects herself and counts the days until she can ask Dinah to a return visit without sounding too pushy. Or too keen.

CHAPTER SIXTEEN

Vixens Mere.
Bombardier.
Dawn breaking over the basin. Few moorhens in the reeds,
petting heavily and thinking about nest building. Nearly
everyone else is still in the land of Nod.
Karen Jones.

She knows she really should lay abed awhile and try to sleep
on because last night hadn't been a good one for Karen Jones.
She'd watched some telly, tried to read a magazine, but her
floating home, not *their* floating home now, has a hollow feel
to it. She throws back the bed covers and starts her morning
routine with going to the window to look at the day. But as
always, her eyes are drawn to the curve of the marina and the
old jetty. It's like she can't escape its fascination; she knows
its planks under her feet, its smooth handrails, its look of
the gallows raised over the water. She's stood on the timber
boards where Harry had taken his last breaths of God's air.
Karen had even sunk her hand into the water, sieved it with
her fingers, tried to net a memory of him.

'Oh Harry. Did it have to end like this?'

But she knows it had to. His sacrifice was for the both
of them. Harry had reached the end of his tether, he'd had
enough. His body was failing, his eyes were moving into
darkness and he was becoming more incomplete with each
passing day. It was Harry's chosen time while he could still

make his own decision, before he would have to ask for help. For her help. There was to be no gun-barrel in his mouth, no blast of shot and blood-spattered body to find; no handfuls of pills, no cold white corpse to haunt the Bombardier. Harry had removed himself, doing what had been on the cards from the moment the bomb had exploded under his armoured vehicle. He'd silenced the ticking clock and he'd spared her because Harry was a soldier making the ultimate sacrifice for her and his mates. Karen had stroked his ice-cold face in the morgue, smoothed his hair as he lay, a ramrod sentry in his box, whispered a bitter thank you for the return of her life.

But today, even though it's not been a good night, she watches the early sun sparkling on the water. This morning is still and bright and splashed with daffodils , the air is cool and sharp in her mouth. Karen Jones savours the beginning of the day with an easing of her conscience for being alive. She sits on her boat, pours herself a coffee, lights a cigarette, and catches a movement on the towpath. She shades her eyes, squints into the distance, 'Like Harry does,' she thinks. But then she recognises who that casual walk belongs to. Her heart takes a guilty jolt as she remembers what it was like to be held, to impatiently undress, be undressed, in a desperate passion that would not wait. Oh, why does it feel like she's being unfaithful? Again.

'Please, not now. Please not now.'

But the unbidden feelings of skin on skin, the touch of a man, of this man's touch, are on her body, inside her body. Desire flickers with the treacheries that memories bring.

'All this time,' she thinks, 'and it's never gone away.'

Summer Walker.
On the towpath in view of Bombardier.
Brodie Stewart.
You were going to give it another week or so here and then

head east in thoughts of the Broads and wide waters, but Art's been on and you need money and he needs some merchandise for his shop.

'Need to keep you in the spotlight. People are asking for you. Quite collectable you are.'

So you'll stay on a for a while because you have to be settled while you work on this piece. You want it to be special, this idea that trespassed from the long-ago into the present. It's to be a homage to Seanmhair and you see a shawl-wrapped, slightly-stooped old lady, hand on the shoulder of a growing boy, and a dog trailing behind them. It's going to be set on a downhill incline of a stony track. And the wood will be? You give that some thought, think that later you'll take yourself around to Ed's, there's always stacks of timber around his buildings.

In that later – a couple of hours on – Big Ed answers your enquiry with, 'There's an old walnut trunk, Brodie. Under the lean-to. Took it down …?' He thinks hard, scratches his beard. Remembers. 'Christ, was it that long ago? Should be well seasoned anyway.'

He says that you're welcome to a chunk of this valuable timber and fires up his chain saw, slices a two foot length off the thick trunk. He won't take a penny for it, 'but if you wouldn't mind carving a little something for Milly to put on her shelf? A bird or something?'

With the talking of Milly, she puts in an appearance, wants Ed to know that, 'What with all that fucking noise,' (she means Ed's extremely loud chain saw) 'the goat's shot off into the woods.'

You think that age might be lining Milly's face, slowing her down, but she still retains a mighty powerful voice. Ed says that he'll take a look after she's served up a brew and Milly asks, 'What about you, Brodie?'

'Please, Milly.'

So you sit and share a pot of tea and a plate of home-made biscuits with them and talk about the dumping of Sandra Day, and poor Jed, and that it must have been down to Mark Rawlins. Who else? 'But they're never going to find out anything, not after all that time in the water,' Milly says with a silent thanking to God added on. But she remembers an unknowing Pigman Pete reckoning on Sandra Day's disappearance. *'Oh, she'll be back. You know her. One day she'll show her face again.'*

And she has, in a way, although – Milly silently chides herself for the uncharitable – not the face she was expecting to show.

Keeping on the topic of doom and gloom, Big Ed says that Karen Jones seems to be bearing up. 'You know. Considering.' You say that it's a shame for her, and that you didn't really know Harry, only met him briefly, but he seemed a nice bloke. You wonder what she'll do now?

Milly shrugs, tells that Ethan said Karen can stay as long as she wants on Vixens Mere. Milly looks across the water and says, 'Though I wouldn't want to be here if my Ed had done something like Harry did.' Ed reckons that Milly'll drive him to it eventually, the way she keeps on. Milly scoffs that he'll never sink, what with all that blubber he's wearing around his waist. Ed clears the plate of biscuits and, while he's still munching, he asks if there's any more in the offin'?

'You'll have to get off your fat arse and get them yourself,' Milly says and adds, 'And you can bring me back a fag.'

Big Ed goes on his errand and you ask Milly about Moses, how he's doing at school, and what a polite lad he is. She doesn't answer for a minute, almost like she's not heard. Then it seems as though your polite questions have upset her, hurt her. It's a different Milly who suddenly stands up, snaps her own question at you, an accusation of, 'You don't know, do you Brodie? You just don't fucking know.'

You're ambushed by this sudden changing of attitude, perplexed by a delivery that doesn't fit the Milly you're used to.

185

'Know what, Milly?'

But she's walking away and her hand is across her mouth as though she doesn't want the words to escape but they burst from her.

'Ask her,' she says. 'Ask Karen. Ask the fucking widow woman.' But her fading voice belies the harshness of her words, subdues their bitterness.

Milly moves out of the picture, brushes past the incoming plate of biscuits, Big Ed, and a pair of favoured roll-ups.

'Milly?' He looks after her and then at you for an explanation. 'Brodie?'

You feel as puzzled as he looks, say, 'I just asked about Moses, Ed. That's all.'

Ed doesn't answer for a moment and then he says, 'There's stuff going on, Brodie.'

You tell him that you're sorry if you've upset Milly. You can't see how, but if there's anything you can do to make it right? Big Ed sighs heavily, parks himself down, lights a roll-up, passes it to you, and says quietly, 'The stuff going on, Brodie; it's to do with you.'

'Me? What to do with me?'

'You need to talk to Karen.'

'That's what Milly said. But about what, Ed?'

'About Moses, Brodie.'

'Moses? Why would I need to do that?'

Big Ed says, 'You need to. She's the only one who can tell you. Well, should tell you.'

There's a weighting of sadness spreading over Big Ed. His head's dropped forward and his shoulders have slumped. He sighs deeply, stands up, and then looks at you and there's a bleakness spilling from his eyes. 'I better get to Milly,' he says and leaves you with the mystery of wondering whatever's going on here, and what's it to do with you, the fucking widow woman, and Moses?

Then these thoughts slow down, take a consideration, and you're starting to put a terrible suspicion together in your head.

'You need to talk to Karen about Moses.'

Bombardier.
Karen Jones.
Inside the galley kitchen. Couple of peeled potatoes on the worktop. Half a cabbage keeping them company in the sink. In the oven a single pork chop is warming through. A lonely meal for one, and loneliness is what keeps Karen Jones company in this time of widowhood. Steve Wright's Sunday Love Songs is playing in the background and it's not helping her mood; these tributes to undying love.

She can't seem to raise any enthusiasm for food and today's no exception. It's there, all for the eating – or will be – but she just can't be bothered. She sits at the table, unshowered, hair unbrushed, and sips from a mug of coffee. She eyes the temptation of a packet of Blue Superkings, and thinks, 'What's it fucking matter?' So she draws another one out and lights up. She's on her third drag when there's the giveaway signs that someone's coming aboard; the slight tremor of the barge, an inch of tilt out of the level. There's a pause when there should be knock, as though a mind's hesitating on this Sunday morning. Karen Jones waits until she hears a quiet rap of a request to open the door.

It's the last person she expected to see and she takes a step back as she says, 'Brodie!' but even in her surprise her hand goes to the mess of her hair. 'Brodie. I didn't expect ...' *Didn't expect to see you on my doorstep.* 'What ...?' God, she can't even finish a sentence.

Brodie is serious, unsmiling. 'Look, I have to know something, Karen.'

'Know something, Brodie?'

'About Moses, Karen. I have to be sure.' There's an earnestness threaded into his question.

Moses? Her breath catches in her throat and their eyes lock together, and she can't help but return the question that they both know the answer to.

'Moses?'

So it's here, the time for truth has finally arrived after all these years. It's stalked her on the canals, pattered on the water, pecked at her mind. Never left her. It whispers to her, 'Tell him, Karen. Get this over with. It can't hurt Harry now.'

But she's not going to answer here, she can't tell this truth with the ghost of Harry Jones peering over her shoulder, hearing of her betrayal in the sacredness of their home. She wants to take it away from Bombardier, compose herself, make Brodie understand just how it was; that he was the unknowing accomplice to a crime of deceit. Karen Jones doesn't want a bitter recrimination, a thin-lipped judgement, she wants him to understand. But she also wants the comfort of someone slipping his arms around her and saying, 'It's all right. It'll be all right.' She wants human touch in a sharing between two people who, briefly, were once as close as two people could possibly be.

'I'll come to you. I'll explain everything. But not here. Please not here, Brodie.'

Summer Walker.
Late afternoon.
Sun's sinking fast and shadows are clouding Vixens water. It looks cold, and easily deep enough to swallow a man. In the kitchen, the kettle's on the hob and on a cupboard shelf a bottle of something stronger waits in reserve.
Karen Jones and Brodie.
Karen Jones has smartened herself up, changed for the occasion, and, except for the smudges under her eyes, she could

be considered an ordinary – but very attractive – woman approaching the middle-age of her life. She's here to tell a secret that's no longer a secret: the story of Moses. But first the offer of tea, of waiting for the steeping, the pouring, the sipping, of fleetingly meeting each other's eyes and both knowing that the other remembered what came before. Karen Jones takes a cigarette – 'don't mind, do you?' – lights up with a visibly huge draw and then begins the story that leads to Moses.

CHAPTER SEVENTEEN

Vixens Mere at the beginning of March about fifteen years ago.
Karen Jones.

She's watching from the Bombardier as Summer Walker slips its moorings and slowly glides towards the narrow exit of the marina. Mick's on the roof, Brodie's on the tiller, and he raises his arm in a farewell and Karen lifts her hand to a goodbye to all that was so overwhelmingly tempting to a lonely woman. She's going to miss him. Badly. Knows that it's an end to sneaking up the gangplank in the lateness of night like a teenager doing the landing shuffle. Knows there'll be no sharing of an afterwards cigarette in their world within a world. Knows she won't be doing this again. But what Karen Jones doesn't know yet is that she's well and truly pregnant.

Now Karen Jones is used to missing her times of the month; she's one of those women who is always very irregular – long periods without a period – and so it's nothing unusual. 'And what with Harry and all the stress, all that's been going on it's only to be expected.' So she doesn't dwell on the subject, doesn't give it a thought until she nearly chokes on her break- fast's return journey early one morning. By then the unknowing father is on some distant stretch of water, taking in the warmth of late spring. He'll be making his living chiselling life's images from oak, ash, and walnut. And Karen Jones will be loving her husband, caring for him between his operations.

In his return to his normal life Harry shuffles on a stick around Vixens Mere, trying to make it a bit further each day. He applies the steely discipline of his soldier's background, the discipline that made him a warrior, that'll carry him onwards in a hopeless quest for normality. Occasionally Karen will catch the briefness of his smile; their eyes will meet and the pain and years will melt from his face. He'll be the man in uniform who turned to her at the altar, the upright soldier who said goodbye at the train station and promised a return in six months. But it wasn't the same Harry who came back; there's things that can't be helped by a surgeon's knife and stainless-steel rods.

'It's in here, Karen. In here.' Harry taps his temple, talks about blurred vision, spends afternoons nursing his head and feeding himself codeine. She brings him cool water, lays down beside him. Comforts. Advances her career as a carer. But sometimes she'll sit alone on deck and look to the still water where Summer Walker had been moored. She will dream, guiltily relive the loving of the flesh, because with Harry there's none of that, can't ever be; there's love without the loving. So Karen Jones survives on her memories, of sometimes lifting the carved wooden boy, stroking the figurine and knowing that Brodie's hands had so lovingly carved and caressed him into form. Like he'd caressed her in their secret passion.

Vixens Mere.

High summer.

Six months after the Christmas party and around four months after Brodie left for pastures new.

Karen Jones.

The beginning of July is hot, sultry, sticky. Harry Jones is back in hospital, most probably for eight weeks min, awaiting another operation. His prognosis is still the same – unsure. The only surety Karen Jones has is that her future child weighs about a pound, and is about the size of a grapefruit in her womb. Karen Jones is one of those women who don't show their condition until the very late stages, although she does think her stomach may have started to thicken. There's something else that's causing discomfort to Karen and that's the fact her morning sickness – a late onset symptom of her condition – continues well past the first trimester of her pregnancy.

She's been sick again today; she didn't even make the sink before her stomach violently disgorged yesterday's intake. It purged itself of all half-digested foodstuffs in a sudden outburst that burned her throat, very nearly choked her, and sprayed just about everywhere in the kitchen. Afterwards, Karen Jones wipes her mouth, sits down with a glass of cold water, and knows what feeling 'like death warmed up' actually means. For half an hour she sits, letting her body begin to put itself to rights again, before she gets out the bucket and disinfectant and cleans up the mess. As she works, she catches an image of herself in the mirror, soggy cloth in hand, unruly hair, grey-faced, dressing gown hanging open, showing off her breasts. 'Like an unglamourous tart,' she thinks to herself, before she adds 'vomit-breathed' to her description. Karen Jones thinks bitterly, 'You wouldn't be so keen if you could see me now, would you, Brodie?'

And he can't see her, won't see her for well over a decade, though neither of them know that part yet, because she's paid the piper and called the tune. She sits at the table, lights up a cigarette, swears it's for the last time 'cos of the unborn, gags on the first drag, and then cries quietly to herself. Karen Jones just can't see any way out of the mess she's in. She's praying for a miracle, a resolution to an impossible position. Then she checks the clock, showers, smartens up, and steps out into the day. Karen Jones takes herself, and the fruit of her unfaithfulness, on a visit to see her wounded soldier husband; a hero of the realm.

Twice a week Karen Jones has been making this arduous

journey. It's a tiring travel of train and bus, and becoming more so as the child within her steals his share of her goodness. God she feels so tired, so drained, as she mulls over a miracle to waylay her situation. But the words of confession keep intruding into her mind, like she's learning lines in a play.

'I'm sorry, so sorry, Harry, but I'm pregnant and I don't know what I'm going to do.' She'll watch the words smite him, this man who loves her more than life itself. She'll present a situation that'll crush both of them, litter it with apology after apology, beg – will she beg? – forgiveness. She rehearses until she's word perfect; she wants to present an uninterrupted monologue for the understanding, for a forgiveness. There can be no more avoidance for Karen Jones; it's time for truth.

Manchester Hospital.

Harry and Karen Jones.

Harry walks towards her very slowly but with much less effort after this final operation to straighten him up. He has a broad smile of welcome for her and the sight of him, his presence, makes her heart lurch like it did in the old days. Though not entirely for the same reason. And then he's clumsily, briefly, embracing her through the stiffness of his limbs as she tries to hold in her stomach.

She manages, 'Harry, you look so good '

Harry's jokey, 'You don't look too bad yourself, Karen' tapers off towards a quizzical 'Sorta different though.'

Karen's snappy 'I've put a bit weight on, Harry.' (I'm carrying another man's child, Harry, and in a few minutes I'll be destroying your world) barely cuts into Harry's enthusiastic, 'I'm really on the mend, Karen. Feel so much better.'

He's cheerful, rubs his hands together, says, 'Let's get a cup of char.' The Army's still in his speech.

Karen starts to say, 'Look we need to talk, Harry,' but his eagerness overrides her.

'We'll have a chat over tea and cake,' he says. He wants to show her that the operation, the weeks of physiotherapy, have helped him so much that he 'feels like a new man, Karen.'

In the hospital cafe she sits and waits as Harry orders up. He takes delivery of a tray, of a pot of tea, slices of lemon drizzle cake and she watches him make his way to the table. He's smiling is Harry, he's so happy, looking like his life's beginning again. Then she watches his smile, his happiness, abruptly change to one of bewilderment, to his mouth working out a 'Karen' with a terrible fear colouring the single word. Then his eyes roll back into his head and he crumples to the floor like he's been shot. And the debris of this occasion is scattered around him; shattered remnants of the tea for two. Of his dreams. He's sprawled and as still as death on the floor and it seems that the IED detonated in a foreign land has finally completed its deadly mission.

All night Karen stays on at the hospital, a night of worry and drama while they're putting Harry's unresponsive form through a battery of tests. Then an MRI scan reveals a swelling on his brain. Karen, in the world of temporary removal, listens as the on-call consultant tells her, 'We think it's a probably a seizure, Mrs Jones, but we can't rule out the cause of it being an infection, a blood clot even, what with all your husband has been through.' Then he looks at Karen, pierces her with an unblinking gaze. 'But it's not good, Mrs Jones. Not good at all.' He takes an inordinately long pull of breath before he continues: 'I'm sorry, Mrs Jones, but you should prepare yourself.' He pauses because these words are so very hard for him to say; they need breaking up into swallowable lumps, understandable chunks. 'It's very unlikely that Harry is going to regain consciousness again. Very unlikely.'

Then the future Moses delivers her a very real hefty kick in the stomach that causes her to wince. 'I'm here,' he reminds her. 'I'm here for you. Me and you.'

Karen curses herself for experiencing one tiny smidgeon of relief. Harry will never need to know.

She goes in to see Harry in ICU before she takes the dreaded journey back to Vixens Mere. He's already changing, relaxing into his proneness – starched as white as his bed-clothes – drip in each arm, steady hiss and suck of mechanical ventilation of his lungs. She smooths his hair from his forehead, tells him how much she loves him, wonders if this a final goodbye. Then she leaves him to his coma and the fog of his frozen brain. She has to catch her transport back to Broome, where she'll join her shipmate of loneliness onboard the Bombardier.

All through the final trimester of her pregnancy Karen Jones will make this pilgrimage: stuffy hot summer hours on jolting public transport, a sweaty uncomfortable journey to where there might be a raised eyebrow in a suspicion of her condi-tion. But Karen Jones lowers her eyes, draws her voluminous clothes around herself, even if she's not fooling everyone. The nurses might be curious, might-tittle tattle a little between themselves, might bring her a cool drink as she sits in the rhythmic beat of the ventilator. But Karen's not their business; the seriously ill and the dying are. Harry Jones is. It seems to Karen that her discomforts are a penance she should willingly pay, as though she's putting a little something on the other side of the scales; these visits to a man who's dead and not dead.
　　'Condition unchanged, Mrs Jones.'
　　Bit like hers she thinks.

So she'll make the journey to Manchester twice a week, and she won't miss one until Moses decides that the time has arrived for his premier appearance. But for now the summer of deceit will continue at Vixens Mere and Karen Jones makes her plans for an existence without Harry; a living with just her and her baby. At night, in her dreamworld, she visits Iris and Fred Needham, presents them their surprise grandchild, slips his photograph into the family history of canal folk. And she thinks that's what she'll do, she'll bring her child up on the cut, just the two of them wandering the waterways like her forefathers had for all those years. A life without Harry. But that poor useless bed-bound out-of-this-world Harry has other ideas .

Bombardier.
It's been another warm day for September and Karen Jones is sitting on the path by her mooring and dunking her swollen ankles in the water. She thinks that if she could only have a cigarette, she'd be in heaven. Well not exactly heaven but she could be in one of those places where she could hide herself and leave the cruel world outside the door. She's left the telly on and she can hear the news through the open window of the Bombardier. She catches 'Indian summer' 'no rain forecast for a week'. Karen Jones gets to her feet slowly and carefully and just as she's pushing herself upright she feels like something's popped inside her and there's a sensation of wetting herself, of dripping through her knickers. She totters stiffed-legged, two boats down, to the Crystal Lady.

'Milly,' she calls and Milly, enjoying a cuppa in the prow of her boat, takes one look at Karen Jones, and nods her head as she says, 'You've started.' Milly's next word is a high-pitched call for Big Ed and he pokes his head out the door, shouts out, 'What the fuck are you shouting about, Milly?'

'She's on her way, Ed. Get the van started.'

In a swift glance, Big Ed takes in a wet-legged Karen, a soggy patch forming between her legs. For a big man Ed's surprisingly quick, he's across to his vehicle as Milly leads Karen gently on with a 'There's no rush, girl. No rush.'

* * *

It's only a short drive to Broome Hospital and Karen's sitting on one of Ed's work-coats, shoved under her to a casual 'Lift yer arse, Karen'. She can feel the wetness of her clothes moulding around that arse. Ed's driving with a smouldering, and rather soggy, roll-up in his mouth and Karen says that there's nothing more she'd like right now. It's a desperate, 'Let me have a drag, Ed. Please?'

Ed looks at her like he shouldn't or she shouldn't but Milly, centre seated, says that it's not going to make any difference now 'cos the little bugger's probably half way out anyway. Karen says that she still has her knickers on and Milly says to take them off if it'll make her more comfortable. Big Ed shudders, reckons that if Karen can hold things in until they get to the hospital he'd appreciate it; he eats his sandwiches in here. He tells her to keep the roll-up if that'll help settle things and thinks he'll cremate his work-coat as soon as he's back at Vixens. Which will be as soon as he's dropped Milly and Karen outside of the Maternity Unit in the warm sunshine of this Indian summer. Well, not really as soon as because firstly he'll roll himself a thick joint, and untab a beer, to take his mind off the shock of womanly things.

Karen asks, 'You'll stay, Milly?'

"Course I will.'

'No. I mean stay with me. When it comes.'

'Course I will. I'll be holding your hand.'

Which is what they tell the midwife on the ward.

'I'm her birthing partner,' Milly says.

The midwife, crisp, clean, efficient, and looking even younger than Karen, says that her husband was the other side of the country when she had her baby. 'He couldn't make it back in time.' She's taking Karen's blood pressure as she's talking and she says to Karen, 'Still, it's good to see your mother's going to be with you.'

Milly actually looks behind herself for someone before she realizes her meaning.

'Cheeky fucking madam,' she mutters.

So Milly stays with Karen, helps in the birthing, takes on the separate roles of absent father and absent husband. She thinks that this likely widow is going to have a lot on her plate over the coming days; but at least this will be something out of the way.

'One door closes, another one opens,' Milly tells Big Ed later that night. That's after she's described the baby's – no name as yet – birth in a lurid exaggeration of the event, and it's putting Ed off his toast and egg supper.

'Marvellous to see. His little head poking out. Bit bloody though. You'd never have thought he'd manage to squeeze out of that little ...'

Ed's just unplugged a soldier from his very runny egg and he asks for a respite 'cos Milly's descriptive powers are making him feel a bit sick. But Milly's in full flow and her portrayal of the afterbirth slithering out after the child caps it for him.

'Think I'll go out for a smoke, Milly.'

'But you haven't finished your supper, Ed.'

'Give it to the fucking goat,' Ed growls on his way out.

Vixens Mere.

Late afternoon the next day.

Karen Jones and the unnamed baby – seven pounds, thirteen ounces – have had another ride home this time, in Big Ed's transit van. Ed's made Karen sit on an old sack because, after Milly's telling of the event, he definitely doesn't want anything untoward leaking onto his seat, especially as the weather's warmed up. Now the newborn is sleeping peacefully onboard Bombardier in his carry cot.

* * *

Manchester Hospital. A week later.

ICU ward. Ultra-sterile surrounding. Warm. Constant temperature control. Outside, dusk is falling and so is the infamous Manchester drizzle. Indian summer well and truly over.

Nurse Collins.

SRN Collins is checking on those that need her special care. She has half a dozen patients: two that won't see the end of the week and another three, badly damaged, who are going to be draining resources for the foreseeable. Then there's Harry Jones who's forecast not to wake up but is stubbornly refusing to relinquish life. 'He's a fighter; it's the soldier in him,' she thinks. Her father – God rest his soul – had been an army officer and she'd been brought up in a military household. Perhaps that's why she feels such an affinity for Harry Jones. Oh, she's professional with all her patients – does her duty, checks out their vitals – but she lingers with Harry. She washes him gently, moistens his lips, talks to him as though he can hear her. She tells him of her father's postings to Cyprus, of an exchange to Canada. Of a sniper's bullet in a country lane in County Armagh. She doesn't want to think about that, pushes it away. She says of Canada, 'It was so cold there, Harry. So cold. And nothing but snow and forest for miles and miles. Green and white. Everything was green and white. Dad brought back a sledge and we ...'

She's taken his hand as she's talking, manipulating his fingers between hers. And then there's a contraction onto her hand, so slight that's she's unsure she's even felt it. 'Harry,' she says, 'if you can hear me, squeeze.'

There it is again, a slow gentle squeeze of the fingers and then another and another.

'You're coming back, Harry. You're coming back,' and

despite all her professionalism, all that she's seen in her career, a tear drops from SRN Collins's eye and breaks when it hits Harry's pale hand.

Now there'll be extra monitoring, consultant assessment, and an improvement to Harry that borders on the miraculous. In a week's time Harry will see into the world again, mumble his first words for months.

'Karen,' he'll say. 'Karen.'

But today, there'll be a phone call to a stunned woman who has been preparing herself for widowhood only a few days into motherhood.

Crystal Lady.

Kitchen.

Cup o' tea time.

Karen, Milly and Big Ed.

The afternoon's drawing to a close. Karen is feeding the week-old soon-to-be-named baby Moses. He has a healthy appetite and he's firmly latched onto her breast, sucking for dear life; pleasurable but sorely painful for the new mother. Milly says that she'll take her cup of tea outside because she's going to have a cigarette with it. 'It just doesn't taste the same without a fag and a good cough.' But before Milly can get out of the door Karen Jones's mobile lights up and she hands baby to Milly who catches one side of the conversation as she cradles him.

'Yes. Speaking.' There's a second or two of listening then, 'Harry? He's what? What?'

Karen Jones's mouth, her panicked voice, is working but her eyes are shocked and wide. The fingers that were buttoning up her blouse have frozen. Then it's a whispered thank you and a goodbye.

Milly thinks that's it. Harry's a goner. This is what poor Karen's been preparing herself for over the last few months and, even before the actual event, she's already well down the grieving road. Milly and Ed had talked about it and Ed said that when Harry snuffs it, it'll be an anti-climax because it's like it's already happened.

Milly says, 'Sit yourself down Karen. I'll get you a nip of something?'

Karen sinks into her seat, shakes her head slowly, numbly. 'Oh Milly, what am I going to do?'

Milly, who's heard the clump of Big Ed's boots on the gangplank, reckons it might be a good idea for Karen to finish buttoning up her blouse 'cos all her goods are on display and Ed's at a funny age.

So Big Ed walks breezily in, and not reading any signs, starts to say, 'Pete's come back with some monster pork chops. I'm going to fire up the barbecue and ...' And then he catches Milly's warning look and nod towards Karen.

Milly says, 'Karen's had some bad news.'

Ed takes in the atmosphere, jumps to the same conclusion as Milly, says he's sorry to hear that. He thinks perhaps he should give her a hug but she's rather exposed in the boob division so it's best he doesn't. He can't help filing the glimpse of nipple to memory though. Then he says, 'I hope Harry didn't suffer, Karen.'

Karen Jones is shaking her head again, slowly. Disbelievingly. 'It's not bad news. He's not dead. Harry's waking up, Ed. He's waking up.'

But there's no hint of elation in her voice and she takes Baby from a puzzling Milly and says that if they don't mind, she'll go home to the Bombardier; she'd rather be alone right now. Karen Jones, twenty-five years old, and so very nearly a convenient widow.

But Harry's nowhere near out of the woods because as his consultant, clinically efficient Mr Brown, puts it to Karen Jones the next day: 'Harry will need constant care, Mrs Jones.

He's delicate in his body and here.' Mr Brown touches his head. 'He needs peace and quiet. No sudden exertions and no sudden shocks.'

Then he asks, 'You and Harry haven't any children, have you?' and Karen shakes her head in a half lie and Mr Brown says that's good because Harry is going to be full-time work.

'You'll have to make sacrifices, Mrs Jones.' Mr Brown shakes his head. 'And there are no guarantees, Mrs Jones. No guarantees.'

What Mr Brown is saying is that Harry could be shaking hands with the Grim Reaper anytime. Likely sooner rather than later.

The Shed.

Day or so later.

Barbecue in progress.

In attendance: Pigman Pete, Milly with Baby, Big Ed, little motherless Jed, Mark Rawlins and the tenant from the Morning Star whose name no one ever remembers.

Milly and Ed are cooking Pete's bounty. Pork and crackling are wafting in the air. Wine and beer and bread are on the side as is Moses because Karen isn't due back from Manchester for an hour. She's hoping she doesn't have a leakage on the bus.

Milly, leaning towards Ed, and for Ed's ears only, says of Karen, 'I don't know what she's going to do now.'

Big Ed shrugs, takes a pull of beer, turns over a slab of pork. 'At the horns of a dilemma, isn't she, Milly?'

In the goodness of Milly she says, 'I'd do anything to help that poor girl, Ed. She's been like a daughter to me.' A tear sneaks from Milly's eye, tracks down her cheek. She wipes it, and her runny nose, with the sleeve of her dress, takes a snort of a sniff and holds out her glass for Ed to refill. Which he does to the brim.

'Steady on, Ed. You trying to get me drunk?'

Big Ed says yes he is and he's thinking that a tipsy Milly might be more receptive to some physical comfort later on. Do her a favour. Take her mind off things. Every cloud and all that. That's Ed though; he lightens the occasion. But when him and Milly – last two still standing at one a.m. – sit down for a final smoke under the stars, he wonders to Milly, 'What do you reckon she'll do then?'

Milly says, 'Well, she can't have Harry and the baby can she, Ed?'

Big Ed ponders for a moment. 'Don't suppose she can.' He doesn't say but it's in his mind that it might have been easier – would have been certainly simpler – if Harry Jones hadn't woken up at all. In Milly's mind are the two things that Karen Jones can't possibly put together; one of them will have to be broken asunder.

Vixens Mere. Present day.
Summer Walker.
Karen Jones and Brodie Stewart.
Pulling heavily on her cigarette Karen Jones says, 'I couldn't do anything else. I gave my child away, Brodie. And yours. I gave away your child. I gave away our child.'

You're silent, still digesting, and Karen Jones says, 'I can understand if you hate me.' She shakes her head, 'I don't want you to but … you know.' She shrugs, suddenly stands up from the table. *It's all too much. This is too much* is written on her face.

'I'd better go, Brodie.'

'You don't have to.'

'I do. It's late and …'

'You don't have to, Karen.'

She doesn't have to because this night your lives are tangled together, always will be because of chance and fortune. Here in the confines of Summer Walker, shut away from the world, you take her hand, draw her towards you, reawaken the loving from so long ago, feel the softness of her body, the taste of her mouth. In the dark warmth of your bed Karen Jones finishes her story, like she's cleansing herself of that time. The loose ends are woven together after the leaving of her beloved child.

Karen Jones had taken the Bombardier out of Vixens marina and slowly – due to her delicate post-birth condition – to Moses's unknowing grandparents on their canal-side house. She borrows their water to provide a coming home dock to Harry for when his strength will have tipped to manageable. Her father says for her to stay as long as she likes and Karen's mother feeds her up because Karen's as pale as a ghost, 'Whatever have you been doing with yourself, my girl?'

For a month Karen sleeps ashore in her spinster's room, builds up body and mind, tries to block her ears to the cries of her phantom child. She thinks she's going mad because she spends hours scanning the old framed photographs on the wall of memories. Sometimes she imagines that Moses is with his ancestors. She peeps into generations, into cargoes of timber, coal, coils of rope, arrays of twenty-gallon drums, raggedy children stepped in height, a blurred baby in a mother's arms, but he's not there. She dreads each passing day in which Moses will be changing, growing. Growing away from her. And what if she doesn't recognise him? What if in years to come she walks by her child in the street? But into her mind comes the solution. A compromise; the mooring that Bombardier will fill each winter for three months at his place of conception. She'll return to her Bethlehem to be an unrecognised mother bearing a Christmas gift every year, and poor innocent invalid Harry will be a part of something he will remain ignorant of to his dying day.

And you've come back to Vixens Mere. And Harry is dead. And now what, Karen?

CHAPTER EIGHTEEN

Broome Town.
A bed-sit room.
Carl Thomson.

The bedsit is newly occupied by Carl Thomson in an old town-house of reduced splendour that once belonged to wealthy Mr Barrington-Edwards, a long-ago benefactor of Broome. He would turn in his grave to see what is traded on the wide ornate staircase of this ancient building. He would certainly raise an eyebrow at the amount of snow, poppers, speed, ketamine and the like that's dispensed here. Barrington-Edwards might even think that his dealings in sugar and men and women in the 1700s was a much morally cleaner trade.

Carl Thomson has been having a good run lately. He's hit his targets all over town and beyond. He's made enough money for this change of address, to purchase a widescreen telly for a bargain price – a mate picked it from the road when it fell off the back of a lorry – and a cheap run-around car. He can spend without watching the pennies too closely and, all in all, Carl Thomson should be enjoying the most successful spell of his chequered career. Should be. But for two things; his ex, Anna, and that long streak of urine that's her boyfriend. The thought of how he's been turned over by them grates continually on his nerves. Talk about boiling blood. This is unfinished business and Carl Thomson's done a few drive-by reconnoitres. He'd even ventured a nonchalant walk halfway down the track towards the moorings on Vixens Mere, a walk that petered out when he encountered a 'hairy fat old bastard with a beard.'

'You looking for someone?' Big Ed doesn't mean to sound aggressive but Billy the Kid has chewed through his tether, done a runner, and pissed Ed off for the third time this week.

'Jed and Anna,' says Carl Thomson.

'They're not here. They've gone on the bus. Scan or something.'

'Scan?'

'For the baby. Twenty week scan or something.'

Carl Thomson says, 'Oh yeah, the baby.' He breaks the passage of his words for a moment and then adds, 'Will you tell them Carl was asking?'

A distracted Ed, scanning around for Billy, says, 'Carl?'

'Carl Thomson. Tell them Carl Thomson was asking.'

He starts back up the track and Big Ed calls after him, 'If you see a fucking goat whack its arse and send the bastard home.'

'Will do.' Carl Thomson humours the hairy old boy and thinks, 'Fucking goat?' He also thinks that Ed may be a sandwich short of a picnic. 'Strange crew down here,' he muses.

On the road back to Broome he thinks that he'll have to get into Jed's place on the sly, take what's his, and then have a satisfactory – for him anyway – settlement with fist and boot. Carl Thomson is not an archetypical bully; he won't back down to anyone. In fact some of his associates refer to him as Killer Carl and they reckon the only thing that could stop him would be a bullet. Or something very close to that method of slaying.

Big Ed and Milly.
Back down on their premises Milly asks Ed, 'Who was that, then?'

'Someone wanted Jed and Anna.'

'Didn't like the look of him,' Milly says. But it's more than that. It's like she's caught a sniff of Carl Thomson; a scent of something bad that Milly can't quite explain.

Ed says, 'Don't expect he liked the look of you either.'

'No, Ed, I mean there's something about him.' Milly draws the words out slowly, fades them into a lame finish, 'Like he's not very nice.'

'Seemed all right to me,' says Ed who's seen a few unsavouries visit Jed over the years. He doesn't give it another thought until later on when Milly's waylaid Jed and Anna for an update on the baby situation just before they can take a step on board Home Sweet Home. Anna, bursting with excitement at her advancing motherhood, holds a scan photo to Milly.

'Look! It's a boy, Milly. Like you said. Look, you can see his head and everything.'

Everything includes the obviousness of his sex that Milly can't help but notice. Little Anna the waif – and now not a stray – is bubbling. 'They said he's really healthy, Milly. Nothing wrong with him. Didn't they Jed?'

Jed manages to cut in on her chatter and shrugs a, 'Yeah Anna.' He's trying to act nonchalant but it's bordering on boredom. All this baby talk.

Then Big Ed remembers the visitor, starts to relay the message.

'A guy was here. Asking for you two.'

Jed says, 'A guy?'

'Youngish. Tall. Said his name was … um … Carl something.'

Jed says quietly, 'Carl Thomson.'

'That's it. Carl Thomson. That's who was asking.'

Milly sees the smile slide from Anna's face, sees the stiffening of Jed's posture. Feels a terrible fear has suddenly invaded them. There's a moment of utter stillness, utter silence before Anna's hesitant, 'He was here? He was here?'

Even Big Ed has now caught the atmosphere. 'Well, yeah. Anything wrong?'

Jed says, 'It's OK. Just some stuff we got to sort out with him. Better get inside, Anna.'

Now Big Ed and Milly are left wondering what trouble is brewing and Big Ed, scratching his beard, muses, 'They were scared.'

Milly says, 'They were terrified, Ed.' And she can't understand why there's such a dread in her stomach. It's like she's picked up on something malevolent stalking the marina, weighting the air and waiting to strike. Internally she asks, 'Why do I feel like this? What the fuck's going on?'

It's not as though her and Ed haven't got enough on their plate. Milly's been almost overwhelmed and she needs to conjure up a quiet, restful night for her and Ed. First, they'll make the most of Moses, listen to his tunes, sing along – well Milly will – and cook him up a monster portion of egg and chips. She'll spoil him 'cos – she gulps when this thought pushes into her mind – who knows what'll happen now, and how much longer Moses will exclusively belong to her and Ed?

So, later, there's a few drinks, a couple of spliffs, and then they reminisce, lose themselves in the carefree past when they were young and the music was free. Then it's to the beloved past where Moses, brown as a berry, barefooted, and wearing only a drooping nappy, takes his first faltering steps on the towpath around Vixens Mere.

Milly lowers her head, puts a hand over her eyes, wishes she just could step on and off a roundabout of her favourite places, favourite times, softly cries for a life that's passing much too quickly. Big Ed blames the Strongbow cider for her maudlin mood but, all the same he detabs two more cans and says that they'll finish these and it'll be time for bed. But Ed goes to bed alone because Milly takes her mood on a silent walk along the waterside and up through the dark woods. She sits herself down on the trunk of a fallen tree and whispers aloud all her thoughts and worries; she wants the fairies, and the elves, and the daemons of the night to hear her story. In the silence of the woods, Milly's sure she can hear them listening, and this certainty is not influenced at all by the cider and dope she's consumed. When, an hour later, she snuggles up to Big Ed's warm and comfortable bulk, Milly's spirits have started to lift a little; she's gleaned relief from uploading her woes into the great consciousness, scattering them over the still waters of an understanding Vixens Mere.

The next morning is an inroad into a grey, soggy day, with flurries of rain pattering onto the roof of Crystal Lady. After Big Ed has taken himself to work, and Moses has drifted off to school, Milly goes to her cupboard in the bedroom and from the top shelf she takes a battered red OXO tin. She spills its contents onto the bed, trawls through yellowed newspaper clippings, photos of her younger self, photos of an even hairier Ed. Then she picks out Moses's birth certificate, unfolds it, smooths it out. Milly reads aloud the name of mother – Karen Jones – and the entry of 'Father Unknown.'
'But we know who that is, Karen. Don't we?'

It's a secret that's not really a secret anymore.

Big Ed's in for a lunch of cheese and tomato sandwiches and Milly joins him with a cup of tea and an empty plate.

'You not hungry, Milly?'

'Don't feel like eating,' she says and they both know the reason why. But Moses, when he bursts in after school, is ravenous.

The door's flung back onto its hinges and he's into the kitchen like a whirlwind, a wet whirlwind with bedraggled hair and damp clothes. Moses's school bag clatters to the floor.

'What's for tea, Mum? I'm starving.'

Milly's at the oven, checking Moses's favourite dish of shepherds' pie. 'It'll be ten minutes. Give your Dad a shout.'

The shout's delivered and a damp Big Ed ambles in, stubs out his fag, settles in his seat. The table's laid, and the pie's cooling on the top. This could be construed as a happy domestic scene, a normal part of their life that's been replicated thousands of times. But this time it's different because what's been gnawing away at Milly can't wait any longer. From the pocket of her dress she draws out Moses's certificate of birth, holds it out to him.

'Here, Moses.'

'What's this, Mum?'

'It's yours, Moses. This is yours.'

'Mine?'

'Take it, Moses. Just take it.' Milly's frightened that her voice is starting to fragment.

They watch him, Ed and Milly do, as Moses unfolds the document, studies it on the kitchen table. They see his puzzlement, his frown forming, the question forming, 'Karen Jones? But isn't that the same name as Mrs Jones ...?' Moses gestures in the direction of Bombardier.

'One and the same,' says Ed.

Milly wants to say, 'She's your mother,' but she feels that she'd choke on the last word and she can only nod along to Ed's explanation. There hasn't been a hiding of Moses's heritage, more like a non-telling. But they knew it would raise its head one day, and now that day is here.

The story's told of Moses, Karen Jones, and Brodie Stewart, as the pie grows cold on the side. This fourteen-year-old's life is revealed from day one until there's nothing left to say. Mother and Father are out of cover and Milly is tear-streaked and Big Ed has a lump in his throat. Now there's a deep silence and a space in time for Moses to silently pick up his guitar, take himself to the shed.

'We'll let him be for an hour, Milly,' Big Ed says. He suddenly sounds tired and old.

Ed's right, Milly knows he's right, and this day she hoped would never arrive is already well and truly into its dawning.

The Shed.

Moses sits in the window of the Shed, watching over Vixens Mere as he gently, soothingly, strums the strings of his guitar. Everything's changed but everything looks the same. The rain's stopped and the water's flat and still. Any other time it would be a perfect evening to stalk the elusive pike; the legendary monster that haunts the deep water and keeps the souls of Harry Jones and Sandra Day company. Moses thinks that he could still get in an hour before the light fades completely. He toys with the idea of fishing out his rod but it's without his usual enthusiasm; these are changed times. So he'll just sit here, pluck out a tune, try to lose himself in his music. But he can't get Milly's hurt – he's never seen her cry before – out of his mind. He needs the comfort of her, to feel the familiar reassurance of her. Like when he came home from school bruised and black-eyed after Dan Lawrence – in the year above Moses – had slated Ed and Milly, and Moses himself, as Hippy Gippys, said they cooked up crows and rooks, took the carrion off the road. In defence of his family, Moses had been steamrollered in the playing field and trodden into the grass. He feels like that now and, although he's inches taller than Milly, and up to the bridge of Ed's nose, he suddenly wants that comfort and reassurance again.

They're still as he left them on the Crystal Lady; Big Ed is standing sipping tea from his mug and Milly is slumped in her chair. Moses is straight over to her, slips an arm around her. 'Mum,' he says and it's enough to bring a smile to her face and the words, 'My boy,' to her mouth. Then she's hugging him as only a mother can hug a son and she tells him it's going to be all right. Moses knows it will be because he belongs in Ed's and Milly's world, safe and secure with all those years of care and loving behind them.

'Let's have some pie,' says Moses, and Milly smiles. Gets out of her chair to heat it back up.

But before this, when Moses was at the shed window, he saw Karen Jones walking along the towpath, pausing by Summer Walker, hesitantly step onto and disappear into the craft. He wonders how the conversation between Karen Jones and Brodie will sound, what they'll be saying about him?

Summer Walker.
The same moment that Moses is sitting in the window of the shed.
Brodie Stewart.

You've sheeted the cover over the bow of the barge and you're working – mallet and chisel – on the piece of walnut that Big Ed had cut out for you. Shapes are forming, becoming discernible. The light's dimming and you reckon to give it another quarter of an hour and then call it a day. Mick, curled up on a blanket and spotted with wood chips, raises his head from his snooze and gives out a short bark of warning then, duty done, drops back to resume his slumber. You pause in your work, wait for the tread on the gangplank, for the voice of Karen Jones to say, 'I was walking by. I heard you working and ...' Her hair is damp and she looks tired and drawn, blanched with sadness. '... and. Oh Brodie, I'm sorry. I just need some company.'

Karen Jones is still fragile, on the edge of breaking. So it's to be an invite in, the offer of coffee and a cigarette, and the solace of a shoulder to cry on. It's a solace that lasts all through the night but it doesn't matter because there's no one left alive to hurt.

Karen Jones is talking quietly into the dark, unburdening herself.

'Every year, every time we came back here, I would look at Moses and think how alike they were, my boy and the boy you carved. I even called him Moses to myself. It helped me, Brodie. He helped me. He was my comfort.'

Karen Jones settles her body against you. She's warm and soft in the night and she ponders for a while and then she shivers slightly and says, 'It's almost as though you knew what Moses would look like, Brodie.'

You tell her that it's late and she's got a vivid imagination and you need to get some sleep.

Later, when Karen Jones is deep in healing slumber, you wonder how you could have carved such a likeness to the unseen and the unborn. But you know really, don't you?

CHAPTER NINETEEN

Morning Star.
Lorrie.
Before she leaves for work this morning Lorrie checks her bank balance. Again. In fact it's the tenth time since yesterday. She also re-reads the letter from her solicitor.

'... *deposited into your account the sum of £22,913.23 (twenty-two thousand nine hundred thirteen pounds and twenty three pence), being the first of three equal instalments due of the sum of £70,000 (seventy thousand) agreed with Ms Petronella Auclair following our disbursements of ...*'

It's not just the money for Lorrie, it's like an official confirmation that it's all done and dusted with Petra, an ending to the wasted years. Or it will be when the balance is paid but Lorrie's on the road out so she should feel more upbeat than she does; she's a good-looking girl, single, and she's a healthy bank balance. But what she needs is cheering up, a good night out, a nice meal, and a few drinks with a pretty girl, someone to make her laugh. She phones Dinah.

'Are you doing anything tonight? Only I've had a lucky strike. Need someone to help me celebrate.' Then she gives Dinah a get-out clause, 'Though if you're busy?'

'I was going to wash my hair but if you're offering a free meal ...'

'And drinks.'

Dinah laughs, 'This is getting better, Lorrie. Have you won the lottery?'

'No. No. Somebody just paid me something that was owed.'

That's enough for now and Lorrie doesn't know if she'll add any more of an explanation later; payment for failure is sometimes hard to admit. For herself and for Petra she thinks, and then immediately strikes away the image of Petra before any sympathy can take a hold. Lorrie replaces her with a petite farmer's daughter who has a coarse sense of humour.

Lorrie's schedule for today has fitted together nicely; a morning shift at the supermarket, an afternoon's training at Broome's Boxing Club, and an evening with Dinah.

'A perfect day,' she tells herself as she gels her hair into spikes, admires her reflection in the mirror and reminds herself of Trainer Tony's words: *You're a fine-looking woman, Lorrie.*'

'If I am,' she asks the mirror 'Why am I alone?'

Broome Boxing Club.
Afternoon.
Lorrie.

There's the usual gym aromas of smelly footwear, sweaty torsos, Deep Heat embrocation, and depleted deodorant sprays. An underpopulated arena. A few diehards and a couple of very keen nippers who should really be at school.

Lorrie's had a fairly quiet couple of hours; she's worked herself slowly into her solo routine, covering the normal keep-fit exercises, and now she's graduated to giving the heavy bag what for. Lorrie's concentrating on imaginary body and head, hooking, jabbing, through punching. Forward and back and …

'Sharpen your lateral movement, Lorrie.'

Tony's put in an appearance; immaculate and cool, for now at least, in his track-suit attire.

'Come on, Lorrie. I'll give you a go on the pads,' and he does. But this is a more intense Tony. He works her hard, keeping her on the move, shoving her around, crowding her. Her sweatshirt's clinging to her torso and perspiration is running down her face. There's a dotting of sweat dripping to the floor.

'Christ, Tony. You trying to kill me?' comes out more as a breathless statement than as a question.

'Less talk, more work, Lorrie,' Tony says as he calls out the shots. 'Uppercut. Left right left combo.' This continues until, 'Last half minute. Go for it, Lorrie. Twenty seconds ... ten ... straight punching now ... straight.' He pauses a moment and says, deadpan, 'God, I wish you were straight, Lorrie.'

Lorrie chokes on a laugh, stops the action, lets her arms down, finds enough breath to gasp out, 'It still wouldn't be you, Tony.' Then, making it sound like a serious afterthought, Lorrie adds, 'I might give Marvel first poke though.'

Tony reckons that it'd be a first for Marvel as, 'Never seen the ugly bastard with a woman,' and then he says, 'Something in the office to show you, Lorrie.'

This something is the second envelope for Lorrie on this day and it's a confirmation that Lorrie has successfully passed her medical and is now licensed to compete in the Ladies' ranks of the Amateur Boxing Association.

Lorrie had taken her medical a couple of weeks previously; blood test, urine sample, and the like – cardio, reflex, teeth. The doctor, a Ms Khan, an attractive middle-aged woman – jet black hair and coal black eyes – had commented on Lorrie's exceptional muscle tone.

'Don't often see such definition on a female body,' she said admiringly and she'd actually stroked Lorrie's bicep and sighed, 'Wish I'd taken care of myself a little better when I was younger.'

Lorrie says, 'You don't look too bad now,' and there had been a meeting of eyes and moment of awareness that passed between them. As Lorrie's leaving the consulting room, her hand on the door, Doctor Khan says, 'You know it's a pity that you're a patient, Lorrie.'

Lorrie thinks it's a pity as well because she wouldn't mind a personal examination by Dr Khan.

'Well?' says Tony, pointing at the ABA's letter of permission, 'No excuse now is there, Lorrie?'

'Suppose not.'

'I'll get you sorted then. You sure you're up for it?'

Lorrie says, 'I'm up for it, Tony.'

After tonight's over, Lorrie promises herself – yet again – that she'll increase her training, give up her occasional cigarettes, leave the demon drink undrunk, hit the pillow at ten o'clock of an evening, and take a run every morning before work. But prior to all of this happening there's just one more night left for wine, women, and song. Well, wine and song anyway because the woman she really wants doesn't seem to be attainable.

It's a nice night with Dinah, casual and relaxed, catching up on the news. Bottle of Italian white on the table and a filling of spaghetti carbonara in their bellies.

Dinah says that there's been nothing from Barry, not a word, and not a penny of what's owed. 'For all I know he's crawled down a hole and died.'

Lorrie says that's Dinah wishful thinking and Dinah wonders if Milly would put a curse on Barry if she sorted her a bag of weed. Then she tells Lorrie that she'd gone with Ethan to the Fighting Cocks for a Sunday night cider – a couple for Dinah and several more than that for Ethan. Dinah had drawn some attention from a young farmer. 'Eyes across the bar and all that,' she tells Lorrie.

Dinah had asked Ethan, 'Who's that over there? Tall guy. Fair hair.'

'Oh, that's Old Bernie Guy's boy. Lives over Stoughford way.'

'Name, Dad? What's his name? And don't look.' Which immediately Ethan does.

'Young Bernie.' Ethan says and doesn't add the, 'of course, what else could it be?' but it sounds like it's there anyway. 'When Old Bernie Guy shuffles off – shouldn't be long now, he's getting on a bit – Young Bernie'll have the best part of three hundred acres under his wellies. Good ground too and ...'

'Dad.'

'What, Dinah?'

'I only asked for his name, not a summary of his assets. I'm not up for bloody marrying the man.'

'You could do worse you know, Dinah.'

Dinah thinks that she did do worse and she says, 'I'll get you another cider, Dad.' She mutters to herself, 'Perhaps it'll shut you up.' But when she comes back Ethan had been joined by Young Bernie and, when Ethan goes 'to water the garden,' Young Bernie asks for Dinah's phone and typed his number in.

'If you fancy a drink sometime Dinah, give me a call?' He gives her a nice smile, a country smile, and she says she might think about it.

Dinah takes a loud slurp of her wine, giggles and flicks her hair. 'Gave me a boost though, knowing I could pull if I wanted to, Lorrie.'

Lorrie knows she mustn't, really shouldn't, but she can't stop a flit of jealousy cross her heart.

They sit and talk for a while longer, call up another bottle, and Lorrie outlines the 'something that was owed' that's given her a reason for this evening's invitation.

'I got some money from my share of the house today, Dinah.'

'Lucky you, Lorrie. What are you going to do with it?'

'Hadn't really given it much thought.' A few seconds of musing out loud then, 'Be a good deposit on another home, I suppose.'

'Oh Lorrie that doesn't mean .... you'll be moving on?' There seems to be an alarm in Dinah's tone that Lorrie can't help feeling a little pleased at. She says, 'Moving on? No, I don't think so. I like it here. (*I like you Dinah*.) Might change the car though.'

Then she tells Dinah about passing her medical and how Tony's fixing her up a bout in the near future and that Dinah 'could come and watch if you want. Cheer me on.' Lorrie laughs, 'and you could bring your new admirer along.'

Dinah grimaces, 'Don't think I'll be doing that. He's not my type, Lorrie.'

Lorrie means to be flippant with a light-hearted, 'And what is your type then, Dinah?' but it comes out like a serious enquiry. Like it's a loaded question. Dinah takes it in her stride, looks to Lorrie, holds her eyes. She smiles. 'Who knows, Lorrie? Perhaps I haven't made my mind up yet.'

There's the toss of her hair again and Lorrie, reading into an extremely tenuous innuendo – or not – wonders, 'Is Dinah flirting with me?'

Brenton.
Fifty miles from Vixens Mere.
Lorrie and Petra's home town where they bought the house together.
The Horse's Head Hotel & Bar.
Petra.

Some of Lorrie's former boxing chums are having a drink at the Horse's Head. Petra and a friend have just had a meal and Petra's paying a visit to the Ladies' room.

Petra looks into the mirror above the sinks, and begins touching up her make-up. Alongside Petra a stocky woman pushing middle-age is washing her hands. Their eyes meet in the mirror.

'Hi, Petra.' Petra's eyes narrow to a query that's answered

with, 'It's me. Anthea. You know. Used to go to the gym with Lorrie.' She laughs, 'Christ, I haven't changed that much, have I?'

Petra now recognises an older, heavier woman than the one who used to give Lorrie a lift to training. *'You've let yourself go a bit,'* Petra thinks. About three stones worth.

'Anthea. Of course. Anthea.' Then there's a brief hug that's not brief enough for Petra.

Anthea says, 'Good to see Lorrie's lacing up the gloves again. Too much talent to go to waste that one. Some of our lot are going down to the show.'

'Lorrie's fighting again?'

Anthea sees the blankness on Petra's face. 'Oh, didn't you know? Are you two not … like together?'

'We broke up a little while ago. Still good friends though,' Petra lies, adds, 'And where did you say Lorrie was boxing?'

Anthea hadn't said but she does now and Petra says, 'Might see you there, then?'

'Look forward to it, Petra.'

Then Anthea's shouldering her bulky form out of the Ladies, and Petra's silently saying to her departure, 'To think I used to be jealous of you.'

CHAPTER TWENTY

Widmouth Country Club and Sports Complex.
Lorrie's first bout in over three years.
Boxing ring set up in centre of hall-sized room. Rows of seats but most of the audience standing. Bout just ended. Canvas dotted with claret. Applause for the two fighters leaving the ring, one grinning and one grimacing. Tony and Lorrie climb through ropes, take their corner. There's been a few no-shows, and a vehicle breakdown, which has meant Lorrie's bout with the Welsh bruiser Megan Morgan has been brought forward an hour. A combination of this advancement and Dinah running late means that she's going to miss Lorrie's comeback fight.
Lorrie vs Megan Morgan.

Lorrie's first look at her opponent is from across the ring. She sees Megan Morgan – couple of inches shorter, stockier build than herself – pacing, loosening her arms, twisting her neck, thumping the red dragon of Wales on her chest. Then it's face to face for MC's intros and, before the referee calls them in, Lorrie gets a last-second pep talk from Tony.

'Don't try and do too much first on, Lorrie. Use yer reach. Feel her out.'

On any other occasion the last comment would have been taken as an innuendo but this Tony is talking quickly, unsmilingly, and in deadly earnest. Lorrie manages a, 'Christ, you're more nervous than me, Tony,' before he pushes her gumshield in. 'Go, girl,' he says and Lorrie almost expects a slap on her arse for a gee-up.

Lorrie, like Tony's advised, uses her reach. It's enough of an advantage to keep Megan Morgan at a distance most of the time, pile up a few points. But this Welsh girl's a determined fighter who doesn't mind taking one to give one. The first round is pretty even and the second is going to the same pattern – Lorrie on her bike, keeping her guard up, Ms Morgan moving forward, fighting at her pace. That's until Lorrie's manoeuvred into a corner and takes a couple of heavy blows to her face before she slips away and the bell sounds out.

In her corner Lorrie swigs from her water bottle, spits a bloody mouthful into the wash bucket. Tony says, 'Let yourself go now, Lorrie. Speed it up. Throw your shots. Don't want to leave this to the judges. OK?'

She nods and gets out half of 'OK' before her gumshield is jammed back into her mouth. Tony flaps a last-second towelling at Lorrie as she takes a deep breath and eases herself into a change of tactics, *into a place where the noise of the crowd becomes muted, voices are blurs of sound; a place of slow motion where the lights are burning brighter, sharper, putting Megan Morgan and her red dragon into clear focus. It seems to Lorrie that she herself has grown, that she can reach over, through the guard of her opponent with impunity. There's all the time in the world to beat her to the punch, time and time again, thud thud thud, until there's blood gushing from the Welsh girl's nose and her right eye is a slit of vision. Megan Morgan is a Welsh Braveheart but enough is enough and the referee is stepping between them, waving that it's all over bar the shouting.*

It's now the raising of Lorrie's arm in triumph, the applause of the crowd, and Tony's arms wrapped around her, lifting her up from the canvas, squeezing her in triumph.

* * *

'You did it, Lorrie. You did it.'

Lorrie, struggling to breathe in the strength of his grip, and in her excitement, and not even sure if he'll hear, says, 'No *we* did it, Tony. *We* did it. You and me.'

Sister and brother. Destined to be always so.

Back in the dressing room, with Tony as attentive company, Lorrie takes a long swallow of water.

'You were special tonight, Lorrie. They're all talking about your performance.' Tony's all smiles, radiating his pride in her and, by proxy, pride in himself. He says, 'Well, how did it feel, Lorrie, winning like that?'

How did it feel? If she was to tell the truth Lorrie would answer, 'Too good, Tony. Too good. Good enough to frighten me,' but she reverts to the coverall of, 'It was OK, Tony.'

Lorrie, aware of sweat drying none too pleasantly on her body, stands up, takes her towel, shampoo, and the like from her gym bag. 'If you don't mind, I need to take a shower.'

Tony says hopefully, 'I could wash your back, Lorrie. If you like?'

She says, 'I don't like, Tony, so fuck off and get the drinks in.'

Lorrie and Petra.

In the fifteen minutes that Lorrie has spent soaping herself clean another bout has ended quickly and dramatically – a first round KO in a middleweight contest – and created a natural interlude for a fair portion of the audience to rush to fill with a pint of the best. It's a crowded bar area where there's no sign of Tony, and Lorrie joins the random order for the serving. She wants to slake her thirst and then watch the remainder of the show. She has the glow of victory warming her from the inside, and she knows that she's being recognised; wet hair slicked back, left eye closing rapidly. She gets nods of recognition from the boxing community, a 'Well done, girl' from an old bruiser whose waist measurement coincides with his age. There's no sign of Dinah just yet but there's Tony, pint in each hand.

'One for me and one for you, Lorrie. To celebrate.'

Lorrie takes her glass and says, 'I'll drink to that, Tony.'

It seems that Tony's already sank a few more swifties and he thinks he'd better steady up ''cos of the drive home.' They talk about the fight and Tony says there's a few things that could be ironed out, 'but you were impressive Lorrie. That last round, those power punches, you really whacked her. Where did it come from?'

Lorrie says, 'It was easy, Tony. I imagined it was you.'

He laughs, closes the distance between them with a clumsy cuddle, the big brother that Lorrie never had. Lorrie feels a rush of sisterly love for her adopted sibling as she gently pushes him away. 'Get off me, you big softie. People'll talk.'

Tony's usual, instant response would have been, 'Let's give them something to talk about then,' but something's caught his attention behind her. He says, 'Jesus, will you look at that?'

Lorrie, curiosity getting the better of her, turns to see the very last person she expected to set eyes on in the world. Petra. She's making an entrance, sashaying between the customers of the bar. Petra, dark hair pinned off her face, slinkily dressed, colourful, gorgeously attractive, and drawing sidelong glances of admiration. Then Petra, now within touching distance, says, 'Hello, Lorrie,' and offers her hand for a welcome that Lorrie reluctantly takes.

'What do you want, Petra?'

'I need to talk to you, Lorrie.'

Petra glances an 'Alone' at Tony who's desperately awaiting a formal introduction and who actually says, 'Aren't you going to introduce me to your friend, Lorrie?' Lorrie's sharp 'No, I'm not,' carries his marching orders and Tony, realising something serious is afoot, backs off with, 'I'll catch up with you later then.'

Petra says, 'I'm over there, Lorrie.'

She motions to a table with a drink perched on it, her coat draped over a chair. They sit and Petra, taking a swallow of her drink, says, 'This is difficult for me, Lorrie. Can we just talk for a minute before I ...?'

Lorrie shrugs, 'Well, let's start with: What do you want? And how did you know I'd be here?'

Petra answers the second question with, 'It wasn't difficult, Lorrie. A little birdie told me. Well, she's actually quite a big bird now. Remember Anthea? She used to fancy you like mad.' A beginning of a laugh. 'Used to make me quite jealous.' The 'quite jealous' is delivered without reference to Petra's outbursts, the countless accusations that denial only seemed to inflame.

''Course I remember. But what do *you* want, Petra?'

'A catch-up, Lorrie.' She hastens into, 'And there's nothing wrong with an old friend looking up an old friend, is there?'

Old friends? An old friend with sparkling eyes. Generous mouth. Sexily, wickedly put together body. Drop dead gorgeous and knowing it and giving out the signal: 'I'm available, Lorrie. Hungrily available.'

Stop. Don't even think about it, Lorrie. You can never go back there.

Remember how I used to run the bath for you, Lorrie? You'd come home after the gym, exhausted and bruised, looking forward to a good soaking in the 'hot as you can stand it' water. Didn't you, Lorrie? I'd bring you a bottle of cool beer and perch on the side of the bath, wash your body, smooth away all your aches and pains until you were soft and pliable under my hands. And we know what follows, Lorrie, because I'm drying you on our bed with the soft fluffy towel and you're lying on your back being spoilt, being pampered, until the kissing, the long sweet kissing, starts and my lips are on your mouth, on your breasts. All over your body. I'm telling you just how much I love you and what I'm going to do to you and what you must do to me. You want to. You must do. I want the touch of you, the taste of you, on my body. In my mouth. How long is it since you were with a woman like me, Lorrie? How long since you've been loved like this?

Petra sips her drink, purses her lips. 'Lately, I don't know why, you've been in my head. You know, the way things happened.' She crosses her hands on her heart in a true confession. 'It was my fault, Lorrie. My fault. I've been thinking about how badly it ended for us.'

'There's no us, Petra. Not any more,' Lorrie says, sharp but sad. *Mean it, Lorrie. Stay strong and mean it.*

'Look, I never wanted you to hate me. I know I was that bitch,' she laughs, 'the wicked witch of the east.' The Petra of the old tricks slowly, daringly, reaches across the table and touches Lorrie's hand, searches for a grip, entwines their fingers, sighs, 'What I'm trying to say is that I'm sorry, Lorrie, and that I've missed you.' She's searching Lorrie's face as she closes the distance between, gives Lorrie the scent of a familiar sweet perfume.

'Haven't you missed me at all?' In another time, another place, this question would have been coyly teasing, a breathless preamble to, '*Why don't you show me how much, Lorrie.*'

Lorrie firmly untangles their fingers, says, 'I've nothing for you, Petra.'

'Nothing? You sure? Not a meet-up for a drink? A meal? A phone call even? You were a big part of my life, Lorrie. A big part.'

'I'm sorry, but nothing, Petra. Nothing.' Lorrie is surprised by the firmness of her own voice.

Petra studies Lorrie's face. 'Really? You really mean it, Lorrie?' There's a disbelief in her tone. 'But I thought – I was hoping – when we saw each other we could at least be friends.' *That word again that doesn't mean what she means.*

Lorrie can't do with this sparring any more. It's old ground that was covered a hundred times but it's not going to end like it used to.

'Look Petra, no more trying to soften me up. Is there something else you really want?' Lorrie's had enough, she can feel the bruising on her cheek, the swelling on her eye growing more painful with each passing minute. Her whole body has started to ache and her words are tiring. 'Just tell me, Petra. Please just spit it out.'

Petra, visibly taking a deep breath, says, 'It's the money, Lorrie. Not just that, though,' Lorrie knows it is. 'I'm finding it difficult to raise it all so soon. I need more time.' Her voice is almost into pleading and her dark eyes are holding Lorrie's as she tries the old trick of, 'And I miss you, Lorrie. I do.'

Lorrie thinks '*Like hell you miss me,*' and she says, 'It was agreed, Petra.'

'But I need more time. I'm on my own; I pay all the bills, Lorrie. Mortgage, council tax. Car to run.'

Lorrie resists delivering the cutting *Poor you* to say, 'Well, sell the house then.'

'But I can't, Lorrie. I don't want to. It's my home. It was *our* home. Remember?' Then pushing into a bitter accusation of, 'It's not like you're skint, is it Lorrie?'

Lorrie's looking at a suddenly frustrated but a more fragile Petra, a glittering of tears in her eyes. Lorrie's reminded of half an hour before when she had put her arms around Megan Morgan in sympathy for her losing; a woman who had wanted to batter Lorrie to a standstill forgiven with an embrace. And that's what Petra is, a loser, but she's not getting the consolation of an embrace just now, instead she's getting what Lorrie's solicitor would, and will strongly, advise against. It starts with, 'I'll think about it, Petra.'

'You will, Lorrie? Oh, thank you. You don't know what a load off my mind that is.'

'But … hang on, Petra, I only said that I'd …'

But Petra's full on, seizing on what she wants to hear: 'I knew you'd help me, Lorrie. I knew you would.' Petra reaches for Lorrie's hand again to grasp a 'Thank you. Thank you,' and Lorrie doesn't let the touch linger long enough for any interpretation of encouragement. Now Lorrie knows that it's all been said, achieved. Petra's got part of what she came here for and now Lorrie has a desperate need for a cigarette. Petra says that she'll join Lorrie then she'll head homewards. And will Lorrie contact her solicitor, change the terms of payment? Agree an extension, another year of time to pay? There's a dumb resigned nod from Lorrie who feels more battered than she has ever been in the ring. Petra says that if Lorrie really does ever want a meet-up or just a chat? And that leads into 'let's have that cigarette 'cos I'm gasping.'

What's in a cigarette and a civilised goodbye in the dimly lit car park of the Widmouth Country Club? What's in it is Petra leaning against her car, taking a long pull of nicotine, and asking: 'So have you met someone, Lorrie?'

'Sort of.' That's not quite a lie. 'Early days though. You?'

'On and off, Lorrie. Can't seem to settle. Not since … well. You know.' She draws in another drag and drops her cigarette butt into the gravel, grinds it out. 'Well, better go, I suppose,' and her words sound like there should be a question mark at the end of them.

After all that's passed between them it seems churlish not to offer a brief touch of lips, an embrace, a forgiving and a forgetting with someone you once loved. Someone you hated, and couldn't ever love again. So the brief kiss isn't brief; it's a lingering closeness; a pouring of warmth and sweetness and regrets. Lorrie thinks that it's the saddest kiss she's ever shared in her life. In this final goodbye Lorrie is vaguely aware of headlights slowly sweeping over them. Then that's it. All done. All finished. They're apart and Petra is driving away with what she came for and, in a couple of hours, Lorrie will be tucking herself into her lonely bed for a restless night and a solo flight.

'Fuck it. Just fuck it,' she says to the silent carpark. Which isn't exactly silent because there's a slamming of a vehicle door and the clacking sound of heels approaching and Dinah saying, 'Lorrie. Really sorry I'm late. Disaster of a day I've had.' Dinah's talking quickly, nervously.

'Doesn't matter, Dinah. I went on early anyway.'

'Oh. I'm sorry. Did you win?'

'Yeah. Bit of a battle though. Stopped a few hits.'

The third sorry of the night is in: 'Oh Lorrie, I'm sorry I missed it. I might have had to watch through my fingers though. You know. Like in a horror film.' Dinah giggles, says that she's never been to a boxing show before.

'Well, let's go in and I'll buy you a drink. Bore you with the details. I'll even show you my bruises.'

Lorrie thinks that Dinah's enthusiastic, 'Oh yes please, Lorrie,' sounds like it's an innuendo and then Lorrie thinks, '*I wonder if she saw me and Petra?*' like it's something to be guilty about. Then it's 'What the fuck's the matter with me?' but she knows that Petra's unsettled her mind, as she always does.

Then it's inside for a drink and to watch the last bout of the evening and for Tony, who's obviously knocked back a few more, sidling up and whispering in Lorrie's ear, 'What's your secret?'

'Secret?'

He nods at Dinah who's threading herself towards the bar. 'Yeah. Secret. You leave with a gorgeous girl on your arm and come back with a different one.' He takes a swig of his beer and adds in a mock rueful tone: 'Perhaps I'd have more success if I didn't have a dick either, Lorrie.'

Lorrie, lightening up, says, 'I'll cut it off for you if you want, Tony. If I can find it.'

They laugh. Tony wanders off to find someone 'who doesn't talk like a fucking butcher, Lorrie.'

The last bout is stopped on a second minute cut after a bad clash of heads and that's it for the evening. The ring's emptied, canvas is shadowed with blood and sweat, and the referee is making a beeline for the bar.

Lorrie says, 'Not much for you to see, Dinah.'

Dinah shakes her head, starts with, 'It's OK, Lorrie. Not your fault, is it? Maybe next...'

She stops because they've been joined by Megan Morgan who's bustled into their personal space to say her goodbye.

'Excuse me,' she says in her soft Welsh accent and offers out a handshake. 'Well done, Lorrie. Best girl won. This time anyway.'

Lorrie says, 'It was a tough one, Megan.'

Megan looks to Dinah, appraises her, gives a low whistle. 'This your partner, Lorrie? Lucky you.' She takes Dinah's hand. 'I'm Megan,' she says, and forward girl that she is, says to Dinah, 'Wish I could find someone as pretty as you.' She grimaces and laughs at herself. 'But, you know. With my battered face.'

Dinah, smiling, says, 'We're friends. Me and Lorrie. We're just friends.'

Megan's 'Really?' carries a hint of disbelief. 'But you two look so good together.'

Then she's turned and gone and and Lorrie says, 'Sorry, Dinah. You know. That she thought we were ...'

'At least she said *I* was pretty, Lorrie.' Dinah tilts her head, preening.

It's in Lorrie's mouth before she can check it. 'You are, Dinah. You're something else,' and Dinah says, 'Do you really think so, Lorrie?' and Lorrie's unsure if this is a kidding time or not. She's still trying to put an answer together when Dinah teases: 'Am I as pretty as the woman you were kissing in the car park, Lorrie?'

Lorrie smiles, says she doesn't know because it was too dark to see and it's left there with no more questions asked and no more answers given.

At half ten the show's over, the hall's emptying, leaving echoes of arranged rematches amidst the after-chat. It's going home time for the flattened noses and the cauliflowered ears, for the muscles that have turned to fat, and for the shuffling walk of numbing brains. Tony has already asked for Dinah's phone number – ignored – and Lorrie says, 'See. Someone else who thinks you're pretty, Dinah,' and they raise eyebrows at each other in a good-natured way. But Tony has not only asked for Dinah's number, he's also asked for a lift back to Broome.

'Bit risky. Me driving. I've probably had one too many. Have to leave my motor here.' He tuts at himself for being a bad boy and there's a slur in his tut that betrays the 'one too many' as the many too many. There's also a noticeable swaying of his body as he's talking.

Dinah says, 'You can have a ride as long as you promise not to throw up in my car.'

Tony promises and adds, 'You can drop me at Glow Worms if you like. Marvel's on duty. I could give him a hand for the last hour.'

Lorrie reckons that one more drunk in the club won't matter much to Marvel and, if there's any problems, he'll throw Tony out with the rest of them. She's also a little disappointed he's snagged a lift with them because she was looking forward to the drive back with Dinah; the comfortable warmth of the car, the closeness of Dinah, stealing sidelong glances at that pretty young face, and maybe just reaching across to touch her. *No. No. Stop it there, Lorrie. For the second time this night, stop it.*

It's a ride to Broome with Tony, who is instantly asleep and snoring on the journey, then wakened into grogginess and helped out onto the pavement outside the Glow Worm. Marvel's in the foyer jawing to a group of lads and Tony, stumbling his way in, trips over the step, falls like a pine tree, and scatters the congregation like skittles.

Lorrie says, 'Oh dear. Marvel's not going to be a happy bunny now.'

They leave the scene with something to chuckle about on the trip to Vixens. Lorrie feels quite content because all in all it's not been a bad night for her, apart from Petra that is. She's come out tops in her bout, she's had an evening with Dinah, and Tony's provided the cabaret.

Down at Vixens Dinah pulls up the car, leaves the engine running.

'You want to come in for a coffee, Dinah?' Lorrie pitches it casually, perhaps a little hopefully.

'I'd like to but no thanks, Lorrie. I better get back. I've an early start tomorrow. Market day. Dad'll want a hand first thing.'

'Oh. OK. Well thanks for the lift and I'll call you. Yes?'

'Yeah. Fine, Lorrie and ...' Dinah leans across from her driver's seat and presses her lips softly, briefly, onto Lorrie's mouth. It's a butterfly kiss with no lingering follow-on intent. Dinah says, inclusive of humour, as Lorrie slides out of the car, 'You're lucky, Lorrie. That's two girls you've kissed tonight.'

Then Dinah's away, the taillights bouncing away on the

rough track and Lorrie fumbles for her cigarettes, lights one up, and sits on the side rail of The Morning Star. She stares across the Mere.

Tonight the waters are still and dark, deep and mysterious. Lorrie wonders what it would be like to slowly wade into those cold waters, every pocket crammed with nuts, bolts and scraps of metal, weighted into a one-way ticket to meet the Lord. Or to lay in the mud, cloaked in tarpaulin, and sinking into silt for all those years while life went on above and around.

Lorrie mutters 'Jesus' to herself and thinks that she'll be giving herself nightmares if she's not careful. She turns her mind to more pleasant things, the evening past, the tilt of Dinah's head, a glimpse of her white teeth as she teases, *'Am I as pretty as the girl you were kissing in the car park?'*

There's the sound of footsteps approaching on the gravel path and it's Milly on one of her nocturnal walks. She's humming some old seventies tune, at least Lorrie thinks that's what it might be. Alongside the Morning Star Milly pauses, calls out to the dark figure, 'You all right, Lorrie? Out here on your own this time of night?'

'Like you are, Milly.'

'I need space to sort out my head stuff.'

'And me, Milly. And me.'

'Well shift your butt over and give me a fag.'

They sit and smoke, look across the flat black water. Lorrie says that she's going to take a fortnight off training now the fight's over, and live like a normal human being.

'Eat what I want. Drink what I want. Smoke when I want. For a while anyway.'

Milly says, 'You missed something out, Lorrie.'

'What's that?'

'A bit of the other, Lorrie.'

Lorrie colours. 'Not much chance of that,' she says with an edge of bitterness but lightens it with, 'Unless you can make me a love potion, Milly.'

Milly says that if she could do that she'd make one up for Ed, ''Cos he's gone off the boil a bit lately.' She sighs regretfully, 'God, when I think what we used to get up to.'

For a moment a horrified Lorrie thinks Milly is going to elaborate but Milly says that it's getting hard on her arse sitting here and her bed's a-calling.

Lorrie stays out long enough to light up another cigarette – she knows she'll be having a hack in the morning – and thinks about warm beds and sleepy partners. She thinks about Petra's warm bed in the room where they painted the walls, painted themselves, giggled like schoolgirls, when the loving was fresh and new, and where she will never sleep again. But what's for Lorrie tonight is the settling under her duvet in her lonely room where she'll lay and dream of things past, and imagine a future that's being built on wishes and hopes, and dreams which might just come true one day.

It starts to rain. Lorrie hears it gently drumming onto the skylight in a steady soothing passage of fall, soothing enough to ease her into slumber.

CHAPTER TWENTY-ONE

Bombardier.
Saturday afternoon.
An hour before the light fades and ends a dull, dreary, wet day.
Karen Jones.
What a day. She's sick to death of the endless rain, of looking out the window and seeing Vixens Mere pockmarked by yet another bout of precipitation.

'Whoever thinks that there's a romance to the patter of raindrops on the roof needs their head tested.' She almost tacks a 'Harry' at the end out of the habit of years. And he's still here is Harry. He's in the pictures on the wall, the unslept bed, the cooking for one. Sometimes, like today, she feels claustrophobic, hemmed in by Harry's nonexistence.

Karen Jones turns on the radio and it's a sad song about a lost love. She switches it off and lights another cigarette, pours an early glass of Prosecco, gives herself a pep talk. 'C'mon Karen, cheer up. Make yourself do something.' This something is a hot shower, a gentle towelling in the radius of the stove, yet another cigarette and another glass of Prosecco but because it's on an empty stomach, it puts her in the world of slight removal.

'When I was nineteen,' she tells the absent Harry with another swig of wine, 'I'd be getting ready for a date with you. Mum would be knocking on the bathroom door. *How much longer are you going to be in there, Karen?* 'I'd be putting on my underwear.' She slips on her knickers, clips up her bra. 'Picking out something sexy for you, Harry.'

Karen Jones opens her wardrobe, tosses out jeans and tops, until, 'Here it is.' Here is a dress she's not worn in ten years. It's sheer, light green, and perhaps a little tight now. She sniffs it, decides it needs a run over with a warm iron and a spray of perfume. Then she brushes her hair out, lets it fall to her shoulders, peers in the mirror to spot grey hairs, the faint imprint of crows' feet. But Karen knows, feels, that she looks good, that she would turn heads. She could go somewhere, anywhere, instead of being here on her own; all dressed up and no place to go. Karen Jones has a sudden surge of anger. She's got to get out, get off this barge, or else she'll go stark raving mad. She cannot bear the thought of yet another night sitting alone. Another night of wasted life. Fuck it. She'll order a taxi, go into Broome to the Victoria Hotel, treat herself to a three-course meal, spoil herself for once, be in public, talk to people. Ten minutes later the process is well underway.

Taxi ordered for seven. Meal down for eight. Taxi booked for the ride home at eleven. All done. Just the waiting to get over with, which means some more drink. Steady on, Karen. You'll be pissed before you get there. Thinking and wondering if ...?

At six thirty she phones Brodie.

'I'm going into Broome. Got a taxi coming at seven. Would you like to come with me?' There's a silence longer than she would have liked and into it her voice sounds small and sad. 'Please Brodie, I just need some company.'

The transference of that need is so compelling that when the taxi leaves Vixens Mere for Broome it has two passengers at seven o'clock instead of just one.

At a half past that hour, in the rather warm restaurant bar of the Victoria Hotel, Karen Jones takes off her shapeless overcoat to reveal what's underneath; the figure hugging light green dress that shows off the shape of her. Brodie Stewart looks at her, really looks at her, and he says softly, 'You're beautiful, Karen. You're beautiful.' And his words touch her soul, send a shiver of desire down her body. She knows where this night is going, how it's going to end. But she doesn't want it to finish in the cramped cabin on board the Summer Walker, she wants it to end in a double bed with crisp white sheets, precluded by a hot sudsy bath with a glass of cool wine in her hand. She wants strong fingers gently massaging her shoulders, and warm lips pressed to her open mouth. Karen Jones, for the first time in so many years, is looking to be pampered, treated like a loved woman. The only pause is when Brodie softly asks: 'You sure it's all right, Karen?' *Don't want another little Moses, do we?*

'It's all right. You know ... pill,' is whispered into the clinging onset of passion because Karen Jones just can't let a mistruth interfere with the perfection of this night. And after all she is thirty-nine years old and taking this chance is not like it was before, is it?

Vixens Mere.
Same Saturday evening but just after Karen Jones and Brodie Stewart have arrived in Broome.
Weather pattern continuing. Rain sheeting down.
Lorrie has left for her shift on the door at the Glow Worm.
  Pigman Pete, Milly, and Big Ed are on for a heavy meal and drinking session at the Bull and Dragon public house approximately four miles away from Crystal Lady.

Home Sweet Home.
Three hours after Big Ed and his passengers have departed.
Still raining dogs and cats.
Anna and Jed.
This is the night for stoking up the fire, enjoying the warmth

and the distraction of the telly. At least it is for Anna and her swelling belly. She's sitting alone with her worries on this filthy night, because Jed, the main source of her worrying has had to revert to his old ways. They need money; money to live, to pay the mooring fees, the council tax, and last but by no means least, money to try to put the blocks on Carl Thomson.

Jed had been helping Big Ed but the weather has been so shite these last few weeks there's been no work. In the words of Big Ed, 'I'm not getting up on a fucking roof in these conditions.' Even when the weather is good Big Ed's old bones are not, so what was a casual job for Jed has become even looser. The problem for Jed, and Anna, is that Jed has no experience of anything really except petty dealing. Another problem is that someone has already stepped into his dealer's shoes and Jed has to start again from ground zero. A new boss, Lenny Lines, has given him a fresh start, and some monetary credit, and Jed's out flogging his wares to strangers.

'Just till we get on our feet, Anna.'

But that doesn't look like happening in a hurry; Jed's being drawn deeper into the mire. That's because Lenny Lines also deals in mobile phones, SIM cards, watches, and items of jewellery. With Jed in tow it means he has somewhere, and someone, who can assist in the storage, the shifting, and selling of the produce.

'Come on,' he says to Jed. 'I'm overloaded here, help me out and I'll help you out.' From a case of watches he holds up a brand new Lexican. 'Sell this and there's fifty bar in it for you. This one,' a Bulovi this time, 'and there's seventy-five.' Another. 'A ton on this one.'

Jed, aware of the ground shifting under his feet, says he'll think about it but Lennie Lines has trapped him because, 'What's there to think about, Jed? It's all or nothing. People are queueing up to do business with me. Well?'

There's a sigh of assent from Jed and later a bag of goodies is stowed under the bed in his Dad's old room. So when Jed hits the town on this particular wet evening he has twenty parcels of coke and three misappropriated timepieces on his person. (That's what the law would say if they were to take a feel of his collar tonight.)

Anna, on her lonesome this rain-filled night, watches the telly, watches the clock, and waits for her phone to light up with the news that Jed's on his way home. She's not going to have to wait long because a sodden Jed, wet coat, wet shoes, wet everything, is finding it difficult to shift his merchandise. He heads for home early, phones Anna to, 'Do us some bread and butter, Anna,' because he's going to pick up some fish and chips on the way home and he shouldn't be much more than half an hour if he steps it out.

Anna watches the end of the Saturday evening film. Then she fills the kettle ready for the hob, sorts out a towel and some fresh clothes for Jed, sits back in her soft chair and waits for her man. 'He'll be a little while yet.' She's warm and comfortable. Her eyes droop and, before she knows it, she's drifted into forty winks.

Outskirts of Broome.
Rain pissing down.
Carl Thomson doing the rounds.
The wipers of his car are well worn and they're producing more smear than clear. It's also one more subject to heap onto Carl Thomson's paranoia. He thinks his mind is very close to exploding. Occasionally, as he drives, he hits the heel of his hand onto his forehead.

This has been a bad day and it's not been alleviated by him getting well and truly stoked-up; stoked-up and extremely angry. He's lined and snorted when he should be selling, and he's dipped into enough weed to give himself the mother of all appetites. (To add to this is that he's had absolutely nothing in his guts since a bowl of cornflakes yesterday morning.) He's also been let down on a couple of deals and he needs money. Desperately. Now. Carl Thomson's driving with his window down, taking deep breaths of wet air to try to clear his head of bad thoughts, and this is why he catches the whiff of the Best Fish and Chips in Town and it adds to his ravenous hunger. He pulls his motor over, pulls up the hood of his hoodie, and joins the end of a queue that is only just inside the steamy and very crowded chippy. But half in and half out of the threshold he pauses. His eyes narrow because at the counter is Jed. *That lanky streak of piss.* It's all Carl Thomson can do to stop himself jumping the queue and flattening the bastard. He steadies himself, watches for a minute as the girl at the counter, young, pretty, flirty, and who obviously knows Jed for a regular, asks, 'Salt and vinegar?'

'Please.'

A dust and a shake and a laugh. 'Treating her tonight then, Jed?'

'I always show her a good time.'

A coy 'Not sure I'd be happy with just fish and chips.'

There's a couple of young lads behind Jed, one of them mutters, 'S'spect she'd have to have a sausage as well.'

Someone else mentions a saveloy and the girl says, 'I heard that, you cheeky beggar,' and reckons that someone's little chipolata wouldn't do her any damage. 'Wouldn't know if it was in or not,' she scathes.

Carl Thomson slips from the queue, forgoes his meal, puts his hunger on hold because there's now more important things afoot. He takes himself back to his car, drives off to the edge of the town, down the lanes, and pulls onto the verge at the top of the track to Vixens Mere. He takes a monster snort of snow and rolls himself a massive joint. This combination offers a tremendous boost to his natural psychosis and, huddled into his seat, he angrily waits and hates. He hates the music on the radio. He hates the driving of the rain across the windscreen, the rare motor splashing past with its fucking blinding headlights. But most of all he hates Anna and he hates Jed; reason enough to do some serious damage to the both of them. So tonight things have fallen into place and the action time arrives when a very wet, and hooded Jed steps a hurrying footfall onto the rutted track down to Vixens Mere.

Vixens Mere.
Carl Thomson, Jed, and Anna.
Carl Thomson slides silently out of the car, follows a few yards behind Jed, who, head down against the rain and wind, isn't aware of anyone until he's onto the towpath and under the stuttering lamplight by Home Sweet Home. Carl Thomson has closed the distance between them to mere feet and he calls out loud enough to carry over the elements, 'Hi, Jed. Nice to see you again.'

At the sound of this voice Jed stalls, turns, then literally freezes on the spot. Only his mouth seems to be working as he asks the question they both know the answer to. 'What ... What do you want?'

'You know what I fucking want. I want my money.'

Jed stutters out the words, 'I can give you fifty to go on with.'

'That's not enough.' Carl Thomson's voice rises to a jolting, 'That's nowhere near a fucking enough. You cunt.'

'It's all I have but look, I got watches. Take one of these.' Jed squeezes his hand under his coat, pulls out the Lexican, lets loose a whiff of fish and chips. He holds out the watch. 'Here, take it. Go on, take it.'

Jed's trying to sell time but it's not going to be bought. No way.

Carl Thomson says, 'What? And have Lennie come after

me? You think I'm fucking stupid or something? Think I don't know how things work around here?'

'I'll cover it. Lennie won't know. I won't tell. I promise I won't.'

'Too late for your fucking promises.'

As he's talking he's reduced the gap between them to touching distance. He snatches at Jed's arm, latches onto it like a bulldog. Jed can feel Carl Thomson's tension, anger, fury, coursing through his steel grip.

'We're going inside your fucking boat, Jed. Fucking sort this shit out now.'

'We can't. Anna ...'

'We're going inside.'

'But Anna ...'

'Anna. Fucking Anna. Fuck Anna. I'm going to find out what that thieving little bitch has got in her money box.'

Jed knows that Carl Thomson cannot, just can't, go into their happy home, their haven from the world. Poor waiflike pregnant Anna mustn't face this monster. Jed struggles, pulls against his captor and the opportunity – his only one so it happens – presents itself for his free hand to swing into the face of Carl Thomson. It actually lands on his bony forehead and hurts Jed more than its recipient. The problem for all concerned now is the losing of any pretence of control. Carl Thomson explodes, flips, and the most one-sided fight that Vixens Mere has ever witnessed begins.

There's the bodily lifting of Jed and him being slammed against the flank of his home, flung to the path to spill out a warmish meal of North Sea cod and Maris Piper fries. Two hefty kicks to the body follow and then Carl Thomson plants himself astride Jed and pounds his fists onto Jed's face like a maniac. These are furious blows, star-inducing thuds of hard knuckle onto jaw and nose. Jed's still managing to twist his head, wriggle his shoulders, stave away some punches with his arms, but he can't free himself from beneath this raging inferno and the strength is draining from his body.

Home Sweet Home.
A few minutes before the confrontation between Jed and Carl Thomson and running into the present.
Anna.

She awakes with a start, realizes the half hour's up and Jed will be home very soon and she's not even sliced the bread yet. She blames her extended catnap on being pregnant and now, moving quickly considering her belly has grown considerably in the last two months, she takes a loaf from the breadbin, a serrated knife – the thin flexible variety, not very sharp, from the drawer. She's on the first slicing when, above the volume of the television, she thinks she hears a shout, like a row's starting. Then there's a hollow thud on the flank of Home Sweet Home, like someone's been flung violently against the barge. Anna, a terrible dread churning up in her expanded stomach, and Jed's name on her mouth, is out of the door and onto the towpath. (It could later be construed as intentional, or unintentional, that the thin breadknife is still in her hand.) In the towpath light, its power diluted by the sweeping rain, Carl Thomson, paranoia fuelled by chemical substances, is giving Jed Rawlins the hiding of his life.

This is what Anna sees: the pummelling of Jed, the rise and fall of Carl Thomson's fists into the face of her beloved. She screams a high-pitched wail of terror.

'Stop. Stop. Stop.'

But Carl Thomson won't stop and frightened panic-stricken Anna, desperately craving the end of this horror show, is onto Carl Thomson, trying to drag him off with one hand and stabbing him with the other. It's a frenzy of blows. But the serrated, and extremely flexible bread knife, hasn't been designed for this job. It buckles and bends and doesn't really penetrate. (All that Anna's frenzied strokes will result in is a series of shallow random cuts, a seepage of blood through Carl Thomson's wet coat.) There's the falling of rain, the halo around the path-light, mud underfoot, scattered fish and chips trampled into the ground and, accompanying every strike with the knife, a hysterical scream from Anna.

Jed's quietened, he's stopped struggling. He's completely out of it. He lies face up and his eyes are filled with mud and rain. His arms are unprotecting; his defences have crumbled. Now Carl Thomson can give Anna his undivided attention. He sweeps her off his back, staggers her, takes his feet. Eyes the knife. Calls her a fucking bitch and moves in on her. Paranoia and chemicals, hatred and brutal combat, have completely overwhelmed his senses. The animal in him has chewed and swallowed any remnants of his reason, so Carl Thomson, never hinged at the best of times, is in a place of no consequence where extreme revenge is going hand in hand with extreme violence. The knife is dropped, twisted from Anna's grip. She manages one more helpless scream for assistance before Carl Thomson's hands are around her throat, his contorted face, his mad mad eyes inches from hers, as he begins to squeeze the life out of 'You fucking bitch.'

And her unborn baby.

CHAPTER TWENTY-TWO

The Shed.
Same night.

Moses has been having a quiet evening; he's quite relaxed, his fingers plucking on his guitar, searching out the notes, joining them link by link. He can lose himself in this and the rain pitching on the roof, sweeping across the window offering no distraction. He'll pause occasionally, take a swig of coke, perhaps jot down a few words to accompany the tune he's working on.

Moses woke up this morning with that tune slipping and snaking inside his head. He'd grunted throughout breakfast, pen and sheet in front of himself, trying to transfer melodic thought to notation. Later it's to Saturday's Music Club session with Mrs Martin, Broome School's music teacher – young and very keen despite the Mrs – who's been working with Moses for two years now. She's discovered that her enthusiasm for the subject has taken her well beyond the formal hours of education.

She places a blank music sheet in front of Moses and he plucks out a song. She asks that he play it as slowly as possible, even stops him between notes. Singles them out.

'That one for there. That's where it goes. Do you hear the sequence. The order?'

She marks them down and then they go over it. Again and

again. Month after month until a whole year has passed. Within this time she'll take a songbook, open it a page, get Moses to play while she softly sings the lyrics. It's lyrics he brings to her one day and almost shyly says, 'I've written this, Miss.'

He hands her a couple of pages of A5 paper and Mrs Martin smooths them out, reads once, reads twice. Moses has written twenty-five lines about a woman who sparkles, shimmers, when she dances in the sunlight, moonlight, firelight. She's a Crystal Lady.

'Need to do a bit more work on it I think, Miss.'

Mrs Martin's still putting her thoughts together. She'd expected to read a lyric poem about young love, a crush on a teacher – Less of that Mrs Martin! – not something as unusual as this. It reads like an old-fashioned ballad and ends when the crystals dull and the light fades in them. It's sad but it's also 'Good, Moses. It's really good.'

'Could I play it for you, Miss?'

This casual schoolboy, this raggedy troubadour, perches on a stool and starts to play the introduction. His voice joins the music and he sings quietly, telling the story of the Crystal Lady until the last line's finished and he strums out the ending of an unsettled soul, restless forever.

He grins at her. 'What do you think, Miss?'

'It was lovely, Moses. Just lovely.' Mrs Martin has a lump in her throat that her words have difficulty getting past. Moses is down from his perch, putting his guitar in its case.

'See you next week, Miss.'

Mrs Martin can only nod.

When Moses has gone Mrs Martin cries softly to herself. It's not exactly like A Star is Born, but it's somewhere in the same arena. She dabs her eyes with her handkerchief, knows it's stupid to cry, but a part of her life she loves will soon be going. School won't hold Moses for much longer; he'll be spreading his wings, sitting somewhere under the stars close to a smoky fire, swigging beer from the bottle, a pretty young girl watching him, singing along. Or he'll be on an underpass with an echo to his voice and a hat under his feet to catch the pennies of strangers. Moses will have the freedom of his youth to come and go as he pleases, seeing the world with his music, and she'll grow old and dry in teaching posts in glass and brick institutions.

When she's home this night Mrs Martin pours herself a large glass of red wine. Her husband says that she's starting early, and is 'Anything the matter?'

'Nothing that another red won't put right,' she says.

But that's not true and she knows it isn't and she says she's going to have a shower. She stands under the stream of hot water and lets it rinse away the falling of her tears.

So this evening Moses has lost himself in his search for the elusive chords and it's only in the silence between notes that he thinks he hears a scream. A woman's scream. Moses cocks an ear and then there it is again, a high-pitched screech of fear cutting a swathe through the wind and the rain. Moses's guitar is carefully, but quickly, laid down. The shed door is pulled open and he steps out into rain to locate the sound of conflict, of a strangled cry of: 'Help me. Please help me.'

What a not-quite-believing Moses sees under the flickering towpath lamp is pregnant waif Anna being held by her throat, shaken like a rag doll. For a few frozen seconds Moses watches in disbelief and in those seconds he catches her struggle, her flailing arms. Her desperate plea. The scene shimmers in Moses's vision like there's murder, a killing in the air. It's closing in, thickening around the spotlight that's shining on this tableau of violence.

It's dreamlike, Moses's exit from the shed, the twenty paces to the strangulation of Anna: the trip, the stagger, when he clips the heap of palings for the picket fence that Ed still hasn't had time to erect. So that's why the four-foot length of tanalised timber – swollen in weight by the absorption of H2O – is in his hands when he's waded into the battle scene. Jed's groaning in the mud, Anna's being throttled by a madman, shaken like a rat, and Moses, doing the only thing he can do, strikes with his wooden broadsword. It lands high on the back of Carl Thomson's head, a glancing blow that skids off the top of his cranium and will undoubtably leave a hairless furrow for years to come. (That's if there are years to come.) But Carl Thomson doesn't relax his grip, it's like the blow has had no effect. He's a pitbull latched onto his prey in a coupling to the death. It's going to take something more than savage to break this grip on an Anna who's wilting, whose struggles are fading. Her arms are hanging down to her sides and only her fingers are twitching. Her time is dying. And Moses has a desperate voice, pitched between command and plea.

'Fucking let her go. Let her go.'

Moses's second swing of his weapon is a panicked swipe, a huge sweeping arc of pressure-treated cedar. Another broadsword delivery but much harder and unintentionally accurate to a millimetre. Moses's inch thick board thuds into the nape of Carl Thomson's taut neck just where his spinal cord and his vertebrae meet his brain stem; the killing spot. It's an instant disconnection, an instant death, that freezes all movement in Carl Thomson's body.

Then he collapses, spills down onto the path, onto the prone form of poor Jed. He's no outstretched arms to break his fall. Anna is coughing, retching, rubbing her throat and Moses is standing there, in the gloom and the rain, with his fingerprints smeared all over the murder weapon. But Moses doesn't yet know that the mark of Cain is going to be imprinted on his forehead. At this moment, he's thinking what to do? What to do? and all those thoughts are directed into his cell phone and relayed to the man who's been a father to him for all of his life. 'Dad. You got to come home. Something bad's happened.'

The last time 'something bad' had happened at Vixens Mere was before Moses was born. Big Ed remembers it well.

Before this phone call, Big Ed and company had been finishing up a 'rare old night' four miles away at the Bull and Dragon. The three of them, Ed, Milly, and Pigman Pete (He's on this outing without Marlene, as she's with her daughter who has produced yet another offspring – the head count can no longer be covered on one hand. Marlene says, 'It's only for a week, Pete. See her back onto her feet.') have had a rather nice pub meal. Here at the Bull and Dragon there are familiar faces and a blazing fire in the public bar. The talking topic is the filthy weather outside but inside it's warm and friendly, and suits the quaffing of several more pints of Banks Bitter, Big Ed and Pigman Pete's drink of choice tonight. Milly is on a cider crusade and, although doing very well, is nagging at Ed's elbow about him steadying up a bit 'cos of driving back. Big Ed reckons that it's OK, no worries, he's only to put the key in the ignition and the old van could find her own way home. The convivial part of the evening ends when Big Ed's phone rings. He fumbles it out of his pocket with one handful of fingers – he's in the Gents and his other hand is preoccupied with the course of direction – and takes Moses's call: 'You got to come back, Dad.'

A slightly befuddled Ed asks, 'Why? What's the matter?'

From Moses there's an urgent garbling of someone attacking Jed and Anna and someone else lying on the path. 'And he's not moving, Dad. Not moving.' Big Ed says that he's on his way and for Moses not to do nothing except to be careful. To his company it's a curt, 'We've got to go,' and Milly's with him, questioning as they hurry across the carpark.

'Is it Moses, Ed?'

'Sort of. Think so. Don't know what's happened. Bit of drama by the sound of it.'

Which isn't a very enlightening answer but is enough to lead to a rapid re-squashing of three bodies into the front of Big Ed's vehicle.

Big Ed puts his foot down and it's a jolting, hair-raising, non-sober ride down the narrow lanes back to Vixens Mere. Ed's phone goes again and Milly answers. But it's not Moses, it's Brodie saying that he's held up in Broome. Won't be back tonight and would someone mind letting Mick out for a piddle? He gets a short shrift, 'Yeah. Yeah. OK, Brodie' and a rapid disconnection. Pete, ignorant to the ongoing atmosphere, is complaining because he's brought his pint with him and he's spilling more than he's drinking. He's also 'sogged' – his word – 'his fucking fag'. The next fuck uttered is by Big Ed and it's to do with Pete keeping his gob shut 'cos there's more important stuff going on right now. Exactly what that is is revealed less than ten minutes later in the aftermath of the Battle of Vixens Mere.

This is what they see under the halo of the towpath light.

The rain's still drifting down and Jed, legs splayed, now propping himself up on the wet ground, is seeping blood from his nose and mouth: a croaking sobbing Anna is mopping at his wounds with a tea towel. Moses is standing guard over the prone form of Carl Thomson, still gripping onto his wooden sword like he's waiting for a twitching of movement to strike again. But there's a stillness to the form of Carl Thomson, he's frozen into his collapse like a toppled snowman in the mud.

For the immediate, for Big Ed and Milly, there's the prising of the weapon from Moses's iron clutch, a hurling away of it, and then Milly holding her sopping wet, shaking boy to her. Big Ed wraps his coat around Moses.

'Let's get him inside, Milly.' *Get him inside out of this shit night where all that could go wrong has gone wrong.*

250

But they don't know just how wrong. Yet.

Pigman Pete helps Jed to his feet, and Jed, groaning, spitting blood from his split lips, grips to Pete like a blind man. Which he nearly is because both of his eyes are virtually closed, thanks to the damage administered by Carl Thomson. In the stepping to the gangplank of Home Sweet Home Jed staggers under Pete's support, which doesn't help Pete much because eight pints of best bitter hasn't exactly done wonders for Pete's own legwork. A sobbing Anna leads the way onto the barge, helps to lay the wounded Jed onto the sofa. In the light they can see more clearly the damage done to poor Jed but despite this he still manages to croak for a 'smoke, Anna. A smoke.'

Pete says perhaps they should get Jed to A & E but Jed shakes his head, as vehemently as he can in his condition. It's a hoarse, 'No Pete. No. I'll be all right.' Pete thinks that Milly'll look in on him. She'll know what to do. Meanwhile there's that other matter laying so still in the wet ground on the edge of the towpath.

The other matter is being curiously inspected by Big Ed who's prodding it with his foot.

'Don't like this,' says Big Ed to Pigman Pete.

'Who is it? What happened then?'

From a nervous Moses Big Ed's had a brief explanation of a fight and 'He was strangling her, Dad. Hands round her throat. I hit him, Dad. With the wood.' Big Ed actually feels quite proud of his boy for helping out their friend. That's only until there's not a flicker of response to the gentle probing of Big Ed's right boot. And now Milly, leaving Moses with a massive brandy and milk and promising to be 'only gone a few minutes' has brought a flashlight to bear on the scene. She says 'Let's get him up to the shed. Find out what's going

251

on.' Big Ed and Pete lift and drag the floppy Carl Thomson into the building, flick the lights on, lay him out on the floor for Milly to note the blue of his lips. She puts her ear to his mouth, a hand on his heart. Nothing. She looks to Ed, to Pete.

'He's dead,' she says like she can't believe it. 'He's dead. What the fuck are we going to do?'

The 'we' is inclusive of the battered Jed, pregnant Anna who's carrying Carl Thomson's fingerprints as a necklace, and then there's Moses who rode to the rescue of a damsel in distress and committed murder.

There's a person, a body here, that's been struck in the face – Jed's work. Stabbed countless times, albeit shallowly but with plenty of blood flow, using a serrated breadknife – Anna's work. Hit twice with a wooden stave, once across the skull and again in that perfect spot where a trained assassin would strike – Moses's work.

If ever the crime of murder carried the label of joint enterprise it has to be this one. Open and shut case. A drug-dealers' falling out. A young hooligan. Make an example of them. Lock 'em up and throw away the key. So that'll be three lives – and an unborn one – ruined for years and years to come. Perhaps forever. When all of the evidence is added together it has to seem that a concerted effort was made to intentionally kill Carl Thomson. That's if you were a policeman, and that's if you ever were to find out what's gone on in this wet and stormy night at Vixens Mere.

The Shed is now a mortuary and the corpse is stretched out on the concrete floor surrounded by three reluctant viewers: Milly, Big Ed, and Pigman Pete.

Milly says to big Ed, 'We have to get rid of him.'

'Get rid of him. What? Bury him? Burn him?'

'He's got to disappear. No trace. There can't be a trace, Ed.'

Milly sits down and they pass the thinking cap and cigarettes between themselves. Back and forward. Forward and back. Cigarettes and ideas against the backdrop of a corpse on the floor.

They think out a six-foot hole in Hunters Woods. A sinking in the deepest part of Vixens. (It's not so crowded down there now.) A huge bonfire. A funeral pyre. A forty-mile drive to the seaside with a dead body in the back of the van. Milly has her head in her hands; if ever she needed help from the Other World it's now. There's a silence here only interrupted by the occasional, 'What if?' and then Pigman Pete says, brightly considering the circumstances, 'I know, Milly,' because into his mind has flitted the long-ago tales of children who were maimed because they went to deliver a bucket of swill at feed time, of Bertie Saunders and his pair of sows. *Only found a tooth, mind. That's all.* And a tooth wouldn't be difficult to get shot of if it came to that.

'What do you know, Pete?'

'I know what to do with this.' Pete motions to the stab-ridden and bloody body. 'With him.'

'What Pete. What?'

'Pigs eat everything, Milly. I can feed him to the pigs. Feed him to my ladies.'

Big Ed says, 'But he's a fair old lump, Pete. It'll take them a week to get rid of him. And we … '

Pete says enthusiastically, 'No we'll cut him up. Saw him up.' Pete's warming to the subject. 'Give 'em a bit at a time.'

Big Ed ponders on the thought of manageable chunks, thinks they're desperate enough to give it a pop. Milly, stifling a retch at the thought of what's being proposed, says that if they don't mind she really should go back to the Crystal Lady to watch over Moses while 'you two do what needs to be done.' She leaves them talking about saws and choppers while she does what she needs to do.

* * *

There are scenes of Milly's life that have embedded themselves into her consciousness: *fifteen years old and stepping out into the dawning of a summer's day. Looking back and knowing she'll never be going back. Sleeping rough. Sleeping in squats where timber boards and doors have been burnt in the fireplaces. Losing days and weeks to chemical dreams. Huddling up to a stranger for nighttime warmth. Passing smokes around in a mini bus packed with hot bodies. Throb of base at music festivals. Waking in Big Ed's van and beginning life again.*

And then Moses's first smile into her face.

And now this which she'll remember forever and ever.

Aboard the Crystal Lady Milly sits with a pale and subdued Moses. Her hand is on his shoulder when all she really wants is to envelop him, smother him, keep him safe from the darkness. There's a slight tremor to Moses's voice as he asks, 'What's happening, Mum? Who was it? Has he woke up?'

Milly shakes her head and says very slowly, 'He can't wake up, Moses. He's dead.'

Milly can't really believe she's saying these words to her boy. She wants to take away Moses's fear, his hurt. His responsibility. But she is going to shield him and it starts after his, 'Was it 'cos I hit ...?'

Milly is straight in – although she can't know for sure – with, 'No. No. Not your fault. He lost too much blood, Moses. That's why he died.' And only a postmortem could disprove her statement. That's if there was ever going to be one. (Which is looking more unlikely by the minute.) She asks Moses to swear on Big Ed's life that he'll never – never ever – tell a soul about what's happened. Moses, a little affronted, a little affected by Milly's serving of plenty of brandy in his hot milk, and not forgetting he's half a dozen inches taller than Milly, says he doesn't need to, he's not a kid. He's not slow on the uptake. He understands what's gone down. Moses is pulling himself together. Taking a perspective. (Who knows, he might even get a song out of this evening?)

Milly, at the stove now, brings a second pan of milk to the boil this night and tips it, along with another more than generous tilt of brandy, into a large mug. She also claims a huge slug of the liquor for herself and wipes her lips with the back of her hand.

'Get this down you, Moses. It'll help you sleep.'

Moses settles in front of the stove, mug in his hand, as Milly leaves for the next staging post. He thinks brandy and milk is a pleasant enough drink and he takes a swallow that Pigman Pete would be proud of and thinks that he just might do his self another when this one's finished.

To Anna and Jed it's nearly the same story to tell but Milly's thinking to break it more slowly because of Anna's condition.

Milly opens with: 'That bloke who caused all the trouble, he's gone.'

Anna says in panic, 'But he'll come for us again.' She puts her hands over her face, mumbles fearfully through her fingers, 'Especially after this, Milly.'

'Trust me, Anna. He won't be coming back.'

Jed's been easing himself to sitting on the settee and before Milly can get out her words of explanation, he's out with the doubt that hurts his swollen mouth.

'You can't know that, Milly. You don't fucking know what he's like.'

Milly thinks that she now knows Carl Thomson well enough now to identify his bloody corpse. Milly, done with pussy-footing about, angry and tired, and worried sick about Moses because of what has been brought to her door by these two, snaps out: 'I do fucking know that he won't be back. He's dead, Jed. Stone cold fucking dead.' There it's out again and in this time to Jed and Anna it sounds even more real. Stone cold dead. The meaning behind Milly's words chill the air. There's no honeying of these words, just an enormity that visibly strikes Jed and Anna.

Anna's cry of 'Dead? Oh, Jed what are we going to do?' is more a wail of anguish. 'What's going to happen to us, Milly?'

Milly says that they have to be trusting. Things are in hand and it's just a matter of lying doggo for a while. That's all, and that's what she hopes. They've just got to leave it to Big Ed and Pete and she's not going to provide any details of the disposal of Carl Thomson. It makes Milly feel sick just thinking about it anyway.

Then Milly takes herself on a short walk to stand on the edge of Vixens Mere and draw on a nice thick cigarette; she needs a few head-clearing minutes on her own. The rain is still drifting down in a thick drizzle and there's mud under her feet. Mud and blood. Mud and blood draining into the dark silent waters of Vixens Mere. It must be so near to bursting with secrets that any more might gag in its throat.

CHAPTER TWENTY-THREE

The Shed.
Lights blazing and windows blanketed in.
One o'clock in the morning.
Pigman Pete, Big Ed and the body of Carl Thomson.
Carl Thomson has been mugged of the contents of his pockets; cigarettes, roll of banknotes, loose change, car keys. He's been stripped naked and is hanging upside down from a roof beam. He has also been disembowelled – all internals are in a couple of squishy builders' heavy duty plastic bags. Pigman Pete has removed Carl Thomson's head and arms and is dropping him to the floor so that he can separate legs from his torso. A polythene sheet under the corpse is puddled with blood. The stench inside the Shed is more than awful.

Pete's thinking that it's a good job he's got his wellies and overalls on; this is a lot messier than what he thought it would be. At Broome's Pork Products they hang the carcass for a day or so to let the body drain. Pete doesn't have that luxury here and there's a generous splashing of blood down his front, his hands and sleeves, his paddling wellies. He has a very thick roll-up – courtesy of Big Ed's special baccy tin – wedged into his mouth but it's hardly taking the edge off the aroma of Carl Thomson's spilled internal body parts.

There's an hour or more of a second joint enterprise offence of the night in the cutting and sawing and chopping, packing away severed arms and legs, head, split down and quartered torso, and then the ex-drug dealer, ex-violent thug, ex-nesting cuckoo – ex-everything in fact, including living – is separated into five of Big Ed's heavy duty, and most importantly, waterproof builders' bags. (Throughout all of this exercise Pete's worked with the overriding feeling that he's somehow repaying Milly and Ed for all the kindness they've shown him over the years. They rescued him. Without them he'd have died in a ditch a long time ago. This is his chance to show them, to help them, and his heart swells with love for his adopted family. He's doing something good for them, he's getting them out of the shit.) The plastic sheet, and other detritus is put by for the burning, and the butchering tools, 'Can't see me using them again,' accompanied by a shudder of Big Ed's shoulders, will join them. All the clothing worn by everyone in attendance will be gathered and added to the pyre. Then it'll be all done. All tidied. All traces eliminated in a week that's going to be a very long one. One small hiccup though is the car that carried Carl Thomson to his execution is parked at the entrance to Vixens Mere.

It's nine o'clock of the morning after and a sleep-deprived Big Ed is driving a yawning Milly to the shops to 'get a few things to eat. Get Moses a couple of his favourite cream doughnuts.' Then Ed, half listening to Milly, sees the vehicle, jams on the anchors, mutters, 'Christ, the car, Milly. Do you reckon it's *his* car?'

This car, dirty, scratched, half-bald tyres, cracked wing mirrors, is parked haphazardly (and hurriedly and angrily with oaths and curses the night before) on the green verge. Milly says in resignation, as though she knows, 'Reckon it could be, Ed.'

There's one way to find out and that's to take Carl Thomson's keys from the glove compartment – they were awaiting disposal in a random rubbish bin – and try the fob.

(Carl Thomson's roll of banknotes will find a much better home.) The answer is that the car doors click open and Ed and Milly take a dekko inside. Unclean is too kind a word to describe an interior that's strewn with empty crisp packets, spilled biscuits, dumped curry containers, upended beer cans, and some things that are just not describable. Milly, getting a whiff, says, 'What a fucking stink,' and Big Ed thinks he's smelt much worse within a stone's throw of here.

'We've got to shift it, Milly.'

The shifting is a few hundred yards down the lane onto, and off a woodland track. There's a quick prayer that no one will discover its remote hiding place. But that's only until late tonight – or a very early morning – when Big Ed will remove the vehicle, drive it to Broome Common where most of the area's stolen cars are set alight. Ed will prise off the number plates, pour five gallons of diesel over the seats and fire the car, let it blaze into the night sky; another statistic put down to joy riders. And that will be that. For the car anyway.

Vixens Mere.
Monday.
Six o'clock in the morning.
Pigman Pete.

Dawn's yet to break. Pete lifts a sealed builders' bag into the back of his work van (he's unsure what bodily part – or parts – of Carl Thomson he's taking for an early ride) and sets off to work.

It's a cautious drive through the lanes and into the yard of Broome's Pork Products for Pigman Pete. Pre-dawn, only the perimeter and door-lamps shed a subdued glow into the dark. Pete parks behind the entrance of Breeding Sows' Unit – the area not overseen by security cameras where him and Singing Sam take their baccy breaks – and then he lights up a cigarette, hawks up something indescribable, while he has a crafty look around just to check that no-one's about. Pete gives himself the all-clear and he's to the back of the van for the unloading. Then into the Unit to the pen where a dozen huge, ravenously hungry, and extremely pregnant sows have pricked up their ears and started squealing for their initial course of breakfast. But first my lovely ladies, it's this. Pete untapes the neck of the sack and upends it into the corral. Carl Thomson's partial remains have heated up inside the plastic bag and a waft of infragrant air hits Pete. He gags and closes his throat as he shakes out a foot to the knee, severed upper leg, and a messy wriggling of intestine, into the straw and shit.

Carl Thomson – these parts of him anyway – is mobbed, torn even more apart in tug o'wars, slobbered over, crunched up, gulped into bellies to provide sustenance for the next, and very imminent, generation of porkers. In ten minutes there's nothing left, 'Not a sausage,' Pete thinks, which is probably not the best of analogies to use. Now his herd are looking to him in appealing pink-eyed anticipation for their breakfast proper. Pete spreads the much sweeter smelling feedstuffs of ground barley, wheat, and corn along the feeding troughs. There's a gentler grunting, snuffling, and chewing in a more contented orderly feeding of this second helping. But another thought for Pete is that he'll never look at his ladies in the same way again; they've crossed a line and behaved like animals.

The next four mornings follow the same pattern: pick up the cuts of meat, tip out a joint of flesh, or a quarter of torso, guts, and watch his ladies wolf it down. Pete wonders if it's his imagination but do his pigs seem perkier, more alert, better conditioned? These unknowing accomplices, due to farrow in the next few days, look a picture of health. Mr Long – proprietor of Broome Pork Products – pays the unit an afternoon visit, comments on Pete's porcine herd.

'Well done, young man.' Everyone's young to eighty-year-old Mr Long. 'You're doing a marvellous job. Marvellous. Never seen such healthy animals. Keep it up. Keep it up.'

For Pete the worst – the fifth and final – episode of gruesome disposal is Carl Thomson's hairy head. Pete drops it in amongst his charges and for half a minute they eye it up. It also seems that the expired drug-dealer eyes them back because one of Carl Thomson's eyes, a milky white marble, is fully open and the other looks halfway through a blink. Gives Pete a touch of the creeps. The sows surround the head with curiosity, nudge it with their noses, push it between each other, take a nibble, a tear of blackening flesh. Pass it back again.

'Come on, girls. Get on with it. It's not Match of the fucking Day.'

Pete wants it over, the last shred of evidence accounted for. He wants to say to Big Ed and Milly – the two people he loves most on this earth, now followed closely by Marlene – that it's all done. He's helped his best friends through a very difficult patch and he's feeling so grateful for their gratitude that it's warming him from the inside.

In a different sort of warming to task, the heavily pregnant breeding sows have now gobbled down Carl Thomson's ears. His nose has gone and his lips are chewed off. All the soft flesh and hair is stripped away, swallowed, and only the brain-leaching cranium is left to crunch to splinters between competing hungry, and very powerful, jaws. Very soon there isn't a trace left of Carl Thomson's bodyless head. That's it. All done. Finished with relief. Pete sneaks out the back for a fag as the factory-farm staff are filtering onsite.

Singing Sam – whose working day always starts with a roll-up out the back – joins Pete.

'You're early again, Pete. You looking for a pay rise?' This is accompanied by a bout of coughing from the very depths of his lungs.

Pete says, 'Like to get ahead I do, Sam,' and Sam stubs out his cigarette, sighs, reckons he should make his start as well.

'See you later, Pete.'

What Sam means is 'see you in an hour,' when they take their next clandestine tobacco break.

Back inside his working quarters, observed in contentment by his replete brood, Pete begins to shovel, scrape, and brush the floor of the sows' area. He dumps the sows' dumps into a trailer, can't help thinking about old Bertie Saunders, thinks he'll keep a watch out for any stray molars. Then to take his mind off current events Pete forwards himself to the evening, to the welcome return of the amply proportioned Marlene.

After his shift and back at Saddleback, Pete's spruced himself up. He's had a long warm shower, shampooed his sparse hair, shaved his face until it's as smooth as a baby's bottom, soaped and flannelled everywhere that matters, paying particular attention to his manhood, doused himself in deodorant, and dressed himself in his cleanest attire. He picks up a case of strong lager en route to Marlene's and presents himself on her doorstep at seven thirty on the dot.

'Pete,' and the pleasure shows in her voice at seeing him. 'I've missed you,' she says.

Pete is halfway through, 'Me too,' as she's pulling him into her hallway and clasping her arms around him. Pete's reciprocating but his arms aren't quite long enough to completely encircle her. Still, his face is where he's been dreaming of for the last few days.

'Dinner's in the oven but let's have a drink first,' Marlene says.

Two Stellas are swiftly detabbed and the couple take to the sofa and sit, glued together, as Pete wallows in his lager and the closeness of their love. Heaven. The air is infused with the scents of Pete's deodorant, Marlene's powerful perfume, a hinting of alcohol, a cloud of lust, and ... and of roasting pork sizzling in the hot oven, bathing in its own juices.

Marlene says, 'Your favourite. Got a monster joint specially for you. I know how you like the crackling, Pete. Be loads of it.'

Intruding into Pete's consciousness are the images of his pink-eyed porcines crunching up the last remains – the head – of Carl Thomson. Pete feels bile start to rise from his stomach and he puts his hand over his mouth, burps, and says, 'I don't feel very well, Marlene.'

She peers closely at him, tells him he does look a little green about the gills but, 'You'll soon perk up when you get some of my decent grub inside you.' She laughs. 'Least I hope so; we got some catching up to do, my Handsome.' (This is accompanied by a very personal fondling.)

There's to be no excuses to forestall a re-consummation of their relationship tonight and Pete quickly downs several beers: 'My, you've got a thirst on, Pete,' to blunt his taste buds and give him the hope of reaching the evening's main prize without throwing up over the dining table. Or Marlene's magnificent bosom.

Vixens Mere.
Sunday morning.
Eight o'clock.
Milly and Big Ed et al.

The Shed has been splashed out with diesel. Anything with even the most tenuous connection to the slaying of the Broome drug-dealer is heaped inside. Carl Thomson's residue taints the timbers, has soaked into the planking. Bad karma abounds.

At the door of the Shed Big Ed says to Milly, 'Let's get this over with' and he holds his lighter to a sheaf of newspaper until it flares into a torch then, stepping inside, Ed fires a heap of liberally doused burnables. He watches the catching, thinks it's a bit on the slow side and prods it with his foot. The disturbance creates an instant response and there's a whoomph, a conflagration that singes his eyebrows and his beard. Big Ed shoots out of the door, rubs his eyes and, stifling a cough, woolly hat askew, emerges in a cloud of smoke. Milly thinks, 'Like a genie out the lamp.' Oh, but if only he was that genie, she could make a wish that none of this had ever happened. Big Ed, coughing taking over, says, 'Christ, I need a fag after that,' and Milly passes over her roll-up. Then they watch as the flames take a hold, the fire starts to roar, and a plume of black smoke heads for the skies. The glass in the windows shatter, the felted roof twists into itself, the creosoted timbers crackle for the devil, the plank walls collapse. Everything burns: the evenings of fun and flirting and singing and drinking feed the flames; all the nights sitting quietly around the wood burner, sipping from a bottle and chewing the fat; a gentle plucking of a guitar and a voice singing softly along; the rasp of saw on bone, the cleave of a hatchet, the slicing of flesh. The charnel house burns.

Now the audience has grown because a bonfire is an open invitation to a gathering. Flames will always draw people and this one draws Moses and Jed and Anna. (Not Pigman Pete. He's having a warm and comfortable lie-in at Marlene's). It also draws Brodie, Karen Jones and Lorrie. There are two teams in the audience: those who know why there's a Sunday morning inferno and those that don't. The Don't Knows are joined by Ethan James on his tractor.

'Fucking hell,' he says to Ed. 'You could have warned me you were going to do this. I nearly called the fire brigade.'

Milly says, 'Too much rot in it. Falling apart, Ethan. Time for a new one.'

Of course it wasn't falling apart but it stank of death: the floor was stained with streaks of blood, and the timbers carried the microscopic spores of butchering.

Ethan, still moaning, goes back to his work in the fields. The others drift away, and Milly and Big Ed pull the bonfire together, sweat in its heat, squint in its flaring. They turn the ends in, make sure that all their sins are burnt to ash. Ed says that their new shed will be built 'Over there.' He waves at a spot thirty feet away. 'Not on here. Definitely not on here.'

The burnt patch of ground seems to stay barren for a long time before weeds and sparse grass make inroads into its black heart. One thing that Milly notices though, is that even Billy the Kid skirts that piece of ground. 'Like Billy knows it's cursed,' she thinks. Milly won't even look in that direction in the moonlight in case she sees the swaying ghost of a hanging man.

Crystal Lady.
Two weeks after the killing of Carl Thomson.
Four o'clock in the morning.
Rising wind from southwest rippling the waters of Vixens Mere.
Slight rocking of the barge.
Moses and Seanmhair.

Moses is into his third nightmare of the week. He's stayed awake for as long as possible every night since Carl's death. He has dark circles under his eyes and his body is a listless slave to orders. If he was going to school he'd be nodding off at his desk.

In Moses's dream he's waiting under the lamplight on the towpath. He knows that he's waiting for Carl Thomson. Outside of the light the darkness is thick and heavy, heaving like the sea and, as Moses watches, it lightens, parts, and Carl Thomson shambles out of the dark. His head is tilted to one side like his neck is broken. Like he's a zombie in a scene from a horror movie; white-eyed with a twisted broken body. He's holding out his hands, palms upwards, and Moses knows why he's here, what he wants. Revenge. But Moses is frozen, can't move a limb, as Carl Thomson shuffles forward, closer, closer, almost touching, until Moses can feel the breath on his face; stinging hot breath. Scorching hot breath that drives him out of this dream and to an awakening on Crystal Lady.

Moses lies in his bed, watching the clock push towards the fourth hour. He's going to make sure he stays awake because he can't, just can't, go back there tonight. In two or three hours Big Ed will be clattering around the kitchen and Moses usually joins him, nibbles at a slice of toast, takes a sip of tea. Big Ed will say, 'Sleep all right, Moses?' and he'll lie, 'Not bad, Dad. Not bad.'

Thirty minutes past four is the last telling of time for Moses tonight and that is through drooping lids, slits of vision. His bed is warm, and exhaustion is staking its claim over him. He yawns, feels himself starting to go. Stop. Stop. A half-hearted stop because the fight's draining out of Moses and he's slowly sinking into … into another dream, a different dream, where *there's a hand on his forehead, fingers gently circling, stroking his skin. Comforting. There're words, gentle words in a strange Scottish accent. An old woman's soft voice matching the stroking of those words.*

'It's all right. There's nothing going to hurt you.'

Moses is a child sitting on a grassed bank by a dusty track that runs downhill to fade in the distance. The old woman of the voice is cradling his small body to her, holding him, protecting him. Keeping him safe.

'Sleep, Moses. Go to sleep. It's all right.'

Then Moses does just that. He sleeps deeply, soundly, without any incursion of Carl Thomson. He sleeps past break-fast time. Milly pokes her head in the door, sees he's still in the land of Nod and leaves him there. When Moses wakes, feeling much more like the fourteen-year-old he is, the dream is still fresh in his head. With the image of the old woman comes a name, like he knows her. *Seanmhair.* He says it several times to himself, commits it to a memory that easily holds a catalogue of tunes and lyrics.

Eight o'clock.
Crystal Lady's kitchen.
Moses is still sleeping.
Milly says to Big Ed over the breakfast that Moses is missing this morning, 'Did you hear anything last night?'

Big Ed, halfway through a fried egg sandwich – bacon's off the menu for a while yet – asks, 'Hear anything? Like what, Milly?'

Milly, never missing an opportunity for a dig, says, ''Bout half four, five maybe, when you'd stopped snoring for a minute. Sure I heard ...' ponders for a moment, 'like someone's voice from Moses's room but when I got up for a piddle I listened at his door. Silent as the grave.'

Big Ed says perhaps he'd sneaked a girl in there and Milly reckons that'll be the last thing on his mind considering what's happened.

'I was only joking, Milly. Trying to lighten things up.'

There's a moment's silence and Milly says, 'Ed, I'm sorry. It's just that ... you know.'

Ed knows. He knows that every time he passes a police-car, he'll watch in his mirror for a flash of headlights, a blue light, the wail of a siren. He follows the news on television, checks out Broome Community Facepage.

'Think I'm getting paranoid,' he tells Milly.

Milly says that a bit of paranoia will keep them on their toes. After all, they have assisted in the disposal of two bodies although, 'For the right reasons, Ed. For the right reasons.'

But sometimes Ed, looking for reassurance that everything is dead and buried – or as good as – will ask her to read the

Tarot. Milly'll spread the cards for his selection, explain the predictions as she pulls his fortune together, 'See this one paired with that one on that one means ...'

'Means nothing to worry about, eh, Milly?'

'Nothing to worry about, Ed.'

'Once more then, Milly. Just to be sure.'

'Fuck's sake, Ed. How many more fucking times?'

There are a few more fucking times but the night of Carl Thomson – like the long ago night of Sandra Day – will slowly fade by degrees until, although it can never be forgotten, everyone will go about their daily business, carrying on as normal. Milly says what else can they do? So that's what they do.

Vixens Mere.
Some more time gone by.

All the guilty parties are relaxing, dropping into everyday life again. Moses has put some time in at school. Big Ed – 'cos the weather's dried up – has been up to Foxes Farm and at long last rebuilt Ethan James's wall. Dinah reckons Hadrian's Wall took less time to build than Ed's. Ed mutters under his breath that they should have got the fucker here to do it then. Aloud he says that considering we live in a welfare state the welfare here is pretty poor. Dinah says if Ed wants a cup of tea he's only got to ask. Ed says that he hopes it includes a couple of chocolate biscuits as well; the sugar will give him some energy. Dinah says that he can have the whole fucking packet if it hurries him up.

Moses.

Seanmhair. The word has stayed with Moses and since *that* night he hasn't had a bad dream; he's had good dreams in the sameness of that verge on a dusty track. He can add the dog, the donkey, and the raggedy old woman. But when

Moses asks Big Ed of the word that's taken residence in his head, Big Ed says, 'Sean – m – hair? Sounds foreign to me, Moses. Any ideas, Milly?'

Milly shakes her head. 'Is it something from school?'

Moses doesn't think he'll tell them about his dreams, it seems it's a secret to keep. Like what happened to Carl Thomson. A secret that must be kept forever.

CHAPTER TWENTY-FOUR

Home Sweet Home.
Anna and Jed.
The wounds have healed; Anna's necklace of bruises has faded, Jed's scrapes and cuts have disappeared. In fact there's nothing physical, not a mark left of the night when Carl Thomson came to call; not even a scrap of Carl Thomson himself. But the residue of what happened remains and Anna, baby bump starting to show even more, has hardly set foot on land for the past month. She feels safer on the barge, she can pull up the drawbridge – gangplank actually – and she can lock the door at night, shut herself away, until Jed returns from his nighttime activities. There's been a few disagreements about Jed plying his trade in the dark corners of Broome. 'I thought that now we don't owe anything to ... to *him*,' Anna can't say the name, can't even think it. 'You could give up. Get a job.' That's what Jed is still promising, to become a regular person.

'We could go somewhere else, Jed, where no-one knows us. Make a fresh start. Me, you and ... and him.' Anna pats her belly. 'Please, Jed. You know, after all that's happened.'

Jed hovers on the brink of decision, sitting on the fence, waiting for something to push him one way or the other. What he doesn't know is that nudge number one is sneaking up on him very quickly.

* * *

Broome.
L&L Furniture Depositary Warehouse.
Eleven o'clock in the morning.
Lennie Lines and Jed.

In his office, sitting above his second-hand but as 'Good as New' furniture store, and behind the pretensions of a huge oak desk, Lennie Lines fixes Jed with a warm benevolent gaze from the smiling presence of his well-fed face.

'Trustworthy you are, Jed. Honest as the day. Great help to me.' As he's dishing out the compliments he's sliding a wrap of white powder across the desk. 'Have this one on me, Jed.' Lennie Lines rolls a twenty pound note into a tight tube, passes it to Jed. Jed partakes without hesitation because, guiltily and unbeknown to Anna, he's starting to drift back to more than the occasional snort. He takes a long satisfying suck up his nose, anticipating the reward of the hit. There's some chat about this and about that and then Lennie Lines says, 'Don't suppose you've seen that Carl Thomson about?'

The question jolts Jed, refreshes some terrible memories, and he has to settle himself before he says he hasn't come across Carl Thomson for a while now.

'Bit strange, really. Bastard seems to have just disappeared,' Lennie Lines muses. 'He owed me so we went to his gaff, cleaned it out. Settled the debt,' He leans back in his chair, points to Jed's place on the desk, the white dust. 'That was his. What you're on now,' he laughs. 'And that. The score.' Jed unrolls the note, makes to give it back to Lennie Lines.

Lennie says for Jed to keep it. 'Have it on Thomson,' he says. 'I don't think we'll be seeing him again in a hurry.'

Jed knows that they won't be seeing Carl Thomson again. Ever. And now he can't touch anything of Carl Thomson's. No. No. And again No. As the images of that night, the fists pounding into his face, the throttling of Anna, her fear for the unborn, the screams of panic and terror, the delivery of the death blow from Moses and the weight of Carl Thomson's body – because that's what it had become in a split second – collapsing on him. The rain softly drifting into a stunned and bruised silence, an acknowledgement that something terrible has happened here.

Then Jed, white trail into his nose, a high in his head, PTSD burrowing into his mind, can't do it. Can't have another sniff of Carl Thomson's coke, can't take the twenty pound of Carl Thomson's money. He can call it revulsion or realisation, whatever fits. But there's something very wrong here. It's like he's looking into the depths of where his life's leading him, and it's a path away from Anna and the unborn.

Jed stands up, thrusts his chair back with unthinking violence. It screeches on the wooden floor. This sudden action jolts himself and startles Lennie Lines.

'For fuck's sake; whatever's the matter, Jed?'

'I can't do this, Lennie. I can't do it no more.'

'What? Can't do fucking what, Jed?'

'This. I'm done, Lennie.'

Jed wrenches open his jacket, yanks out wraps of coke, packets of weed, a couple of watches, a wad of notes, says to a bemused Lennie, 'Few more bits at home. I'll drop them in.'

'What the fuck's going on, Jed?'

'I'm giving up. I'm resigning.'

Lennie, amazed at first and now taking the situation in says, 'You're resigning? You can't resign, Jed.' Then slowly and deliberately, 'Think about it, Jed. Give yourself a day to think about it.' Then, even more slowly and deliberately he tacks on, 'I don't think you'd be wise to pull out, Jed.'

But Jed's shaking his head, his mouth is twisting, his lips are trembling, like he's about to cry, like he's breaking down; his voice is laced with desperation: 'I gotta do it, Lennie. I gotta stop.'

He could explain that he has to get out before a habit becomes a necessity again, before Anna is tied to another loser.

Before another child becomes fatherless. Before he ends up like Carl Thomson. Or like his mother, at the bottom of the mere.

Lennie's looking at Jed, recognising that he's a lost cause, at least for Lennie's cause. Thinks that it's a shame 'cos he quite likes Jed. Still, business is business and it must come first.

'Ok,' Lennie relaxes, 'Bring the rest of the goods back here,' he looks at the clock on the wall, 'at eleven tomorrow morning. Everything. And on the dot, mind. And Jed? You won't let me down, will you? 'Cos what you're doing is bad enough on its own.'

'No Lennie. I won't let you down. I just want out.'

Broome.
Eleven o'clock on the promised day.
Lennie Lines's office above the furniture store.
Jed and Lennie Lines.
On Lennie's desk, in an Aldi Bag-for-Life, is Lennie's returned merchandise.

Jed says, 'It's all there, Lennie. You can check it if you want?'

'Don't need to. I trust you, Jed. Now you're sure ...?'

'I'm sure, Lennie.'

'Nothing I can do to persuade you? 'Cos you're causing me a few problems and I don't like problems.'

Lennie's moved to the window over the yard, above the steps, where five minutes earlier he watched Jed entering.

'Sorry, there's nothing, Lennie.'

'Well, it's a goodbye then, Jed.'

There's to be no farewell shaking of hands, no bonus for good service, just a loud sigh of dismissal from Lennie Lines and a silent sigh of relief from Jed. Whew, glad that's over.

But it's not over because down in the yard a big man, Dave Probert, Lennie's trouble-sorter extraordinaire – monster sized and shaven skulled – has stepped out in front of Jed, stopped him dead in his tracks. From his vantage point Lennie Lines watches this film without sound unwind. Dave Probert says something to Jed that causes Jed to look up to the window, to the profile of Lennie Lines who raises his hand, pauses it, drops it like he's starting a race. Ready. Steady. Go. The Go is a signal to begin the second beating in as many months for poor Jed Rawlins.

It starts with a cruel hard blow to Jed's face. Dave Probert's outsize knuckles flatten Jed's nose, cut open his lips, slash above his eyes, before Jed collapses to the ground. This is a cold professional beating, targeted blows, and booming kicks that leaves a corner of the yard puddled with blood, snot and vomit. Jed ends up curled into a ball, trying to protect his face, his vitals, from this merciless attrition, whimpering like a whipped dog. *If I get out of this alive, Dad. I promise you never again. Never again.* After the deliverance of Lennie's disapproval Big Dave Probert steps back, wipes his boot on Jed's flank. He gives a thumbs up to the watcher in the window, gets a replica in answer and then grabs Jed by the collar of his coat and hauls him to his unsteady feet. Into Jed's battered face he growls a warning: 'Now you fuck off and don't let me see you around here again. Got it?'

Through split lips Jed mumbles, 'Got it. I got it,' and then he's escorted off the premises, shoved out onto the road, too bruised, too hurting, to worry about the curiosity of strangers in their peering faces and their fleeting enquiries: 'You all right mate?' 'You been in an accident?' 'Do you want me to call an ambulance, young man?'

All Jed wants to do is just get home. He has this vision of laying on his sofa and Anna, gentle caring Anna, dipping cotton wool into a bowl of warm water, washing his wounds, soothing his pain. But that's a long walk to home and his limbs are stiffening, his vision's blurring, and his head's pounding. Jed sits himself onto a low brick wall at the end of a drive, tugs out his phone and calls Ed.

'Jed? What can I do for you?'

'Can you do me a favour, Ed?' The words are slow, painful to speak.

'A favour? Sure. Anything except money, Jed,' he chuckles and then, cottoning on, he asks, 'You sound a bit ... well a bit funny. You all right?'

'No Ed, I'm not. Can you pick me up, take me home. Please?'

'What? Yeah. Sure. Where are you?'

'Corner of Stanton Road. By the library.' His voice is not much more than a croak. 'Can you hurry, Ed?'

'Be there in a quarter,' Big Ed says and his next sentence, the promised fifteen minutes later is, 'Christ, Jed, what the fuck's happened to you?'

Jed is a mess still in development and most of it shows on his face; the crookedness of his nose, the boot-mark between eyes that are closing to slits, drying blood under his nostrils, smeared blood on his face, a crimson collar on his shirt.

'Got beat up, Ed.' He's fully croaking now.

Big Ed thinks that could be an understatement and he's also suddenly worried that trouble could be returning to Vixens marina. He's loaded Jed into his van, belted him up, before he asks, 'This anything to do with ... you know. What happened?'

'No, Ed. Nothing. Completely different.' Which it is in a way and it's also not in a way.

'You sure? 'Cos if it is I'll ...' *I'll what? What will I do? Escape from trouble. Take to the cut again at my age with Milly and Moses in tow, find a quiet backwater far, far away? Sleep with a gun under the bed? I'll what? Fuck knows what.*

'No, Ed. It's done. I'm done. I really mean it, Ed. It's all finished.' Then Jed says, very quietly and on the verge of tears, 'I've made a promise to my Dad, Ed.'

Ed has a vision of Mark Rawlins coming aboard the Crystal Lady bringing with him the most terrible news in the world and saying, 'When I'm gone you will keep an eye on Jed for me, won't you? Couldn't bear anything to happen to him.' Milly and Big Ed make their promise, sort of keep their promise.

Ed takes another look at Jed's battered features.

'I think we better call in the A&E, Jed. Get you patched up.'

'I want to go ...' is as far as Jed gets because Big Ed says that there's to be no argument. 'Look at the fucking state of you.' So that's where he's taking him, the A&E. Like it or not. Then Big Ed rolls up two cigarettes, lights them up, passes one to Jed, and starts the van for the journey to Broome Hospital. He thinks he'll drop Milly a call, let her give Anna a heads-up to soften the blow, the least they can do considering her condition.

Crystal Lady.
Milly and Anna are sharing a midday cup of tea with biscuits. Milly says that in a murder case (she's seen this on the telly) the first twenty-four hours are crucial and that Carl Thomson has been departed, 'for over a month or more now. So there's nothing to worry about.'

'But what about cold cases?' Anna has also been watching the telly, a series about important evidence being discovered decades after the event.

'Pete says there's not a hair left of him. Pigs munched up every last part.' She shudders, takes the lid off her rolling tin, digs out papers and tobacco, asks Anna, 'Don't mind if I do? I'll blow the smoke away from you.' Anna, into her tenth week of abstinence from nicotine, would quite like the smoke blown towards her.

Anna says, 'If it wasn't for Moses, Milly ...' She thinks for a moment, shudders, remembers the hands around her throat, the fingers throttling her windpipe. 'Me and Jed, we'd never tell on him you know. He was helping us. He saved us.'

Anna instinctively touches her stomach to include the unborn in the us.

Milly says, 'Just thank God all the trouble's over, Anna.'

Then Big Ed's phone call arrives.

CHAPTER TWENTY-FIVE

Foxes Farm.
Evening. About six.
Dinah and Lorrie.

Dinner's done. Dishes in the washer. Dinah's spread out plans and sketches on the kitchen table. Ethan's leaving, going to check out some prospective bullocks on a farm across the way. Might stop for a cider on the return journey. Lorrie's had a training session with Tony and has called into Foxes on the way home.

It's a subdued Dinah that lets Lorrie in the door, though not subdued enough to stop herself snapping at the growling collie twins, 'You know who she is so shut the fuck up.'

'Drink?' Dinah tilts a glass in Lorrie's direction.

Lorrie shakes her head, hair still damp from her shower, and says, 'No. In training, Dinah. Tony's been putting put me through the mill.'

'Well, I will.' Dinah pours herself a generous measure of Merlot.

Lorrie says, 'Is everything all right?'

Dinah takes a swig – no genteel sip for her tonight – of her wine, pulls a face, gestures to the sheets of drawings on the kitchen table. 'It's just that ...'

'What? Tell me, Dinah.'

'This. All this.' Dinah's at the table stabbing at sheets of paper with her fingers. There's a tremor of a sob in her voice.

'They were in Dad's office while he was clearing stuff out. Asked if I still wanted them?'

Lorrie says, 'Show me, Dinah,' and Dinah shows her the sketches of Vixens Mere marina that she and Barry – he'd drawn them up – had planned for their future. 'It's what we were going to do, Lorrie. Not straight away. But bit by bit.'

The drawings are not to scale; they're loosely drawn in quite an artistic way: Vixens Mere lined with several more barges, a picnic area biting into the woods, café with a terrace extending over the water, toilet and shower block. Lorrie thinks what's sad is the two figures – set on a rise – holding hands and looking over the basin; the long tumbling hair of the woman – Dinah – and the obviously over-sized, over muscular, man – Barry. Lorrie entertains a scoffing thought of, 'He certainly fancies himself,' but she says aloud, 'They're good, Dinah.'

'Yeah. Barry had a good eye,' says Dinah, tracing out the lines of the sketches. She adds, rather ruefully Lorrie thinks, 'and he had good hands.' Then she grabs the papers, screws them up in a fury, throws them on the floor. 'The bastard,' she says, 'The fucking bastard.' Dinah's head is in her hands and her body is trembling. This is much more noticeable to Lorrie when her arm is around Dinah's shoulders and she's offering the comforting embrace of a friend.

There's a sob, punctuated with, 'I'm sorry, Lorrie. I didn't mean to go off like that.'

Dinah braces herself upright and Lorrie lets her arm slowly, regretfully, slip from her shoulders. Dinah says another sorry and that she shouldn't let *him* still get to her like that but, 'It's still hard sometimes.' She draws her sleeve across her teary eyes, her snotty nose, says, 'Stay for an hour, Lorrie. Keep me company. Please, Lorrie?'

Lorrie says that it'll be an hour at tops because she's on the early rota in the morning.

Dinah tops up her glass, tilts the bottle of wine towards Lorrie, and asks a question that Lorrie wishes could be taken another way, 'Sure I can't tempt you, Lorrie? One glass won't set you back much, will it?'

'All right, just the one. A small one.'

Three generous glasses and an hour and a half later Lorrie's asking, 'Don't suppose you've got a spare fag, Dinah?'

It's while Lorrie is smoking that fag that she unscrews one of the sketches, smooths it out on the table, studies it, thinks about it – and through the enabling effects of alcohol – muses, 'It's a good idea, Dinah,' while she begrudgingly thinks that Barry actually might have had something about him.

Dinah sighs, 'Who knows, Lorrie. Perhaps one day? Anyway, who do I know with money and time?'

Lorrie thinks, 'Well there's me for a start,' (Petra's keeping her word about coming across with the money. Another wodge has arrived into Lorrie's account) but she's not about to say that out loud; she's not about to risk her payoff, and her heart, when her life is starting to take form again after the disaster of Petra. Then there's the sound of a motor, the crushing of gravel, as Ethan James crunches to a stop outside his farmhouse door and automatically activates the collie twins. Through the racket of excited yapping Lorrie manages, 'I better go now, Dinah.'

Dinah says, 'I'll call you.' She takes Lorrie's hand. 'Oh, and thank you for cheering me up, Lorrie. For listening to me. You're a good friend.' There's a slow moment of time as Dinah stretches up to Lorrie's mouth to give her the briefest, sweetest, of kisses.

Following day.
Lorrie.
Her eight-hour shift starts at six the next morning with a workmate, Celia – young and sparkling and much too loud

for Lorrie's delicate head – beginning with a stocktaking tour of the supermarket shelves; Celia on the iPad and Lorrie doing the counting. It's a boring thankless task that's only a partial cover for Lorrie's increasing yawns.

'Reckon you must've had a late night, Lorrie?' Celia's question is loaded with a *I think I know what you were up to.*

'Could say that.' Lorrie doesn't really want to talk, just wants to get the job over. Her head starts to ache; she's going to need a couple of paracetamols very soon.

'Where'd you go? Somewhere nice?'

'Friend's place.'

'I was at my boyfriend's last night. Go there most nights now. We're thinking about moving in together. His Mum's not too keen though, says we're on the young side but he's twenty and I'll be nineteen next year. What do you think, Lorrie? Are we too young?'

Lorrie is trying to count a shelf of assorted biscuits and finding it difficult to hold the number. She's rapidly losing the will to live.

'No, Celia.'

'What? Not too young?'

'No.'

Lorrie thinks that if Celia was her daughter, she'd have been pushed out of the nest a long time ago. 'And I'd have helped her pack.' Lorrie laughs to herself. That's a couple of lines to share with Dinah when she sees her again. When. She touches her lips, imagines Dinah's soft mouth in a fleeting daydream. Until: 'How many, Lorrie?'

'Uh. Mmm. Thirty two.'

'Right. Thirty-two.' Celia taps the iPad. 'Oh.'

'Oh what, Celia?'

'It's disappeared.'

'Disappeared?' then 'For fuck's sake, Celia,' slips out and Celia says that she's sorry and her bottom lip begins to tremble.

Lorrie says that she didn't mean to swear and if they swap roles? This works a lot better even though Celia insists on counting loudly, and not very quickly, but at least it's killed any conversation. Lorrie sighs. It's still going to be a long shift; two o'clock can't come quickly enough but come it does and inside of twenty minutes Lorrie is back home on the Morning Star.

Lorrie, on a guilt trip over breaking her training by downing wine and smoking cigarettes – yet again – has decided that her penance for her misdeed has to be a good long run to sweat away last night's sins of guilty pleasure.

'Five miles, Lorrie. That should do it,' she tells herself as she changes into her shorts and top to fit the mild afternoon. She can't help giving herself the once over in the mirror and her reflection shows a tall, rangy, shorn of any fat, and very attractive woman. Lorrie pleasantly notes that all her exercising has certainly perked up her bottom as well. Her image tells her that, 'You could be every woman's dream, Lorrie. Every woman except the woman you want.'

She sets her stopwatch and starts at a good pace, concentrates on settling into a rhythm. She takes the towpath, leaves it at the top end of Vixens, cuts into the track through Hunters Woods, and then past Foxes Farm and into a circuit of the lanes. For half this distance it's an uphill climb that pulls back Lorrie's pace, makes her swear to no more fags or booze ever again. Or perhaps when she's in training. She also makes believe that she's in the ring and the minutes are ticking away, and she must not flag.

Tony's onto her. 'Come on, Lorrie. This is when it counts. This is what makes the difference. Push, Lorrie. Come on. Push. Harder. Harder. No pain, no gain, Lorrie.'

Lorrie wants to tell the voice in her head to shut the fuck up but she doesn't have the breath. She doesn't get that back properly until she's crested the last rise and is on the relief of downhill coasting. God, that was hard going. She glances at her stopwatch, checks her time. Not too bad considering. Now the telling part is behind her, the last mile is really a relaxing wind-down, a long-strided lope. Lorrie drops this to a jog as she approaches Foxes Farm, sees Dinah's car parked up, and reckons to beg a drink. She taps on the door and Dinah, a surprised smile on her face, says, 'Lorrie. I was going to ring you.'

'I've saved you a call then. Any chance of a glass of water?'

'Yeah. Sure. Come in.'

Lorrie follows Dinah into the kitchen, aware of her soggy underarms, perspiration-patched top soaking into her shorts. And Dinah's not dressed like the girl she was last night. She's in her work clothes and she's more like the Dinah that Lorrie – dare she say it – is falling for; the cheeky farmgirl with streaks of something unmentionable on her jeans and a smear of dirt across her cheek.

Lorrie says, 'I'm a bit sweaty, Dinah.'

Dinah, now at the sink, running a cool stream of water into a glass says, 'That's all right, I'm used to the pong of animals.' She laughs, 'I don't mean that you're one, Lorrie.'

She gives Lorrie the glass and for Lorrie it's a swift upending and that she, 'must jump in the shower.' Dinah says that's exactly what she's going to do but she wasn't planning on sharing and she wants to smell nice 'cos she's got an appointment at the bank in Broome in an hour.

'Going to take the plans for Vixens, see what the Business Manager thinks.'

The plans are on the table, looking a lot smoother than they did last night. An impish grin from Dinah: 'I ran the iron over them when I was doing Dad's shirts. Had a bit of an accident, though.' She shows Lorrie Barry's badly scorched image, wonders if she's voodooed him? 'Fucking hope so.' Lorrie silently fucking hopes so as well.

'Give me a call later, Dinah. Let me know how you get on?'

That's where they leave it for now and what was going to be a gentle trot back to Vixens Mere is virtually a sprint for Lorrie; she feels full of life, exuberance. Lorrie bounds aboard the Morning Star, strips naked, runs the shower as hot as she can stand it, slowly soaps herself all over, lingers on her breasts, between her legs, and then, in her imagination, she's sharing a shower, gently washing the bubbles from Dinah's soft skin, soothing down her lovely form. She tells herself, 'I've got to stop this, I'm not a fucking teenager.'

But Lorrie doesn't stop it, not until she's finished.

CHAPTER TWENTY-SIX

Vixens Mere.
Very early morning.
Sun just peeping over Hunters Woods. Stillness of dawn hanging in the air.
Moses and Milly.

No school and no work for Moses today, he's giving them both a miss. He's set up two fishing rods on the far end of Vixens. One rod is to ledger for tench, or hopefully a very rare barbell, and the other, fitted with much lighter line and sensitive float, is for taking a few roach out of their wet environment. Now Moses is set up, and comfortably relaxed in his fishing chair, he thinks he'll open up his lunch-bag, pour a hot sweet coffee – lovingly prepared by Milly – perhaps sample a ham sandwich and slice of Farmhouse cake – also prepared by Milly who said, as he was going to go out of the door first thing this morning, 'Anything else you need just give me a call on the mobile.'

'Mum, I'm only a hundred metres away. I could shout to you.'

Milly says, with the emphasis on metres, 'A hundred metres. What's that in old money then?'

Moses laughs, 'Over there, Mum. Over there,' and points beyond the jetty.

Milly says that she's going to be baking some cheese scones and she'll bring them over while they're still warm 'cos she knows how much he likes them. Before he leaves Milly hugs him fiercely, briefly and hungrily.

He hugs her back. 'See you later, Mum.'

'See you later, Moses,' and Milly turns away; she doesn't want Moses to see what's written on her face. Then she watches him go, loaded up to the gunnels with his fishing paraphernalia, this son who isn't only hers and Ed's anymore. She has a sudden unreasonable sear of hatred for the man who walked the end of his existence into Vixens Mere, curtailed her time of exclusivity with her son. She wishes Harry Jones was alive, that he would have lived forever.

Summer Walker.
Brodie Stewart.

You awake early. You always have in all the time that it's possible to remember, from the frost-bitten shelters of winter to the sparkling of summer dew on the heather. Seanmhair said that even as a bairn you couldn't wait for the day to begin.

'You'd be off, you and that old dog. Hardly time for a crust of bread or a sup of tea in your stomach.'

You see her now; her thin frame, weatherbeaten face wreathed in a smile of condonement for the mischief you and the dog could seek out; a raid on a garden allotment, a bag of potatoes, a belly of apples inside your shirt, a rabbit poached from a hutch. Always an apprehensive, 'You sure no-one seen yer?'

This question, her voice from the past life is hanging in the air, nibbling at the edges of the present. You answer her with assurance, 'No one's seen me.'

In the beginning of this day – today – you're sitting in the prow of Summer Walker, your first cup of tea and cigarette is being taken together. You're watching the sky lighten, the glittering of the sun on the water of Vixens Mere, the bordering trees emerging out of the deep woods. You scan around, pick out the sleeping crafts of Home Sweet Home, Crystal Lady, Saddleback, and Bombardier. You think about Karen Jones lying sleepily in her bed, raising her hand to her mouth, stifling a yawn, and you imagine how welcome the warmth of her sleepy body would feel if you were to peel back the covers, slip in beside her. Lay alongside her. But the laying alongside is always at Summer Walker, except for that one night in Broome. 'Not in mine, Brodie. You do understand? You don't mind?' The watchful ghost of Harry Jones still sits at the table in the Bombardier. He always will; guilt is a permanent fixture there. You see all this, think all this, in the earlyness of this morning but your eyes are constantly drawn to the figure of Moses fishing beyond the jetty. You stand up. This is going to be the time; tea's drunk, cigarette butt's flicked into the water. This is going to be time to speak to Moses.

You can say that you're taking Mick for a walk around Vixens marina to give his, and your, legs a good stretch out. You can also say that you need to take your head away from your work in hand for a spell, add some distance and perspective to the carving that's coming to its form through your hands. You laugh, touch it, say goodbye as though it's alive, like it's going to miss you for an hour's absence. You almost expect an answer, that's how familiar this figurine in walnut has become. Karen, on calling yesterday asks, 'Who is she? Who's the boy?' and you say that she's an old lady you used to know. And the boy? She studies him, says he looks like he could be the brother of her carved boy. There's a likeness? You shrug a usual don't know because explanations are too complicated in your life.

Art, of Art and Crafts, has been pushing you for more pieces – objects d'art, he calls them – anything.

'One or two people have been asking. Want your stuff. So when can I expect something?'

'Couple of weeks, Art. Hopefully anyway.'

'OK. Look forward to it. Oh, and Brodie?'

'Yes.'

'Strange thing the other day. I was at this sale and some decent stuff came up. One piece, same sort of style as you.' He laughs 'Could have sworn it was yours. But it was old, pretty old. No history though, no carver's mark.'

Moses must be aware of your approach but he concentrates on his float until you're close enough to be unavoidable. He's waiting for you to speak.

You say 'Morning, Moses. You're about early.'

Fresh-faced and young, he looks to you with, 'Best time of day for fishing, Brodie.'

'Any luck yet?'

'Few nibbles.'

You watch as Moses draws his line in, plucks out a couple of maggots from his bait tin, skewers the wrigglies on his hook, flicks his line out again. But now the small talk's over and you plunge straight in with, 'You know about me and Karen, Moses. You know who we are.' *Mother and father to you, Moses.*

You say it gently and without looking away from his settling float Moses says just as gently, 'I know, Brodie.'

You start the talking and what you can't tell him is what it's like to be a displaced father because you never knew you were. What you can tell him is that things, 'Needn't be any different between us two.' You've no claims on him, but if you can help him in any way?

'I got everything I want from Mum and Dad,' he says quietly.

It's not dismissive of your offer but you know that it's true, that it's right; you haven't even been a bit player in this young man's life but 'I'd like to think we could be friends, Moses.'

'I'd like that as well,' he says. 'To be friends, Brodie.'

You offer out your hand to a friendship with your son

because that's all that's on offer for now. Or ever, maybe. It's a firm squeeze of fingers and then you say you should be going, finish walking the dog. You're turning away when Moses says a goodbye of, 'See you later.' He adds a, 'Mate' with a grin and you say, 'Yeah, later,' agree with the 'Mate,' and his grin broadens, spreads over his face. But underneath this easiness there's a query on his lips; there's something else to come. Moses asks you, 'Do you know what Seanmhair means, Brodie?'

'Where did you hear that, Moses?'

The question is more like a demand than a query because it's shaken you hearing that word from your son's mouth. It doesn't belong here on the waterside in this place of settled people. There's a slight embarrassment from Moses now as he answers. He looks to his fishing float as he speaks, mumbles really, 'I've been like dreaming lately. There's an old woman and it's like it's her name.'

Seanmhair's not going away. Never going away. Always keeping the portal open.

You can only tell him the truth. 'It means grandmother, Moses.'

Moses thinks for a moment, working things out in his head. 'Oh... Grandmother. What ...?'

'It's Gaelic, Moses.'

'Oh,' and then it's a sudden question of: 'Have I got a grandmother? You know seeing what ...?'

You could say yes and deflect, cover a half-truth, with the mention of Iris Needham but he's asking you, not Karen Jones. He wants to know from you. You hesitate on a shake of your head because many, many years ago there was a mother for you, a grandmother for Moses, *a thin woman of a bony embrace who walks slower than the trudging donkey, stops on a steep rise to catch her breath, puts her hand on your shoulder, says, 'Let's wait here awhile, bonny lad,' and you sit together while she takes a sip of water. There's always a hand to her chest and pain to her face, but then she'll gather herself, take a deep breath before the moving on. One morning she wakes up as grey as her blanket, reckons that daemons were trying to steal her soul as she slept. Seanmhair hushes her, says she shouldn't be talking like that in front of you. But a week later the daemons do come, do take her soul.*

She's buried on a lonely mountain churchyard, abandoned for years now, overgrown with furze and heather and stunted trees. But you know exactly where she lies and one day you'll stand together at her graveside and pay your respects. You and Moses.

In this future time, Moses will be taller than you, and all the secrets won't be secrets anymore. You'll walk the old ways with him, sit beside a flickering fire, shelter in a ruined croft, point to where the mussels anchor their lives to the riverbed. You'll open your hand, show him the freshwater pearl that Seanmhair gave you, say to him, 'It's yours now. Look after it forever.'

You'll use her words in the passing down of something that will always be held in the beating heart of family blood.

So to the question of a grandmother, you leave him with, 'Not on my side. Not now, Moses.'

Moses nods at your answer and then shifts his attention to his fishing. You stand at the edge of Vixens for a few moments longer before the calling up of Mick for company. In those moments, in the cool of this early morning, you're suddenly aware of how still, how hushed, is Vixens Mere; not a moorhen ploughing a wake, not a ripple on the water. It almost feels as though it's listening, waiting for more of your words to gather in, to siphon your images, and swallow them in its cold depths. You break that spell with a loud call to your dog.

'Come on, Mick. Time to go. Catch you later, Moses.'

'Yeah. OK, Brodie. See you.'

As you take the track into Hunters Woods you're thinking to

yourself that this is going to be all right; Moses is no snarling resentful teenager, he's accepting of circumstance. It makes you think that Big Ed and Milly – Mum and Dad – have done a good job, have raised him to be a decent grown-up. You give Mick a run, let him have a good snuffle through the undergrowth, and then it's back to Vixens Mere where the tang of burning wood and coke tell of the waking barges. There's a trailing of smoke from your Summer Walker, from Home Sweet Home, and it smells like the Crystal Lady is incinerating old socks. From Bombardier there's not a wisp to signify that a fire's been lit. Now you could walk on by, give Karen Jones a call later, let her know you've talked to Moses, but on an impulse you cross to her threshold.

Bombardier.
Karen Jones and Brodie Stewart.
Karen, still in her nightdress, is rubbing the sleep from her eyes as she opens the cabin door to you. Her clock has struck the nine – she's overslept – a few minutes ago, and her bed is still warm. Her hair is tousled, uncombed, and she's close to looking wanton. Gorgeously wanton, like she was in the bedroom of the Victoria Hotel in Broome.

'Brodie,' she yawns. 'You're about early,' and the inferred question is, 'What brings you here?'

'Took Mick for a walk,' and you answer the silent query with, 'I've been talking to Moses.'

'You what? Oh Brodie, is it all right? What did he say?' *What did our son say?*

There's an eagerness to her for news and you think that you're on cusp of being asked inside. But Karen Jones glances over her shoulder like there's someone behind her, says that the conversation can happen on Summer Walker.

'I'll get a coat, come to yours.' She's closing the door. 'You can make us a cup of tea, Brodie.'

* * *

Over that cup of tea Karen talks about Moses, watching him from a distance, never sure quite what to say when their paths cross.

'I'd like to ask him about things. School. His music. But the words are hard to find. And he's my son, Brodie and ...' she shrugs in resignation, pulls her coat tighter around herself, 'and I think it was easier before he knew.'

In that before he knew, Karen and Harry Jones would come to Vixens Mere every winter. They'd leave behind the overnight stops on the Avon and Kennet canal, the summer drifting on the Bath waters, the forays into the Broads, the mooring-up for a month at Fred and Iris Needham's off the cut, all managed on a wounded soldier's pension and a carer's allowance.

'You always want to come back here,' Harry would sometimes grumble at Vixens Mere and Karen Jones would make the case – her case – that it might just as well be here as anywhere. And it's cheap, and they've regular friends at Vixens – the Rawlins family, that guy on Morning Star, Ethan James, Big Ed and Milly. And Moses.

Karen Jones sees Moses crawl – misses his first steps; sees him pedal his bike – misses his first day at school: sees him growing in yearly snapshots of visiting – misses his first public performance on his guitar at Broome Academy. The pride in this boy – her boy – is by proxy, through Milly's disclosures of progress.

And now, even though the secret isn't a secret anymore, nothing has really changed. Karen Jones doubts it ever will; Harry Jones took his life too late to make a difference.

So what was Moses like this morning? You say that he was pleasant, polite. Seems a good lad. Normal conversation. You pour out a fresh cup of tea, offer her a cigarette, a light.

Karen Jones takes a drag, blows out a plume of smoke, takes a sip of tea, says, 'I'm going to stay here, Brodie. See Ethan about a permanent mooring.'

She doesn't have to give her reasons why and you don't have to give yours when you say that March will find you out on the cut.

'But you'll be back?'

'You know I will, Karen. Especially now. You know. Moses.'

She nearly asks, *What about me? Am I not reason enough?*

Karen Jones is looking for a truth, trying to see what's behind your eyes. You know she wonders about your life, who you really are; this person you never talk about. But this morning you're a man who wants her, who wants the warmth and the comfort of a woman. Karen Jones can give that willingly. She stands from the table, unbuttons her coat, shows that there's nothing underneath it except the beauty of her body. And her ulterior motives.

CHAPTER TWENTY-SEVEN

Broome.
Evening.
A quiet corner of the Merryman Inn.
Jed.

It's about eight o'clock when pubs and clubs haven't yet started to liven up. People are in and out the doors and the market for early chemical lifts is opening for the dealers. But not for Jed, he's trying to persuade some former associates to provide him with substances to sell.

This is the fourth venue for Jed tonight and he gets the same response as he did at the previous ones.

'All I'm asking for is enough to make few bob; half a dozen pearls, that's all.'

He's asking Slim Jim and Johnny Reynolds – they're the other two parts of this skinny trio who've covered for each other over the last few years. They go back to the days when, fresh out of school, keenness and innocent faces were an invaluable asset in this game. Although never again for Jed; his bruises may have faded but his nose will be crooked for the rest of his life.

Slim Jim says, 'You know we can't, Jed.' He looks to Johnny Reynolds to draw him in for support, who repeats Slim Jim's words. 'You know we can't, Jed.'

But Jed's become increasingly desperate over the evening and these two are last on his list for a small upturn of fortune.

'I need the cash. Look, no-one will know.'

Slim Jim rolls his eyes skywards. 'Lennie will know, Jed. He knows everything. He'll skin us alive if we help you.'

Johnny Reynolds nods in agreement, says, 'He's put the word out on you, Jed. We can't do nothing.' He glances furtively around the bar. 'We're taking a chance even talking to you now.'

'So you won't help me?'

'We can't, Jed.' There's a shake of his head and an apology in Slim Jim's tone. Johnny Reynolds adds an honest, 'Sorry Jed, but that's how it is.'

So it's a leper's departure from the Last Chance Saloon for a dejected Jed; he leaves his erstwhile friends to their nefarious employment, makes a slow trail back home. He'd stop for a pint on the way but he can't afford it and, on his lonely walk, he begins to stress about what he should do for the best, for Anna, for himself, and for the life that's growing inside of her. This when the second, and final, nudge pushes into his reasoning.

Vixens Mere.
Gentle playing of guitar coming from Crystal Lady.
Lighted windows in Morning Star and Bombardier.
Summer Walker and Saddleback in darkness. Pigman Pete is staying over at Marlene's.
A tang of burning wood and coal drifting in a pale settling smoke over the water.
Home Sweet Home.
Jed and Anna.

Outside of his barge Jed shudders, takes two long strides over the spot where Carl Thomson took his last breath, and then onto Home Sweet Home and into the warmth of the kitchen.

There's always a welcome from Anna, a delight in her eyes to see him back in one piece. Unwounded. She stretches up to kiss him, hugs him briefly, asks, 'Do you want a coffee?'

There's a big sigh from Jed and a, 'Might as well,' that draws an enquiring look from Anna. 'Not good in town?'

Jed sits at the table, strokes his forehead like he has a migraine. 'Fucking hopeless, Anna. It's fucking hopeless. No one wants to know me.'

Anna says, 'It's my fault, Jed. I brought all this on you.'

Her voice is trembling and she's wearing the face that caused him to invite her to his home.

'No. Not yours, Anna. It's his fault. Fucking Carl Thomson.' Jed stumbles on the name that's rarely spoken.

'Yes, but if I hadn't ...'

The hadn't doesn't need explaining, it's been the monkey on her back since she packed her bag, took a K of Carl Thomson's money, and met up with a soft-hearted lad on a dark wet street. And the softness is showing through as Jed, defeated by events, says, 'I can't try anymore, Anna. No one'll help me. Old mates. No one. Lennie's on my case all the time.'

'There must be something we can do, Jed?'

Then Jed speaks what's in his mind, what he was working out on his walk back to Home Sweet Home, what has been in his mind ever since Dave Probert's size thirteens stomped all over his body. Jed speaks slowly, softly, of not wanting to be here anymore, of feeling a black dread every time he steps over the ghost of Carl Thomson sprawled on the towpath, of reliving his four-year-old self peeping through the crack of the door, of his mother lying in the cold dark water, 'Out there, Anna. Out there.' He tells of watching his back on every foray into Broome. Jed is becoming wary of his own shadow and says, 'We've got to get away, Anna. Go somewhere where nobody knows us. Leave all this behind.'

'Go away? But we got no money or nothing, Jed.'

'We have. We've got this.' He rakes a glance around the cramped kitchen cabin of Home Sweet Home and Anna picks up on his intention.

'This? You mean sell the ship, Jed?'

'Barge, Anna. It's a barge,' and he manages a grin as she laughs at his pretend sensitivity.

Now the talk is of starting again far away, of finding a proper job. Maybe even becoming a proper person. Jed could buy a car, make life a lot easier. 'Shopping and that,' like a normal young couple. The wonder to Anna is that it's all within reach. She has a picture float into her mind of the both of them walking on the pavements in an unknown town, sharing turns at pushing a pram, at giving her child the life that she never had. Anna cries again this night but the tears are for a future happiness. She says, not quite rid of disbelief but merging on excited acceptance, 'Oh Jed, do you really think we could we do this?'

'We have to, Anna.'

They have to because there isn't a choice anymore because, to tell the truth, tonight in Broome confirmed the thoughts that have been bubbling in Jed's mind ever since Lennie Lines's minder gave him a good going over. Jed's pissed off with skulking into town with his hood pulled over his head. He's fed up with being cut dead by old acquaintances, by everyone, being told no dice when he offers to do some selling. Although he can actually show his face in Broome, realistically Jed is persona non grata on the streets; Lennie Lines has branded Jed's caste on his forehead for everyone to see, made him an untouchable. That's unless the touching is another hiding coming his way.

Tomorrow he'll talk to Big Ed about selling Home Sweet Home, let Ethan and Dinah James know the score; they might be interested? Jed's thinking of the recently renovated – and quickly rented out – Morning Star. Jed and Anna's accommodation is well up together for an oldish barge. Mark Rawlins had kept Home Sweet Home shipshape and Bristol fashion; regular blacking of the hull, superstructure metal cleared of rust, painted regularly. He had been proud of his residence on the water.

So the word is to go out but it'll have to be on the QT because if certain people in Broome get a sniff of a lucrative transaction they'll gather like jackals to tear the meat from the bones.

Anna says, 'How long do you reckon before we can go?'

Jed shrugs a 'Dunno. Month or two maybe.'

'Please make it quick, Jed. Please. 'Cos what if someone comes looking for you again. What if ...'

She's nervous is Anna; she's terrified of a knock on the door that might bring retribution in an unlawful, or lawful, boarding party.

'Don't worry, it'll be all right, Anna. We'll keep our heads down.'

Jed is starting to feel confident, like they're moving out of the danger zone. He wants Anna to share his optimism, draws her to him, strokes her hair, soothes, relaxes her. But he's also aware of the bump of her belly against him. Jed says, 'I'm not going to be able to reach you soon, Anna,' and she says that they'll have to try a new position then. As she's speaking, he's looking into her street urchin's face and she breaks into a fleeting cheeky smile. He thinks she looks beautiful and he knows that he loves her.

Broome.
The Glow Worm.
Soon after nine o'clock.
Tickets only Annual Pirate's Night. So called because there's a connection to a 17th century buccaneer, William Besom, who captured a Spanish galleon and buried the spoils of his enter-prise – reputedly a massive haul of gold – somewhere near the town. Pirates' dress code and a prize – a large bottle of Captain Morgan's Spiced Rum – for the most authentic costume.

* * *

*Dance floor and bar well populated with male and female –
and a few in between – pirates.*

On the door of the Glow Worm: Marvel, Tony, and Lorrie.
Marvel, his usual happy self, reckons that tonight gives
everyone a chance to look like a dickhead. Tony says for
him to, 'Lighten up. It's only a bit of fun,' as he's eyeing two
Jill Sparrow lovelies; cavalier-boots, low cut blouses, and
midriff exposures. He nudges Lorrie, whistles through his
teeth, mutters, 'Take a look at them.'

'Perv,' says Lorrie.

Tony comes back with, 'Don't tell me you wouldn't if you
had the chance, Lorrie?'

'Might think about it,' Lorrie laughs and Marvel – earwig-
ging – says that his money's on Lorrie to pull; she's much
better looking than Tony. A compliment from Marvel is a
pretty rare thing and Lorrie says she'll treasure it. Marvel
chuckles, thinks that she's cracked a good joke considering
the pirate theme.

Through the foyer and into the venue proper Jack Sparrows
follow Jill Sparrows follow Blackbeards follow Buccaneer
wenches. There's yellow and red bandanas, black pirate
hats, multi-coloured eye patches, long legs in fishnet tights,
and long legs in stockings and garters, flashed from under
short, flouncy dresses. It's a fun dressing up, drinking up
night that won't end until one o'clock when the last pirates
are put ashore.

The parade in eases off about nine and Lorrie's on her own
in the foyer. Tony and Marvel are patrolling the dance floor,
'Propping up the bar more like,' Lorrie thinks, scanning entry
passes and checking the punters in.

'Right, that's six tickets,' Lorrie counts with her finger,
ticking them off. 'You. You. You. And you. And ...'

'Me, Lorrie,' calls out Dinah.

She's in the group of half a dozen of the same agers. They're all in the theme attire but to Lorrie, Dinah looks stunning. She's dressed in a knee high split-skirt, a tight white blouse – very low fronted – and large hat distinguished by a skull and crossbones. A pair of gold hooped earrings add to her film star looks. To Lorrie, Dinah and her friends look so young, so vital, so in love with living, that she suddenly feels an old drudge at her twenty-eight years of age, and herself in a plain charcoal jacket, light shirt, and trousers. (And a red bow-tie. Don't forget the only splash of colour you're wearing.) Then she feels an itch of resentment for those years that were not carefree and fun-filled and, although it's not exactly reasonable, blames Petra for that lost time.

Dinah's motley crew, brimming with energy and straining for the off, push through to join the music. But Dinah hangs back, says to Lorrie, 'Do you like my outfit, Lorrie?'

There's been a pause in entrants and Dinah's crowd have disappeared ahead of her and it's a few moments of being alone in the foyer.

Do you like my outfit, Lorrie?

Dinah swirls around, her skirt flares, and the golden loops in her ears swing and shimmer. 'Well, do you?'

Lorrie says the first thing, the truest thing, that comes into her head. She says her thoughts out aloud. 'I think that you look gorgeous, Dinah. Gorgeous.'

'Do you really think so, Lorrie. Really?'

Lorrie, not sure she's said quite the right thing, reinforces it anyway with another, 'Really.'

'Nice to know it was worth the effort, Lorrie,' and then Dinah gives her one more twirl and waltzes off into the hall. (What with the noise of people and music and merriment Lorrie won't really have a chance to talk to her again until chucking-out time, when an obviously inebriated Dinah informs her that the lift she was expecting is not going to materialise because her so-called friend – Cow! – who was meant to be dropping her back 'has pulled Captain Kid and she's in line for a good old Jolly Rogering. Sorry, Lorrie. Bit crude that. Can I ride home with you?'

Meanwhile it's one of those nights at the Glow Worm when everyone seems to be in a happy mood. There's been no drama, not even a mild scuffle. It's a good time being had by all, a merry melee of dancing action influenced by alcohol and ... 'Well there's bound to be other stuff floating about,' says Tony as him and Lorrie, on the rounds in the Ladies', check the toilet lids, the dispensers, the window sills, for the tell-tale signs of white powder. There's a dusting on the cisterns in a couple of cubicles but 'nothing to worry about,' she tells Tony. He reckons that a party had gone on in the Gents. 'Looks like they've been bagging up flour in there,' Tony says.

It's now all noise and action on the floor. The music's cranked up, the disco lights are in kaleidoscope mode, the bar counter is arrayed with glasses and bottles. The bar staff, a team of top of the range pros, are serving at full throttle but find time to slide a pint across to Tony and a cola to Lorrie. It's a big swallow for Tony and then he leads the way into the fray.

Lorrie can feel this is a good night. Yes, it's loud but not to the point of deafening. There's screeching laughter, good-natured horseplay, and no sign of any trouble brewing. They're ambushed on the floor by, 'Come on, Tony. Show us your shapes.'

Tony, not backward at coming forward, is in his element at all the attention he's receiving as he's – most willingly – passed from partner to partner. Lorrie's roped into a group of lady pirates who've hitched up their skirts and turned their shape-making into a rather revealing can-can. These are a set of Glow Worm regulars – tall and short, fat and thin, married and divorced – who are always out for a laugh.

They surround Lorrie, cajole her into joining them, draw her into the mood of revelry.

Lorrie is light on her feet, up on toes, picking up the rhythm of the music like she picks up the rhythm of the ring – although her high-kicking trousered legs are not showing tomorrow's washing, not like those of her uninhibited friends. It's an exhilarating five minutes that ends with the advent of a slow ballad on the sound system, and in a series of fleeting good-natured smooches with her party friends. (It's not fleeting enough to prevent one of them – the description 'large lady' is being rather kind – saying admiringly to Lorrie: 'If I was a bloke dancing with you Lorrie, I'd have a hard on,' and giving her a rib crushing hug.) As lovely as it is to actually have some fun – with the bonus of female contact – Lorrie has to get back to what she's being paid for or else Marvel will be onto her.

Lorrie and Dinah

The music's stopped, the bar's closed, the venue's cleared, the fire-doors are checked and the building's secure. It's a goodbye to Marvel and Tony: 'Don't forget training tomorrow night, Lorrie,' and into the car-park behind the nightclub where Dinah's waiting behind the glow of a cigarette. Then it's a dark drive to Foxes Farmhouse with Dinah, high on rum slammers and chattering like a magpie, saying what a night it had been, and Lorrie must come in for a coffee and a fag.

'That's too tempting to resist, Dinah.'

Dinah teases, 'You including me as well then, Lorrie?'

Lorrie laughs out a, 'Might be,' because this is how the joshing between them has evolved, and tonight it's more than assisted by Dinah's alcohol consumption.

In these small hours they sit opposite each other in the farmhouse kitchen – a smartly suited attractive woman, sober as a judge in fact, and a ravishing buccaneeress who looks like she's just stepped off the set of Pirates of the Caribbean, and has partaken of too much grog. For this unlikely pairing it's the sharing of the coffee pot and a couple of cigarettes: 'I really shouldn't, Dinah. I am in training.' But training and beauty sleep are out of the window tonight because Dinah's heard that Jed Rawlins is selling Home Sweet Home. Although it's not a time for the mentioning, and her words are stumbling over each other, she says that the bank's not keen on her ideas for Vixens Mere.

'Dad says that he'll help me but he's got enough on his plate. What with the farm and everything.' Dinah tacks on an opinion of her ex-boyfriend, 'Fucking Barry.'

It's more than late now and Lorrie, much as she sympathises, doesn't want to become involved in a Barry HateFest this time of night; she really wants to get a few hours' sleep before the sun lifts over Hunters Woods. But Dinah's at the stage of inebriation where she's slipping down into the maudlin. She's not going to let Lorrie go until she's told her that, 'You're a friend, Lorrie. My best friend. You helped me through all the shit with Barry and …' Dinah is searching around now in the way that the affected do. 'You've given me lifts, and … and yeah, you're my best friend.' And her eyes are shining and a tear spills onto her face.

Lorrie says, 'It's all right, Dinah,' and she opens her arms protectively and Dinah comes into a holding that's gentle, and close, and deserving of another, 'It's all right.' Dinah's sniffing and apologising for her snotty nose and more.

'Sorry, Lorrie. I don't want you to think …?'

Lorrie laughs lightly. 'It's OK, Dinah. No need to be sorry. That's what friends are for.'

But it may be becoming a different sort of friendship now because Dinah's whispering into the closeness between them like they're conspirators.

Dinah sniffs. 'Can I tell you something, Lorrie?'

''Course you can, Dinah.'

'Anything?'

'Anything at all.'

As much as Lorrie's relishing this contact she's aware that it's very late – she's had a long day – and that tomorrow Tony will push her to new physical limits. So as lovely as this is with Dinah, Lorrie thinks that she needs to get her head down (she instantly wishes she'd kept that thought to herself) for some rest. But then Dinah whispers, 'I was jealous, Lorrie.'

'Jealous?' *What the fuck does she mean? Jealous?*

'When I saw you and that girl kissing in the car park, Lorrie. I was jealous.'

The headlamps of Dinah's car sweeping across them, pinning them, showing beauty and beauty, face into face, melded together. Longing, desire, and regret captured briefly in the scanning of the spotlight like in an old-time movie. What Dinah didn't expect though was the jolt in her stomach – a sort of thrill and a sort of deep envy marrying together.

Lorrie says very softly, 'You were jealous?'

Dinah's in too deep to back out; honesty is not for the avoiding now.

'Yes, Lorrie, I was jealous,' and spelling it out – it seems to Dinah more obviously than she needs, 'I wanted it to be me.'

'You sure, Dinah, because you're …'

'I know I'm drunk but I mean it, Lorrie. I mean it.'

Dinah's voice has gone up a few octaves, like she's worried about a rejection, and Lorrie's, 'Look we should talk about this tomorrow, Dinah,' sounds like that could be on the cards but Dinah's come too far to back down.

'Kiss me, Lorrie? Kiss me like you kissed her?'

Then Dinah slowly, apprehensively, lifts her face to Lorrie's, closes her eyes, touches lips to lips. Lorrie mentally mutters an, 'Oh, fuck it.' Her reserve, her reasons why this is the wrong time, wrong place, dissolves. Of course it can't be a replica of what was shared with Petra; this is different, exclusive, a first enquiry for loving from Dinah. And it's the beginning of all that Lorrie wants, even if she tells herself, later, that she never imagined that a taste of heaven would be so salty. So sticky. So snotty.

CHAPTER TWENTY-EIGHT

Home Sweet Home.
Bright Sunday morning.
Banging and hammering and sawing. Big Ed has a new shed
well under construction.
Lorrie, Jed, and Anna.

Lorrie's spent an hour in bed this morning wondering why the fuck Ed burnt down a perfectly good shed only to build a new one, and is now, on this supposed day of rest, making enough noise to wake the dead. She's also wondering if she's about to add to her extensive catalogue of errors. She's sent a text to Dinah: *How are you? No regrets?* and wonders if that's too strong, and too early. God, she feel like she's fourteen again and sending messages to Sally Dennis from under her bedclothes. She's balanced this decision with the old adage of nothing ventured, nothing gained. (She's also added her own caveat of nothing ventured, nothing lost.)

Lorrie is up and dressed and sipping tea before her phone pings a reply: *Fine. But halfway through scraping the yard. Bullocks have been shitting for England! I'll call round down for a coffee later. And no regrets xx*

Lorrie is going to take it easy this morning; she knows that Tony is going to be on her for a tough afternoon session. 'Need to keep yourself together, Lorrie. Stuff coming up.' So Lorrie will have a walk, chat to her neighbours, see how much longer Big Ed is going to be smashing nails into his building.

Not much longer it seems because Milly's come out at the top of her voice about not being able to hear Steve Wright's Love Songs on the radio 'cos of 'the fucking racket you're making.'

Also out in the morning sunshine are Jed and Anna, sitting in the bow cockpit, sharing a pair of long faces.

Lorrie asks, 'Any joy with the boat?' and wishes she hadn't because long faces become longer. It turns out there has been interest but what Jed needs is a lightning sale.

'Want to be out of here asap, Lorrie. Need a cash sale,' Jed says.

Jed is nervous, he's picking at his nails, running his fingers through his hair. Anna's drumming her foot and sniffing like she's still using.

'That bad, eh?'

'Just want to be gone, Lorrie.'

Lorrie thinks that if she'd been the recipient of the couple of good hidings like Jed's sustained lately she'd 'Just want to be gone,' as well. Out of curiosity, Lorrie asks the price for Home Sweet Home 'cos it's quite a tidy looking barge. Jed's answer of, 'Thirty K' is almost immediately followed by a desperate: 'But I'd take less, Lorrie.' Like she's shown anything more than a polite enquiry? It seems that as a professional dealer Jed isn't overly successful at bargaining on the street or on the marina. From a departing Lorrie it's a, 'Sorry. Not in my plans, Jed.'

On her stroll Lorrie stifles a yawn. A late night and no lie-in due to Big Ed's cursing and hammering first thing has jaded Lorrie a little. But Big Ed's cheery 'Good Morning' and invitation of 'Come and have a look around, Lorrie' and a bawled instruction for Milly to 'Get the kettle on' is contagious. Lorrie bucks up, takes a guided tour of sawdust underfoot, window and door openings cut out of the timber framing, roof already felted and tacked.

'Another couple of weeks and it'll be done,' Ed says with satisfaction.

There's also for Ed the satisfaction that he was paid for taking a stable block down and disposing of it. He's disposed of it all right, he's re-erected most of it here. A win-win for Big Ed.

It's a quick cuppa and the refusal of a fag and then Lorrie follows the path up into Hunters Woods. She can look over the whole of Vixens Mere from here, see the moorings of Summer Walker, Crystal Lady, Saddleback, her own Morning Star. And of course, Home Sweet Home, the barge that'll soon – hopefully for Jed and Anna and baby bump – be under new ownership. Lorrie thinks of Dinah's plans, her dreams for Vixens Mere. And that makes Lorrie think of Dinah's dreams spread out onto the table at the farmhouse. She looks down on Vixens Mere again, picks out Home Sweet Home.

'Don't, Lorrie. Don't even think of it.'

But she already has.

Vixens Mere.
Cool evening.
New Shed Party. 'Bring bottles and food.'
Barbecue more than well alight and Big Ed has already char-grilled sausages and is in the process of cremating a griddle of chops.
Inside, a long pine table – courtesy of a house clearance – is loaded with bread rolls and plates of offerings.
Couple of sofas, easy chairs etcetera, courtesy of the same clearance.
Music 60s/70s/80s pitched so as not to kill conversation.
Big Ed, Milly et al.

Milly, more than a few cans of Strongbow under her belt, is sprawled comfortably – and not too ladylike, into a massive armchair that Big Ed deemed too good to take to the dump. (That's along with everything else that will 'surely be useful one day, Milly' and is filling space until it's only fit for burning.)

Milly's enjoying the warmth of the wood burner, and is scanning the room, all the familiar faces making up the numbers that will soon be depleted. She's going to miss them. Miss Pigman Pete who, at the moment, is locked into a slow dance with Marlene. His face is buried, well almost enveloped, by her two best attributes and Milly reckons to herself that Pete could be in danger of suffocation if he doesn't come up for air soon. He certainly wouldn't hear the fire alarm. Pete is going to move into Marlene's terraced house in Broome where she'll feed him up like a porker. That's one down. Two down is Jed. Poor battered bent-nosed Jed who desperately needs a fresh start away from all the drama that's happened here. He'll be taking himself, and young pregnant Anna, many miles from here. 'He's no choice and,' although Milly might miss him, 'at least he won't be bringing any more trouble back to Vixens.' She feels a bit guilty about that thought because what would Mark Rawlins think of his wayward son, the son her and Ed had promised to keep an eye on? Well, they had in a way, hadn't they? Milly shudders, remembering Carl Thomson's nocturnal visit. Jesus. Shove that right away, Milly. Put it along with Sandra Day, wrapped in Ed's tarpaulin and feeding the fishes for all those years.

Milly catches Moses's eye across the room, shakes her Strongbow can at him, gets the nod and goes back to her musing. Now according to the old superstition, and Milly is very superstitious, things always happen in threes and, 'Number three of the leaving,' Milly tells herself, 'has got to be Brodie,' the man who comes and goes, drifts in and out of others' lives. Milly knows for sure he's drifted in and out of Karen Jones a few times.

That's it then, the magic three accounted for, another Strongbow in her hand, and Moses is now cutched up beside her in the armchair. She loves the closeness of him, the scent of her boy.

309

'You all right, Moses?'

'Yeah, I'm all right, Mum,' and there's not a pause before the word of Mum, no hesitation. It flows naturally into meaning. Moses's arm goes around her and he gives her a son's squeeze, a loving squeeze.

Karen Jones.

Her eyes are drawn to Moses, captures his picture with Milly; her with the long loose skirt, dark blouse, crystal earrings, and a bandana almost covering her grey head. And Moses, lanky height, long-haired, with no tilt to fashion in the mixture of his vagabond's clothing. She thinks they look like a pair of gypsy fortune tellers.

Then Karen Jones has to turn away because all that she has missed is welling into her throat, into her eyes; she knows that she can't sit in Milly's place. Maybe not ever. But later she catches up with Moses and the talk is the same as always with the awkwardness between them, the unspoken remaining hidden while the spoken is the usual stilted stuff of, 'How's your music going? I hear you playing sometimes.' A cheery, 'Sounds good, Moses.'

From him she gets, 'Thanks, Karen,' and then he leaves her with a smile. Warm enough to melt her, cool enough to keep her uncertain of her status.

But one day soon, Moses, things will be easier between us. I won't just be the mother who kept you a secret. Kept myself a secret. One day soon, Moses. I hope.

In a couple of hours, when most of the company will be four sheets to the wind, the lovely, sad, and vulnerable Karen Jones leans in close to Brodie and, hoping the timing is right, says, 'I want you to take me back to yours. I want you to love me, Brodie.' She doesn't have to add, 'Please,' but she does and she doesn't need to add the reasons why and she doesn't. And Brodie doesn't need to know.

* * *

Big Ed, relieved of cremation duties by Lorrie and Dinah, is admiring the handiwork of his new shed from the inside: the plank lined walls, the boarded ceiling, the exposed trusses and tie beams, shelves for Milly's assorted ornaments of jars and brightly coloured jugs and vases. Milly has also taken control of the walls with several murals – actually pretty good – of the moon and stars and Hunters Woods reflected onto the dark waters of Vixens Mere. There's also an image of Crystal Lady capped with snow, trapped in ice; a vertical pluming of smoke rising into the cold blue of a winter's sky.

Big Ed tells himself rather smugly, 'Yes, I've made a good job of this building. Well, me and Moses and a bit of labour from Jed. And I'm going to miss Jed. Doubt we'll see him again once he's gone. Probably for the best though. Probably best for all of us.'

Big Ed, like Milly, is also counting those others that'll soon be missing from Vixens Mere. He wonders who the new faces will be at Home Sweet Home and Saddleback, who'll be starting a new life on their stretch of water. The thought of a new life makes Big Ed remember his old life, the travelling days, the impermanency of van life, of summer nights in a grassy field with a throb of a bass in the distance, the company sitting around a crackling fire, passing around smokes. Milly beside him, so young, so fresh, so loving; all of them sharing the little they possessed, and what Ed now realises is the most important asset of all. Youth.

Big Ed thinks that he's getting too sentimental, perhaps he should steady up on the drink. He seeks out Milly, wraps his arms around her. Holds her tightly.

'What's that for?' Milly's surprised, pleased by this show of affection. Big Ed tells her that she looked much too pretty to resist and she laughs, says that flattery will get him everywhere, in fact anywhere, that he cares to go. What he doesn't tell her is that he wanted to touch something, a connection, that stretched back to all those years in the past of the flickering firelight, the squelching mud of gatherings when the morass was ankle deep, when rainbow lights danced across the sky as the music clashed loud and brash and smothered mind and soul. That's what Big Ed wanted.

Later the beer's still flowing steadily and Big Ed offers Ethan Jones another bottle of San Miguel.

'Shouldn't really,' Ethan says. 'Got to be up early in the morning. Animals to feed.'

Big Ed laughs that it's not stopped him before and Ethan tries to disremember the mornings of climbing out of bed feeling like death warmed up, of bollocking the bullocks as they tried to shunt him out of the way to reach the spreading of breakfast hay. He clinks bottles with Big Ed, says,

'Last one, Ed, then I must make a move.'

They both know that's not going to happen and they'll still be sitting around the fire in the small hours chewing the fat while Ethan has yet another 'last one.' But after Ethan's done, filled to the brim, and he's making tracks home with an occasional stumble, he'll pass by the sleeping barges. He'll stop, breathe in the night, cast his eyes over the still dark water, remember how him and Mrs Jenny James would walk down here with Dinah in her pushchair twenty years ago; hot Sunday afternoons strolling and making plans for the future, the farm, Vixens Mere. 'That turned out well, didn't it, Ethan?' he tells himself. Still, he has Dinah – his favourite daughter, as he calls her – but there's been a concern lately because she's become a little secretive. It's not that Ethan's a prier but Dinah's had a few away nights recently and the enquiry of Ethan's raised eyebrows first thing in the morning are met with a shake of her head, and a silent, 'Don't ask, Dad.'

Ethan hopes that she's met someone who deserves her, not

like that bastard Barry. He pauses again, alongside Morning Star, looks over the silent floating homes. He can't possibly know that Dinah is sleeping the rest of the night away almost within touching distance.

Summer Walker.
At the same time.
Brodie Stewart.

Karen Jones is lying beside you, warm and soft, quietly breathing, and you're staring into the dark ceiling, thinking about the morning and another goodbye. Lately spring has been drifting in on the softest of breezes and the familiar urge is taking its usual hold. It's strong in you, this demand to be satisfied, this restless wandering along the waterways through locks and endless miles of the cut. There's to be one more night, this night, with Karen Jones and all the tender loving she provides. She disconcerts you this woman; she's touched you like no-one else ever has and you can dream sometimes of living within all of her life, of waking to her in the times to come. Until her hair is grey on the pillow, until one morning Karen Jones is an old woman, shrivelled under the bedclothes. Then you'll have the bitter reminder that she doesn't have, can never have, the years that you carry within your soul.

It's a clear morning on another leaving and the sunshine is already warming the day. Seanmhair takes your hand, squeezes it gently, tells you to be careful on your journey, to keep yourself apart from 'this.' She looks in your eyes, touches her heart. 'Don't let anyone in,' she says. 'It's the better that you don't.'

But you have.

Vixens Mere.
Saturday.
Warm May morning.

Dinah and Lorrie: new partners in enterprise, (thanks to

Petra coughing up) are painting the superstructure of Home Sweet Home. Jed, Anna, and future baby, have put many miles between themselves and Broome. An untenanted Saddleback is next on the list for a thorough clean out. 'More like a fumigation,' Dinah laughs to Lorrie, and a lick of the paintbrush. Summer Walker's berth is empty.

Crystal Lady.
Karen and Milly.
Karen Jones has laid herself out on Milly's sofa and Milly's hovering her most powerful purple crystal – taken from her special box of tricks – on a fine cotton line over Karen's stomach for the second time in fifteen years. The sun's peeping in at the scene and the crystal sparkles with its energy. But the stone stays motionless for a minute, two minutes, until Milly's bound to ask, 'You sure you're pregnant, Karen?'

'Yes, Milly.'

'How far gone do you think you are? When was the last time the painters were in?'

There is a doubt in Milly's mind and it's reinforced when Karen says that she doesn't really know. 'I haven't seen a doctor yet but I just know I am, Milly. I just know it.'

Milly thinks that wanting and knowing are completely different things.

Milly says, 'Well, I don't think ...'

'Don't stop yet, Milly. Please try a bit longer.'

The last time that the two of them were in this situation Moses was forming himself, and then there was a definite, almost instant, response. Milly's not sure anything is beginning here, in fact she thinks that Karen's deluding herself and that this is a waste of ... the crystal moves in the slightest of swings and a current of shock runs up Milly's arm. 'We got something,' she whispers aloud and all around them there's a gathering of silence, a listening to the beating heart of a newly formed soul. Then the glittering crystal starts a slow orbit, an anticlockwise circle of prediction.

'Oh Milly, what is it? Tell me what it is.'

'I think it's going to be a girl, Karen.' Milly watches the slow revolving of the pendant for another half of a minute, just to be as sure as she can be, then gathers up the tools of her trade. She gently, lovingly, boxes them again. Puts them to bed.

'Thank you, Milly. Thank you.' Karen sits up, tears spilling down her cheeks. She wipes her eyes with the back of her hand as Milly sinks into her chair, takes a deep breath.

'God, that took it out of me, Karen. Whew, I need a smoke.'

She helps herself from Big Ed's baccy tin on the side, rolls one up, offers it to Karen.

'No. No, thanks. Better not.'

'Don't suppose you should,' says Milly and she takes a good look at her client and thinks that Karen seems to have started blooming already; she has a faint flush to her cheeks and a faint smile on her lips. Milly thinks it's a bit premature for this air of motherhood; there's a long way to go yet.

Karen Jones gently strokes her stomach. She's thinking, willing to this child that she'll be 'Mine. All mine.' She loves it already with a fierce love that won't ever be for letting go. Never. Karen Jones won't be giving this child away. This child conceived in deceit will be hers in honesty. Totally hers. She won't have to lie awake at night in the wondering, worrying, about her offspring from a distance because this girl child will be sleeping softly beside her at night. Breath to breath. Living and growing.

Milly says, 'You going to let Brodie know?'

'He'll find out when he comes back here, Milly.'

Karen Jones and Moses watching Summer Walker slipping out of Vixens water in the mist of early morning. Karen Jones is trying desperately to hold in her tears and she's managing well enough until Moses unexpectedly takes her hand, squeezes it, says, 'He'll come back, Karen.'

And then she does cry. And it's for two reasons.

'Be a nice surprise for him, then,' Milly says a little sharply. 'Bit like the last time.'

Karen Jones thinks that it'll be a surprise all right, what with all her untruths about precautions taken, about the swallowing of a daily pill. She's getting what she schemed for, a child to make her a real mother. And Brodie? She might love him in this strange way they have, but she loves this unborn more. She thinks she'll call the child Mary. Mary Stewart. Seems to fit together well. She wonders why the Christian name Mary pushed itself forward so fittingly for her little girl. She searches in her memory but can't find a connection.

Milly hopes, for Karen Jones's sake, that Brodie doesn't stay away for fifteen years like he did before. If it's for that long, her and Ed may very well have popped their clogs and she won't be alive to see the finish of the tale. And Milly does like an ending.

EPILOGUE

Vixens Mere.
Four years on.
Autumn's arrived early and it's cool for October. Afternoon sun is glinting in the water. Bordering trees, drooping willow and upright ash, are shedding their leaves onto the water. Moorhens are scrabbling in the fading reeds; a pair of handsome drakes are having a set-to, watched by a nonchalant and extremely plain hen.

There's been changes to Vixens in these last four years; changes in that Home Sweet Home and Saddleback are both tenanted with new faces; parking at the top of the track has been enlarged. Development, slowly but certainly surely, has advanced. Three more electric hook-ups, septic tank and drainage updated, two showers, male and female WCs and a toilet sluice. Scrubs and trees have been cleared from the top end of Vixens to allow easier fishing access. Underwater snags have been dragged out. Nothing untoward – no corpses now, thank the Lord – for tackle to snare on. Big Ed has been a Godsend as a builder and digger operator. New jetty and decking are waiting for available funds.

Summer Walker is slowly nosing in as it has every year for the last five. Mick, muzzle even greyer, bones even stiffer, this time around is in the prow of the barge sniffing familiar air.

* * *

Brodie Stewart.

You see them on the path, watching you in. A welcoming committee; Karen Jones, hand shielding her eyes against the sun; Moses, mop of hair, lanky frame six inches taller than his mother, and Mary in the pushchair. There's an aura of closeness to this trio of family watching you draw to the bank, leap to the shore. First, you slip your arms around the sweetness of Karen Jones, then it's an embrace for Moses and then you kneel to the level of your daughter, this child you haven't seen since March. She takes your gaze and looks back at you and the startle of her blue eyes narrow in curiosity. Then you lift her, feel her firm young body relax in your arms. You know that Karen Jones has a sparkling of tears in her eyes and you know it's because of you, because you've kept your promise for another year. Now your shy young daughter puts her face to yours and you feel the warmth of her breath. She brings her mouth to your ear to whisper softly in perfect old Gaelic, *'Athiar.'* Father.

For a moment you're back in the high mountain air in the third spring of your life and your father's lifted you to himself, enveloped you in his strong arms. And the smell of the road is on him, strong and powerful, dusty and clinging, and it's washed with the sharp stirring of silted water from the cut. It's like you remember.

Like it'll always be on you.

Hunters Woods.
A few years later.
Small hours of the morning.
Half a moon, unsure if its waxing or waning, keeping high clouds at bay.
Glow of a cigarette in the dark.
Milly.
She comes up here most nights lately, drags her ageing bones

to her vantage point over the sleeping barges, the dark mirror of Vixens Mere. Here in the stillness of the night she can sit in silence, think how things are changing; think how her and Ed are changing: Big Ed starting to stoop with the weight of the years: herself bone-thin and finding the hills a bit of struggle nowadays.

'We're getting old, Milly,' Ed sometimes says to her and it makes her want to weep out loud. She doesn't want this change; she doesn't want their lives to be running down to an ending. If she could pick a perfect time in a perfect place, it would be just her, Ed, and Moses, in the whole of the world. But now Moses is coming and going from Vixens Mere taking himself, his guitar, his tunes, to festivals and venues in a scattering of counties. Sometimes, if it's not too far away, they'll fire up the old van and visit for the day, mix with the music, mingle with the youth they once were; two old hippies casting about for someone to recognise in the faces of the crowd. Listening to the applause for their son.

'For God's sake, Milly,' she tells herself. 'Don't be so fucking maudlin.'

She fishes a roll-up from her pocket, thinks she'll sit here until it's smoked, and sit and listen and take a watch in the night. What she hears is the whispering of the trees in the breeze, the hooting of a lonely owl, a scrabbling in the brush. What she sees is Vixens Mere below her as calm and flat as a sheet of glass. Not a ripple of movement except for … Milly wipes her eyes, squints … except for a disturbance of the moon-silver circle in the middle of the mere. Like something's stirring in the depths, reaching for the light.

Description of Vixens Mere transcribed from the notebook of Stanley Drake (Capt.) poet, writer, and local historian, soon after his return from the Great War of 1914 - 1918.

Vixens Mere can be found on ancient maps, a rough square of blue water. In those times it would have been measured by three chains of length and three chains in breadth. The depth was probably running from shallow to a fathom and a half. But it's more than old this pool; there's endless years of memories layered into each other, melded together. The will-o'-the-wisps, the spirits of the water, drift up on a full moon, peep above the surface, whisper into the black night of a time when there was no time.

The remains of settlements are close by, maybe half a dozen buildings, long crumbled to vague stunted outlines in Hunters Woods, overgrown with brush and ivy, and rooted with oak, ash, and plane; trees of the forest. But Vixens Mere didn't disappear with the inhabitants. It slept on through countless summers and frozen winters, its ancient slumbers undisturbed except for deer lapping on its shore and wildfowl nesting in the reeds.

There were fish, and eels that slimed into the cool deep. Children paddled in its shallows, lovers sat on its banks, watching their reflection in the mirroring water.

That's how it may have stayed forever if, on a hot day of a summer, the navvies hadn't pitched up their tents, erected their huts, and began to carve this pool into a canal basin with shovels, picks, planks, and wheelbarrows. The surveyor, Mr Clark, and the foreman of the navvy gang, Desmond O'Mara, set up profiles and sight lines, eyed through the T of the travellers, and their men, rough and tough, muscle and sinew, weathered by sun and storm, swarmed over the site.

These workers chopped and dug, drove into the earth, deeper, wider. These men fought like dogs, cursed like heretics, and sang in praise of the Irish, the Scots, the Welsh, the English, and the Almighty, as they wheeled out the spoil, lined the banks with clay and stone, packed a towpath around the basin.

When the works were completed, a mason chiselled the date 1830 into a stone entrance pillar of its recognition. Then they broke the dam, let the veins of the canals flood in, married Vixens Mere with the morphic resonance of all waters: the liquid highways of the Exeter Ship canal, the picturesque Avon and Kennet, the quiet backwaters, the twenty-nine locks at Caen Hill: the endless traffic of brightly painted barges hauling coal, iron, gravel, timber, and familied by the gypsies of these canals, their urchins sprawling on the cargo, adding raggedy decoration to the boats. But then there's the growing hiss of steam in the distance and the clever money starts to shift from water to rail. Mr Clark reads the early signs and gains employment with Great Western Railways. He puts in a good word for Desmond O'Mara who manages another decade of labour as a Gangerman, laying sleepers for the tracks, before taking himself home to Cork just in time for the failure of the potato harvest.

Vixens Mere is included in the sale of the surrounding farmland in 1907 and by now it's a pleasant and out the way situation and, as the years pass, more memories are added to this brooding pool: the shallow wakes of the ins and the outs, silhouettes of floating craft against a filtered sun, swimmers kicking away from the pull of the deep, baited lines and struggling fish. These memories slowly swirl in its depth, living on as the world changes, ever since the first flooding of water joined the watery soul of this place.

Joined with the slow beating of its aqueous heart.

Acknowledgements

A special thanks to my lovely wife Debbie for enduring the person I became when I was putting together this novel. She walked the canals with me, listened to the story form, and encouraged me beyond belief.

I would like to thank Catherine Evans at Inkspot Publishing for having faith in my work and for her and Charlotte Harris's judicious editing of my book. I would also like to thank Taryn de Meillon for her wonderful illustrations, and Kate de Meillon for the unenviable task of publicising *Under Vixens Mere* on social media. I am grateful to all at Inkspot Publishing for the time, care, and enthusiasm they have applied in bringing my book to the marketplace.

Thanks also to Ruth Hogan, for her enthusiasm and encouragement.

One more mention must go to my agent Peter Buckman, whose perception, candour and irreverent humour always ease my literary journeys.